THE ONE KINGDOM

Book One of The Swans' War

Sean Russell

www.orbitbooks.co.uk

An *Orbit* Book

First published in Great Britain by Orbit 2001
This edition published by Orbit 2002

Copyright © Sean Russell 2001

Teaser from forthcoming title *The Isle of Battle*
Copyright © Sean Russell 2002

The moral right of the author has been asserted.

A CIP catalogue record for this book is available from
the British Library.

ISBN 1 84149 088 1

Typeset in Perpetua by
Palimpsest Book Production Limited, Polmont, Stirlingshire
Printed and bound in Great Britain by
Mackays of Chatham plc, Chatham, Kent

Orbit
An imprint of
Time Warner Books UK
Brettenham House
Lancaster Place
London WC2E 7EN

To my children I bequeath my hatred of the Renné, for all the atrocities they have committed against us, and all that they will commit.

The Final Testament of Abril Wills

ONE

In the moving landscape only the men were still. They sat at the long table atop Summer's Hill as motionless as stones in a running stream.

Around them the wind was in flight, more joyous than a swallow, as heedless as a child. It swept down onto the new green oats and raked through the hay, making waves and patterns like sand on a riverbed. Gusts bent and swayed the trees, pulling away the spring leaves and spinning them up into the wind-washed sky. But in the center of this the men remained still.

Dease was relieved that he and Samul had prevailed, and the others had agreed to meet here, where the countryside was visible for almost half a league. He didn't want to take the least chance that they would be overheard—it was enough that they had to listen to themselves.

"I would say there is not one among the Wills who can even unhorse him, let alone manage what we need," Samul said—Samul, who almost never spoke out in the family assemblies, preferring to seed his ideas in the minds of others so that he might watch quietly. Samul the cunning, Dease thought of him.

Beld shifted on his bench. "Toren is so sympathetic to the Wills that I think they should not even want to cause him a bruise, let alone do him harm."

Dease noticed that the others looked a little uncomfortable whenever Beldor spoke. No matter what their feelings in this, no one else hated Toren the way that Beld did. Several were Toren's admirers, in many ways.

"I fear we can't trust to others to do it for us," Samul said softly. "I think the earlier plan the best. We let our cousin win the tournament, as he is likely to do anyway, and then do the deed at night so that it looks like revenge. That would be best. It will see our dear cousin removed from the succession and place the blame clearly on the Wills."

"It will hardly be clear," Dease said, unwilling to hide his distaste for what they planned, "not that it will matter. Everyone is ready to believe the Wills capable of the worst treachery."

"Then that is what we'll do, Cousins," Beld said, sitting back a little on his bench. "I worry only that some might lose their nerve." He looked around the table. "That hard decisions do not come easy to everyone."

"You can name me, Beld," Dease said. "We all know of whom you speak. You're hardly subtle."

"But subtlety is not what's needed," Beld answered, sitting forward quickly, his temper flaring. Dease could see his cousin's muscles tensing beneath his tunic. "Deeds are what's required, Cousin, and I'm not sure you can stomach that, being such an admirer of Toren's and all."

Dease met his cousin's gaze easily, not looking away or even looking particularly intimidated, and very few were not intimidated by Beld. He was a great bear of a man, but even more so, he looked like someone barely in control of a vast and raging anger—which was, in fact, the truth.

"I do admire him," Dease said simply. "In many ways he is the best of us, and not just on the tournament field."

Beld banged his fists on the table. "But Toren will give us over to the Wills! He thinks that they can be won over by charm and words, and they will be convinced to give up their feud of nine generations. He will gift them the Isle of Battle, which is no different than giving them the wealth to raise an army. Toren thinks that all we have to do is renounce our claim to the throne—as simple as that—and they will do the same, and all will be well with the world." He looked around at the others quickly. "Give up our claim! I've heard him say it myself. Does he know what the Wills would do to us if they were ever to ascend the throne? They would not forget the past. They would not forgive. Toren will see the Renné name eradicated from Ayr, that's what Toren's . . . *statecraft* will accomplish. But it isn't our name that I want to see forgotten. No, I for one have had enough of his conciliation. I—"

"Enough, Beld!" Dease interrupted. "We've all heard you rant before. Spare us, this day."

Beld lunged up from the bench, but Arden and Samul grabbed his massive arms, and he let them pull him back onto the bench.

"Enough of this," Samul said, his voice, as always, firm and reasonable. "Don't bait him, Dease; we can't afford division now."

"Yes, I know, but let's not try to justify what we do as noble, Samul. It is the most vile treachery. We are about to murder our own cousin, and though I admit it's necessary to our preservation, still, I can't pretend it is anything but what it is. You all know I've tried to reason with Toren. I've spent countless hours in this vain pursuit, and I sometimes think he came nearer to convincing me, than me to him." He splayed a large hand on the table, looking down at it sadly. "But I'm sure now that he will not be convinced to give up this folly. So we must either follow him to disaster or resort to treachery. For the future of our family, I choose treachery, but I have no doubt that I am a blackguard—a murderer and a traitor. And if we are discovered, don't imagine that our family will think otherwise, for they would rather honorable ruin than this ignominy that we have chosen."

The stillness returned, as the wind ranged around them, swaying the branches of the tree overhead so that shadow and sunlight chased each other madly across the table and over the grim faces of the gathered men.

"Are you with us, yea or nay, Dease?" Samul asked at last.

Dease looked up, a little surprised by the question. "I'm with you, yea and nay, Cousin, but I'm with you."

Samul stared down at the table before him. "Then,"

he said softly, "we have only to decide who will do it and how."

"I'll gladly take this infamy on myself, Cousins," Beld said, trying, but failing, to hide his satisfaction.

"No," Dease said firmly. "This is not an act born of hatred. I will do this thing"—he took a breath—"for I love him best."

Beld began to protest, but Samul silenced him. "Then you will both go. Dease will do the deed, and Beld will witness. And we will all pledge ourselves to silence or to hang together, if that is what comes—but it will be as though each of us had committed the act himself. Do you agree?"

No movement, and then each man nodded his head in turn, some more reluctantly than others. Silence settled around them again.

"How do you propose to do it, Cousin?" Arden asked quietly. He was the youngest of them, barely more than twenty, and spoke his mind the least, though Dease knew that he was not the least thoughtful.

Dease looked up from the table, the sorrow of the death already etched on his face. "During the archery trials at the Westbrook Fair I will steal arrows from the Wills. . . ." He paused to take a sudden breath. "And I will use them to shoot Toren through the heart. He will die quickly."

No one made comment, but they sat with the weight of what they would do and what they had become pressing down on them.

A gust of wind moved the branches overhead so that
the leaves hissed. A dark bird clung determinedly to its
perch, protesting the disturbance.

"Once," Arden began, his voice filled with affection
and sadness, "Toren unseated me at the tournament in
Waye, and afterward——"

"Don't begin that!" Dease said, turning to his cousin.
"Don't even think of beginning that! You have no right.
None of us has any right."

When the men went to untether their horses, the
wind, which had not paused to draw breath all morning, sighed once and died away. So the cousins rode down
the hill into a newly still world, where the only sounds
were their horses passing, for the men spoke not at all.

The silence left after the death of the wind was like the
world in mourning. Even the birds gave up their songs.

Dease rode along a lane shaded by plane trees, enduring his sorrow.

Like the countryside after the wind's death, he felt
emptied, hollow. Silence invaded him. Silence and bitterness.

Out of his sadness and remorse came feelings of anger
and resentment toward his cousin. Why was Toren forcing them to this? Could he not have listened to reason?
Could he not have heeded the warnings—for Dease had
tried to warn him.

Unfortunately, Toren did not believe that anyone's

opinions had more validity than his own——a family weakness.

Beld suffered the same problem, and he had not half the intellect of Toren. It was difficult for Dease to admit that he agreed with Beldor this time, though Beld's opinions were mere reactions, not arrived at by careful consideration——perhaps there had been no thought at all. Dease realized that more than anything he wished that their problem could be solved by Beld's death. That death he would not feel such sorrow over.

The idea that Beld would accompany him——no doubt to savor the death of the cousin he hated——did not sit well with Dease. He wondered if Beld could suffer an accident on the tilt field that summer. It wasn't impossible.

But, no; one murder was enough, even though Beld was more deserving of it than Toren——at least in some ways. Dease shut his eyes and tried to clear these thoughts from his brain. When he opened them he looked around and saw something moving across a field.

It was Arden's head bobbing just above the green oats. His young cousin was trotting along beyond the field, trying to outpace him, no doubt. Planning to intercept him.

He will want to talk, Dease realized, and then hoped the others would not see them. It could not help but look suspicious. Why had Arden not ridden off with him in the first place? Everyone would have thought that innocent enough.

This is what comes of being a conspirator, he realized: you live in fear of suspicion.

At the corner of the next field Arden caught him, his face red in the sun, his look a bit embarrassed. Dease was certain that the decision they had made did not seem real to Arden yet. It was all just talk, as most things were with young men.

"Cousin," Arden said as he reined his horse in, and then nothing. Silent like the world around them. "May I ride with you awhile?"

Dease nodded and the two fell in side by side, riding down the long row of trees, from shadow to light to shadow again.

"You're not happy with the decision," Dease said at last.

"No one is happy . . . No one but Beld, that is." He played with his mare's mane. "I still hope that Toren can be convinced to change his mind. There is time. The Westbrook Fair is some months off." He looked up at Dease, clearly an appeal. "He won't listen to me, but don't you give up, Dease. Toren might be brought to his senses yet."

Dease nodded, though it was not in agreement. "I will try, but I fear my constant badgering has begun to antagonize him."

They rode on through the still day, each of them lost in thought. Dease looked at his cousin. He had grown into a fair young man, or at least that was what the women thought. Blond and blue eyed like so many

Renné, with skin fair as a child's. Arden was strongly built, like his father—or so he would be when he reached his full weight. Dease had not seen Arden on the tilt field in some time, but he was hearing reports that his young cousin would do the Renné proud this season.

Suddenly Arden raised his head. "I have one concern, Dease." He said this so earnestly that Dease found himself leaning over to hear what would be said next. "What if Beldor's interest in this is not so simple as it seems? We all know he hates Toren—that is not in question—but after Toren is dead the succession falls to Kel. And after Kel only you stand between Beldor and the throne. And if the feud begins again . . ."

"There is no throne," Dease reminded him.

Arden looked at him oddly, as though trying to plumb his thoughts. "Perhaps, but who does Beldor hate most next to Toren?"

Dease nodded. It was no secret. Beld hated him. Hated him for their difference. Beld, the man of action, could not bear Dease's thoughtfulness. His love of music and art were offensive to a man of arms. Such interests weakened a man. He had heard Beld say it. And the fact that Dease always triumphed over Beld on the tilt field drove his cousin to fury.

"Everyone has had this same thought, Arden. Beld knew I wouldn't let him do this thing. I wonder if he wanted to be seen to offer. Who would suspect the man offering to commit the murder of treachery? But, in fact, we all do. I've never turned my back to cousin Beld."

"Samul and I have our eye on him, Cousin," Arden said. "If some accident befalls you after Toren is gone, we've made a pact. We shall not let Beldor come into the succession. We will not."

Hearing this, Dease closed his eyes. His sorrow kicked inside him. Such was the choice they'd made this afternoon upon Summer's Hill.

✝ W O

The ruined tower stood above the old battlefield at Telanon Bridge, an empty-eyed sentinel overlooking a meadow of spring flowers and slumbering ghosts. A cooling breeze bore the scent of ice and snow down from the nearby mountains, and the trees bordering the old battlefield began the furtive whispering which haunted the winds by night.

From the crumbling battlements Tam watched the shadow of great Eldhorn wash over the hills: night's tide flowing, silent and relentless. Shadows pooled in the valleys and made islands of hilltops still lit by the sun.

Below, a fire crackled, and Tam heard the muffled voices of his cousin and Baore as they prepared the meal. Smoke, caught by eddies and drafts from the ancient stoneworks, drifted through the ruin like the spirit of regret that seemed to dwell in this place. "The young begin their journeys with joyful hearts," Tam quoted to himself, "the old with regrets."

Yet his heart was not filled with joy. The world beyond his home, the Vale of Lakes, was strange and not much spoken of by the people of the Vale—despite the fact that all of their ancestors had come from that outside world.

Driven here by war, Tam reminded himself.

All the most important things you'll do in this life will exact a price in one way or another, his grandfather liked to say. *Once you've made up your mind, pay the price and get on with it.* Of course, his grandfather had never traveled more than a day's walk from the Vale.

To the south Tam could see the dark river twist and fall and then disappear behind the ragged edge of a wooded hill—the River Wynnd, gathering speed for its long journey to the sea.

Tam closed his eyes and thought of the map he'd traced on his grandfather's table. Beyond the old tower lay the wildlands—league after league of deeply forested hills—which eventually gave way to rolling meadows, then fields in their frames of hedgerows and drystone walls. Here one would find the villages of the lowlanders, houses of weathered stone washed up along the riverbank.

Tam opened his eyes and gazed into the distant south where small clouds blossomed on the horizon. No point getting ahead of himself. They would not go so far. Not halfway through the wildlands was a small, isolated village—Inniseth—and between there and here lay a fortnight of speeding, twisting river.

Tam let his eye follow the river back; a brief, effortless journey. Immediately beneath him the delicate curve of the old bridge arced like an arrow's flight across the chasm, its stone lighter in color and harder than the rock of the cliffs—carried here from quarries far away.

"The man who spends his time gazing at far horizons and not helping with the preparation of his meal shall soon hunger after more than distant lands." This was Tam's cousin, Fynnol, calling up from below, another of his spontaneous pieces of "ancient" lore and wisdom.

"I thought it was me who shot the grouse?" Tam called down.

"Giving you a chance to show off your skill yet again. And when did we begin to count grouse hunting as work? It's play, and therefore doesn't go in the ledger."

Tam could just make out his cousin staring up through the spray of new leaves, his face creased with humor, as it usually was. Fynnol of the quick wit and quicker laugh. Tam didn't think he could win this small duel of words. Few could best Fynnol there. "I shall be down immediately, then."

Tam took one more look around the hills that were coming back to life after winter, and then climbed down from his perch. The three young men had made their camp here for five days in what they thought might once have been a dining hall, though the walls were now covered with lichen and wild ivy, and the roof was the vault of the ever-changing sky. Fynnol hunched over a fire burned down to coals, and with great concentration, turned a pair of spitted grouse. Ten feet away, Baore sat against the stone wall, carefully polishing a bronze dagger hilt unearthed that morning.

"Do you realize, Cousins," Fynnol said, "that we have escaped the Vale? We are free of it!" He laughed. "No more Wella Messt knowing every little thing we do—and sharing it with everyone beneath the living sun. No more cows to milk, hogs to slop, corn to plant. My only regret is that we plan to return so soon."

"We shall likely not be back before midsummer's day," Tam said, "especially if we can't find what we want in Inniseth."

"I want nothing more than to get away! Far, far away," Fynnol said, and then glanced over at his cousin, Baore, who shifted uncomfortably. Tam crouched down by the fire, but Fynnol cocked his head toward the food bags. "Tubers await your attentions."

Tam nodded, but his focus was on their companion. Baore was bent over, looking closely at the dagger handle in the fading light. He was a man whose hands could not be still. Even when they sat around the fire telling stories in the evening, Baore would be honing fishhooks or sewing a tear in a shirt. He was never without some small job of work in hand.

Quiet then, as each bent to his task. There was a bit of awkwardness between the three this evening, and Tam was not quite sure what the cause might be. Baore was silent—more so than usual—and Fynnol, ever aware of his cousin's moods, was more talkative and animated.

Tam wondered if Baore might be having second thoughts about their journey down the river. After three years of talking endlessly about their plans, how could

Baore say that the Vale looked fairer to him than any adventure? Certainly he didn't dare say it to Fynnol, whose judgments of their place of birth had become more and more harsh as their day of departure approached.

It was ironic, Tam thought, for of the three of them Baore looked the most like an adventurer: large jawed and crooked nosed, with an impressive breadth of shoulder and a height that few men equaled. Appearance belied the truth, though, for Baore was gentle by nature and a bit slow and unsure when it came to speaking his mind. *Just waiting for a good woman to make up his mind for him,* Fynnol always said, and Tam feared that judgment was not far wrong. Fynnol called Baore "the draft horse," and it was more true than flattering—strong, easy of nature, loyal, and solid on the earth. *If the gate is left open, our draft horse would not think to go out,* Fynnol once said, and Baore appeared to be proving him right. Perhaps he would need to be led—or driven.

Tam looked over at the big Valeman. With his blond hair (which Fynnol described as *willful*) and downy youth's beard, Baore brought to mind nothing so much as a hay mow battered by a windstorm.

Conversation over dinner was a bit forced, Fynnol talking excitedly about the journey and taking wicked pleasure in mocking the people they were leaving behind. If Baore was their draft horse, then Tam thought Fynnol was the crow of the group—cunning and wary, but swift and filled with hidden purpose. And like the crow, Fynnol was little concerned with his effect on others. Tam looked from one to the other, marveling that these two were cousins. One clever and prone to scheming, the other solid and steady. And yet here they were, about to set out on this adventure together—Fynnol's adventure— for though he was not blessed with the personality of a leader, Tam knew it had been Fynnol's zeal that had pressed them forward.

"I have decided," Fynnol said suddenly, "that I would like a gray mare that will be the envy of all the Vale and who will give me foals that men will clamor to buy."

"I thought you were set on a bay stallion with a star on his forehead?" Tam teased.

"That was before I thought it out straight, Tamlyn." Fynnol was eating a leg of grouse with greasy fingers, and waved the gnawed bone to make his point. "Gray is the color of early morning, so shall bring me good luck, for it is about beginnings; and a mare will give me foals of which I shall take my pick, thereby being sure to have another horse just as good. Or maybe better. A gray mare. That's what I shall have."

"Well, you can't name a gray mare 'Evening Star' if gray is the color of morning," Baore said, forcing himself to join the banter, trying to shake off his mood, for he was not grave by nature.

"Baore speaks the truth. And why is gray not the color of evening as well?"

"Because the color of evening is purple, Tamlyn, as everyone who has ever read a book well knows. And as to the name, I have another just as good. 'Greystone,' after my grandmother's family. Solid as the earth, but light on the tongue. Greystone."

"You always have things worked out so perfectly," Tam said. "And then, when you change your mind, you soon have them worked out just as perfectly again."

"Oh, more perfectly, Cousin. More perfectly."

To their left someone cleared his throat, and everyone turned to find a man standing just at the edge of the firelight. For an instant no one moved they were so surprised.

"As you have everything worked out to such perfection," the man said in a warm voice, "perhaps you will not mind sharing some of it with a stranger? The light of your fire would be welcome."

All three Valemen were on their feet, Baore with a heavy staff in his hands. The man took one look at this giant, who had risen before him, and stepped quickly into the light, extending both his hands palm outward.

"You've no reason to fear me," he said, a smile appearing from behind a neatly trimmed beard. "I'm a peaceful traveler, and shall gladly give my sword and bow into your keeping to prove it." He unbuckled a scabbard and held it out toward Baore.

"Keep your sword," Tam said after a second. "We make travelers welcome in this corner of the world."

Despite Tam's words the man stood his sword against the stone wall before approaching the fire. Tam thought him neatly turned out for a traveler. Not a hunter or trapper, he was quite sure. Though the stranger dressed for the wood and looked comfortable in his role, he had a hint of the city about him——or so Tam imagined, for he had never been to a city himself.

"I thought I heard the vowels of the Valemen here." He smiled again. "I'm Alaan, and you are Tam, I think, and Baore and Fynnol." He laughed at their reaction. "I apologize, but I sat and listened to you speak long enough to be sure you weren't brigands or fugitives. Most men you meet in the hills are kindly, honest men, such as yourselves, but not all, and I have become more cautious as I grow older."

Tam gestured to a place by the fire. "It is a rough table we set, but we've more than enough on it to feed four."

"I've a horse tethered out in the dark," Alaan said. "Let me find him and I'll be back."

Fynnol cast a look over at the man's sword leaning against the stone. "Is that the weapon of a hunter, Cousin," he said quietly, "or is that the sword of a man-at-arms?"

Tam looked over at the long blade, with its unadorned hilt and pommel. "'Tis as you say, but there are three of us and one of him, and if he wanted to rob us he would have only to empty our boat as we slept, as he must know if he's been listening."

They sat back down to their meal, and in a moment Alaan reappeared, leading a heavily burdened horse. This he tended to and tethered outside the hall, speaking softly to the beast. When he came to the fire he bore a drinking skin and several bags.

"I have a wine here that has not killed me yet and some other things that I might offer to your fair table, for any table with kindly men about it seems fair to me. I can't tell you how often I've eaten my supper with only my horse for company these past months. He is intelligent for his kind, but still he talks only of food and mares and how much his hooves pain him at the end of each long day, and I have heard enough of that."

"You may be disappointed here," Fynnol said. "We were just speaking of mares ourselves."

The man smiled and poured them each some wine, which was far better than his claims, and shared some goat cheese mixed with herbs none of them knew, and by the time they had tasted his food and drink he was a welcome guest indeed. Polite questions were asked as they ate, though the food and wine took up much of their attention.

"Where is it you travel to, Alaan?" Fynnol asked as they sprawled about the fire after their meal. "Or do you come to visit us in the Vale of Lakes to see the beauty of the waters?"

The man laughed pleasantly, like a man genuinely glad to find company. "I am not stopping in the Vale this time, though I have done so in the past. Does Delgert Gallon still dwell by the Neck?"

"He does indeed," Baore said, surprised, "though he's old and mostly deaf these days, and growing frail."

"Gallon is Baore's aunt's cousin's brother, or some such thing," Fynnol added.

"I'm sorry to hear he is not hale." Alaan shook his head, the smile disappearing. "But I go south this time."

"As do we," Fynnol said, "though we can't join you on your journey, for we go by boat."

Tam saw Alaan's eyebrows lift a little.

"You don't fear the river, then?" he said evenly.

"If you're speaking of the fast water and gorges," Fynnol said, "we fear them as much as any man should. If you're talking about the old wives' tales . . . We're more afraid of the old wives, to be honest."

Alaan nodded but made an odd little grimace. "Then I shall not regale you with old wives' tales."

There was a moment of silence, and then Baore said softly, "You don't believe these stories, do you?"

Alaan kept his attention on his cup for a moment, his face impassive in the flickering firelight. "It is a strange old river, I'll tell you that," he said at last. "And I've been down it once. That is how I know old Gallon—he sold me a boat some years ago and I followed the river, though not quite to the sea as I'd hoped." He smeared a bit of bread in the juices in his bowl. "How far will you venture?"

"To Inniseth."

Alaan nodded, thinking. "You'll likely encounter few difficulties between here and there, that is, if you pass through the Lion's Maw without harm." He glanced at Fynnol. "Will you pay the Lion for passage, or is that an old wives' tale as well?"

Before Fynnol could speak Baore interrupted. "I'll

pay," he said. "'Tis only a coin, and many a man who's kept his silver has come to harm in the Maw."

"It is only a coin!" Fynnol scoffed. Then said to Alaan, "I wouldn't throw any of my hard-earned money into the river, though Tam and Baore may do as they please."

"And you, Alaan," Baore said, "did you pay the Lion for passage?"

"I did, and I would do so again, were I to travel that way. And when you see the water racing through the Maw and hear the Lion's roar . . . why, even Fynnol might change his mind." He smiled as though he jested. "But I'm sure you'll survive it. You've likely spent your lives in boats. Beware the River Wynnd, though, for it will take you places unexpected and show you things you might rather not see."

The three Valemen glanced at one another, Baore uncertain, but Fynnol not quite suppressing a smirk.

"Is it true the people of Inniseth sacrifice their dead to the river and will not venture near it after dark?" Baore asked.

Alaan smiled. "Well, it is hardly a sacrifice. They pour the ashes of their dead into the river and will not be buried in the ground. They believe that is the worst curse you can place on a family—to bury one of them in the ground. It is their punishment for murderers. But it is true the ritual of sending the ashes down the river is partly done to appease the river or its spirits in some strange way. Outsiders are not welcome at their funeral rites, so I can't say what is done, but they seem to believe they've made a pact with the river: it will leave them in peace during their lives if they are surrendered to it in death."

Fynnol laughed, but Tam and Baore did not join in and he fell quickly silent.

"And do they not venture near the river after dark?" Baore asked.

"Well, the town lies on the high ground across the river from the fields, which flood in spring. Each day the people must go there to work. It's true that they'll not cross the river after dark and that those who live nearest to the water bolt their doors and gates at night and leave no windows open on the river side." Alaan looked around at the others and suddenly smiled. "But these are old wives' tales and I promised not to indulge in those."

The traveler looked off into the darkness, concentrating as though listening. Tam wondered where the man might be going and where he had come from. There were signs in his speech that he was a man of education, and clearly he'd traveled. It was hard to say why such a man was here, so far from the inhabited lowlands, for the Vale was one of the few settlements in a vast wilderness. Occasionally men would appear, traveling up the old road seeking gold and silver in the far valleys, but the mines there had been emptied long ago and few men carried anything but disappointment home again.

"You've been digging in the old battlefields and mounds, I take it?" Alaan nodded to the artifacts that Baore had been cleaning. When no one answered right away: "There must be many a broken blade and shield still buried beneath the earth hereabout, though I would guess that time has left little of it in peace. Will you carry it down the river to sell? I ask only because I know a man who takes an interest in such things and might like to see what you have."

"We don't disturb the mounds," Tam said quietly, "just the open meadow of the battlefield. Anything of iron or steel has long ago decayed to dirt. We find the occasional streak of rust where a sword might have lain, but I would imagine few objects of any size were left on the field—shields and swords and armor would have gone into the mounds with the dead."

"What do you find, then?"

Tam saw Fynnol give him a warning look, but Alaan noted it as well and held up his hands as he had earlier.

"It is wise to be wary of strangers. You need tell me nothing."

"It's not that we've found anything of great value," Fynnol said quickly. "The odd coin, sharpening stones, some buckles, and strangely, a few bits of women's jewelry . . ."

"Oh, that is not so strange," Alaan said. "Knights often wore some piece of their ladylove's jewelry into battle as a token of their feelings and as a charm against injury. Gold and silver will long outlast steel and iron, or even copper and bronze, so you would be most likely to find them. Jewels, of course, last even longer."

"We've found no jewels," Tam said, "though we would

wish otherwise. It is our plan to visit Inniseth. We'll buy horses there and ride back."

"You'll find good stock at Inniseth, though the Wold of Kerns might treat you better, but it is further on, of course. You must have discovered some fine things if you will go so far to trade them for horses?"

Tam shrugged. "It is partly the journey. We've never been beyond the hills and would like to see a little of the lowlands while we may."

"Before you marry, you mean, and settle down to the serious business of populating the wildlands?"

The young men all smiled a bit shyly.

"Well, it's a good thing to see the world," Alaan said, his tone a little more serious. "But you must take care. Travel causes some affliction of the eye, and after a while no place it rests looks like home. No woman the right woman." His face became more serious. "I speak from experience. Have you found anything marked with the devices of Knights of the Vow?"

"Just this one thing, and of that we are not certain." Tam gestured to Baore who looked surprised for an instant, then handed over the dagger handle he had been polishing. Tam passed it to the stranger. "'Tis so faint one can hardly tell, but is that not the swan and the lion?"

Alaan held the handle close to the fire, turning it slowly. He poured a little wine into the ashes at the fire's edge and stirred them with a stick. Taking up a bit of this paste, he rubbed it over the crest on the handle, a few faintly etched lines appearing as though by magic.

"Most would think this belonged to a Knight of the Vow," he said after a moment, "but I'm sure it didn't. It's hard to tell, as you say, especially in this light, but this is not the swan and the lion. Oh, it is similar, and intentionally so, but this is a crane. Do you see? The arms of the princes of Alethon—allies of the Knights through many years of struggle. The last prince fell at the Battle of Telanon Bridge. Here." He waved the handle toward the dark wood. "But there is an even more compelling reason. The devices of the Knights changed over the years. The swan and the lion they were given by King Thynne when first they formed, but this was replaced in later years by the silveroak tree, and finally by a fan of silveroak leaves. If this handle bore the swan and the lion it would be very ancient indeed. So ancient that I hardly think it would have survived so long in the ground. But it is a valuable piece all the same. Don't take less than five eagles for it. Who will you sell it to?"

"There is a man named Truk in Inniseth town," Fynnol said. "He is said to pay fairly for such things."

"Morgan Truk has never paid fairly for anything in his life!" Alaan laughed.

"You've heard of him?"

"I *know* him. He is as kindly an old bandit as you will ever meet. But he will pay you a tenth what he can get for it himself, that is certain. And don't think of buying horses from him. As I sit here, he will charge you four times as much as any other man. Don't be taken in by his gentle manner."

The three Valemen glanced at one another.

"You say this is worth five eagles?" Fynnol asked.

"Oh, easily. It would sell in Westbrook for three times that. So if you sell it in Inniseth town you must consider their efforts to carry it downriver and find a buyer. If Truk won't give you five for it tell him you travel to the fair at Westbrook. That will change his tune. I should be glad to look over what you've found and give you my own opinion of its worth, if that would be of any help."

"That would be kind of you," said Baore, looking around at the others, obviously delighted to hear that they might make significantly more than they'd expected. Perhaps the journey would look more attractive to him now, Tam thought.

"It's all down in the boat," Tam said. "If you have time in the morning, it can be seen properly."

"I have time, and it is the least I can do to repay your kind hospitality." Alaan looked around the dark walls. "I would guess many a man has made his camp here and spent his days searching for the treasure of the Knights of the Vow. Is that what you truly seek?"

Embarrassed silence from the three young men, and then Tam spoke up. "When we were young and first came here we had such dreams, but we found only a few trinkets. Then we learned that the lowlanders valued antiquities, so we have come back each year after planting and spent some time digging and sifting through the soil. It will pay us back now, or so we hope."

"Tam's grandfather tells us that there was no treasure.

That there weren't even any Knights of the Vow at the battle fought here," Fynnol said.

Alaan shifted where he sat, gazing into the fire. "Well, that might or might not be true. This was a tower of the Knights, as you no doubt know, for they kept guard over the gold and silver that came from the mines high up in the mountains. Rich, those mines once were, and the Battle of Telanon Bridge was fought for their control. It is said the Knights no longer safeguarded the treasure then, for their toll had grown for this service and the King forbade them to continue it. But even so, there is an old song that suggests at least one Knight fought here, at the battle."

Alaan cleared his throat and then began to sing in a pure, clear tenor.

"Through crimson leaves and failing light,
And battle lost upon the ridge.
Dark birds fell like leaves from flight.
As four rode over Telanon Bridge.

The first was a knight who'd broken a vow,
And one was a captain whose shield bore an oak.
The third hid a wound that robbed him of life,
And last came a child in his dead father's cloak.

A treasure they bore more valued than gold
A treasure they bore from the battle-seared ridge
Four riders went forth,
Four riders went forth over Telanon Bridge.

Through wildlands in winter they carried their charge
No friend to succor them in bitterest cold.
Of those sent to warn them, none were met
And three riders arrived at the black Duke's hold.

A treasure they bore more valued than gold,
A treasure they bore from the battle-seared ridge.
No riders returned to tell the tale
Of the four who crossed over Telanon Bridge."

Tam glanced out an opening in the stone, where stars hung among the branches of the trees. The river voice echoed in the gorge below, and a nighthawk *peened* over the keep.

"The song is incomplete, but it is clear that the child is the treasure, unlike many another version of the same lyric. It was originally recorded in Eaorel, but it was well rendered as I have sung it. But you see, 'one was a captain whose shield bore an oak.' A Knight of the Vow, one would have to admit. Though of course it is only a song." Alaan shifted to stretch his legs, stiff as though he had been riding long days.

They fell silent and a small gust whispered through the trees, speaking a tongue Tam could not understand. For a moment they all seemed to listen.

"I've heard an old song much like that," Tam said. "My grandfather knows many old tales and songs, and taught them to my father, though only a few were sung to me. My grandfather lost his heart for teaching them when my father passed on." Tam was embarrassed suddenly to be telling this to a stranger, but Alaan's kindly manner and obvious interest seemed to draw him out.

Alaan began to gently rub one knee. "Perhaps you can sing some of these songs, for I've an interest in old lyrics." He would perhaps have said more, but a bird alighted in a window opening overhead, half lost in shadow. The stranger extended his hand and made odd noises, partly whistling and partly the noises some made to babies. The bird, which seemed to be a small crow, strutted nervously on its perch but would not come down.

"He is shy with strangers," Alaan said, giving up.

"This is your crow?"

"Mine, yes, but not a crow. A whist. Perhaps a cousin to the crow and the jay, but smaller and with a far prettier song, though when he is alarmed he makes the warning cry that gives him his name. The whist will also fly at night. I don't know what it is they hunt in the darkness, but they go abroad in the hours when only the nighthawks and owls are hunting. I found Jac, for that is his name, in the trunk of a tree that had been struck by lightning—the only survivor of his family, I fear. I raised him and have not been able to rid myself of him since. Where I go, he goes, though he is endless trouble: a thief of any small thing that glints, though the gods know what he does with them. Often I don't see him for days, but he always returns." The stranger reached into one of his bags and took out a few nuts that he spread on the ground.

"You know the older languages?" Tam asked, wondering about Alaan's comments on the history of the song.

"You see before you the bane of several worthy scholars. I fear I was a bitter disappointment to them, but I have a weakness for the old songs and tales all the same."

The whist dropped to the ground then, scooped up a bill full of nuts, and leapt back to its perch with only three beats of its wings.

"He seems dark blue in the firelight," Fynnol said, always observant.

"Yes, in the right light he can seem blue, at other times dark gray, but usually black. A good color for a bird that flies at night."

Tam looked up at the bird as it worked quickly on the nuts it had dropped on the ledge. "Aren't the whist from Forlyn? You've traveled far if you have been there."

"Far, yes." Alaan turned to Tam, his look both surprised and curious. "How long has your family been in the Vale, Tam?"

"My great-grandfather was the first. From Kell, it's said, though I'm not sure anyone really knows."

"A family that passes down the old songs and doesn't remember their own history? What is your family name?"

"Loell."

"Not an uncommon name in the Vale, I should imagine," Alaan said. "From the Helfing Wold to begin with, though spread across all the lands now." He kept his eyes fixed on Tam. A fluttering of wings caused everyone to look up just in time to see the whist disappearing into blackness.

"Now I'll worry that he will be an owl's dinner until he appears again," Alaan said, shaking his head. "And what manner of life did your ancestors follow in Kell?"

Tam shrugged. "Men-at-arms is what I suspect, though no one seems to be sure."

"And your father, you say, passed on?"

Tam nodded. "When I was a boy."

"I'm sorry to hear it," Alaan said softly, and began to poke at the fire with a small stick. "After the last wars many a man left his past behind and took on a common name. Their descendants can be found in all the little corners of the land between the mountains. Better not to stir the fire," he said, doing just that. "Not that anyone cares now." A flame flickered up from Alaan's efforts, wavering before them like a snake. "It is astonishing what is lost in war: places of learning are destroyed, libraries burned, people of knowledge put to the sword or starve or die of disease or any of the other hundred scourges that travel in war's train. Before the Renné and the Wills split the kingdom, the land between the mountains was a civilized realm . . ." He stopped, as though embarrassed by this outburst.

"Do the Renné and Wills still carry on their feud?" Baore asked.

Alaan pulled his stick out of the fire, a small flame attached to the end. "Oh, there is a peace of sorts, though I believe they will never give it up," he said. "The Wills are so reduced in circumstances these last years that they've not been able to keep an army. Would that the same thing befell the Renné and then we could all rest easily—for a while. Perhaps they will one day realize that this fool's feud is what brought them to their present states—two families much reduced in circumstances if not in pride.

"For the most part, now, they compete only on the tilt field, and with the Renné and Wills quiet, there is a peace of sorts over much of the rest of the land between the mountains. I pray it lasts a little longer." Alaan blew out the flame on his stick, gazed at it a moment, then tossed it on the fire. His charming facade seemed to have slipped away and he looked tired and grim. "I think it's time for me to sleep, as much as I hate to give up your pleasant company. Do you keep watch here?"

Tam shook his head, and the stranger rose, thanking them again for their kindness before going to the bundles he had removed from his horse. When he had disappeared beyond a wall to find some privacy, Fynnol turned to Tam.

"Well, what do you make of him, Cousin?"

Tam cocked his head to one side. "I think you would spend many years with Alaan before you would know what to make of him."

"He seemed to think your family were renegades of some kind," Fynnol said, teasing.

"Every family in the Vale came escaping something," Tam said. "I never thought my family's story any different.

Shall we sleep?" he said, rising. Baore looked up at him and then quickly away. Tam wondered if there would be three setting out downriver the next morning.

After they had rolled into their blankets Tam lay awake, looking up at the crescent moon, unable to sleep. *We're all from away,* his grandfather had said when Tam had asked him if it was true their family was not originally from the Vale. *Some more recently than we—but all from away. It is nothing to be ashamed of, nor is there any great mystery. Like so many after the great war, my father was forced to flee, and brought his family north. We have earned our place here, Tam, and the people of the Vale—those who came before and those who found their way here after—have been good to us.*

He would say little more than that and likely that would have satisfied Tam—but they practiced the arts of war with a deadly earnestness in the Vale. Every boy spent uncounted hours learning to ride, bear a lance, and fight with the sword. The bowmen of the Vale were as good as any in the land between the mountains, Tam heard men boast. It was true that the people of the Vale had been forced to protect themselves over the years, but such proficiency in war did not come from farmers and tradesmen.

Often his father had ridden out to patrol the road. There was some unrest in the distant south then, and a steady, thin stream of stragglers flowed up the old road, most looking for peace and safety—but not all. Tam was only a boy at the time, but he remembered his father leaving. All that returned was word of his death. He'd been buried beneath some unmarked mound, and no one remembered where it was.

The earth rolled over in its sleep and hid the crescent moon behind the shoulder of a distant hill, and Tam felt sleep coming over him. A last memory of his father wending his way up the path from their door, the horses' hooves sounding dully on the packed earth—the poor beasts moving slowly and hanging their heads as though reluctant to leave.

Tam came awake to a hand on his shoulder, shaking him gently.

"Fath—?"

"Make no sound," Alaan said. "There are men in the wood nearby, and they don't approach like men who wish us well."

Tam sat up, straining to hear. The fire was ash now, emitting no light, but the smell of it was strong. Starlight fell on the ruin of the old tower, and, far below, the river tumbled among the rocks. The hollow sound of a boot on wood echoed dully, as though someone found unexpected roots in the darkness.

"I hear them," Tam whispered. He would normally not be frightened of men in the dark—for likely they were doing as Alaan had done and making sure Tam and his companions were not cutthroats—but Alaan was clearly alarmed. He had a sword in his hand and seemed poised to use it.

Why do they seek him? Tam wondered. A low *whist-whist* sounded above him. Alaan's bird.

"I might have brought you ill fortune without meaning to," Alaan said, keeping his voice low. "If you have a blade or a bow best to find it now."

Tam pulled on his boots and snatched up his bow while Alaan woke the others. He crouched low, staring into the darkness. There were too many openings in the tumbledown walls. His eyes flicked from one to the other to another.

Something in the darkness. There is nothing so frightening as something hiding in the darkness.

"Who are they?" he heard Fynnol ask, as he scrambled up.

"Men to be avoided, I fear," Alaan said. "Follow me. Take nothing but weapons."

He led them out of the ruin through an empty window, and the four went as silently as they could into the trees. Tam designated himself rear guard, straining to hear the sounds of pursuit.

What if Alaan is an outlaw? Tam wondered.

But he followed this thought no further. Heavy boot steps echoed through the ruin behind them.

"We are headed toward cliffs," Tam heard Fynnol hiss.

"I know a path," Alaan answered, not slowing.

Branches whipped at Tam's eyes, and bits of torn spiderweb netted his face. He plunged on, following the others in almost total darkness. How Alaan kept to the trail was a mystery.

Suddenly there was more light ahead, an opening in the trees—the road where it met the bridgehead, Tam was certain.

Alaan brought them to a stop and turned back toward the others. "There are only three men on the bridge. They weren't expecting us to come this way."

"But how did we get here?" Fynnol whispered. "There are bluffs between the bridge and the ruin."

Alaan ignored this. "Listen to me. You've never encountered men like these. They are relentless in pursuit of their ends. Better they never know who you are. I will drive the men off the bridge. Cross over and don't stop until you're back in the Vale. Do you hear?"

But Tam heard a noise from the wood. "They are behind us!" he whispered.

The sound had not gone unnoticed by the men on the bridge. One of them called out, and Alaan answered as though he were a friend. And then he burst out into the open. Three men in dark surcoats stood at the bridgehead, swords and iron helms glinting in the starlight. Alaan didn't hesitate but was upon them, crying out as he swung his blade.

The men did not stand their ground but fell away, one stumbling and falling to his knees. Alaan's sword flashed in the starlight and the fallen man sprawled facedown and did not move.

A second man lost his sword and jumped back, clasping a hand to his arm, shouting in panic. Alaan drove the last man off the bridge and shouted to the Valemen.

"Cross over. Quickly! Don't wait for me."

Fynnol did not need to be urged and dashed onto the bridge. Baore looked back over his shoulder, as though he would not leave Alaan alone, but Tam pushed him ahead, and the two bolted onto the span behind Fynnol.

"Not our fight," Tam managed as they went, but the sounds of shouting and struggle behind made him wonder if they did the right thing. If Alaan was an outlaw why had he sent them on and stayed to block the bridge?

Tam stopped, pulled an arrow from his quiver, and let fly at the men swarming down onto the bridge. And then another and a third. A shaft sparked off the stone balustrade a foot from Tam, prompting Baore to grab Tam by the shoulder and drag him on.

The last sight he had was of the brigands hacking terribly at a figure down on the stone, his cloak fluttering in the breeze and cold starlight.

Then the men rallied and rushed out onto the bridge, chain mail ringing dully at each step. Tam and Baore ran. But as they reached the far bank they heard men pounding down the old road toward them.

"After me," Tam hissed, and plunged into the underwood. There was a steep path that led down to the river here. Even knowing where it was Tam had trouble staying on the trail. He was sure that anyone unfamiliar with it wouldn't dare try to follow.

In a few moments they were on a sloping rock at the water's edge, where they bent double trying to recover their wind. They could hear men above them calling out and others on the bridge answering. Then an arrow glanced off the rock by Fynnol's foot.

"They're shooting from the bridge!" he yelled, leaping back into the shadow of the cliff. Something trundled through the bush, and then a good-sized rock splashed into the river. Arrows continued to fall.

Fynnol did not wait to consider the best course of action but plunged into the water, pulling himself along the cliff, struggling to keep his feet beneath him on the slippery stones.

"They're still coming down," Baore gasped as he jumped in after Fynnol.

Tam spent two arrows shooting up at the men on the bridge, and followed the others into the water. He regretted leading them to the river now. If they went downstream with the current the men on the bridge would likely shoot them as they passed, but to struggle upstream against the flow was going to be possible only for a while. He heard the first man land on the rock at the water's edge and more come.

With some effort Tam had kept his bowstring dry.

"Steady me!" he said to Baore, and felt one strong hand take hold of his clothing at his back. Tam let go of the rock, but Baore would not let the current carry him away. He nocked an arrow and shot at the man he could just see, not twenty paces off.

He heard the man cry out, and saw his shadow fall. A second man appeared, crouching on the rock. Tam shot again, and this man scrambled back up the path, out of sight.

Tam gave his treasured yaka bow to the river then, and turned to follow the others. He could hear them breathing fast ahead of him, coughing up mouthfuls of the cold, metallic river. Cursing in their panic.

Up, Tam thought. *We have to go up.*

The cliff was striated and cracked, with hardy shrubs and ferns growing on the smallest ledges and from the narrow fissures. Here and there small pines and cedars seemed to grow from the rock itself. They might scramble up and hide, Tam thought. It might be possible.

Arrows continued to search for them in the dark, and occasionally one would float past Tam. He hoped the others hadn't been hurt. An edge of rock came to Tam's hand, and he stared up. A fang of stone leaned out slightly from the cliff—perhaps seven feet high—and a tree seemed to grow out from behind it. They could go up there, perhaps higher.

"Fynnol," he whispered, trying to pitch his voice over the river but not loud enough for others to hear. "Come back. We have to go up here." Perhaps Baore could go on fighting the river, but Fynnol could not last much longer, Tam was sure, and he would not be far behind.

He felt Baore bump into him in the darkness, and heard Fynnol suck in a mouthful of water.

"We'll go up and hide beneath this tree. Give me a leg up." Tam dragged himself up, his wet boots slipping on the stone.

The branch of cedar touched his head gently, as though alerting him to its presence in the dark, and he took hold of this offered hand and pulled himself up. He scrambled over the top of this rock and down into a fissure behind, pulling Fynnol after him, and then the two of them took Baore's hands. The big Valeman tumbled in on top of them.

They hunched down, shivering from the river, trying to make no sound. It was too dark to see the others' faces, but Tam could hear their quick breathing, sense them fighting panic. He strained to hear the sounds of their hunters in the dark. There was the occasional shout in the night, but these grew less frequent with time and Tam felt the edge of his fear blunt a little. They made themselves as comfortable as they could in their lair and waited.

Tam watched the last stars gutter in the gray, and then the familiar world emerged. Tam was sure they could not be seen where they hid, for the branches of the tree concealed them from anyone on the cliff or the bridge, and they were above any man who would venture into the river. But what to do, that was the question. They could hardly stay here forever.

"I say we keep still and watch until noon," Fynnol said. "If we see nothing, we go straight back to the Vale."

"I'm with you, Cousin," Baore said softly. "We need to warn the others that there are such men about."

"Such men?" Tam asked. "But who were they, and why did they murder Alaan?"

No one had an answer.

Tam could not believe that the man who had shared their fire only the night before was dead, perhaps lured to that death by a desire for companionship—for it had certainly been their fire that had drawn the men in the darkness. "Alaan said he knew old Gallon. Perhaps we can find out something from him, or at least find some way to send a message to Alaan's kin."

Tam crawled up to the edge of the rock and looked out through the branches of the tree.

"What do you see?" Fynnol asked, ever impatient.

"No men. No——" Tam stopped, sure that he was not looking at the right place on the bank, but after a moment he was forced to admit the truth. "There is no luck for us! The boat is gone!"

Fynnol and Baore scrambled up beside him. Tam heard Fynnol groan, but Baore said nothing. He and Tam sank back down behind the rock. Still none of them spoke. The loss of the boat and their long-held dream to journey down the river was overshadowed by their relief at being alive. Fynnol kept watch, and Tam and Baore sat quietly with their thoughts.

"I'll feel the fool cowering here if these bandits are gone," Fynnol whispered down to them. "Hey up! What's that I hear?"

The three fell silent, trying to separate the voice of the river from some faint sound . . .

"Is it a flute?" Baore asked.

"Singing. I'm sure I heard singing," Tam said.

A moment later one of the great horses of the Fáel appeared, twenty-two hands tall, and behind it one of the wanderers' colorful carts. On the high seat Tam could see a man and woman, raven-black hair wafting in the breeze funneling down the gorge.

Black wanderers the people of the Vale called them, for the color of their hair and eyes. *Fever bringers* they were called as well for the night fever they were said to have spread across the land between the mountains.

"I would say it is safe for us to venture out," Fynnol said, heaving himself up the rock and down into the running river. He looked back up at the others, grinning. "I don't think even brave brigands would risk angering our wandering friends."

"Do not assume they are friends, Fynnol," Tam cautioned as he followed his cousin into the water. "These might not be the Fáel we know."

The current took hold of Tam and carried him quickly down to the path—the place he had shot a man the night before—but if blood had been spilled upon the rocks the river had washed them clean. The events of the night seemed unreal suddenly, as though it had all been a bad dream and nothing more. The path seemed especially steep after a cold night spent cramped and frightened. Fynnol stopped once to rest. Eventually they emerged into a clearing just as one of the great carts rolled by.

No matter how many times he saw the massive horses of the Fáel Tam could not get used to them. The largest draft horses bred in the Vale stood eighteen hands, and these were full four hands taller, and some were six! At the shoulder they stood a foot taller than Baore.

Dark-haired children ran along beside the carts, and one—a girl of ten or twelve—took hold of the turning wheel, as tall as a man, and placing her feet quickly on the rim, turned a full circle before letting go. The origin of the cartwheel, Tam thought.

Up on the high seat of the wagon the older folk rode, awash in sunshine. Tam always thought the Fáel, in their bright flowing clothes and tinkling jewelry, looked like birds of the air compared to the dull colors of the men and women of the Vale. And like the birds, they traveled to and fro across the land between the mountains, coming north in spring and returning to the distant south before winter.

Shiftless vagabonds and worse they were called by the hardworking people of the Vale, though never to their faces. The curse of a wanderer was feared.

Usually the Fáel kept to themselves, but once a party of them had been caught by an early and nasty winter and had struggled through to the Vale, where they had wintered in the haylofts of various barns, unsettling many of the inhabitants, though fascinating a few. More than one young woman had lost her heart to the travelers' charms, and more than one Valeman made a fool of himself over a Fáel woman. And Tam understood why. Had he not been only a boy he would have likely done the same himself.

But the Fáel had their own sense of honor, and the

people of the Vale—their "rescuers"—they treated differently ever after. Not that the people of the Vale were welcomed into the world of the Fáel, but at least they weren't treated with the disdain the Fáel reserved for others.

One of the massive carts pulled up as Tam and his companions appeared, the great horse taking a few steps to stop, like a ship under way.

The Fáel who drove the cart looked down on them guardedly. "You must be Valemen," he said. "I had heard your dress was shabby but . . ." The Valemen noticed their clothing for the first time: wet, torn, and filthy.

The Fáel children scurried up onto the high seat beside him, gazing with intense curiosity at the strangers. The Fáel said a single word in his own tongue to his wife, who laughed and then quickly covered her mouth.

"And I had heard the Fáel were more polite to people who had saved their lives," Fynnol said quickly.

"And that is true. But you have never saved mine or anyone in my family's. And you smell like the river." The man smiled at Fynnol. "I assume you are lost," he said and pointed off down the road. "The Vale is a few hours' walk in that direction."

Tam cut off Fynnol's retort. "We are far worse than lost. We were set upon by brigands in the night and our companion was murdered."

The mockery in the wanderer's face evaporated, and immediately he sent his oldest child running off.

"How many were they—these brigands?"

Tam shrugged, looking at the others. "It was dark and they surprised us in our sleep. Twenty, at least, I would say?"

Baore and Fynnol nodded.

The man tilted his head and snorted derisively. "These were not brigands! How would twenty men survive by raiding the north road? No one travels here but my people once every few years and the odd poor fool looking for gold in the mountains."

"Nevertheless, we were set upon by armed men and they were intent on murdering us."

The Fáel shared a look with his wife. Just then a boy in his early teens ran up and spoke to the man in their own language.

"We will raise our tents here tonight," the Fáel said. "And you can tell your story to the others. Do you fear these men are still about?"

Tam shrugged. "I don't know. We were camped at the old tower and haven't ventured back. We spent the night hiding among the rocks in the river."

The man handed the reins to his wife and, fetching a sword and bow from the cart, clambered down quickly.

"Who is the bowman among you?" he asked.

"Tam," Fynnol said quickly.

He handed his bow and quiver to Tam. "Show me this place," he said, and set off along the line of carts, sword in hand.

Word was spreading quickly of what had happened, and the faces that watched them pass were grim and not friendly. The Fáel, whose name was Tuan, led the way quickly over the bridge, passing perhaps another dozen wagons as they went. Two young men, both armed with swords and bows, dropped into place behind them; and on every cart bows appeared and children were lifted up into the backs of the carts where their round, serious faces appeared, watching the strangers pass.

They found their camp in utter ruin—bags torn open, the contents spread everywhere. Alaan's horse and bags were gone. Only his scabbard was found in a corner where he must have discarded it the previous night.

"Alaan, you say." The Fáel looked around the ruin, no longer unwilling to believe their story. "What sort of man was he?"

"He was well spoken," Fynnol answered, "well spoken and though he appeared at home in the wood he seemed a man bred to a different life." Fynnol stopped to think, creasing his forehead. "He had a pet bird with him—a whist, he called it. We never learned what brought him here or where he was going. I guess I thought we'd learn that in the morning, for he seemed in no hurry, nor did he appear concerned that he might be pursued."

"And what was it you were doing here?" Tuan asked, eyeing Fynnol.

"We were visiting with the ghosts of fallen warriors. In the Vale we believe this will make us strong."

Tam flashed an angry look at his cousin. "We were digging for artifacts in the meadows. We've done it these past three years and were going to take what we'd found down the river to trade for horses. But our boat is gone."

Tuan tilted his head a little, then looked off toward the river. "It seems unlikely these men came by water," he said.

Tam agreed with this: the river flowed directly out of the Vale and to journey any distance against the flow would have been impossible.

"So one would hazard that they had come on horseback. It seems rather odd that men on horseback would bother to steal your boat." He crouched down, staring at the ground. "Perhaps your boat floated off on its own. If the river spirits are willing you might find it stranded downstream a little."

Tam and Fynnol glanced at each other, and Fynnol shook his head almost imperceptibly. Neither of them thought their boat had taken to the river on its own. It had been firmly beached and soundly tied to a tree.

Tuan stood, looking around the ruin, lost in thought, his dark eyes filled with sudden cares. "Gather up your belongings," he said, pushing a pile of clothing toward Fynnol with his foot. "The others will want to hear your story."

"Perhaps we will do as you suggest," Tam said, "and search downriver. As you say, our boat might have run up on a gravel bar. Stranger things have happened."

"Take my bow," the Fáel said. "Who knows what might still be lurking in the forest."

THREE

Five hours of fighting through thick underwood convinced them their boat was gone. Just a league away lay the Five Gorges, and without steady hands to guide the boat, the rocks would have it. Their precious cargo, the fruits of all their labor, would go to the bottom, never to be seen again by men.

"I still don't know how Alaan managed to get from the ruin to the bridge without us plunging over a cliff," Fynnol said. It wasn't the first time he'd returned to this topic.

"It was dark and we were all frightened and half asleep," Baore said. "We must have come closer to the road than we realized."

Fynnol shook his head. "No, we went out the east window, toward the river. We couldn't have been that turned around." He looked to Tam for support.

"You're right, Fynnol. We escaped out the east window, but we must have gotten confused in the dark. Either that or there is a path down the cliffs that we've never found, and a surprisingly gently sloped one at that."

The walk back to the bridge was completed in silence,

and it was near to evening when the Valemen made their way into the camp of the Fáel. The wanderers looked up as the outsiders appeared, and then whispered among themselves.

"Perhaps we shouldn't stay here this night," Fynnol said, and Baore nodded his agreement.

"Let's find Tuan and talk to him a moment," Tam said. "If we don't sleep here, we're left with the open woods or the ruin. Neither appeals."

Memories came back to Tam of the family of black wanderers who'd spent the winter in his grandfather's hayloft. He remembered going out there of an evening, clutching his grandfather's hand, curious and frightened, as though they were visiting a family of bears. The Fáel seemed to have burrowed a home out of the golden hay, sleeping in the loft and living on the wooden floor beneath the massive old beams.

Someone called his name, and there, among the hostile faces, Tam saw one smiling and familiar: Aliel. He felt oddly embarrassed, uncertain if she would greet him as a friend or treat him as the Fáel treated outsiders.

"Look!" Aliel said to no one in particular. "See what happens when Vale children escape being eaten by the Fáel. They become giants!" She waved a hand at Baore.

Aliel embraced Tam and left a soft kiss on his cheek, holding him at arm's length and gazing at him as though he were a long-lost nephew. Her dark eyes shone, and a smile as sweet as morning spread across her face.

"We've often wondered what happened to Tam and

his curious cousin." She surprised Fynnol by nodding to him. "Oh, you've not changed so much," she said. But then her manner became suddenly serious. "But you've lost a friend," she said softly.

"Hardly a friend," Tam said. "He was a stranger who joined us at our fire. Who he was or where he came from we don't know."

"Well," Aliel said, taking his arm and drawing him into the encampment, "sup with rogues and you will share their deserts."

Fynnol laughed, flashing Aliel a smile of appreciation.

Aliel was not tall, smaller than Fynnol, but she was lithe and graceful as the Fáel tended to be. Like many of her people, Aliel's eyes and mouth seemed too large for her face, her nose too long; but Tam thought it gave a kind of drama to her beauty. She wore her long hair unbound, and jewelry dangled and sparkled about her.

Tam introduced Baore, remembering that Baore's father had wanted nothing to do with the black wanderers who had appeared at the gate in the late autumn snow. Baore took Aliel's hand with slight reluctance, but Aliel seemed not to notice and spoke with him as though he were an old friend.

They all took stools by Aliel's fire, and she stirred the contents of an iron pot that hung over the flames, then added a seasoning that was pungent and strange. Around the camp Tam saw the other Fáel casting glances their way. Aliel's obvious friendship had not made these glances more welcoming.

"Pay them no heed," Aliel said, not looking up from her cooking. "They are suspicious of your people—thinking that you will rob them or steal their horses. They don't know you."

"Nor do they care to know us," Fynnol said.

"That is true. They're happy with their own fancies and superstitions. My people are like yours in this way. Should I assume your day's labors have left you hungry?" She began filling bowls.

Aliel's husband, Cian, arrived at this moment, and Aliel poured him a basin of steaming water. He took a cloth and carefully washed his face and hands, looking up from his efforts to regard Tam.

"You will look like your grandfather one day," Cian said to Tam, apparently pleased to see the Valemen. Although Tam had once thought of the Fáel as all appearing much the same, when they had stayed the winter he had realized that wasn't true. Cian was a perfect example of this, for his skin was lighter and his face surprisingly round without the high cheekbones and fine, long nose.

"Tell us of your grandfather, Tam," Cian said. "Is he well?"

"He is, though his hair is gray now and he walks a little slower—though just as far."

"Give him our blessing when you see him, and tell him we've never forgotten his kindness."

"You should visit him yourself, Cian," Tam said. "He would be delighted to see you again."

Cian was suddenly absorbed in the washing of his hands. "We would like to visit him, Tam," Cian said quietly, "but these we travel with . . . they would never understand."

Fynnol caught Tam's eye, eyebrows rising.

Aliel served the meal at a low table, and they sat on rugs laid over the spring grass. Tam shut his eyes and let the first mouthful of his meal linger. He breathed in the aroma of it, a clear memory of his first Fáel supper coming back to him.

Aliel poured them all a light, clear wine, then raised her cup. "I'm glad of this chance to have you to ourselves for a while. Genn will want to speak with you. Any news of brigands on our favored roads is a concern. Let's drink to . . . well, let us drink to the river, for last night it gave you refuge."

"To the river," the Valemen said with feeling, and raised their glasses.

"Who is Genn?" Tam asked.

"She is our . . . guide, I suppose you would say. Don't be concerned. Genn knows how many of us wouldn't have survived if not for people like your grandfather, Tam." She began slicing a dense loaf of bread, which Tam realized must have been made without an oven. "Tell us about the Vale. Have you had other winters like the one that brought us to you?"

For half an hour the Fáel tried to pretend they were interested in the doings of the Vale and Tam tried to find something to tell them. Finally Cian took pity on him.

"We should let these young men eat before Genn calls for them," Cian said. "Best not to go hungry."

They ate in silence for a while, Aliel humming an odd, haunting tune, meeting their gazes now and then with her beautiful smile. As they ate, dusk stole into the Fáel encampment, muting colors, brightening fires. The tents, formed like miniature pavilions, stood out against the growing shadows, their soft colors seeming to glow in the gloom.

Tam looked past Cian and Aliel at the other Fáel moving about the encampment: the graceful women in their long, flowing skirts and intricately embroidered vests, their golden-brown arms bare. The Fáel women seemed terribly exotic and beautiful to Tam. So unlike the practical women of the Vale in their no-nonsense clothing, hair pulled into a single, tight braid.

The dress of the men was only slightly less exotic, for they favored brightly colored vests over shirts with billowing sleeves. Even now, at the end of the day, the Fáel had a lightness to their step. They didn't seem exhausted by their toil, as did the men and women of the Vale. Yet they were industrious, despite their reputation. They produced beautiful fabrics, jewelry, instruments, and the finest bows in the land between the mountains.

In the growing dark, the great horses shifted, hooves making a muted sound upon the soft earth. Tam could see Cian and Aliel's horse staked out nearby, cropping the grasses contentedly. It was said that the Fáel valued their horses above their children, and certainly when they had wintered in the Vale Tam had been left with the impression that the horses were members of the families. The Fáel took no chance that their precious horses might breed with those of the Valemen—leaving any half-breeds behind.

They were well-tended beasts, and much alike in color and conformation. Silky black manes and tails, varying degrees of white on their faces, shiny coats of burnished brown shading toward deep chestnut, and feathered white feet. Like most draft horses they were of calm disposition.

Cian looked up as someone came near and nodded to him. "It is time to meet Genn," he said, rising. "Aliel and I will accompany you."

Tam was half expecting to meet "elders," but the Fáel they were introduced to hardly fit the image: one was a fairly young man they called Cynddl, not more than thirty despite his gray hair; and Genn was a woman of perhaps fifty years—hardly elders. They sat in chairs woven of willow wands set beneath the spreading branches of a great beech. Colored candle lanterns swayed on cords, illuminating the Fáel and the sweeping structure of the tree.

Tam felt a bit self-conscious sitting there with the dark Fáel eyes gazing at him. Genn had wrapped a finely woven shawl about her shoulders, and perched so elegantly on her chair that Tam felt clumsy and oafish just sitting near her. Tam didn't remember her from the Fáel visit to the

Vale, but Aliel and Cian deferred to her and listened respectfully.

"I'm surprised your people would let you go digging on a field of battle," she said. "There are things in such places that should never be disturbed: old enmities, malignities that have festered over all the years the ground has been closed. Battlefields are places to be wary of. You can't know what you might unearth."

Having experienced the arrogance of the Fáel before, Tam knew there was nothing to be gained by reacting in anger. "We sought only to find a few trinkets we might trade downriver for horses," Tam said. "Certainly we meant no harm."

"Let us hope you've done none. I'm also told you were set upon by brigands . . ." She looked at each of them in turn, as though this attack was somehow their own doing. She brushed a wave of graying hair back from her face. "Highwaymen don't ply their trade where roads are seldom traveled. Tell me how this happened."

Baore and Fynnol both turned to Tam, silently electing him spokesman. He told the story, surprised at how tight his voice became when he related their flight across the bridge and down into the river. When he was done Genn carefully straightened her skirt, saying nothing for a moment. "You say these men were all in the same dark surcoats and wore helms?" she asked at last.

Tam nodded.

"Well, it would seem unlikely they were brigands, then. This was the livery of some noble family."

Tam hadn't considered this, for the nearest noble families lived many weeks' journey away. "I've never seen a man dressed in livery, but perhaps you're right."

The Fáel cast glances back and forth, and then Genn spoke again. "It would seem most likely that your chance companion, Alaan, had stolen something or offended some powerful family. Charm, you say he had, and though it is not the exclusive attribute of rogues, it is a trait they all must have in abundance. I fear, without meaning to, you fell in with a fleeing rascal. It would explain why he had traveled so far into the wilds. Unlike our people, few will come so far just for the journey."

Tam shifted in his chair, considering what she'd said.

"Alaan didn't act like a man being pursued," Fynnol said quickly. He leaned forward, his sharp features set and determined. "And when the men appeared, he held the bridge so that we might escape. Hardly the action of a rogue. He could have slipped away when first he heard these men and left us to our own fate."

"Thieves and rogues are not all cut of one cloth," Genn said. "Some have a strange kind of honor, and even among your people only a few are utterly without remorse. It's not impossible that, though Alaan might steal from a wealthy family, he would not see innocent young men murdered for his crime. The world is large. Such men exist."

Cian cleared his throat. He was so soft voiced and quiet of demeanor that Tam had forgotten that this concealed the truth about him: he was nobody's fool, and quite capable of letting you know it. "Excuse me, Genn, but I think Fynnol is right. They say Alaan did not act like a man pursued; certainly if he had been chased into the wildlands he would have been more wary."

"Perhaps." Genn shrugged. "Though he might have believed he had outdistanced his pursuers or that they'd given up the chase. More importantly, I don't think these men who fell upon him were robbers. They were men in pursuit of Alaan and no one else. Oh, they were prepared to cut down men who appeared to be Alaan's accomplices, but once they had Alaan they left these others in peace. It might be that they found their stolen goods in Alaan's baggage. I'm sure they're making their way south as we speak."

"I am surprised that you didn't meet these men on the road," Tam said. "As you say, they would have gone south, back to their homes."

He could see the Fáel react to this. They were a secretive people and, by reputation, quite willing to lie to strangers.

"We did not see them," Genn said after a moment, "but the men walking out before us saw signs of them. A troop of mounted men had turned aside into the forest. They must have heard us, though why they would avoid us I cannot say."

"It makes me wonder if they had rightful cause to be hunting Alaan or to deliver judgment," Fynnol said.

Genn shrugged. "The affairs of your people are of little concern to us—just or unjust."

Cynddl caught Genn's eye. "But what of the whist?" he asked quietly.

Genn shifted in her chair. She wore at least one ring on each finger, and now she tapped them one at a time upon the arm of her chair. "If this man had kept a crow or a jay there would be no cause for concern," she said. "But a whist is a bird of omen, to both your people and to ours. You must know the legends . . .?" she said to the Valemen.

"We don't," Tam said, a bit embarrassed by this admission.

Genn regarded him a moment and then shook her head. "Well, they're old tales. Tales of both our peoples." She resettled herself in her chair. Darkness was now complete and the faces of the Fáel were lit only by the colored lanterns.

"During the earliest wars of men, long before the one kingdom was forged, when the princes still ruled their own lands, there was a prince—a renowned warrior named Derborgil. He went to war against Prince Siforé, though his own mother was filled with foreboding and begged him to make peace.

"But Derborgil was a proud man and a warrior above all else, and he mustered his armies and set out for the borders of Siforé, who had offended him. It was a terrible war, long and with many men lost on both sides.

"To the despair of all, before each battle a dark bird appeared and flew overhead or perched upon Derborgil's standard and cried out *whist* once for every man who would die that day. The men dreaded the coming of the whist and its terrible count, but none would slay it out of fear, for they believed it an unnatural creature. But Derborgil took his long bow and, before a battle, shot the whist as it came down from the sky, crying as it did, *whist, whist*. He cut off its wings and adorned his helm with them, saying, 'Now I am the crier of death.'

"He led them into battle then, a terrible fight that lasted a day and a night and the next day as well. Finally Derborgil won through to Siforé and slew him after a long struggle. But when he looked around he saw the field was silent and still. Only he remained of all the men of the warring armies. He knew then that his mother's premonition had been true, and he threw himself upon his sword.

"When those who watched came onto the field of battle to seek their fallen brothers and husbands, they found no sign of Derborgil though they had marked where he had fallen." Genn paused. "Suddenly, they heard a bird crying in the darkness, over and over, *whist, whist*.

"In the land of Forlyn the crying of a whist is still believed to herald death, and though they consider the bird the worst omen they won't harm it, knowing the fate of Derborgil."

Genn gazed intently at the three Valemen. "But your people misunderstand the tale. The whist only foretold the deaths, it didn't cause them. When the whist spoke they refused to listen." Genn looked around at the others, tugging her shawl close about her shoulders. "But still, the whist is not a good omen to your people.

"The other story is older yet," Genn said into the silence, "but concerns our people. And the ancestors of Cynddl in particular, so I will let him tell the story."

Tam thought Cynddl hardly looked Fáel. His skin was almost pale, his hair gray and cut short, though his eyebrows were thick and black. He seemed to have no vanity, unlike the other Fáel men and women Tam had known, nor did he seem to harbor any resentment toward the "outsiders." Though he had only been in the man's presence for a few moments, Tam had the impression that Cynddl was not much concerned with matters believed to be of import by either of their peoples.

"The whist . . ." Cynddl began, his voice seeming too old to belong to its owner—a complex voice, so laden with experience that one believed it immediately. "The whist was an omen for our people, too, though of a different sort. In the days we now remember only in poetry and song, it was the whist that found us wandering the seas. We hadn't gone our separate ways, then, but were all *Fáel-scena*, 'seafarers,' unlike the landfarers some of us have become. Invaders had driven us from the islands we loved, out into the open ocean.

"Cynddlyn led our people then, and he was the finest sailor of his day. It was said he had once lain with a sea maiden and she told him the secrets of the sea. It is from Cynddlyn that my own family descends," he said, though more with reverence than pride.

"The supply of fresh water dwindled and no rain came

to fill the sailors' casks. They were desolate and near to giving up all hope of finding land, when a bird came down from the sky to perch in the rigging of the ship, exhausted and lost like the Fáel. Cynddlyn knew this wasn't an ocean bird but a bird of the land, blown out to sea.

"They watched him while he perched, resting, staying just out of reach of anyone who approached. And then he took flight again toward the horizon and Cynddlyn ordered his ships to follow. By day they could see the bird, dark against the sky, and by night they could hear him singing—a beautiful liquid pealing.

"After three days of sailing, on a night when moon and stars were hidden, the song of the bird changed to a terrible, forlorn cry: *whist, whist*. Cynddlyn ordered his ships about, but in the darkness and running sea his signal was lost and all but three of the ships were wrecked upon rocks.

"When the sun rose they could see, far off, mountains. Those who had heeded the warning of the whist were saved, but the rest were lost." Cynddl looked at each of the Valemen in turn. "And so you see the whist has not quite the same meaning to us. It led us here out of the trackless sea—those who heeded its warning."

No one said anything for a moment.

"I have never heard of a man taking a whist for a companion," Genn said quietly. She looked at Tam. "Have you?"

Tam shook his head.

"It seems an odd choice, given the whist's reputation. Have you seen this bird or heard its cry since last night?"

"We haven't," Tam said.

Genn looked at Cynddl, and Tam wondered what passed between them, unspoken. She turned back to the Valemen.

"Well, we are satisfied these men-at-arms meant no harm to anyone else. Your people will be glad of that." The rings on both her hands sounded sharply on the wooden chair. "What will you do now that your boat is lost and your artifacts with it?"

The three Valemen glanced at one another. No one had yet said it aloud. "Our journey is finished before it began," Tam said softly. He could see Fynnol close his eyes a moment, and when he opened them again he stared down at the ground.

The Fáel shared glances among themselves.

"Perhaps it is not all loss," Genn said gently. She nodded at the young Fáel. "Cynddl is a story finder— one of the most gifted I've ever known. We carried him north with us so that he could travel the river and gather what stories remain from the ancient kingdoms. We'd hoped to find boatmen in the Vale who would take him downriver, for Cynddl has no experience of fast water. It is his plan to buy a boat and pay the boatmen. I don't know if this would equal the price of horses but perhaps you could consider it?"

Fynnol glanced quickly up at Tam, hope kindling in his eyes.

"We would have to speak of this among ourselves," Tam said.

"Tomorrow would be soon enough, I think," Genn said, glancing at Cynddl who nodded.

"I knew them only as boys," Aliel said, "but I don't think their people would let them undertake the river if they hadn't the skills to manage it."

The news of the brigands had silenced the camp that evening, and there was almost no one about. A cool breeze wafted down the slopes of the nearby mountains to wander among the tents, unwelcome.

"What do you think of them, Genn?" Cynddl asked.

Genn pondered this. It was like her not to respond to even the simplest question without thinking a moment first. She looked up. "I'm sure they are much alike, these Valemen. And at least two of these Aliel has known. I should think they will do."

Cynddl shifted in his chair. Aliel thought him odd for a story finder—not quite so distant, almost warm.

"This journey I'm undertaking is not so simple, Genn, as you well know. I'm hesitant to take *anyone* along, and do so only of necessity. I go to find the stories of sorcerers," he said softly, "and even sorcerers long dead are dangerous in their own way. Did Rath not tell you that? The tales of some are to be feared. That is a lesson story finders have learned again and again. Some stories are best left undisturbed."

There was no music or dancing in the Fáel encampment that night. Armed archers walked the edge of the meadow, and still others stood guard over the road and the bridge. Genn might have said she didn't believe these men-at-arms posed a threat to anyone but Alaan, but it appeared she was not really so confident of this. The Valemen's offer to stand guard was turned down, and they rolled themselves in blankets beneath Cian and Aliel's cart.

"It is a chance to have all our plans renewed, just when we thought all was lost," Fynnol said. "How can we pass it up, Tam?"

"Baore is the boat builder," Tam said. "Without Baore we all stay in the Vale."

"Baore . . .?" Fynnol's voice came out of the dark. There was no response but measured breathing. Baore was asleep, or pretending to be so.

"I will see to Baore," Fynnol said firmly.

Horses moved in the dark, and wind pawed softly at the tents. Somewhere nearby Tam was sure he could just hear a couple in the act of love, and the sounds of the woman's pleasure would not let him sleep.

"Did I hear you speaking still?" a voice said. Cynddl crouched down beside the cart's wheel—barely a silhouette in the faint starlight. "I hope I'm not mistaken and have wakened you?"

"We are lying awake, waiting our chance to steal your horses," Fynnol said.

Tam punched Fynnol, then rolled on his side, propping

himself up on an elbow. Baore shifted in his sleep but did not wake.

"And I have come to offer you horses," Cynddl said quietly. "An offer you can ponder as you lie awake. I'm told that beyond the Wold of Kerns the river is easily navigable—even for a Fáel who's spent very little time in boats. The Wold is also said to breed fine horses. Take me there and I'll give you the silver to buy three good mounts. I can't promise you the best stock the Wold will offer, but you'll have three horses that won't disappoint you. That's the price I offer for a well-found boat and your skills as rivermen from here to the Wold." He paused. "I should warn you though: I won't make this journey with quite the speed you might plan to make it yourselves. I'll stop along the way and spend a few days here and there."

"But what will you do on this journey?" Fynnol asked.

"If you took as much delight in the words of others as you do in your own, Fynnol, you would've heard. I am a story finder. I'll listen for the stories of the race that once lived in the wildlands—stories that are only faint echoes, now. I'll do the same here, at Telanon Bridge. I'll spend this night out on the old battlefield, and tomorrow and the next night and perhaps the one after that as well. Who knows what tales I might find in such a place? Consider what I've said. Horses freely offered might even be better than stolen Fáel horses. Sleep well."

With that he rose and slipped silently back into the encampment. But none of the Valemen slept.

FOUR

"The river boat is a simple craft," Baore explained, "flat bottomed and without bent frames. If you'll both lend a hand we'll be afloat again in less than a fortnight. You'll see."

"Afloat and carrying a perfect fool down the river," Fynnol said, then raised a finger. "But a fool with silver, thankfully."

"He didn't seem terribly foolish to me," Tam said.

"Well, what else would you call a man who sits and listens for the stories of a place to come to him? I had a great-aunt who heard voices, and we didn't glorify her with the term 'story finder.' She was mad, and no one was confused about it."

Fynnol had been as good as his word, taking Baore aside that morning and convincing him that Cynddl's offer was too good to be passed up. Tam was always amazed at Fynnol's powers of persuasion. His cousin would have his adventure and his gray mare. There would be no denying him.

They came to the Stone Gate——a natural wall through which a tunnel had been carved, closed at either end with iron-clad gates of heavy oak. To one side, a stone bluff rose, too steep to climb; to the other a cliff dropped away to the racing water below.

Despite the intimidating entrance to the Vale, the gates were closed only at night. They were tended by the Dilts family, who had long held this post; and though many thought they were less than diligent, in these comparatively peaceful times no harm had come of it.

They woke old Dilts, who was asleep beneath a tree, and told him their strange tale of brigands and murder, which did not seem to create the expected effect. It was soon clear he didn't believe a word of what was said.

"I thought you'd lose your boat in the first gorge," he said, and went back to his dreaming.

The three carried on, shaking their heads and hoping they could convince some other who held sway over Dilts, for there were men outside the Vale who viewed murder differently than the people who lived this side of the Stone Gate, that was certain.

"'A man too wise to heed warnings will die a fool,'" Fynnol said. "And a lesson that will be. We should go down to the nook at Dingle Shale. We're sure to catch a boat going north from there."

"You two go down if you like," Tam said, "but I want to go by Delgert Gallon's and pay a visit."

Fynnol lifted an eyebrow at this. "You think he knows more about our traveler?"

"Perhaps. His was the only name Alaan mentioned."

"I mark it as odd that he would know only an old

busybody like Gallon," Fynnol said. "But then who, other than ourselves, is worth talking to in the Vale?"

Tam shrugged. He caught a ride on a passing wagon, and sat in back with a gaggle of giggling children, leaving Fynnol and Baore to look for a boat at Dingle Shale. Tam watched them disappear down the old road—two cousins, small and great, dark and fair.

The wagon came at last to the road to Delgert Gallon's, and Tam took his leave, the children waving good-bye and breaking into song as the wagon lumbered on.

Gallon was a tanner who had been driven from his trade by age and an increasingly foul temper. Tam had met him but once, years ago, but the Vale was not so large that people concerned themselves much with formal introductions. Old Gallon was asleep in a chair in his garden—a common practice this afternoon, it seemed—but one of his daughters shook him gently until his eyes opened.

Despite the careful treatment, he woke in bad humor and glared at Tam. "And what is it you want?" he said sourly. He was a wiry old man, all bone, with muscles like taut cords tying his frame together. His cheekbones were so prominent and his eyes so deep sunk that he had a slightly crazed look, Tam thought, which suited his ill humor well.

"My friends and I were set upon by brigands at the ruin by Telanon Bridge, and a stranger who had stopped with us was murdered . . ."

"What's this you say?" The old man sat up in his chair, rubbing the sleep from his eyes with hands tanned like old leather. His daughter brought tea, staying nearby to hear the story.

"We were——"

"Now wait, lad. Set your story aright. Who exactly were you with?"

"My cousin, Fynnol Loell, and his cousin, Baore Talon. We had gone out to the old battlefield to look for artifacts, and last night a stranger joined us. He called himself Alaan."

"Alaan!" The man shot a look at his daughter. "Not the rogue with the bird?"

"A whist, yes. He called it Jac."

The man twisted in his chair with agitation.

"But who was murdered?" the daughter asked.

"This same Alaan I named."

She put a hand to her mouth, and the color drained from her face.

"Well, that is the first good news I've heard in a long time!" Gallon said loudly. "And I'm not surprised. The man is a rogue and a thief! Oh, he'd a honeyed tongue, that one. Played me for an old fool. Well, the river take him! That's what I say."

"What did he steal from you?" Tam asked.

"Just every story I'd ever heard. He knows more about our Vale now than you do. Not that that's saying much, I would wager." He glanced at his daughter. "Had the best of my Lizzy and left her with child."

"That's not true!" she protested, recovering a little. "The child is Kendal's."

"Ah, he married out of pity for you and the child to come. More noble than smart, that is certain."

Indignation appeared to propel the daughter from her chair, and she slammed the door to the house so hard a windowpane cracked.

"He was here for a fortnight," Gallon said, only slightly deflated by his daughter's reaction. "Sat by my fire every night and listened to all the doings and stories of the Vale—charmed them out of me. And the whole time he was at my daughters behind my back. The miracle is there's only one child, and that one like his father, too— sneaking and sly." He shivered with disgust. "Dead you say? Good riddance, say I."

"But what could he have found interesting about the Vale?"

The old man looked at him sharply.

"Of course, I'm sure you know things that—" Tam cast about for something "—well, things I should likely want to know myself."

This placated the old man a little. "Well, I'm not telling you, so don't bother asking. But I know things about the Vale and its people. I know that many a family name was not always as it is now and where many a family hailed from before they found themselves in this furthest corner of the world."

"And that's what Alaan wanted to learn?"

"Oh, more than that. He wanted to know which given

names appeared in families again and again. Which families spawned the best swordsmen. He was terrible interested in who'd gone out to fight the brigands and roaming mercenaries after the last war. Oh, he had a lot of questions. He knew when he'd met a man who knew something of value." The old man slammed a fist on the arm of his chair. "Played me for a fool though, he did!" Gallon calmed himself with an effort. "But that's all over now. You're certain he's dead?"

"Yes, I'm afraid he is. We saw the men fall upon him with their blades. We were on the bridge, and fled down into the river. They chased us, too, but we hid among the rocks and they gave up looking. Stole poor Baore's boat, though, or sent it down the river."

"Well, it serves you right for digging where you shouldn't and keeping the company of rogues. I'm glad you didn't get yourselves killed, though. You must be Adlar's son."

Tam nodded.

The man eyed him oddly, cocking his head to one side. "Hold out your hands," he said suddenly.

Tam did as he was told.

Gallon stared at his hands for a moment. "You'll do," he said grudgingly. "Did you see the hands of that rogue Alaan? I should never have let him in my door. Hands that had never seen a day's work. Hands not even fit for cleaning house. The hands a . . . *scholar* might have." He said the word "scholar" with a disdain that Tam thought would be hard to equal.

"But what was it that Alaan wanted to know? Surely what given names reoccur in a family would hardly profit a stranger?"

Gallon eyed him suspiciously. "You think that useless knowledge, do you?"

"Well, I'm sure it isn't," Tam said quickly. "I just don't see why some stranger passing through the Vale should want to know it."

Old Gallon shook his head as though Tam were almost too stupid for him to bother with. "Because families who've fled their lord's service in the wars change their surnames; but even so, given names are passed from one generation to the next. Who were you named for?"

"My great-uncle who died before I was born."

"And who was he named after?"

"My great-grandfather, I think."

The old man cocked an eyebrow at him. "If your surname had once been something other than Loell, a man might still find your family by knowing what given names your people favor."

"I take your point, but not why Alaan would care about that."

"Because he was like that bird of his: steal any bright thing it saw. Any bright thing belonging to someone else, it coveted." The old man sat back in his chair and crossed his arms. "But he'll be doing no more of that." The old man sighed with satisfaction. "Your grandfather is well?" he asked suddenly.

"Well enough."

"He's a good man, your grandfather, a good man." He sipped at his tea. "You were going off in a boat down to Inniseth. Isn't that what I heard?"

Tam nodded.

"Well, you're better off here. Take a lesson from what happened to Alaan and stay where you're welcome."

Tam nodded but said nothing, and old Gallon's attention seemed to wander.

They sat a moment longer in silence, and then Tam rose from his chair. "I have to be going if I'm to make it home this day."

The man nodded, not registering what was said, but then he seemed to notice his guest was standing. "Where're you off to?"

"Home."

"Ah. Well, give my regards to your grandfather and stay away from rogues. Come back sometime. I've four more daughters, and they're not all as misguided as my Lizzy, bless her foolish heart."

Tam's grandfather listened silently to the story, never interrupting. By the time Tam was done the old man's face was grayer than barn board. He got up from his chair and went to the big sideboard that dominated the room, his movements stiff and jerky. He poured them both a cup of harsh spirits, then drank his off in one swallow. His eyes were red and watering when he lowered himself back into his chair.

"Thank everything good and kind that you're unharmed," the old man said. "All of you. I lost a wife and a son and that's all the loss a man can bear in one life."

Tam reached out to put a hand on his grandfather's arm, but the old man took the hand in his own—rough and hard from a lifetime of toil. His grandfather took a sudden deep breath, almost a gasp.

Tam was at a loss for something to say, and unsettled by his grandfather's show of emotion. "Why do you think this man Alaan journeyed so far?" Tam asked. "And why was he asking old Gallon about given names reoccurring in families? Who could he have been seeking?"

For a moment the old man said nothing, his face half hidden by a hand gently rubbing his brow. He lifted his cup to drink but found it empty, and set it back down— a sound like a door latch opening. "In wars, Tamlyn, men do things . . . things that haunt them the rest of their lives, if they have any soul at all. It is not always men-at-arms meeting upon a bright field of honor. Villages are burned; common people put to the sword. The men who perform these horrors are sometimes sought out. Vengeance is not the exclusive right of the Renné and the Wills. Alaan might have been searching for such men here—for his own reasons or on behalf of some other. But it seems someone else found him first."

Tam wondered if one ever completely escaped the feeling that crept over him now: he felt like a stupid child. *Such men could find refuge in the Vale?* He tried to imagine who among the people he knew could harbor such a secret past. He looked up and found his grandfather's clouded blue eyes on him.

"You'll go with this story finder, I take it?"

Tam nodded. "It's been our plan now for three years to travel downriver. I don't imagine we'll be set upon by armed men again. It was just bad luck that Alaan came to share our fire."

The old man nodded and let go of Tam's hand. He went stiffly to the sideboard to fill his cup again—then didn't. He leaned against the cabinet, taking the weight off one leg as though it pained him.

"If you want me to stay," Tam said suddenly, "I will."

The old man shook his head. "New rivers find their own courses," he said. "I shan't be telling you where to go or not."

Tam took up the cup the old man had poured him and tipped some of the grain spirits into his mouth. It burned like a hot coal.

"I've a calf to see to," his grandfather said and plucked a hat from a peg, but just as he opened the door, he stopped. "Tam . . .? If anyone starts asking you questions about the people of the Vale, don't be like that old fool Gallon—tell them nothing."

Tam sat utterly still for a moment, then nodded. The old man went out into the clear evening air, and the door latch clicked closed behind him.

FĪVE

oren Renné read by candlelight on the stone terrace of his Westbrook house. Early-blossoming chestnut trees filled the air with their faint fragrance, and leaves trembled like lute strings in the soft night breeze. A moth fluttered into one of the candles at Toren's elbow, and both moth and candle flickered out.

Toren closed the book on his finger and, taking another candle, relit the flame that had expired. He opened his book again, finding the line he had last read, or could last remember, and went back to his reading. In the doorway, a servant cleared his throat.

"Gilbert A'brgail is here, your grace," the old man said.

"Had we a meeting that I've forgotten?"

"He has come without warning."

Toren looked back at his book, sighed, and set it on the table well clear of candle drippings. "Bring him to me."

A'brgail was a dealer in old and rare weapons and armor—a passion of Toren's, who possessed a collection second to none. He'd known him for perhaps seven years, and grown to like him immensely, for A'brgail was a deeply thoughtful man. In fact, "rigorous" was the word Toren would use to describe A'brgail's thinking, and he could say that of very few.

The impressive figure of Gilbert A'brgail appeared in the doorway. He hesitated there, silhouetted by the lights within.

"Sir," Toren said, rising to his feet. A'brgail crossed the terrace and the two clasped hands.

"I hope you will forgive this intrusion, your grace."

"It is a welcome surprise," Toren said. "Will you take some wine?"

A'brgail nodded, and lowered himself into the chair opposite Toren's. Toren had always found Gilbert A'brgail something of a contradiction. Certainly he had the bearing and appearance of a knight—and clearly he'd had the training—but he was modest and humble in demeanor. There was nowhere about the man a hint of pride. His dress was impeccable but unassuming, and he went about his business efficiently and without fanfare.

Toren gazed at A'brgail a moment. A knight of sixty upon whom the years lay lightly—that is what he would guess to see the man. He showed no signs of frailty or excess, no paunch or thinning of the shoulders. Beneath a neatly trimmed beard of white he was strong jawed, and the high forehead indicated the intellect that so impressed Toren. He bore a scar upon his lip that made his mouth turn down a little at the corner, so that it always seemed to be near a frown, and this suited his seriousness admirably. When he spoke his mouth moved crookedly, and Toren had the impression that he enunciated every word with particular care, as though speech required an uncommon concentration.

"And what have you to show me this night?" Toren asked as his servant delivered wine. "I will tell you, everyone who's seen the helm you brought me last visit has tried to buy it."

A'brgail nodded, a crooked smile appearing. "I'm not sure why I sold you that. I'll never find another like it." He shifted in his chair, which was almost too small for him. "But I've something even more rare to show you tonight, though this I *will* not part with."

"As you said about the helm." Toren laughed.

"Nevertheless, there is no coin that will buy this." He took up a package he had laid on a side table. It folded as he raised it, surprising Toren—A'brgail's wares were commonly both solid and sharp edged. Yet this was not a shirt of mail, for Toren could see it had little weight.

Carefully A'brgail unwrapped the cloth. Toren had not noticed before how large and hard knuckled his hands were. They exhibited the lumps and swellings and the crooked fingers of hands that had received many a break and blow. As his appearance suggested, Gilbert A'brgail had not always been a dealer in arms and armor.

From within the folds the older man took a garment of gray—ancient and fraying, Toren could see. Gently he spread it over the back of a third chair and then stood aside, saying nothing.

"Well, it is an old surcoat," Toren said, "but I assume something makes it rare and valuable. Did it belong to a celebrated knight?" It was an ancient garment, Toren guessed, darkened and threadbare, its original color faded and lost.

"Celebrated? No, but look more closely."

Toren rose from his chair, taking up the candlebranch and casting light on the old garment. There was a strange, scattered glitter in its fabric. "I see no devices. Who was its owner?"

"There is a device, but small and difficult to discern by this light." A'brgail gestured to the left breast, and Toren leaned closer with his candles.

"But these are silveroak leaves . . .!"

A'brgail nodded.

"It is the robe of a Knight of the Vow!"

The older man nodded again.

Toren stepped quickly back. "But this is bad luck to even have in my home! Why have you brought this to me?"

"This one bears no ill luck, for it is mine by right."

Toren had taken several steps back, and realized he was glaring at the older man, who registered no insult but remained courteous, even deferential.

"Perhaps you will allow me to tell you a story," he said softly, "and to assure you again that I would never knowingly bring an object of ill luck into the house of Toren Renné." A'brgail took his seat again, putting the fingers of his battered hands together. He touched these to his lip, gently tracing the old wound. "I am a descendant of the man who wore this surcoat," he said quietly. "I swear this to be true by the vow of my ancestor. It has been passed from father to son for generations, hidden and kept from harm, though it has aged all the same."

"But my ancestors destroyed the Knights of the Vow," Toren said. "Destroyed them to a man on the Isle of Battle and at Cooling Keep."

A'brgail looked up, opening his clasped hands. "Not to a man. No. There were Knights not present at either battle. The A'brgail who wore this surcoat was recovering from a wound suffered earlier. And he, like several others, managed to escape the Renné. The land between the mountains was in chaos then, and refugees choked the roads—roads no longer protected by the Knights of the Vow. He found his place among the people fleeing the wars. Beyond the border of the old kingdom my family made their home. All the years since, we've kept this secret." He placed both his battle-broken hands upon the arms of his chair. "And now I'm here telling this to you, the heir to the family who betrayed the Knights of the Vow."

Toren had shifted in his chair, moving so that he could come easily to his feet. "And this is why you have befriended me, so that you might have your revenge . . ."

Gilbert A'brgail laughed and reached for his wineglass. "Revenge? How like a Renné you sound, Lord Toren. The Renné who destroyed the Knights of the Vow have been dead for a century and more. How would I take my revenge upon them? No, you have done me no harm." He looked at Toren over the rim of his glass, a small, crooked smile appearing. "You need not worry. I've not sold you some article once owned by a Knight to bring you ill luck. No, I swear to you, revenge is not my purpose."

"Then why have you befriended me? It is an odd choice of acquaintance, it seems to me."

"So it would appear, but we're alike in some ways. We both wish to redress wrongs done in the past—not to our people but *by* them. Your first thought was that I had come for revenge, but the Knights of the Vow were not destroyed by the Renné. They were brought to ruin by the breaking of their vow."

"A broken vow cannot be remade, Gilbert. Nor can King Thynne's curse be withdrawn. The Knights were destroyed, and, though you tell me some few escaped, the power and authority of the order was lost."

"Yes, it was. But it could be regained. As to the curse of Thynne . . ." He swirled the wine in his glass. "It fell upon those who broke their vow. I believe I am free of it."

"But you are not a Knight of the Vow," Toren said.

A'brgail lowered his glass a little and met Toren's eye. "Am I not?" he said.

Toren took up his own glass and emptied it, glad of the liquid in a dry throat. He was about to ask A'brgail to state more clearly what he meant, but did not: it was clear enough. Instead he said, "What have you come to ask of me, A'brgail?"

The older man reached out and took the ancient surcoat in his hand, rubbing it between finger and thumb. "I have come to ask that, when the time is right, you give your blessing to the rebirth of my ancestor's order."

Toren set his empty goblet down, almost upsetting it as he did so. "Why would I do that? My family would think I'd lost my reason. 'They will join our enemies and have revenge upon us,' they will say. And how will I answer them?"

A'brgail released the folds of the old surcoat. "I don't know. I know only that we will not break our vow twice. And certainly there will be need of the Knights again. At the moment something like peace reigns over the land between the mountains, but we have both made a study of history—peace will not last. Let the noble families war if they wish—it is their right, I'm told, and certainly it is their passion—but have peace beyond the battle-field. Peace ensured as it was in the past—by the Knights of the Vow."

Toren heard himself laugh, though it was short and without pleasure. "If I didn't know you for a sober man, A'brgail, a man of character, I would think you moon-struck. Do you really believe you can revive the Knights of the Vow? I will tell you, this is a corpse long dead."

A'brgail gazed for a moment at the ancient surcoat, then back to Toren. "It has already been done, your grace. The order exists. We have only waited for a propitious time to make ourselves known. Unfortunately, other matters have forced me to reveal this to you before such a time arrived."

Toren reached for the bottle and too quickly poured himself more wine, splashing a little on the table. A'brgail had barely touched his own.

"This is a dangerous thing you've done—and more dangerous to come here and tell me. I would advise you to reveal this to no one else. If my family or the Wills and their allies were to learn this . . . Well, they don't want to see other powers come into being. Powers with uncertain alliances."

A'brgail put his crooked fingers together again, bowed his head, and pressed the first fingers to the inside corners of his eyes. "What you counsel is wise, I know, but we'll not be able to keep our existence secret. I'm afraid the Wills know of us already."

"And how did this come about?"

A'brgail stared for a moment at his half-mended hands, turning them to gaze at the hardened palms. "You see, Lord Toren, we made a terrible mistake . . . *I* made a terrible mistake." He sat back in his chair and took up his goblet, but did not drink. "Let me tell you the story of a man named Hafydd. Hafydd who was once an ally of the Renné."

"Hafydd is dead. My father dealt with him long ago. Cut him down in the field . . . at Quarryston, I seem to remember."

"Harrowdown, to be exact, but Hafydd was not killed.

Oh, he was at Death's gate, certainly, but he was alive still when the battle ended. You see, I was one of the watchers on the hill: a student of war even then. Of the knights who took the field that day, Hafydd was the most skilled, the strongest, as he was on many another field on many another day, I imagine. But his force was greatly outnumbered by the Renné and were slaughtered. All were left for dead—and only a few were not—though by the next morning only Hafydd remained among the living. We tended him and brought him back to strength.

"Changed, he was, for he had been haughty and arrogant before. Now he was humble and thoughtful, spending much time in contemplation. Not everyone trusted this transformation, but I was not one of them." A'brgail made a knotted fist as though he would strike the arm of his chair, but the fist hesitated in the air and then opened and came slowly to rest as light as a bird. "I believed in his transformation, believed Hafydd might become great among my order, even be grand marshal one day. I told him all that I knew of the Knights and their history—much of it unknown to any outside the Order. But he betrayed us in the end, and slipped away with knowledge he should never have been given— knowledge that has made him dangerous. More than dangerous." A'brgail reached over and tugged gently on the surcoat so that it slid slowly off the back of the chair and crumpled onto the seat. He gazed at this a moment and then looked up at Toren. "And now he is returned, calling himself Eremon and serving as a counselor to the

Prince of Innes—who is about to make an alliance with Menwyn Wills."

"Menwyn Wills would not dare do such a thing!" Toren said. "We are in the process of returning the Isle of Battle to the Wills. He would never endanger this by making an alliance with the Prince of Innes!"

"Oh, I think he will. It is being done in secret, and Menwyn Wills thinks you will not learn of it until it is too late. I'm afraid his opinion of you is not high, your grace. As for the Prince, he is under the influence of Hafydd, and you should not underestimate Hafydd's hatred of the Renné. No, his hatred would impress even your family, who may make their own claims in this area.

"Do you know the word, 'eremon'?" A'brgail asked suddenly. "No? It is the name of a thorny bush that grows in the clearings where fire has destroyed the forest. It is said its seed will lie dormant in the earth for hundreds of years, until the heat of the blaze breaks open its case and brings it back to life. . . . Eremon. And this is the name Hafydd has chosen for his return. He is allied with your enemies, and you will not defeat him without the assistance of the Knights of the Vow. I'll be perfectly truthful with you, your grace . . . even with our help I'm not confident of his defeat."

SIX

Elise loved only one person in the world without reservation and hated two others with at least equal passion. This disparity between the number loved and the number hated did not go unnoticed by her—but she was, after all, a Wills, and the Wills family, it was often said, had a certain genius for hatred.

One of the two she hated was about to arrive, and Elise paced across her sitting room, unable to sit still. For a moment she paused to stare out a window and down to the green earth below. Tying the bed sheets together was out of the question. Not only was it too far to the ground, but, despite the reassurances of any number of tales, Elise had no faith in the sheets holding together under the weight.

Of course she could just have a groom ready a horse and ride across the bridge, but by nightfall they would be looking for her, and by noon—or supper time at the latest—she would have been found. And all that would have been accomplished would be to convince her uncle that she was too young to make her own decisions—not that he needed to be convinced. Running away, no matter how appealing, did not seem to be an option—not for her, at least.

"I guess I'll have to attend the Westbrook Tournament, after all," she said rather sadly.

It was the one event of the year that she most dreaded, for it seemed to be a time that family honor absolutely required sacrifice, and though her cousins appeared more than willing to bow to this necessity, she was not so amenable. Of course, they had only to risk their limbs and, less likely, their lives. She, on the other hand, was being asked to sacrifice a great deal more. At least that was how she saw it.

"Your Highness?"

It was one of the conceits of the family that the heir presumptive was still addressed as though he or she were royalty. Elise turned to find her maid in the doorway.

"Your uncle is on the stair."

Elise had several uncles, in fact, but the only one who did not need to be identified by name was Menwyn. He was "*the* uncle," even though he was not the eldest of his brothers. That honor belonged to her father.

"I don't suppose you could tell him I'm ill?"

The maid did not respond either to refuse or agree, but only looked deeply uncomfortable. It was one thing for Elise to lie to Menwyn, but a servant would be taking a great risk.

"Please show him in," Elise said with resignation, to the great relief of her maid.

Elise took up an embroidery hoop that she had not

actually looked at in months, and bent over it in false concentration. Suddenly disgusted by this farce, she flung the hoop aside and went back to staring out the window. He might as well know the truth: she was not industrious as a young, unmarried woman should be, but instead read poetry and played her lute and stared out the window—and, yes, daydreamed.

"Enjoying the scenery, Your Highness?"

"According to my understanding only the members of a royal family are so addressed, Uncle." She could see his pained smile without turning around.

"Before the first restoration, our ancestors were always addressed as the royalty they were. It is a tradition I believe in upholding."

"And if there is no restoration?"

"There will be," he said. "I have no doubts. It was true in the past, and will be true again."

She turned away from the window, unable to continue being so rude, even to Menwyn—she was simply too well brought up. Her uncle smiled at her, that repulsive smile—as though she were a willful child, exasperating at times, but in spite of it he loved her.

But he did not love her. In fact, she suspected he felt much the same toward her as she did toward him: a festering, malignant hatred.

Whenever he stood before her, exhibiting, as he always did, this utterly false concern, images began to appear, unbidden, in her mind. She would see herself bludgeoning Menwyn's narrow little face, breaking his teeth and blackening his eyes. It always unsettled her—ladies were never to countenance such thoughts—but she could not help it.

Elise tried to compose her face to not betray her thoughts. *How surprised he looked when she broke his mouth with her mace. And then, when he raised his hands, she drove them into his face as well, and he fell back, cringing.*

"Your father asked me to speak with you."

Elise felt her jaw tighten at the lie. Her father was her ally and hated Menwyn as much as she . . . Though perhaps that was not quite true: her father's feelings toward his ambitious younger brother were far more complicated. But her father had retreated, now, into music and the books that were read to him. Into the dark and still night that was his entire world.

Her father had been born blind and had been pushed aside in the succession by Menwyn, who was strong and hale and who could see perfectly well—too well, in some ways, for he had an eye for the weaknesses of others. Menwyn was a man who could lead an army into battle; and to the Wills family, that was of great importance, despite the fact that there had been no battles now for many years.

"The Westbrook Tournament is but a few weeks away," he began smoothly, his speech obviously rehearsed. "I have supported your wishes in the past, and understood then that you were not yet ready, but this year I can hardly go against the family again. You are a Wills, Your Highness: we must consider your future and ours. A suitable match must be found."

"With a suitable number of men-at-arms and a suitable fortune," she said, not meaning to taunt, or at least not meaning it to sound so.

Blood ran from his ears as she laid her mace alongside his head.

Menwyn shook his head, looking for all the world like a man injured by what had been said. "Child, you will never know what injustice you do me, how much concern I have for your well-being and your happiness. I have risked insulting some of the most powerful families in Ayr because I respected your desire to remain a girl a few years more. But you are twenty years old now. Past time when one should accept the duties and responsibilities of one's position. You are a Wills, not the daughter of some tradesman. None of us have married on a whim, yet most of us have found contentment in our unions."

She could not bear it when he spoke the truth, or at least partial truth—as close as Menwyn likely ever came. Not everyone had found happiness in their "unions" and some endured something more akin to lengthy illness, but many *had* found contentment.

"But I will not choose your husband, as Your Highness well knows. That decision will be made by your father. I am only here as messenger. I can tell you that the flower of the nobility will be at the Westbrook Tournament: all the other great families and all their sons. Elise," he said, suddenly dropping the sham of royal address, "childhood has run its course."

This last line chilled her more than anything he had said, not because she wished to remain a child—she did not—but because everything Menwyn would require of her would be justified thus. Because she was no longer a child, because she must shoulder her responsibilities, put aside her own desires for the good of the family. She must join in this terrible illusion that they were still royalty, deprived of their rightful place. An illusion to which all things must be sacrificed.

She knew well that everything Menwyn said was deception or an outright lie, not that it would be of any use to protest. Menwyn did not much care to be reminded of his exact words from other conversations. He simply denied them. Elise sometimes thought the man so deluded that he actually believed whatever his current version of the truth happened to be.

Over the last three years it had been Uncle Menwyn pressing to have her wed—and despite his protestations, she suspected he had already chosen her groom to be, the son of a powerful man with ambitions of his own. A duke who wanted his grandson to rule even greater estates than they now possessed, perhaps even a kingdom—who could say? He would not be the first to believe that adding some Wills blood to his family's would provide the justification he needed to invade a neighbor; for, after all, Ayr in all of its entirety had once been their dominion.

Menwyn was staring at her, his brows knitted. He was a master at reading the reactions of others, at tailoring

his words to the moment. She tried to make her face
blank and unreadable.

"I think you shall see, Elise, that this year the young
men are fairer than ever. All the ladies say so. Among
them we shall find you a prince."

She almost laughed out loud at this.

There did seem to be an unusually promising group
of brutal young men in this generation. Utterly ready to
fight the Renné as though the ghosts of the past rode
onto the field. That was how it seemed to her. Each family
was at war with the other's ancestors, those who had
perpetrated the "great injustice" upon the other. The fact
that it was not the present Renné or Wills made no difference. There was the perennial, unerasable injustice of the
past and it must be engaged in mortal combat at all costs.
If war was not, at present, possible, then the tournament
would make a reasonable substitute.

Why the people of Ayr would ever want to be ruled
by families so stupid she could not understand. But then
that was exactly the point: they did not want to be ruled
by them. It was only a myth of the two families, who
could no more give up the injustices of the past—their
precious injustices—than they could surrender the
dream of restoration in the future. The ultimate victory
over their rivals—restoration. Better even than the utter
annihilation of the other. Just let them ascend the throne
again, with the other family there to witness. It would
make centuries of warfare and uncounted dead seem a
small price—it would be worth that ten times over.

"I simply cannot shield you from your responsibilities any longer," Menwyn said solicitously. "The family will not hear of it."

A protracted silence ensued, which did not seem to discomfit her uncle at all. He continued to look upon her with feigned affection.

"Have you finished?" she asked evenly. Offending Menwyn was one of the few pleasures she had, considering that in the end he would no doubt have his own way. It was the only form of rebellion possible.

His face barely changed. "I bid Your Highness good day."

As soon as the door closed, she yanked a pillow off the divan and screamed into it as loudly as she dared, then flung it across the room.

She went to the window again and looked out over the river valley. The sight calmed her a little. It was so beautiful in the late afternoon light—the stands of trees casting their shadows over the irregular fields, the innumerable shadings of emerging green. It had rained earlier—just a shower—and the world looked freshly scrubbed and pure, the blue sky with its rags of clouds fluttering in the breeze.

Suddenly a bird flitted past her, and then back again, so close she could almost reach out and touch it. It fluttered before her, the sunlight falling on its dark wings— blue-black in this light. It seemed so bold she almost thought it was a tamed bird, escaped from some cage, and held out her hand to it. Without hesitation, it darted at her ring with its opened bill, causing her to pull her hand back.

"Well, you cheeky thing. You would steal my ring, wouldn't you? Go on, you thief. Shoo!" She waved her arms, and somewhat reluctantly the bird was off. In only a second it was beyond the walls, then over the island and crossing the lake to the fields beyond. She could not take her eyes from its determined flight. Another moment and it was lost from view entirely.

If only she could fly like that: out the window and gone before anyone could even saddle a horse. She would have a branch for a bed and the sky for her country. She would be free of this foolish family that could never be rid of its past. Free to choose whom she would. Free.

What would the world look like to someone who did not even know her parents' names? It must seem a glorious place. No obligations but to oneself. No obligations.

SEVEΠ

Elise heard her father before she saw him. There were no candles in his rooms, and dusk was stealing the light away like a cat stealing the breath from a baby.

He was playing upon the harp, not his virtuoso instrument, but still one upon which he was more than competent. Elise paused at the door, listening. It was not a piece she knew, but it seemed to suit the sounds and mood of the evening entirely. The last whisper of falling wind, the lowing of cattle as they made their slow trek back to the barns, a curtain moving in the open window, a nightingale's liquid song. The music became part of all of these sounds, dancing in among them in exquisite counterpoint.

She pushed the door open a fraction more, and the music died away, reverberating for an instant longer in her mind than on the air.

"Elise?"

"How can you know it's me?" she asked, shaking her head. His perceptiveness always astonished her.

"Everyone else knocks, my dear. Even Menwyn."

She laughed. "And I thought it was some . . . some secret sense."

"Well, there is your perfume," he said, holding out his hand.

She crossed the room and put her hand in his. He kissed it and held it to his cheek, closing his eyes tightly as he always did.

She often thought her father would have been a striking man if he did not have that emptiness of expression of the blind. His long face and serious countenance gave him an appearance of sadness, though she knew he was not an unhappy man, merely a thoughtful one.

He was the opposite of her in appearance—dark to her fair. Though she, too, had a somewhat long face, which she tried to hide by the way she wore her hair.

He took her hand away from his face, though did not release it. She loved the warmth and gentleness of his fingers—the hands of an artist.

"And what brings you down here to visit your aging father?"

"You are hardly aging, and do I need a reason other than the pleasure of your company?" She hooked a chair near with her foot—a terribly unladylike act, but she was sure her father would not recognize it as such.

"You may visit me any time you choose, as you well know, whether it is merely for the pleasure of my company, as you put it, or because you need to unburden yourself, but sometimes I sense it is the latter . . ."

She squeezed his hand, wondering where to begin.

"*Menwyn . . .*" he said softly. It was not a question.

She nodded.

"Shall I assume you are nodding agreement?"

This made her smile. "Yes."

"He is our particular bane, isn't he?" her father said conspiratorially. "He is pressing you to accept a suitor?"

"He keeps saying that it is you who will make the decision . . ." she blurted out.

Her father sat back in his chair. "Yes, he would say that."

"But, Father, Menwyn would have me marry . . . *anyone* if his father had enough men-at-arms and was belligerent in nature." She rose from her chair, taking three quick steps in the gathering gloom, but then stopped. "I don't want my marriage to support this senseless feud," she said in a harsh whisper, as though one did not speak such words within these walls.

For a moment her father did not answer. "No," he said in a normal tone. "I don't want that either. We shall have to set ourselves to resist Menwyn, though he will rally all the others against us. You know the truth, Elise: he has isolated me almost entirely. We can count on no one but ourselves." He turned his head toward her as he said this, as though she were visible to him.

She came and put a hand on his shoulder, bending to kiss his cheek. He was ever her supporter.

He reached out and ran his fingers over the strings of the harp, the sound of falling water, and smiled. "You should know, Elise," he said, suddenly serious, "that all of us make appropriate marriages. That does not mean you must marry someone you detest, but even so, you must find a fitting match."

"Yes," she said softly. "You loved Mother, didn't you?"

"More than words can express, almost more than music can."

"But you hardly knew her when you married . . .?" She knew the answer to these questions, but it had become a litany of reassurance.

"I had met her but twice, and spoken to her for less than an hour."

"But you trusted Grandmother's judgment."

"Entirely."

"There is the heart of my problem," she said.

"So it is," her father agreed.

"Father? This is not selfishness. I will marry whom you choose, but I don't want to see the fighting begin again. Do you understand? I will not have my marriage give Menwyn the means to make war. Enough Wills have died to assuage family pride"—she paused and took a long breath—"and others as well."

"I know you are not being selfish, my dear. But, Elise? When it comes to marriage, it is acceptable to be a little selfish." He paused. "And you are not being willful just to spite Menwyn?"

"I don't think so," she said, hoping it was true.

"I don't think so either, as tempting as that would be. We shall have to consider carefully how to proceed. Menwyn is a formidable opponent. He bested me in the past," he said without sign of rancor.

"I was too young to help you then," Elise said, not really feeling that this would mean much.

Her father smiled. "Yes," he said, "you are more stubborn than I. And stubbornness is a trait never to be underestimated."

Carral made his way up the unlit stair. His meeting with Elise had unsettled him substantially, leaving him pacing back and forth across his room for a long time. Mid-eve had rung some time ago, and had shaken him from his worries at least temporarily.

Despite his reassuring words, the truth was he was unable to provide the protection his daughter required. He could not even offer her proper guidance. If her mother had lived . . .

But regrets were of no use. Past events couldn't be changed. One couldn't simply wish the illness upon Menwyn, though the thought had occurred to Carral more than once when his wife lay stricken.

He came up to the closed door, and, though he had not consciously counted the stairs, he knew when he was there. Rather like counting beats in music—one didn't do it consciously, one simply came in at the right moment. You felt it.

He opened the door and immediately sensed the fire. He could hear the wisp of flame and shifting of wood, feel the heat of it, smell the smoke.

He could also smell the food. It was likely cold now,

but that didn't matter. He was fulfilling a time-honored trust. Someone had to consume at least part of the offering left for the castle ghosts. Who did this was never spoken of; indeed, it was often not known by most of the castle's inhabitants. Carral was sure that some believed the food actually *was* eaten by ghosts.

Using his cane, he felt his way across the room in case furniture had been rearranged—an odd propensity of the sighted. The warmth radiating from the hearth was welcome after his climb up the dank stairway, and he settled in the chair, searching the small table for the wine bottle and a glass. He always wished they served better wine to ghosts and had considered leaving a note of complaint—but to have someone write it would reveal his secret and he couldn't have that.

"I hope you aren't of a mind to drink all of that yourself."

Carral jumped he was so startled. "Who is that?"

The voice seemed to have come from across the room, near the window. "Don't you believe in ghosts?" the voice asked. "But clearly not or you wouldn't be drinking that wine."

Carral couldn't identify the voice and he had an unrivaled memory for such things. This one was educated, well modulated; someone conscious of the effect of his tone, his words.

"I don't think I know you, sir," Carral said.

"No . . . no, you don't," came the answer. "I am no friend of your brother's, though, I will tell you that."

"Many can say the same."

"Yes, but would they dare?"

This made Carral laugh. "Well said, whoever you are. If you are indeed a ghost, what brings you to haunt these halls, assuming it is not just your professed lack of friendship for my brother?"

"The reasons are many." The ghost paused. Carral thought he heard the sounds of someone sipping wine. "As I wander among the living I hear a great deal. See a great deal. Men's ambitions are not hidden from me. Your brother, for instance: he wishes to ally himself with the house of Innes."

"The Prince of Innes has long been a friend to the Wills," Carral said.

"That is so, but this Prince is not the man his father was. He looks at his domain and sees that it is prosperous and strong. He doesn't understand that this is the result of his father's pursuit of peace. He does not understand the costs of war, nor does he care to understand. No, this new prince has ambitions beyond the father's, and in this he is aided by his advisors, especially a knight named Eremon. Though he was once known as Hafydd."

"Hafydd? Not *the* Hafydd . . .? He would be ancient if he were still alive."

"Not so ancient as you think, at least not to the eye. You know him?"

"Hafydd, yes, at least I know of him." Could this be true? Carral wondered. "He was among the Renné when

my father fought them at the Battle of Standing Stones.
He was a great knight and he hated us."

"Yes, he was, but his hatred has spread. The Renné are
foremost in his enmity now. They misused him or so he
thinks: betrayed him, even. His resentment has had many
years to fester; for, as you say, he is old. But what he's
lost in age he has gained in cunning and malice. He will
use the Prince of Innes against the Renné, and he will
also use your daughter to that end. He cannot imagine
that she would not be his ally in this."

Carral was stunned to silence. Who was this man and
why was he telling him this? And why did he sound so
convincing?

"There is more," the voice said. "Eremon, once known
as Hafydd, has acquired some of the knowledge once
possessed by the Knights of the Vow."

Carral felt acid boil up in his stomach. "How can this
be? The Renné destroyed the Knights centuries ago."

"Not quite so long ago, and knowledge often survives
men or is rediscovered." The voice had moved now and
stood by the hearth. "Some frightening things have been
born of tragedy: hatreds that survive down through the
generations."

"Life is often tragic," Carral muttered.

"Yes," the stranger said. "Tragedy always seems to be
lurking in the wings, ready to take the stage. How many
opening scenes are blissful: the birth of a beautiful daughter, only to be followed by loss—of a beloved wife, say?
But it might not end there. Beware your brother.

"Eremon and the Prince need the marriage of your daughter to bring the old allies of the Wills into line. They wait, as your own family does, nursing their resentment, keeping alive the wrongs done them by the Renné and their allies. They have only to see the Wills suddenly restored to former strength. Menwyn and the Prince riding at the head of an army, a son of the two families growing to manhood in some safe place. And Eremon whispering in their ears, telling them where their enemy will march, what fortress he will besiege, how great will be his forces, how weak his alliances." As he spoke the floorboards creaked, tracing his passage around the room. He was to Carral's right now.

Carral could not speak, but sat in fear of what this specter would say next. What words would come out of the darkness. He found the bottle and poured himself wine with a trembling hand. Was there a candle burning? Could this other see him?

"So you see, Carral Wills, knowing a ghost can prove valuable."

"Knowing this ghost's purpose would be even more valuable. Why are you telling me these things and why should I believe them?" The ghost cleared its throat not two feet behind Carral. The blind man felt the hair on his neck bristle.

"You should believe them because they are true and you know them to be so. Because you know your brother for what he is, and have no illusions about the intentions of your family."

The floor creaked again and the door swung open, letting in a cold breath of air.

"But who are you?" Carral called out.

The ghost paused. "It is a wise man who believes the evidence of his eyes."

"But I see nothing."

The door swung softly closed and the treads began to creak as the ghost descended.

EIGHT

It was a room to which very few had keys. Dease counted himself honored to be among the few.

As a room it had no particular merit—a small parlor with a hearth and doors leading out onto a narrow balcony. It was the balcony that gave the room all of its importance, for it overlooked a walled garden. Dease had never actually seen the garden by daylight and did not know if it was beautiful or overrun by weeds—somehow he did not think it overrun by weeds.

He pushed open the doors, being sure to rattle them adequately as he did so. When certain he had given proper warning, he stepped out onto the balcony. The night was redolent with the perfume of flowers, and the air had a soft dampness one would never sense above a stone-paved courtyard.

"You have caused my nightingale to fly," a woman said, her warm voice drifting up from below.

Dease stared into the dark garden, letting his eyes adjust to the night. Only fragments of starlight found their way beneath the overhanging trees. It was a garden of shadows.

"I am sorry," Dease said softly. "I'm a poor substitute for a nightingale."

A soft laugh came in reply.

"Llyn? Are you well?"

A second small laugh, lovely as a breeze, came from below. "Of course I am well. And you, good knight? How goes your summer of tournaments?"

"Well enough. Toren has felled me at every turn, so I have been second to the best knight in the land at every tilt."

"And this disheartens you?"

"To the contrary. I am flattered to be in such company."

"But if not for Toren, Lord Dease Renné would be the champion of the field this season . . ."

For a moment he did not know what to answer. "It is always cooler in the shadow, Cousin," Dease said at last.

Did she whisper yes? But the word was lost in a breath of wind and he could not be sure. He could distinguish her now. A ray of moonlight twined in her yellow hair, but her face was hidden. She moved beneath a screen of leaves, though he could still trace her silhouette.

"Is there no family news that you might tell? No gossip?"

"I rely on you for this," Dease said. It was true. Llyn, a daughter of his father's cousin, knew more of the family and their doings than he——more than he ever cared to know, in truth——which was remarkable considering Llyn lived in solitude within the castle. She was tended by three loyal servants——the most discreet servants Dease had ever known.

As a child, Llyn had been horribly burned. Had almost not survived, in fact, and ever since had lived in cloister, hiding herself away. Of all the family, only a few had contact with her at all: Dease, Toren, a few of their female cousins, an aunt or two. Dease did not know the full range of Llyn's acquaintance but it was not large. He felt such pity for her, though she told him repeatedly that pity was both wasted and unwanted.

"I have very little current gossip, though I can tell you much from years gone by."

"How goes your history of the illustrious Renné?"

"Well enough, though I will tell you, Dease, when you begin to look into the history of our family—really look, not just accept our own myths . . . well, it is not such a story of honor and nobility as the minstrels have made of it."

"No," Dease said, closing his eyes a moment. "I suspect you're right."

"If I had realized the effort and time this history would take, I would never have begun it. So much has been lost since the kingdom was split—the great Record Hall of the Kings and many of the chronicles of the noble families as well. All the years of war have blotted out our history, like ink spilled on a page. It is a terrible thing to happen to a people: like not knowing who your parents are and wondering if there is madness in your family or the bleeder's disease."

"There are the songs of the minstrels and the stories people pass down."

"Certainly, yes, but there is often more art than truth in a minstrel's song. As for stories passed down . . . well, look at the stories told by our own family. We are ever the aggrieved, never the wrongdoers, which we both know is not the truth."

"The Fáel have their story finders . . ." Dease ventured.

"Do not laugh, Cousin. That is what I often feel I am doing—finding stories piece by piece." She sighed. "Have you seen much of Beldor this summer?" she asked suddenly.

Dease was a bit thrown by the change of subject. Did Beldor visit Llyn? *Beldor!?*

"Too much," he said quickly.

"Which might be very little, I think . . .?"

Dease nodded, then realized she might not be able to see him in the dark; but before he could speak Llyn went on.

"Many have remarked that Lord Beldor has grown—that he has matured. It is said that he has finally put aside his jealousy and pettiness and does not resent Toren as he did. That he has mastered himself, at last."

Silence followed these words. He could hear her light footfall as she progressed through the garden, the sound of fine gravel shifting beneath her feet. She listened, but he found he could not speak. Did Llyn have some suspicion?

Dease felt as though his sense of balance betrayed him. As though he might lose his perception of up and down and plunge from the balcony. Fall into the bottomless sky.

Llyn was the most insightful individual Dease had ever known. What was she saying about Beldor?

"You do not answer, Dease," she said softly.

"I did not hear a question, Cousin. It is true that Beldor has seemed less resentful of Toren . . . I have thought it rather a relief and hoped this apparent maturation would last."

Llyn did not answer immediately, but only moved quietly through the garden below. "Beldor will not change, Cousin, any more than a mad horse will grow tame. Such an animal might grow sly and bide its time, fearful of the whip, but it will not suddenly become sound of mind or character. Nor will Beldor. I have tried to warn Toren, but he will have none of it. Will you watch over him, Dease? Will you promise me this?"

Dease felt his mouth grow dry. He wanted to gainsay her. Tell her that Beldor's apparent change of heart was true, but he could not. Somehow he thought she would detect the lie, and then what would she believe?

"I will, if you ask it, Llyn." He could never refuse her.

He heard her sigh. "Thank you, Lord Dease," she said warmly. "There are too few men of virtue. Men of their word."

Yes, Dease thought, *and I am not one of them, not any longer*.

"You are silent in your modesty," she said.

"Should I protest?"

"You've no need of false modesty with me. You know your merits better than most—and your shortcomings."

A strain of music drifted over the garden wall, silencing them both. It traveled from some distance and had grown sparse and thin in its journey so that Dease could not quite discern the melody. But even so it seemed to carry a memory with it.

Some years ago, before the Renné costume ball, Dease had sent a gown and mask to Llyn's room. Only he of all who attended had known who the sun spirit was. How beautiful she had looked in her gold mask, the curls of her silky-wheat hair like the rays of the sun. And they had danced and whispered and laughed. And as they danced he had held her, feeling her yield a little with each step, draw a little closer. Before the unmasking she had slipped away.

For a week after she saw no one. They never spoke of it again, and though there was a costume ball each year at high summer, Llyn never attended again. Dease closed his eyes and could feel her close to him.

"Did we dance to this tune, Cousin?" Llyn asked softly.

"I think we did."

Silence followed, and Dease could feel himself willing her to speak, willing her to say what was in her heart—or what she had felt that night.

"I've had a dream," Llyn said, suddenly self-conscious. "Three times I have dreamed that a small bird came and sat upon the railing of the balcony, where you are now. And each time he called once forlornly, *whist*. And each time the doors behind opened and set him to flight. A man stepped out onto the balcony, but I could not say who. And then I awoke." Llyn moved a few paces. "The whist is a foreteller of . . . ill fortune, Cousin."

It was a foreteller of death, Dease knew. "Yes, though to the Fáel it is a good portent."

"No Fáel has a key to my balcony."

"And you have no idea who it might have been?" Suddenly it was important to know. Toren. It must be Toren.

"I cannot say, for he did not speak and was lost in shadow."

"As you are now."

"I'm not lost, Dease."

"No. No, you're not." He took a long breath. "Do you remember our dance, Llyn?"

She didn't answer a moment.

He heard her light footfall crossing the garden. She hesitated at the door. "I remember," she said softly.

Before he could speak he heard the door open and quickly close.

He was alone. For a while Dease stood, watching the fragments of faint moonlight stir about the garden moved by the wind in the leaves above: a rustling of moonlight.

He could not go, hoping for something—perhaps that Llyn would return, but he could not say. And then a bird alit upon the garden wall. Dease caught his breath.

The bell-like song of the nightingale filled the air, so beautiful and true, and somehow this pained him more than anything he could imagine. More than a whist calling out his name.

ΠΙΠΕ

Baore and Fynnol brought the boat to the foot of the fields and beached it on the coarse sand. Tam had seen them coming from afar, the two of them bent to the oars, pulling like puppets.

A cloud shadow swept over the small, breaking waves, turning whitecaps to gray and winging south like a great hunting bird. Tam closed the door to the house, looking around the garden once. Little would change by autumn.

At the foot of the garden he met his grandfather waiting by the gate. The old man was looking older than usual this past week, having twisted his foot so that he limped stiffly.

"I won't walk you down," he said and reached behind the wall to produce a sword in a new sheath. "It was my father's," he said. "After what happened last time you left the Vale I think you should take it."

Tam took the sword by its hilt, feeling it balance easily in his hand. A powerful desire to stay came over him unexpectedly.

"Go carefully," his grandfather said softly, placing a large hand on Tam's shoulder. Tam nodded, stood a moment longer, and then went out through the gate, trotting quickly down the lane toward the lake.

He found Fynnol and Baore lashing the belongings he'd left on the shore into the boat.

"Ah, he's coming after all." Fynnol looked up. "And bearing arms, too." Fynnol pointed at something in the boat. "Baore's brought his shod staff, so I shall have the two of you to protect me . . . and I can't tell you how distressed that leaves me."

Tam lashed the sword to the thwarts, and the three pushed the boat out onto the smooth waters of the lake. Tam looked back toward the house, seeing the dark figure of his grandfather still standing by the garden gate. Tam waved once, even though he knew the old man could not see him so far away, and then settled himself to the forward oars. The line of poplars that followed the lane stood out in the morning sun like golden flames, leading like beacons back up toward his home.

What if, in our absence, war came to the Vale? Tam thought suddenly. But he pushed the thought aside. It was more than unlikely. The Vale was far from the populated areas of old Ayr, and even there peace reigned. The Vale would be safe, waiting for them upon their return.

Fynnol had scrambled into the stern, smiling triumphantly at the two who'd taken up the oars. "Put your backs into it, lads," he said. "It's a long way to Wold of Kerns where our fortune awaits us."

"It is a long way to the bottom, too, Cousin," Baore growled.

Fynnol peered over the side. "Not so far. I can see it quite clearly. Row on," he said, stretching one hand above his head and waving it like a banner. "I'll take my turn soon enough. We're away! Away from this cursed place, walled in by its mountains, shut off from the larger world." He grinned at his companions, foolish with delight, then bounced up to his feet, as though he could see over the hills even now. The boat rocked, and the others steadied it. "How can you look so dour?" Fynnol asked, standing with one foot on the gunwale. "It is a joyous day. But let's beware of strangers and keep watch on our boat both by day and night. We'll tether it to you each evening, Baore. That'll be anchor enough to hold it. Yes, beware of fair-spoken strangers and keep your bows ready."

They passed the length of Shadow Lake and through the Neck into Blue Hawk Lake, the wind at their backs. Sailing scows passed them by, spreading their tanbark sails to the breeze, white foaming about their blunt bows. Farms sailed north, the trees in new leaf drawing like sails. Occasionally someone would raise a hoe and wave, for it was no secret that the young men were setting off into the outside world, despite what had happened on their last attempt.

Tam was sure he had told the story of the attack at Telanon Bridge to every individual in the Vale, and to some more than once. It must have made quite a change from the usual domestic gossip, but everyone thought they were mad to leave a second time. Even their friends were not so sure they should risk it again.

But leave they did. They swept into the river that emptied the lakes, down the green-shadowed gorge past the Stone Gate. The waters flowed more swiftly here; and Tam took his place in the stern, using his oars to back and ferry, guiding them surely between the banks and around the occasional rock.

As they rounded the bend before the bridge they found a figure seated on the bridge rail, dangling his legs calmly over the side. He hailed them as they drew closer, standing up on the parapet.

"There is our story finder—skylarking, apparently," Fynnol said, shading his eyes.

"I'll bring us up on the gravel beyond the bridge," Tam said. In a moment the crunch of wood on small stone brought them to a halt.

Fynnol and Baore jumped out and pulled the boat up a few inches more.

"Are the Fáel still camped here?" Baore asked.

Tam shook his head. "They said they would go on the next day. I can't think why they would change their plan . . ."

The branches of the trees parted and Cynddl appeared, sliding down the embankment, a bag over his shoulder and a bow in either hand. "You made fast work of your boat," he said, eyeing the craft appreciatively. Then he held out one of the bows. "I have brought a gift from Cian and Aliel for Tam."

Tam stepped out of the boat and took the bow in his hands as though it were a great prize. The dark red-brown of the yaka wood was polished to a deep luster, and the wood was warm to the touch, as if it still lived.

"To replace the one you lost to the river," Cynddl said and gave Tam a quiver of beautiful workmanship. Tam drew an arrow out and stopped short, for it was not tipped for hunting but for the piercing of mail.

Tam looked up at the Fáel. "What do they expect us to find upon the river?"

"It isn't what they expect you'll find, Tam, but what they fear you'll find that has prompted this gift." He turned to Baore and Fynnol. "And for you Aliel sent these." Cynddl gave each of them a small bag, beautifully embroidered. "It isn't gold, I'm afraid, but the spices used on the rabbit you so enjoyed. Now you'll be able to cook like the Fáel."

"Cian and Aliel are here?" Tam said.

"No, my people went north days ago. Only I stayed, listening to the whispers. What stories linger hereabout! How I wish I had the whole summer to gather them." He shook his head. "But all I've found in my short stay are fragments—like scenes of a play, most of them sorrowful."

Tam thought Cynddl completely unlike the Fáel he had known: where they were guarded and resentful, Cynddl seemed open and trusting. But he had such an air of terrible loss around him. Even when he smiled there was a sense of melancholy to it. His hair, gray far too early, added to this, of course—and his thin face— but there was something more: a distracted air, as though his mind were elsewhere and little concerned with matters at hand.

"We're at your command," Tam said. "If you wish to stay longer . . ."

But Cynddl shook his head. "No, the stories I've come to collect wait further south." A surprisingly disarming smile appeared. "And Aliel has asked me to keep you from trouble, for I've traveled all across the land between the mountains, and you've barely left your gardens." Cynddl passed his bag to Baore, and Tam noted a blade strapped to the side.

"There aren't many places where a boat can land in this section of the river," Fynnol said, looking around. "Let's have a meal here, where we can sit ashore and make a fire."

"Do you like fish?" Cynddl asked.

The Valemen all agreed that they did.

"Then I'll catch us our meal. I've found all the places where the big bass hide."

He took a small bag from his belongings and disappeared into the trees. A moment later he appeared, barefoot, standing on a rock, a line in his hand with something small flashing on the end.

"Watch for the sly otter who lives in these waters. Twice she has taken my catch. Twice!" He laughed. But today they would not share their meal with otters, and in no time Cynddl had pulled two fish out into the flashing sunlight.

They roasted them over a fire, Cynddl taking charge

of the cooking. To the fish they added fresh bread baked by Baore's mother, which had to be eaten before staleness or river water ruined it.

Tam looked around him at the gorge. Sunlight skipped off the water, and the cliff-top trees made moving shadows on the rock walls and the green river. Beneath the bridge he could just make out the tooth of rock and the tree beneath which they had taken refuge that strange night. It made him shiver to think of it: the men shooting arrows at them in the dark—and Tam shooting back; Alaan down upon the bridge, his attackers over him.

"Where do you expect to find these stories, Cynddl?" Fynnol asked. "Do they just lie about upon the bank awaiting you?"

"No, Fynnol," Cynddl said. "It's me that waits for them. There are places along the river where the lost race built their strongholds. If their stories can still be heard, I'll find them there. For the next few days, though, there'll be no need for me to stop."

Before Fynnol could speak again, Tam interrupted. "We've never been in the wildlands," he said. "Is it very different from here?"

"You live in the wildlands, Tam," Cynddl said, smiling. But then more thoughtfully added, "I've only traveled up the road and never down the river, so I don't know how different it might be. South of here lies a beautiful land— the wildlands you call it, though my people call it Greensprings for the uncounted springs of pure, clear water that pour from the rock." He looked from one

Valeman to another. "Not many people make their homes among the hills of Greensprings now, for it's a strange place, as you've no doubt heard. No one knows what befell the people who lived there long ago, but there is a sense of sadness over the land that's not imagined. You'll feel it yourselves.

"Nothing remains of the ancient people now but the stories that echo in the places where they made their homes; and even these stories are now so faint that even the most gifted story finders can barely hear them.

"Men who've traveled through Greensprings tell strange stories. They claim to have seen and heard unsettling things: voices, the cries of unknown beasts, and lights in the forest and even in the river itself." Cynddl took up a pebble and tossed it into the river. "Most of the land is forest, though there are meadows where grasses and flowers thrive. Twice the road crosses the river—once by bridge and once at the ford at Willowwand.

"It's a rich land but not for farming, for the bones of the earth lie close to the surface. You can see animals in the Greensprings that have disappeared elsewhere. I've seen lion as we traveled and bear and the great hart. Wolves are not uncommon; the silver fox lives there still, though is seldom seen. Birds of all kinds live in Greensprings in summer, even the white eagle that we call the ghostking.

"The trees there must be very old. Some are seen only in the Greensprings and nowhere else in all the known lands. There is silveroak, which is also called knight's tree. Golden beech, waterwillow, cedars of many kinds, great firs taller than every tree but the ancient alollynda. And the rose clan is scattered everywhere: apples and crab apple, wild roses, mountain ash, and wild cherries. Witch hazel we'll see, and perfect laurel trees. Sweetgum, doveplum, tallowwood and hornbeam." He laughed. "It is a long list and I'll point them out as we go." He turned his attention back to his meal, which Tam thought was better than any fish he had eaten and wondered what Cynddl had done to prepare it so.

Cynddl opened his bag and took out a roll of paper, pressed flat in the packing. He unrolled this on a rock. They all gathered around, for it was a Fáel map of the land between the mountains.

Putting his finger on the map, Cynddl said, "We're making our picnic here, by Telanon Bridge." He ran his finger down the meandering line. "I can't vouch for the course of the river. My people haven't traveled this way in generations, so all we know comes from others. Here we meet the north bridge, and from that point on the river is somewhat better known."

Tam stared at the map, feeling his excitement grow. His grandfather had a book of maps, and as a boy Tam had spent many delight-filled hours poring over it. Maps were like doors into the imagination for him—as though he were a great bird looking down on the world from high above. But then, in his imagination, he would swoop down and see the world close up, change into the form of a knight and travel the roads to tournaments.

"A map of possibilities," Tam said aloud.

Everyone looked at him oddly.

"It is what Aliel said when she found me staring at a map as a child. I didn't know what she meant then——it was a map of old Ayr I looked at——but I understood soon after." He nodded toward the map. "And now, perhaps, we'll make some of these possibilities real."

Cynddl looked at Tam and smiled. "The Fáel have a saying: 'Only a perfect fool hopes for adventure.'" He touched the map again. "Once we've passed the ford at Willowwand the river should run much more smoothly. Although the people of the Vale think the lowlands start there, we'll still be among hills for some time. Is it about a fortnight to Inniseth?"

"About that," Fynnol said, "then another ten or twelve days to the Wold of Kerns."

"Then it will take you forty days or more to return. The road runs a long way to the east before swinging back in a great loop to come west to Telanon Bridge." He ran his finger over the land south of Telanon Bridge. "There's said to be an old trail, but it won't accommodate our carts so my people have never taken it. But you might be wise to keep to the road for your return journey. The path might be difficult to follow, or even to find, and if you're lost in the wood you could spend many more days than on the longer way.

"The ruins of Cooling Keep stand here, on an island

where the River Dyrr joins. The last Knights of the Vow perished there, and the battlements were torn down and what could be burned set aflame." Picking up a feather that lay on the ground he ran the quill down the river south of the Wold of Kerns. "The land is beautiful here, too, and still wild by the standards of the old kingdom." The quill moved south, like a winging bird. "The inhabited lands start here, though the border of the old kingdom proper is still far off. These were thought to be the furthest reaches of civilization then, if civilization it could be called. Men who were sent to the outer duchies and principalities to represent the King thought they'd been sentenced to a fate worse than the darkest dungeon. To them anywhere beyond two days' journey from court was a hardship beyond enduring.

"But there are many sights to be seen here: valleys famed for their beauty, lakes the sight of which would break your heart. It's a shame you'll travel only to the Wold. There's a great deal of beauty between there and the sea." He took hold of the map's edge as though he would roll it. "But to Valemen I'm sure the Wold of Kerns will seem far enough. You'll see more than most who live behind the gate, that's certain." He rolled up the map with quick motions, and Tam shook his head, as though he had wakened from a daydream. A dream of the greater world.

They broke up their camp. Cynddl scrambled up toward the trees with their water skins, claiming that he had found a spring that was far sweeter than river water. "As good as mead," he called as he disappeared.

Fynnol turned to Tam, speaking quietly. "Why do you think Cynddl wants to go down the river?"

Tam shook his head, looking over at Baore, who had stopped his task and listened. "You don't believe he's trying to find the lost stories of the ancient kingdoms?"

Fynnol stared up at the trees where their Fáel companion had disappeared. "No more than I believe that throwing coins into the river will keep you from harm."

Cynddl came sliding down the embankment a moment later, their water skins over his shoulders. With one last look around, they pushed the boat out onto the green water and found their places. The current took hold of them and tugged them out into the flowing stream of the sunlit river.

Cynddl's thieving otter took up station behind them in the shadow of one of the banks and followed easily along, its sleek, soft face just breaking the surface.

"See how she comes slinking along," Cynddl said, "like a spy. As if we cannot see her." He laughed. "By road it is twelve days to the ford at Willowwand," he said. "How long will we take to reach there?"

"Five days, perhaps a bit more," Fynnol said. "The river has good speed yet, though the spring rains have passed. We'll see. If we needed to we could row, but we're in no hurry to pass through lands we've never seen before." He glanced over at Cynddl. "Or do you need to travel more quickly?"

Cynddl shook his head, settling himself down on one of their bags. "Life speeds by those who travel in haste."

He shaded his eyes with a hand and gazed off toward the shore like a man prepared to enjoy every minute of their journey.

But Tam noticed the Fáel reached out a hand and made sure his bow was nearby. And he had lashed his bag in such a way that his sword would come easily to hand.

They made their camp on a treed point that kinked the river between two of the Five Gorges: First Gorge, the Valley of Clouds, Deep Gorge, Ruan's Race, and last and most dangerous the Lion's Maw. The night air was still cool so close to the mountains so early in the season. Tam sat near the fire, wrapped in a blanket, listening to the river hasten quickly by. In the distance they could hear the constant conversation of the fast water flowing through the Valley of Clouds.

"You said there were many stories to be found at the old tower," Tam said to Cynddl. "Did you learn of the battle?"

The Fáel story finder shifted where he sat across the fire from Tam. Between them ribbons of flame flared up, then fluttered to nothing in the still night air.

"I was not there long enough to find a story complete." The Fáel held his hands near the fire to warm them. "The name 'story finder' is misleading, I think. The training I received from my elders was almost all in the art of waiting, in patience. Stories come if you know how to listen. You don't dig them up in the way that you dug up objects from the old battlefield.

"The stories of men linger on. They echo in the places where they were told or where they were lived. Over time the echoes grow fainter, and sometimes parts of stories fade to nothing and are never heard again. There is nothing sadder than that.

"If you've learned the lessons of patience and you have the gift of hearing, stories come to you—in fragments, whole lines, feelings, images, sometimes an entire speech. Repeatedly, when I was staying in the tower I would have . . . visions of parts of the battle. I kept seeing a small boy, and then I'd witness the battle through his eyes. I would see men I knew fall . . . my own father." Cynddl shut his eyes a moment and sat very still. "But there were other things as well. I began to have this faint image of knights riding over Telanon Bridge. Six of them, tired and scarred from battle. They were accompanied by no train, no equerries, no carts bearing stores, no relief horses. Six lonely knights riding in silence at dusk, pausing on the bridge to look up at the ruined tower. And what despair they felt! What anguish and regret. But listen as I might I could find nothing more about them. When I close my eyes I see them still, as though they are forever crossing Telanon Bridge, the tired clatter of their horses' hooves echoing over the river.

"It's a bridge that has seen a great deal over the ages. The first bridge at Telanon—for that's the old name of the narrows—was built more than four hundred years ago to carry the bounty of the gold and silver mines down through the wildlands to the north bridge where much of it was taken aboard barges. That bridge was destroyed by the miners when the sons of King Paldon fought for the throne. Probably the destruction of the bridge tipped the balance in that war, for Prince Keln then had no gold to increase his army.

"For almost two hundred years the Knights of the Vow kept a tower by the bridge and safeguarded the long trains of precious metals. But their greed undid them. They kept demanding more and more for this labor, and finally King Korrl forbade them to perform this service ever again.

"One could never reckon the riches that have passed this way, and the produce of the farms in the Vale went to feed the miners and their families in the mountains. When the mines died the Vale became, for a while, a forgotten place. But the long rebellion of the princes against the kings sent many people north hoping to find a place to escape the chaos.

"And then again when the Renné and the Wills split the kingdom and old Ayr was brought to ruin in the hundred years' war, many people fled out to the edges of the land between the mountains. Whole villages were torched then, and the people put to the sword for allegedly harboring the enemy or for no reason at all. The brutality of that time is impossible to imagine, but these old towns still bear their stories like scars. One can hear the screams echoing there to this day." Cynddl looked up from the fire, his jaw tight. "It's very odd that a bridge so far from the inhabited lands is so rich in history and stories."

"Alaan sang us a song about the bridge," Baore said quietly. "It told of a child being spirited away and of a man who might have been a Knight of the Vow."

"Ah, yes. That old song." Cynddl hummed a few bars, and Baore nodded. "I don't know about the Knight of the Vow, but certainly the story is true. The son of the Prince of Alethon was taken away from the battle and was never seen again. Many believe he was delivered to his uncle, who murdered him so that he might inherit his brother's lands and titles, but no one knows for certain."

Fynnol was hardly managing to hide his mirth at this speech. "Are there stories lingering here, on this point of land?" he asked.

The Fáel did not miss the glee in Fynnol's tone. For a moment he looked at the young Valeman, not in anger but as though he were some object of mild curiosity. Fynnol returned the gaze innocently.

"Let me tell you a story of the river," Cynddl said. "It has been speaking all the time I've camped by its bank." He drew himself up a little, the tendrils of flame lighting him with a warm, wavering glow. "It's the story of two brothers, Assal and Wirrth, and happened a long age ago. As young men, they journeyed into the wildlands together, seeking precious metals and gemstones. For many years they sought their fortunes among the hills and streams at the foot of the mountains. Wirrth came to hate the wildlands, which seemed to him to be concealing what they sought and tormenting them with false hopes. He believed their only hope of escape lay in relentless toil. To this end he would work from sunrise to sunset each day, but his brother, Assal, would lay aside his tools when he deemed his daily toil was done. Then he would walk through the wildlands, enchanted by the beauty of the mountains and the rivers and streams. Of an evening he would play an old harp and sing. Resentment grew between the two as their differences hardened.

"Despite this, neither could bear to be alone, so they continued on over the years, their hatred festering and growing. They passed their youth and middle years in their pursuit, and then one day, walking along a small stream at the foot of the mountains, Assal was lost in a thick mist. It was an odd mist, for certainly the sun shone strongly from above and lit the fog so that it glowed white and golden like a cloud at sunset. Before him something moved and Assal was afraid, for there were great bear and mountain lions dwelling nearby.

"But what moved before him seemed to be of the same substance as the mist, white and glowing. 'You seek gold,' came a voice that was like the muttering and hissing of old winds among the rocks and crags. 'I too sought gold,' it said. Assal was not sure if his ears were playing tricks on him, for surely this was only the sound of the breeze.

"'I can show you where the gold hides,' came the voice out of the mist. Assal found he couldn't answer—he was so afraid of this specter which seemed to be part of the mist. He thought he could see it now, almost human in form, with flowing white tresses. 'What is it you want of me?' Assal said at last, so frightened he almost didn't hear what the thing had said. 'Fulfill my bargain with the river and I will show you gold. Gold pure and glittering and easily taken.' 'What bargain?' Assal managed. 'Throw half of all you gain into the Lion's Maw and I will be released.'

"Assal didn't speak but only managed to nod. 'Follow,' said the creature of mist, and there was a movement before him. To follow such a creature was difficult, for Assal could only see where the mists swirled as the creature passed. Up they went into the trees. For some time Assal followed, not sure where they were or where they were going.

"Finally the creature led him to a speaking stream that chattered and burbled down a valley between the mountains. The mist seemed to recede then, drawing up the valley like a coverlet being lifted. 'Remember our bargain,' hissed the creature, and then its words were lost among the winds and the speech of the stream.

"There, in the sunlight, Assal saw something glitter in the water, and when he waded out to look, fetched from the running waters a nugget of the purest gold! He had found a stream that bore gold in both dust and nuggets.

"He was a day finding his way back to Wirrth. 'Here brother,' he said, 'within my palm I hold all that we have dreamed.' And he showed Wirrth the nugget. Wirrth abandoned his toil and subjected the nugget to all the tests that he knew and pronounced it true gold, but when Assal told him the story of its finding Wirrth grew angry and sullen, saying that his brother mocked him or had perhaps lost his reason.

"The two climbed up to the stream and panned all the gold that their boat could bear: a substantial fortune. It took some time and many trips to carry this down to their boat, for the way was difficult. They set off down the river from a place very near to where Telanon Bridge stands today, and soon came to the Five Gorges. Four they managed without incident though their boat was overloaded, but when they came to the last, they argued.

"Wirrth refused to throw any of his gold into the river, saying that Assal had succumbed to madness and this was what came of men who frittered their time away in fancy and idleness. 'You throw your half into the Lion's Maw,' Wirrth shouted, 'but I will not sacrifice the smallest part of my own to your foolishness.'

"As Assal would not give up all of his share and Wirrth would give up none of his, they set out into the final gorge, Assal muttering beneath his breath. A mist hung over the gorge and the voice of the Lion roared so that the rocks trembled.

"But all the while they had been traveling Wirrth had been thinking, and his festering resentment of his brother came at last to a head. He had done all the work over the years. Without him Assal would have starved in the winters. And all this time Assal had mocked him and called him a slave to his toils and worse. Assal did not deserve half a share of their gold, nor even a quarter.

"As they entered the Lion's Maw Assal knelt in the bow with a pole to fend off the rocks, and Wirrth manned the oars in the stern. As they were thrown first this way and that by the wrath of the river, Wirrth contrived to knock his brother over the side with an oar. Assal clung to the gunwale a moment, struggling desperately to pull himself up, but all he managed to do was heel the boat enough that it filled and Wirrth lost control of it. Assal was pulled down into the roiling waters, and then the boat rolled and smashed against stone and all its cargo was sucked down into the whirling waters of the Lion's Maw.

"Wirrth managed to survive by clinging to the wreckage, but he had nothing left but the clothes he wore and a knife on his belt. The boat was badly damaged, and he hadn't the tools to repair it. He went down the river on a makeshift raft, growing frail and sickly as he traveled. A fortnight you say to Inniseth, but Wirrth took twice that time. He never recovered enough to travel north again, nor would he tell any other where his secret stream lay for fear that some other might profit from his labor. And so he passed away and the people of Inniseth committed his ashes to the river, where the story says he is tormented by his brother to this day.

"There, it would seem, is the origin of paying the Lion for passage." Cynddl shrugged off the blanket he had wrapped around his shoulders and rose, stretching his arms up toward the stars. "I'll walk along the bank a bit before I sleep. Rest well, all of you." He gave them a nod that seemed more like a bow and stepped out of the ring of firelight.

Fynnol looked at Tam and smiled. "Well, there you go, Cousin. A creature of mist once led a man to a stream full of gold and that is how we have the foolish custom of throwing good gold and silver into the Lion's Maw to pay for passage."

"There is another story there, Fynnol—the story of a practical man who mocked his brother for telling a fantastic tale of being led to a treasure. Who knows what treasures Cynddl might find as we travel along the river."

Fynnol laughed. "Well, I'm glad to hear that. We could use a treasure, Cousin."

"So we could, but I doubt you'll buy horses with the riches Cynddl finds."

✝ E Π

The island had once boasted greater fortifications, yet like much of the old kingdom after the partition, war had often found its way here. But war hadn't made the long journey, now, in many years, and the island's defenses had not been kept up, partly to save the cost.

Elise stood on the top of a high hill at the lake head, gazing south. She could see the island and its castle clearly, and all the other islands fading away to pale blue-greens as they meandered off into the distance. It was a long lake, more than a league, and she loved the way the hills and islands folded into one another, their colors growing softer and more muted as they dwindled toward the horizon, layer upon layer.

Her cousins lamented their isolation here, constantly pining for the inner principalities and duchies of the old kingdom, but Elise never complained. She thought the life her cousins dreamed of was frivolous and vapid, though perhaps she merely feared what would happen if the Wills made their way back into the center of the old realm.

Intrigue, she thought, *perhaps even war.*

There was enough intrigue already. Her uncle Menwyn saw to that.

She looked over at her maid and the lone guard who rode with her. Though they waited with little show of impatience, they were ready to go back, Elise knew. It seemed they could take a quick look at the scene, proclaim its beauty, and then leave. But Elise was prepared to sit here all day. She loved to watch the vista change. The moving light played across the scene, altering the mood from one moment to the next. One never knew what it would do. And look at those clouds rolling across the far horizon! She could watch them for hours.

The shadow of a cloud flowed over the brocade hills, silent and dark. She watched it progress across the landscape like some shape-shifting creature. And what could such a creature seek?

There was said to be a supernatural beast that dwelt within the lake itself—half fish, half horse, and white as a wave crest. When the wind blew it was often seen, or so people said, galloping among the breaking waves. But Elise had not seen it—at least she was not sure she had—but it was not for lack of looking.

She sighed. Menwyn was right about one thing—she was a daydreamer. Her father claimed, though he always smiled when he said it, that this was man's highest calling, but she knew few others agreed. Of course when you were a musician and composer, famed across all the lands, you could make such claims about the value of daydreaming. Something resulted from it.

She took up her pen again and, dipping it in ink, wrote in her book of days.

Here, the world fades toward a horizon of clouds that rise up in whirls and furrows and cast themselves across the sky. Oh, what subtle plays of light among them—shades of palest yellow and blue and a mauve so translucent your eye is not sure it's there. I sometimes think that the sea is just beyond the farthest hill, and the distant clouds are sea clouds, sailing landward, though of course this is impossible. The sea is many leagues off, unlike the sea of imagination which is right at hand. This could be it below me—a small hand of the ocean reaching far inland toward me. If I were not a Wills, caught up in all the ambitions of my family, would I be so drawn toward the world of the imagination? The world of art and artifice?

She closed her eyes and imagined the court of the old kingdom before her family and the Renné split the country over the succession. Almost, she could see herself there, among the gaiety, the intellectual life . . . almost.

The sound of a horse called her back from the past, and she turned to find a man dismounting. He bore a wicker box such as minstrels used to carry their instruments, though if he were a minstrel he was either of noble birth or quite famed, for he was dressed in fine clothes and had the bearing and confidence of a man of property.

He bowed low toward Elise but addressed her maid.

"I have been sent from the castle to play for Lady Elise, if she will allow it," he said.

Elise smiled. Her father loved to surprise her. "She will," Elise answered, feeling suddenly that an interruption of her contemplation would be welcome.

The stranger took out his instrument, a beautifully made Fáellute, and perched upon the end of the stone bench opposite Elise. Very quickly he tuned it and then turned to her.

> "A firstborn son both fair and kind
> And a second son of different mind
> Taradynn and Tindamor
> Would live to bring their father woe."

Elise knew the song immediately: the song of a younger prince who secretly murdered his brother to take the throne. Taradynn and Tindamor. Carral and Menwyn. Elise sat for a moment in stunned silence. How did he dare to play such a song for her? If Menwyn heard of it they would both have more trouble than they wished—especially this minstrel.

"I do not know if you are more foolish or brave," she said, forcing control of her voice so that her words came out clipped and precise. "Did my father know you would play this song for me?"

"Your father did not send me, lady, though I know and respect him," he said evenly, watching her reaction carefully.

She shook her head in confusion. "Then what kind of madness . . . ?" Elise was at a loss for words.

The minstrel tilted his head toward the lake. "Do you see the party riding up the eastern shore?"

She ran her eye along the edge of the water, and there in the shadow of the wood she saw a dark line of riders.

"The Prince of Innes comes to Braidon Castle, secretly. With him travels his handsome son. I will tell you honestly, lady, that if you are not made of stone you will find him much to your liking. But I have come to warn you. The young prince no more controls the policy of his family than you make policy for the Wills. Compared to the old prince, Menwyn is a fair and reasonable man. Do not be fooled by this prince's manner, which can be courtly and kind when needed. Within his own house he is a tyrant the likes of which you have never known. And he would bend you to his purpose, do not doubt it, for in that place you would have no allies but the young prince, who does his father's bidding, however much he disdains to. That is what I have come to say." The man looked off toward the old watchtower behind them.

"And why does this matter concern you?"

He brought his serious gaze back to her. "It concerns every man and woman who lives between the mountains," he said matter-of-factly.

She turned her attention toward the party approaching through the trees, and suddenly she wanted to rush back to the castle lest some decision be made about her future while she was absent. Elise felt her hand come to her face unbidden.

"Will you ride back with me?" she said, her voice sounding very small and frail.

"I regret that I cannot accept your kind offer, my lady. You see, the Prince has a particular dislike of my art and it were better if I remained here for a few days until he is gone."

She shook her head, rising from the bench, feeling both apprehensive and determined. "You haven't told me your name, sir minstrel," she said.

He rose quickly. "I regret to say, my lady, that any name I give you would not be true. I can make one up if you like. Or you might give me a name of your choosing."

"Then I will call you Gwyden Dore, for the knight who posed as a minstrel to save fair Katlynn." She met his eye, as a well-bred lady should not. "But you should beware, Gwyden Dore, for your namesake perished in his deed."

"So some songs tell, my lady, but still others say he escaped." The man smiled. "I far prefer the latter."

She passed by him and the guard fetched her horse. Elise let herself be helped into the saddle, and then looked toward the minstrel, who bowed low.

The songs in which Gwyden Dore escaped also told that Lady Katlynn ran off with her rescuer. She took one last appraising look at this handsome player and wheeled her horse, setting off at a canter into the wood.

ELEVEΠ

The garden of birds was hidden within a bower concealing a pool of lilies. About the edge of the pool, birds perched like flowers: tall herons, feathers fluttering in the breeze; gladioli cranes; blossom-bright kingfishers; the tiny, secretive herons of riverbanks. In the languid air above, swallows stitched delicate designs.

Tuath dipped the oars silently and propelled herself another boat length, turning her small craft so that she might have another view. A pair of swans with cygnets in tow passed close by, hoping for morsels. The sad flute-like notes of the sorcerer thrush fell like leaves.

"I hear you, Tylyth," she whispered. "You are my favorite, yet. My secret love."

Tuath turned her eyes again to the swallows, watching them weave, wondering what pattern they favored today. She narrowed her eyes and tried to see only the flight, imagining each swallow as a needle pulling invisible thread.

What a gown that would make, she thought, but then tried to push all the thoughts from her mind. It was

never clear what she saw—not consciously understood—yet there seemed to be a pattern, a design. *It is
only inspiration,* her sister claimed, *ritual. The swallows'
flight means nothing.*

Yes, perhaps.

But even so, she believed the swallows' flight was not
random, any more than the plaiting of distinctive nests
was accidental. Closing her eyes, Tuath tried to hold the
flight of the swallows in her mind, searching for the feeling of *yes—yes, that's it* . . .

Sometimes she felt it here, in the garden, and had to
hold it inside her until she came to the hall of weaving,
avoiding everyone lest they speak and chase her precious
revelation away. What torture that was to feel something
so hard-won slip away.

When the *yes* came she pulled the boat quickly to
shore, jumping lightly out and leaving the boat to look
after itself. Keeping her eyes fixed firmly ahead, Tuath
walked deliberately to the hall, looking at no one, raising her hand once to stop another from speaking. The
epiphany wavered—the *yes* becoming a *maybe.* Tuath
stopped where she was, closing her eyes, trying to recap-
ture the flight of the swallows. *There, yes, that was it* . . .
wasn't it?

She hurried on.

The last few yards she almost ran, tearing open the
door and shutting herself quickly in, latching the door
lest her vision escape. A sigh sounded in the silence and
muted light of the Weavers' Hall.

A moment later she found her sister standing on a head-high platform, her needle darting in and out, in and out, glinting in the light slanting through high windows. Tuath didn't stop to look at the tapestry but mounted the stairs to her place and set straight to work. The first few stitches would tell. She closed her eyes to make them, the needle darting back and forth like a bird in flight.

They drank tull at a small table, gazing at the tapestry they made, wondering what the pattern would be.

"It's a strange design," Tuath's sister, Tannis, said. "Disturbing really. Sometimes, when I look at it, I shudder."

"Yes. I have strange dreams about it. The man before the gate—the one bearing the other up—he turns to meet my eyes and I feel a dread creep over me, a fear like I have never known." She did shiver then. "I would give it up but for Nann."

Tuath wondered at the men before the enormous gate. They were in darkness or deep shadow—one man limp, his arm and head hanging down unnaturally, the other bearing him in his arms.

Tannis poured them more tull, her strong, dusky hands lifting the heavy pot with ease. Tuath always marveled that these hands could do such delicate work.

They were twins, Tannis and Tuath, one dark, one light. They had been born of the same mother on the same night. Tannis raven haired and Fáel eyed. Tuath light as snow, eyes like ice reflecting a pale blue sky, skin waxen white revealing the delicate blue branchings beneath. Rivers and streams of blood. Bruises like estuaries.

One dark and solid, like words on the page, the other ghostly, almost insubstantial, yet sisters, born within the same hour.

"I would give it up as well," Tannis said, "if I could . . . but it haunts me like no other we've done. I look at it sometimes and wish I'd never been born a vision weaver."

"Yes, and it has disturbed Nann even more. She tries to hide it, but I can tell. It shows in her face. I'm sure she comes here at night to puzzle over it. Perhaps she dreams of it as well."

Nann helped Rath into the Weavers' Hall, his weight distributed between her arm and his cane, almost none of it, apparently, on his feet.

He has grown so feeble, she thought. *Now when we need him most.*

A chair had been set for him, padded with cushions, a blanket left to cover his thin legs. Nann wasn't quite strong enough to lower him to the chair, and he dropped the last handsbreadth, bouncing like a doll. The old man closed his eyes for a moment, and remained very still.

"Rath . . . ?"

He nodded his head, though his eyes remained closed, his jaw clamped shut. "All right," he whispered, his voice so soft she could barely hear it.

His eyes opened, clouded with age, like overcast skies. Nann stepped out of his way but stayed nearby. The old man leaned forward on his cane, squinting, pressing a crooked finger into the corner of one eye.

Two hundred candles had been lit to illuminate the tapestry. Tannis and Tuath would be dismayed to hear it, for the smoke would ruin the colors, but there was no way to be sure Rath would be well enough to view it by daylight. Who knew what might befall him by morning?

She watched him, wondering what he would see. He stretched his thin neck forward—like a baby bird's, she thought. The shape of his bald head reinforced this impression. Even for a Fáel he was dark skinned, the result of his years of traveling beneath the sun, gathering stories and lore. She found it odd to think that this tiny man before her was so great among her people. He looked like a candle flame about to flicker out.

Rath stared for a long time at the tapestry, saying nothing, his thin face set in its habitual scowl. Finally he stamped his cane on the floor—a pitiful tap. "Why wasn't I shown this before?" he demanded, his wisp of a voice rasping in the almost empty room.

"We thought the pattern too incomplete until now."

"I'm not so blind! It is clear as clear and likely has been so for days—longer!" He lifted his cane in one bony hand and pointed it shakily at the figures stitched before the gate. "Caibre," he said, then aimed it toward the man stepping out of the trees. "Sainth," he said. And finally at the woman who took shape from the river. "Sianon."

Nann closed her eyes. They were names she knew. Names out of stories and legends. Names their story finders had heard whispered when the Fáel first stepped ashore in the land between the mountains. The winds knew those names then, and the rivers and streams. Sorcerers, they were said to have been, Sainth, Caibre, and Sianon: the children of Wyrr, the oldest enchanter of them all. Wyrr, who gathered the knowledge of all who died, and who went into the river in the end, joining his spirit to the water's.

What are the secret branches of the river? The dreams of Wyrr.

"How can you be sure?"

The old man lifted his cane again. "There, in the clouds, a black swan and in its shadow another. The devices of Wyrr who placed the first swan on his banner when Caibre was born. The second, a white swan, for the birth of Sainth. The third, another black swan, was for Sianon. But the white swan disappeared from Wyrr's banner, some tales say, because Sainth fought bitterly with his father, for they were too much alike, father and second son."

"But who is the fourth?" Nann said, pointing, almost afraid to ask.

"What?"

"The other man, there, before the great gate."

Rath bent forward again, leaning heavily on his cane. "I don't know," he said at last. "But the gate . . . That is Death's gate." He sat back in his chair, and covered his eyes with one hand for a moment.

Nann looked at the old man in pity, for he was in sight of that gate even now. She was sure Rath's head was spinning. It was too much for him—even the short walk, the few steps, and now this.

"I've forgotten the story," Nann said when Rath opened his eyes again. "Their father offered them gifts, gifts of their own choosing . . .?"

Rath nodded. "Wyrr was like many fathers; though he was wise, he could see only good in his own children. When he grew old he offered them gifts—of their own choosing, as you say. Caibre, the eldest, wanted to be a greater warrior than he already was, a leader of men. 'Let men fear and obey me,' he said.

"Sainth, the second son, did not care for war but loved music and learning. He wished that he might see all the world.

"Sianon, the youngest, and Caibre's rival for her father's affections, said that she, too, would be a great warrior, but men would follow her and do her bidding out of love." Rath pressed three fingers to the center of his forehead. He was still for a moment, clearly in pain, and then he continued without lowering his hand. "Wyrr warned his children that such gifts would not come without price, and what this price might be he could not predict, but they all chose to take this risk.

"And so it came about that Caibre was feared and obeyed just as he'd wished, but he was no longer master of himself. Once he had begun a thing he could not give it up. He would besiege a castle until his entire army had been spent, then he would raise another army and take it up again. There was no retreat for Caibre. It was a word without meaning to him.

"Sainth was given the ability to travel the world by secret paths that only he could find, but no place was home to him, no woman fair enough to be his bride—for there might always be another fairer—and so he wandered, joyfully at first, but later in sorrow.

"Both women and men loved Sianon and would do anything to gain her favor, but she loved none in return. One man was much like another to her, and even toward her own children she felt nothing. Only her brother Sainth did she love, but this was forbidden."

"Didn't they destroy each other in the end?" Nann asked.

Rath nodded, still pressing the fingers to his brow. "Yes. Wyrr went finally into the river with all that he knew, and Caibre and Sianon made great kingdoms upon either shore. Often they warred, for they hated each other, but always Sainth would come between them and peace would be restored. In the end, though, Caibre could not give up the war, and he killed Sainth when he came suing for peace. And though Sianon warned Caibre that it would be his own death to kill her, he did not care, his hatred for her was that great. They fought a great battle on an island in the middle of the River Wyrr, and weakened from their wounds, both were lost when the fortress collapsed. But it is said they too went into the river in the end, and it sustained them, that they did not truly die but became nagar and dwelt in some netherworld between death and life, sustained by their father's love . . . until now."

Nann stood looking at the tapestry lit by two hundred candles. She pulled a chair near and sat down. She felt as weak as Rath suddenly. For a moment Nann stared at the tableau before them. "We guessed these might be sorcerers—or I believed that, at least—but we never thought for a moment that they could be the children of Wyrr. We sent Cynddl to travel the river seeking the stories of sorcerers. We did not realize . . ." she said softly. "Is it really possible? Perhaps Tannis and Tuath are mistaken?"

Rath removed his hand from his brow and looked up, the clouds in his eyes glowing in the candlelight. His thin neck quivered a little as he lifted his head to examine the tapestry again.

"Possible? Yes. Blame the Knights of the Vow for that. It was they who desired the gifts of the children of Wyrr, warriors that they were." His head slumped down, his neck weak as a baby's. "You've sent my prize pupil into great danger," he said, "and he likely does not even know it. Poor Cynddl! If you had only sent word to me sooner . . ."

Nann closed her eyes for a moment, but the man before the gate stared at her all the same.

"Shall I take you back?" Nann asked.

"No, help me up. I will travel to the River Wynnd."

Nann took hold of his offered arm. "But what will you do there?"

"I will taste the waters," he said, "and see if this can be true."

†TWELVE

T am and his companions perched on a rock and looked down into the folding waters of the Lion's Maw. Foam curled and spun among the shattered rocks, driving through the narrow gorge with a force that shook the ground. Tam gazed down at the speeding water, like the back of a giant serpent sliding by. Around him, the others stared at the scene in silent awe.

"Well, I shall offer my coin and gladly," Cynddl said above the Lion's roar. "You say others have survived it?"

Tam nodded. "Yes, but not easily. Men have been lost here. But there's no other way. The cliffs can't be scaled unless we leave our boat behind—perhaps not even then." Tam pointed down into the gorge. "There's our greatest obstacle: that tongue of rock. Do you see, Baore? The oars must be backed all the way to keep some control, but before that tongue of rock we must slip across the stream or we'll be smashed to bits."

Baore looked at him, his face stiff as stone. "I'll man the oars, if you like," the big Valeman said, "but you're the better waterman, Tam."

Tam nodded, reluctant to admit this truth. He would

have to take them through, though he'd never even been in waters like these. He crouched down by the racing river, as though drawn to be near such power. "If we're unlucky enough to capsize," he said to the others, "hang on to the boat, but be wary. If you're caught between the boat and a rock you'll be crushed. Better to swim free than that."

Tam looked down into the gorge again. For a long moment no one spoke. Tam's mouth was drier than chalk, and the trembling of the ground seemed to course up his legs and drum deep in his chest.

Cynddl took a coin from some pocket in his vest. For a moment he stood looking out at the roiling waters, the coin glittering in his hand. He spun it out over the waters, where it winked in the sunlight as it disappeared into the foam. Tam felt the weight of his own coin, then flicked it as though to see if it would land crown or tail. But he lost it in the glinting water and it sank unnoticed. Baore followed Tam, his coin going farther than the others, out into the quickest water.

For a moment more they stood looking on, no one rushing to the boat, which seemed suddenly very small and flimsy. But there was no going back from here, the river wouldn't allow it. They must go forward or make a home on this rock. Suddenly Fynnol, pale as foam, stepped forward and threw a coin into the water, though it went only a little distance, as though he hadn't the strength to send it farther.

Cynddl caught Tam's eye, raising an eyebrow. But no one said a word to Fynnol.

"Standing here is not making me braver," Baore said, his voice tight and dry. The big Valeman turned away. For an instant the others hesitated, then followed. They slid the boat down the rock, jumping into their places as they went. Fynnol tripped on a thwart as he went aboard and stumbled awkwardly into his place. He sat there rigidly, staring straight ahead, gripping the gunwales fiercely.

The river reached out and took hold of them, yanking the boat out into the speeding current. Tam strained against the oars, but the river did not care. It threw them to one side, then forward again. In the bow Baore took up an oar and braced himself like Assal to fend off rocks. Fynnol had sunk down onto the floorboards, as though he could hide from the Lion.

Suddenly they plunged down, their bow buried, then thrust up again. Heavy spray lashed them, and they were thrown around the boat like dice in a cup. They swept forward faster and faster, and the boat began to yaw. Desperately Tam dug in his oars and brought her round.

He tried to back and slip sideways to avoid a rock, but the river forced them relentlessly forward. They crashed against stone with a grating, rending sound, all of them hurled to one side. Baore shattered his oar against rock and flailed desperately with the broken stub to get them clear.

But then they were past and quickly falling. Crashing down and rising up, thrown this way and that. They held on as though to a bucking horse, spray flying all around, the rocky walls of the gorge flashing past. Twice more they crashed against rock and were torn free by the current. There was so much water sloshing around in the boat that Tam thought they must have been holed.

A jagged ridge of rock appeared and Tam put all of his weight into the oars, but one jammed against stone and slammed into his chest, throwing him back before the tholepin snapped and released the oar. The rock was directly ahead and Tam braced himself, but then, with barely a scrape the rock shot past.

Once more they plunged down, and then suddenly they were in smooth but swiftly flowing water, the terrible roar of the Lion behind them. The others turned to look back at him, relief hardly stronger than fear. Tam heard Fynnol muttering curses over and over as he dragged himself out of the water flooding their boat. Baore still clung to the stump of his broken oar like a man who couldn't quite believe he'd lost a limb.

"Best put ashore as soon as we're able," Baore said. His mow of hair was plastered to his face, and he was gasping as though he'd been holding his breath. "Everthing'll need drying . . . and the boat wants tending to." He patted the thwart gently. "Who knows what hurt she's taken."

Cynddl and Baore bailed with a will, and the water didn't rise again, relieving Tam's fear that they'd been holed.

"Worth a coin for passage," Cynddl said and looked at Fynnol.

The Valeman forced a smile. "What bothers me is knowing that wastrel Lion will likely squander our silver on low lionesses and strong drink . . . to wash down all that water, no doubt."

Even the serious Cynddl laughed. But Fynnol had not been so heedless standing before the Lion.

They were in the gorge for half an hour more, but the river only ran swiftly on. There were no rocks or narrows. Finally they were spit out of the gullet of the Lion and found themselves spinning slowly, drawn into an unexpected backwater. After the chaos of the Maw this place seemed unnaturally still and quiet.

Cattails waved along the shore and water lily leaves fluttered over the boat's wake. Tam breathed in the stench of sun-warmed mud and rotting vegetation. In the bow Baore stood up, pointing with his broken oar, and Tam brought the boat up on a soft, low bank. As they climbed out, there was a splash in the water nearby.

"Paid the Lion, did you?" came a squeaky voice.

Tam looked up to find a man standing in the water within the shadow of an overhanging tree. He wore a ragged cloak over his shoulders and upon his head, a tall, misshapen felt hat crowned with a long feather. His threadbare breeches had been cut off at mid-thigh, exposing spindly legs. He was an old man, thin and wiry, with weathered, dark skin that left Tam wondering if he lived all the time out-of-doors. His features were sharp, the bones of his face prominent, but his eye bright and quick. In his hand he held a short, thin spear and on the end wriggled a small fish.

"Doesn't matter," the man said. "He'll let you go or not

as pleases him. I paid him, you know. People say I didn't, but I did. Paid him twice, but here I am still, washed up on this shore without hope of going on. No hope at all."

"Who in the world are you?" Fynnol said, stepping ashore and staring in wonder.

The man looked down into the water, raising his spear. He took a slow step forward, stiff and long legged, like a heron, Tam thought. What had been done with his fish, Tam hadn't noticed. The man lifted one crooked arm, raising the shreds of his cloak so that it cast a shadow on the water. "Me?" he said, taking another slow step. "Who are you?"

"Why, I am Fynnol and these are my cousins, Tam and Baore. And this is Cynddl, a Fáel story finder."

The man looked up at this, his bright eyes darting back and forth as he regarded Cynddl. "Well, there are stories enough on this river, that's certain—many of them sucked into the Lion's Maw. He ate both my brothers, the Lion did, and spit me out here." His mouth turned down sourly. "But *you* . . . he let all of you live." Some movement caught his eye then and he plunged his spear into the water, but it came up empty.

Fynnol's stance was a little uncertain, Tam noticed, as though he might have to jump back from this stranger at any moment.

"Why can't you go downriver?" Fynnol asked. "Surely all the worst water has been passed."

The man looked up at him, head tilted to one side. "He waits for me yet—the Lion. He waits, but he'll not have me."

"But if you go downstream he is behind you," Baore said. "You'll be perfectly safe."

The man went back to stalking his fish. Tam realized that he was three-fingered—missing the two outside fingers on the hand that held the spear.

"Shows what you know about the river," the man said sullenly. "The three of us—my two brothers and I— went into the Maw, but only two came out. And when we set off down the river again we found ourselves in another gorge."

"But there are only five," Fynnol said quickly. "You had passed the last."

The man shook his head. "The river has more tricks to play than you know, more branches than you think. We found ourselves in the Maw again, and this time only I survived, the boat smashed to splinters. He took my two fingers, the Lion did, and here I've been ever since." He turned around and went stalking patiently back along the bank, his hunched, thin shoulders hiding his bent head. "I won't go down the river now, for he shall have me next. Or so he thinks, but I'm not fool enough for that. No, I am safe here. Only the cold, old river and her singing for company, but that's enough. Better than death, that's certain." And off he went, stiffly lifting one bare foot and then the next, placing them ever so carefully into the water. Making not a ripple where he passed.

For a moment everyone watched him go, too surprised to speak.

"Well, they say the men who live in the wildlands are

all a little strange," Fynnol said, "not fit for human society. But this man . . .!" He looked at Tam and, as though realizing how serious he'd become, grinned broadly. "We passed through the Maw!" He laughed. "And unless the Lion has leapt ahead of us downriver, we'll have smooth water, more or less, from here to the Wold of Kerns!"

Fynnol and Cynddl began to spread all their wet belongings in the sun, while Tam and Baore examined the boat. The four of them tipped the craft over on the beach, and it was a sorry sight. Baore's beautiful hull was scraped and scarred and battered, though not a plank was split or loose.

"It'll take some work," the boatwright said, "but it's not really so bad. We might as well make a camp here this night, for when I am done she'll need some time to dry." He busied himself with his small kit of tools, pulling off his soaking shirt to work. There was little any could do to assist Baore with his task, so they left him alone with his injured charge—a healer of boats—and they swam and fished.

That night they spent beyond the Maw, rolled in blankets beneath the stars, the roar of the Lion not far off and in the background of all their dreams.

Late in the night Tam fell into an unsettling dream. Their boat had overturned in the Lion's Maw, and he was whirled into the foaming white waters, dragged down into green depths where he found a hundred others, pulled this way and that by the currents like straw men in the wind, lost in an endless, ghostly dance. All around them, like leaves in a slow whirl, glittered the coins paid for passage.

He woke to find he was staring at the moon as it floated free of the treetops, the growl of the Lion rolling down the gorge on the small, cool breeze.

Something moved, just beyond their camp in the shadows made by moon and trees. At first Tam was sure it was their heron man come to rob them or perform some other mischief, but no man took shape or emerged from the shadows. Very slowly Tam raised himself up on his elbows.

"You saw it, too?" Cynddl's voice came out of the dark.

"Yes. Was it that odd man we met today?"

"I don't know what it was. No animal, I think. More like . . . Well, I don't know. It was as though there were movement but nothing of substance. Like glass sinking through water."

Tam nodded. "Some trick of moonlight and shadow, I think."

"Perhaps," Cynddl said. "It's not long till morning. Sleep, and I'll sit up and watch."

Tam was about to protest, but Cynddl was already up, his sword to hand. Tam closed his eyes but didn't immediately fall asleep. An unbearable sadness washed over him, a sorrow that would overwhelm a man's heart. But somehow it didn't seem to be his own.

It was the dream, he thought. He had been drowning in sadness, pulled down by its cold, bitter current.

THIRTEEN

Three days after leaving the bridge at Telanon they seemed to be on a different river. The current had lost its sense of urgency and no longer hurried along. For a time in the morning Baore and Fynnol took to rowing, but after a few hours they'd grown used to the slower pace and shipped their oars to watch the land pass quietly by.

The river was beautiful and peaceful here—in such contrast to the Five Gorges that began their journey. Springs bubbled from the banks, and broad-leafed trees appeared more often among the cedar and pine, their new greens shimmering in the sunlight.

For an hour it rained and they sheltered beneath the overhanging canopy of a willow, spreading over their heads the oiled sail cloth that protected their belongings. They watched the pattern of rain on the slick surface of the river and said not a word.

The sadness Tam had felt when they camped beyond the Lion's Maw was still with him, a heaviness of heart that seemed to have no cause. Even when the sun broke through again this weight did not lift.

They saw much wildlife along the banks—hart and bear, the small deer of the valleys, sleek river otters, and the crafty fox. Small gray gulls soared over the river crying forlornly, and ducks trailing strings of chicks paddled along the banks.

"Do you hear that sad song?" Cynddl said suddenly. He sat up from where he lounged. "A song like a leaf falling? That is the sorcerer thrush. You won't see it, not if you spend a year looking. Creep through the wood as you might, just when you think you've found its perch the song will come from somewhere else, though you'll see no bird move. Very few have ever seen a sorcerer thrush, but it's a mark of great favor for those who do."

Islands of cloud were abroad that day and cast their massive shadows upon the sparkling river, stealing away its color and glitter, and the world seemed suddenly terribly somber and not nearly so welcoming. A woodpecker hammered on a hollow trunk, the sound echoing through the shadowed wood like distant thunder.

After their midday meal Cynddl spread his map out on the tarp covering their belongings and began to follow their progress carefully. Late in the afternoon he gestured to a small point of land. "Can you put me ashore here, Baore? I think this is the place I seek."

Baore took up the oars and ran the boat gently up on a narrow band of sand. Tam strung his yaka bow and, hoping to find dinner, took some of his own arrows—tipped for hunting. A natural stair of seven steps worn into the rock led up from the beach, and they found themselves walking through the sparse underwood beneath a canopy of new leaves. Tam had never seen such trees, bent and gnarled as though crippled by disease, yet they were tall with an astonishing spread of crooked branches. The new growth sprouting from these trees seemed incongruous.

They should have no leaves at all, Tam thought, or only dry dead ones.

Cynddl led them back into the wood and up a slight slope, where a dappling of sunlight sprayed across moss and ferns. Every twenty paces or so he would stop and listen, and finally a low, liquid carillon pealed through the grove and in a moment they had come to its source: a small spring in a low embankment from which a clear stream of water flowed.

"Here's the place I seek!" Cynddl said, looking around as though they had discovered some amazing castle out here in the wildlands.

"It appears to be a spring like any other," Fynnol said, though there was not such an edge of mockery in his voice. The Lion's Maw had dulled that, at least for a while.

"So you'd think, but once—an age ago, really—this was a dwelling place of one of the clans that lived in the Greensprings. And before them, a fortress stood here, when there were still great kingdoms on either side of the river." He waved a hand around at the wood. "You won't find signs of buildings now, for the walls have long ago been worn away by wind and rain, but if we're lucky there will be an echo of the peoples still."

Cynddl stepped across the small stream that flowed from the spring, his gaze flitting from stone to fern to stone, as though he expected to find gold shining through the green. "It seems there were two ages of settlement in the Greensprings. The Age of Two Kingdoms, the story finders call the earlier period. The Age of the Clans we call the second. Very little is known of the people who dwelt here while the Two Kingdoms stood. Even when the Fáel first came to the land between the mountains the songs and stories of these people were hardly more than faint whispers. Some believe they were deep in magic and that sorcerers of great craft lived here then. The people were artful, and, though little remains of their craft now, what we have is intricate and of delicate beauty. But they were also warlike, fighting always one kingdom against the other, and in the end, we guess, this brought about their ruin." He turned around, gazing into the trees, as though he looked for stories there.

"The Greensprings was empty of men for a long time after the wars of the Two Kingdoms: ruined and uninhabitable, some stories say, or inhabited by ghouls and spirits of great malice, others say. But the forest grew back, and men returned finally. These clans were infected by the hatred that lay beneath the surface, and warred among themselves until they, too, disappeared." He looked up at the Valemen. "Haven't you felt a terrible sorrow as we've traveled south of the Lion's Maw?"

Baore said he had, but Fynnol shook his head in denial.

Tam said nothing, preferring to keep his feelings to himself—he didn't know why.

"It's the regret of these people who once dwelt here. The emotions of men live on in a place long after men have gone—like ruins of buildings and hearths. The stronger the passion the longer it lingers. Hatred lasts longest of all, I'm sorry to say. But, here, see for yourselves." He cupped a hand and drank from the flowing spring. Tam and Baore did the same, but Fynnol stood back and did not drink.

"Do you taste it—the bitterness? That's not the water. It is the remnants of the malice of men, of the people who lived and died in this place so long ago." Cynddl looked around where the twisted shadows of trees lay on the jumbled rocks and ferns. "I'll spend some time quietly here," he said, "if it won't distress you to stay in such a place for a day or two?"

Fynnol snorted. "I think we can bear it," he said and glanced at the others, shaking his head just perceptibly.

They set up their camp at the stairhead, in a small clearing among the crooked trees. Immediately they began to explore the area, ranging over the rocks and along the riverbanks. As dinnertime drew near, Baore and Fynnol dropped lines into the water, while Tam went into the wood with his bow hoping to find something for the dinner pot.

The bitter taste of the spring still lingered, and Tam found Cynddl's assertion—that this was the hatred of men—disturbed him more than he would have expected.

The idea of drinking the malice of others made him feel a bit ill, as though he had drunk poison.

Tam soon flushed a pheasant, and his yaka bow felled it from flight. He found it among a stand of stoneberry coming into leaf. The limp, warm weight of the bird as he lifted it struck Tam: the way its head lolled and hung heavily down. He smoothed the bright feathers of the neck and wondered if the regret he felt was his own or some emotion lingering from an age before, as Cynddl said such feelings did.

Tam made his way back through the trees, though the underwood was too thick to pass in places, forcing him to go roundabout and lose his way a little. Circling a patch of dense bush he came upon their Fáel companion seated by the spring, lost in thought.

"My apologies, Cynddl. I didn't realize where I was."

The Fáel smiled. "No need to apologize, Tam. Listening for the old stories is often done somewhere deep in the mind, as though beneath the normal currents of thought. No doubt you've had the common experience of puzzling over some problem for hours, then in the middle of dinner the solution comes to you while you're buttering bread. Listening for the old stories can be like that at times."

Unlike most of his people, Cynddl wore almost no jewelry, only a gold band bearing a small stone on the first finger of his left hand. He had removed this and absentmindedly slipped it over one finger, then the next. Tam looked up and found that Cynddl was staring at him.

"Fynnol has undertaken this journey to escape the Vale and go into the wider world," the story finder said. "There he imagines people will be different—exotic and quick-witted perhaps. Though how he imagines he'll find such people in Inniseth or the Wold of Kerns is beyond me. Baore has come because Fynnol badgers him into joining all his enterprises, I suspect." Cynddl raised his eyebrows and Tam nodded.

"Fynnol has found it's almost always good to take along someone large and strong."

"Fynnol is no one's fool. But perhaps Baore wanted to test one of his own boats upon the river as well." Cynddl stopped playing with his ring. "But what of you, Tam? What has brought you down the river?"

"Perhaps I have come to keep my cousins from harm," Tam said quickly.

Cynddl smiled. "Perhaps that is part of it."

"Or maybe I just couldn't bear the thought of them having an adventure without me. How would I feel when they returned with all their stories and I'd spent my summer in the Vale doing what I'd done every other year?"

Cynddl weighed the ring in the palm of his hand. "There's some truth in everything you say, but I think there's more. Perhaps you don't know yourself?"

Tam shrugged. He looked over at the running spring

with its bitter taste of malice. "My father died beyond the gate of the Vale. He was out with a party of hunters seeking hart when they happened upon a company of armed men on horseback. The Valemen approached these riders in friendship, but the riders drew their weapons and fell on them." Tam felt his throat tighten, his voice change. "Only two escaped to warn the gatekeepers. These men-at-arms had come north, perhaps fleeing the wars of the Renné and the Wills—we don't know, but many men have done this and been welcomed in the Vale. These men were planning something else and cut down the hunting party lest they lose the element of surprise. That's what the people of the Vale say, anyway.

"Archers immediately set out—men who knew every woodland path and every rock behind which to hide. These men-at-arms paid the price for their crime. Only a few escaped, fleeing south, from where they came." The spring whispered its bitter tongue and Tam's eye came to rest on the cock pheasant lying so still on a cushion of moss. "I was only a boy, but the outside world and the men who dwelt in it became the stuff of nightmare for me. I am here to see them firsthand . . . I—I don't quite know why."

Cynddl slipped the ring back on his finger. "And you too were attacked by armed men beyond the gate— though you all were unharmed."

"Not all. Alaan fell holding the bridge so that we might escape. So the strangers one meets in the wildlands appear to be of all types: both noble and cruel. Why I should need to journey beyond the Vale to learn that I don't know."

"This is the truth of journeying, Tam: not every new thing you encounter will be in the world outside." Cynddl patted his chest. "Much will be here."

Tam found Baore and Fynnol back in camp and they soon made a target of birch bark on one of the crooked trees and began testing Tam's new bow. Baore was an indifferent archer, but Fynnol was fiercely competitive and, though Tam was acknowledged to be the best young archer in the Vale, Fynnol would not concede defeat easily.

Cynddl appeared in the midst of this contest and fetched his own bow. It was soon clear that he could shoot with Tam; and in the end beat the Valeman, though barely, proving that the fame of the Fáel archers was not without reason.

"You're a very good archer, Tam," Cynddl said as they collected their arrows.

"Cian taught me when I was a boy, and I've had a great deal of time to practice since." He patted his bow. "My gift from Aliel and Cian might have part of the credit."

"But Fynnol shot with the same bow and didn't do nearly so well."

"Fynnol's skill is with words. There he can shoot barbs with the best of them."

"In the Vale, perhaps," Cynddl said quietly. He carefully

parted the branches of a wild rose, searching for stray arrows. "Perhaps here is a reason to go out into the world: one might be the finest bowman in the Vale, but could one stand among the archers competing at the Westbrook Fair?" He glanced over at Tam. "Am I a man among men in my village alone, or is this also true of the wider world? Can I find a place in the larger story?" Cynddl turned back to his endeavor, reaching far into the unwelcoming bush.

Tam felt a bit embarrassed by this turn in the conversation. He wasn't sure why he'd come on this journey and hadn't thought much about it. Adventure, he'd believed it was, but now he wasn't so sure. "Archery seems an odd pursuit for a story finder," Tam said, turning away from these thoughts.

"Not so odd," Cynddl said over his shoulder. "Anything that teaches the mind focus is encouraged. Most are taught to play instruments, as I was as well, but archery was my passion for a time." He slipped his hand slowly back into the heart of the bush and gently withdrew an arrow.

As they returned to the others Tam heard Fynnol and Baore bickering as only cousins or brothers could.

"At least I didn't finish last," Fynnol was saying.

"Now we'll get out the shod staff," Tam said, "and we'll all finish behind Baore."

"What's this?" Cynddl asked.

"Haven't you seen the oak staff Baore keeps tied to the floorboards?"

"The one with the iron tip? I thought it was for fending off rocks or some such thing."

"No, that's the shod staff, or so it's called in the Vale. The ends are clad in iron and weighted with lead. Only the strongest can wield it, and Baore's staff is longer and heavier than most. Fetch it out, Baore, and show Cynddl."

It took a little coaxing, but perhaps smarting from losing at archery and his cousin's taunts, Baore dug out his staff. He was soon demonstrating its uses in the clearing.

"Do you see?" Tam said. "With someone of Baore's strength wielding it the shod staff is a fearsome weapon. It doesn't matter if a man wears mail. Baore can break the bones beneath the iron rings. Try to step under it and he'll drive you to the ground. A swordsman can't cut through the iron, and at that length Baore is a safe distance from even the longest blade."

Baore showed Cynddl how the staff balanced and demonstrated how he could spin it end for end and crack a man's skull, take a sword from a hand, or drive the weighted end hard into a man's chest or head. He could hold it by one end and swing it in a great arc clearing an area a dozen feet broad.

"Baore can sweep a rider from his saddle like that; and only a man of his strength can do this, but I have seen him trip up a horse."

"Perhaps once," Baore said. "You lose your staff, more often."

"You shouldn't tuck this under all the baggage, Baore,"

Cynddl said. "We're in the wildlands, after all. You can still meet lion here."

They made a meal of pheasant and fish that Cynddl cooked in the Fáel manner, and then they sat by the fire, speaking quietly. The light of the waxing moon fell through the twisted branches, entangling them all in a crazy web. Baore had found his whetstone and was busy honing arrowheads, the small motions looking for all the world like he struggled to get free.

Fynnol lounged against a soft pile of their baggage, appearing bored to Tam. "And what stories have you found lying on the ground hereabout?" Fynnol asked Cynddl.

"No stories that are complete," Cynddl said, apparently unaffected by Fynnol's goading. "Though I've tripped over a few things today." He pointed upriver. "An age ago two young girls from this village wandered up the river seeking fairy-caps, a kind of mushroom. Their hunt drew them farther from their homes than they meant to wander. To their horror they happened upon a band of men from one of the clans they were constantly at arms against. Into the river went the girls, striking out for the center and downstream, but the men took up their bows and shot one girl, and the other they dragged from the river unharmed. Unharmed until they had her ashore." Cynddl paused and drew a breath that did not go easily into his lungs. "I won't tell you more than that. Suffice it to say that there lingers here yet the hatred that act produced. It burns here like a fire beneath the land." He leaned back and thumped awkwardly against the tree behind him. He looked at Fynnol. "Count yourself lucky you weren't born a story finder, Fynnol Loell. There's many a story that will rob you of sleep and which no jest can make you forget."

They were all silent then for a long time—only the rasp of steel on stone as Baore pursued his labors. Finally Cynddl excused himself and slipped out of the clearing where they made their camp.

"Have you noticed," Fynnol said when their Fáel companion was beyond hearing, "that we hear nothing but dark tales from our story finder? Perhaps he's only a finder of stories with unhappy endings."

"Perhaps that's because men make so many such stories," Tam said softly.

Fynnol looked up at his cousin. "I'm sorry, Tam. Sometimes I forget what happened to your father."

"And I envy you that, Fynnol," Tam said.

They rolled up in their blankets, glad to have come a little farther from the mountains where the night air wasn't quite so cool.

Tam must have slept for a time. When he woke, the moon had traveled into the west. He saw movement on the edge of the camp, but when he sat up and reached for his sword, he realized it was Cynddl walking back and forth from shadow to moonlight. Tam rolled quietly out of his blankets and approached the story finder.

"Has something wakened you?" Tam whispered.

"Yes, but nothing hereabout. Nothing 'real,' as Fynnol

might say." Cynddl was only a silhouette, but his oddly stooped carriage made him seem at home among the twisted trees.

"It is just this place and the stories that were made here." Cynddl stopped walking and raised his hands, fingers splayed like branches. "The horrors of this place I can't begin to tell, nor would you want to hear."

"Perhaps they're only stories, Cynddl," Tam said.

Tam could see Cynddl's head tilt to one side as he regarded the Valeman. "No, Tam; there are the stories that men tell, and the stories that they live. Here I've found too many stories they lived."

The Fáel went back to his pacing, too agitated to be still. "You should sleep, Tam. Don't take up the habits of a story finder—awake at all hours, lost in thought when one should be enjoying the company of friends. No, sleep now and treasure your companions and your journey. The stories of men are mine to bear."

FOURTEEN

They spent two days beneath the twisted trees, and then Cynddl announced it was time to leave, offering no explanation for his decision. They pressed on at sunrise the next morning beneath a high haze, a sky the indeterminate color of a newborn's eyes.

"Today we'll find the ford at Willowwand, I think." Cynddl was gazing at the map. He looked up at the riverbanks. "The land is starting to appear familiar now, and the river valley has grown broad."

The river carried them along in its lazy current, in no hurry to reach the distant sea, and the day was warm. Everyone lounged as best they could, but Cynddl, who, despite sleeping less than the others, seemed to be the only one alert. Tam was having trouble keeping his eyes open.

The high thin cloud filtered the sunlight and the day seemed very still, the sounds of the forest and river unnaturally clear.

"Tam?" Cynddl said, rousing Tam from his revery. "The current seems faster."

Fynnol, who was curled in the bow, sat up. Suddenly he pointed. *"Rocks!"*

"The ford at Willowwand," Cynddl said. He stood, careful not to rock the boat, and shaded his eyes, looking warily around, his shoulders bunched up, one fist clenched.

"It appears to be clear," he said, though Tam was not sure what he meant.

"Is there water enough for us to pass?" Baore asked.

"What . . . ? Oh, I think so. Stay to the center. At worst we'll have to lighten the load by stepping out and helping the boat along for a few yards."

Without warning, Baore reached out and pulled Cynddl off his feet, and just as he did so an arrow whistled past. Tam threw himself down. Cynddl recovered and already was stringing his bow. Arrows began to strike the sides of the boat and pierce the baggage with soft but unnerving *thups*.

Tam had his bow in hand, but it was hard to move as he sprawled in the stern trying to keep all of himself hidden. He heard Cynddl's bow sing, and then again.

"There!" the Fáel yelled. "Beneath the willows!"

Tam sprang up and loosed an arrow where Cynddl pointed. Men in dark purple tunics scrambled beneath the trees. He heard them shouting and calling out. Fynnol had found his bow as well, and they sent the men on the shore into retreat, more than one figure staggering with an arrow buried hard in flesh.

As soon as the air was clear, Baore shipped a pair of oars and the boat surged forward. The other three watched the banks, arrows nocked. Tam could hear them all breathing hard.

"Have we beaten them off?" Fynnol asked, almost breathless.

"For the moment," Cynddl said. "Has anyone taken hurt?"

No one had, though there were half a dozen arrows protruding from their boat in various places. They'd come to the ford proper now, and the bank was low and open to the east, a meadow of grass and a few trees spreading back into the forest. To the west the forest leaned out over the water, and the road could be seen curving up into the wood. Tam found himself looking furiously about, expecting men behind every tree.

Suddenly, horsemen appeared from out of a grove, galloping fiercely across the grass toward the center of the ford. Tam could hear the drumming of the hooves and see the turf thrown up. Dark horse tails streamed from the riders' helms, and the sun glinted brightly off polished steel. The riders were attempting to intercept the boat before it escaped into deep water. At that same moment, the bowmen emerged from behind the willows, bearing swords and shields now. They, too, raced toward the ford.

"River take them!" Fynnol swore, dropped his bow, and jumped to the oars, pulling with desperate energy.

Tam and Cynddl kept shooting at the swordsmen who ran along the embankment, but the bobbing of the boat as the oarsmen rowed made accuracy all but impossible. Tam tried to gauge the speed of the horsemen, but it was difficult. It almost seemed that they might yet escape, slip through the ford before anyone could reach them.

"We need to save our arrows!" he yelled, reaching out and grabbing Cynddl by the arm.

The horsemen bearing down on them wore black surcoats and carried round shields and the short iron-tipped lances used for boar hunting. Fluttering from the tips of these were red streamers, which Tam knew were meant to absorb the blood from a kill and keep the lance from becoming slick.

"Shoot the horses!" Fynnol yelled.

But Cynddl held up a hand to stop Tam. "Their trappings will protect them." He stared a moment more, then said, "We won't pass ahead of them."

"Yes, we will," Baore shouted. He had torn the seams of his shirt from his efforts so that it hung from him like rags. Tam worried that the oars would not stand up to the strain.

"Again!" Cynddl said, and they released another volley of arrows as the riders reached the shore. The horsemen plunged on in a shower of spray, one toppling from his saddle as an arrow struck. The Fáel bows were deadly at this distance.

Tam looked ahead. They'd come into the ford now, and the oars were finding bottom with each stroke. But the riders had found a deeper channel and this slowed them, giving Tam hope. But then they surged up into shallows and resumed their headlong pursuit, spray flying all around them. Not far behind them the swords-men came. Seven men on foot, four left on horse, for two were floundering in the water, wounded. Tam counted eleven armed men. He sent another arrow into the shield of one of the riders and just then was thrown from his feet as the boat ground to a halt on the river bottom.

Cynddl was the first to recover. He jumped into the water and resumed shooting. The others were quickly over the side, Baore and Fynnol dragging the boat forward, Tam and Cynddl trying to gain them time. A third rider toppled from his saddle slowly, like a falling tree, and then a blossom of spray flew up where he hit the water. Tam loosed an arrow at the men on foot, knowing that if the riders held them up for even a moment, the men on foot would be on them. They couldn't stand against so many.

Suddenly Baore swept up his staff and Cynddl leapt for his sword. The first rider bore down upon them, crimson fluttering at the end of a lowered lance. He went for Baore, who sidestepped deftly, surprising the rider, and then with a mean thrust sent the rider rolling into the shallow water. The man came up to his knees without a helm and went down again as an iron-shod staff cracked his skull.

Cynddl hamstrung the next horse, and the rider fell beneath his crippled beast. But luck was not with them entirely and, trying to escape the lance of the next rider, Fynnol collided with the horse and was thrown a dozen feet. This rider passed, and as he pulled his horse up to return, Tam shot him coldly in the side so that the man

hung over his horse's neck and spurred it on, hoping to
escape a second arrow.

Baore waded quickly to Fynnol, who was floundering in the water, dazed and injured. The big Valeman
picked his cousin up and laid him in the bottom of the
boat. Then, in a surge of strength, he seized the bow and
dragged the boat on.

Tam and Cynddl fired again at the advancing footmen,
but they put up their shields and came on, though slowed
by the river and tired from running. Cynddl fired below
the shields at the men's legs, causing them to crouch and
slow even more. As Tam reached for an arrow in the boat
he saw Fynnol lying there, his face contorted in pain.
But there was no blood and he was certainly conscious.

Cynddl tossed his bow into the stern and helped Baore
drag the boat forward. Suddenly they surged ahead as
the boat came free of the bottom and they ran with it,
leaving Tam as rearguard. He kept pace with the boat,
stopping to fire, then running again. Their attackers
reached shallow water and flew forward, bent low, howling as they came.

"Tam!" Cynddl called, and Tam glanced back to see
the Fáel waving a sword in the air, pulling the boat with
his other hand.

Tam turned and ran, hearing the staccato sound of
men racing through water behind him. As he neared the
boat Baore leapt aboard and took up a pair of oars, and
Cynddl, looking back toward Tam, jumped into the stern,
bracing himself with his sword at the ready.

The water was suddenly over his knees and Tam leapt up with each step, trying to speed forward. Suddenly Cynddl had hold of his arm and dragged him aboard even as he swung his sword. Tam tumbled onto the floorboards, groping for his blade. He heard steel ring on steel.

Tam sprang back up, the boat rocking wildly. Cynddl was pounding his pommel on the helm of a man who had hold of him, while a second ran up, sword raised awaiting a clear stroke. Tam ran his sword up the mail sleeve of Cynddl's attacker and the man howled, springing back and stumbling in front of his companions.

Dazed, Tam looked back, thinking for a second that they had escaped. But then the attackers parted, a horseman charging through them, his lance down. Tam caught a glimpse of the man's face beneath the helm—grim and remorseless, filled with rage over his fallen companions.

Tam was so tired and stunned by what had happened that he wavered there dumbly. Cynddl had collapsed in the boat beside him. Tam grabbed the story finder by the shoulder and hauled him up. But just as the horseman was about to run his lance into one of them, his horse plunged into deep water and came to a near stop.

The man bellowed in anger and frustration. He tried to throw his lance, but his swimming horse turned for the bank unbidden, and the lance passed over them harmlessly.

Tam sat back on their covered baggage, trying desperately to catch his breath. The oars stopped then, and Tam looked back to see Baore lying in the boat, gasping for breath, spent from his efforts. Tam turned back to the horseman and the few men on foot gathered around him. They waved their weapons and cursed the boat as it drew away on the current.

Suddenly, from behind, there came a shout of defiance and triumph, and Tam looked back to find Fynnol standing, clutching his side but holding aloft the horseman's dripping lance that he had plucked from the water. He shook it at their attackers, and then dropped to his knees, tears streaking his face. He sobbed, unashamed.

FIFTEEN

T he men who had attacked them scrambled out of the river and gave chase along the embankment, but were soon defeated by the forest. In half an hour they were lost to sight as they stood upon the shore watching their quarry carried to safety by the river.

Cynddl had Fynnol remove his shirt and found beneath it a massive bruise, though the skin was only just broken in the center of the discoloration.

"That's the last time, Tam, I promise," Fynnol said, wincing. "I'll never wrestle with horses again, though I still think I'd have had the better of the beast had I not slipped."

"You might well have cracked ribs," Cynddl said, "but nothing seems to be broken. Fortune smiled on you at that moment. You could easily have been trampled, and that's nothing to jest about."

Baore leaned over the side and plunged his head into the river, emerging to whip his sopping hair back from his face, spraying everyone. He eyed their Fáel companion. "Those were the men who murdered Alaan at Telanon Bridge," the big Valeman said.

Cynddl shrugged, pulling items from a bag, searching for something.

"You knew they'd be waiting," Tam said.

"I didn't know, but Genn was concerned." Cynddl looked at Tam thoughtfully. "Who can say what those men are searching for? Something stolen and not recovered when they murdered this stranger you met? They might believe you're his accomplices." He glanced at Baore. "Even seen in the dark someone the size of Baore would be remembered."

"They think we have whatever Alaan took from them?"

"I can't tell you what they think. I can't even tell you with certainty that Alaan took something from them, but it seems a likely explanation." Cynddl produced a small leather pouch and began untying the string that closed it.

"Alaan told us these men were unlike any we had ever met," Tam said. "'Relentless in pursuit of their ends,' he warned us, and this would seem to be true. Let me tell you something more, Cynddl: Alaan visited the Vale once before. He came looking for someone or some people whom he seemed to believe might be hiding there. My grandfather thought it likely that Alaan's purpose was revenge. But someone found Alaan first."

Cynddl gave up on the knot, looking up at Tam. "You said nothing of this to Genn."

"I didn't know this until after we returned to the Vale."

Cynddl closed his eyes and pressed his fingers to them a moment. When he took his hands away he let out a long breath. "I wish you had known this before. If these men were trying to stop Alaan from carrying out some act of revenge, and they believe you are his allies in this . . ."

"It explains why they were trying to murder us," Fynnol said, straining against the pain so that the words were pressed flat. He was bent over in the bottom of the boat, his face hidden from the others. "If they were looking for something that had been stolen they might have wanted us alive. There might have been a question or two . . . they wanted answered."

"And they have simply waited here for us?" Baore said. Water still streamed down his face and ran from his eyes. "How in the world would they guess where we were going?"

"Where else is there to go?" Cynddl said. "Here, at the ford, they can watch the river and the road. There's nowhere else to cross." He gestured to the north with the pouch. "These riders left the road and came by another, faster way. We saw their tracks turn into the forest, and there were more of them than we've just met. Some waited here, but I think others have gone on."

Tam stared down at the sun wavering in the river. "Who are these men?"

Cynddl shook his head. "I don't know. They bore no devices that I could see, though I hardly thought to look. Their surcoats were different. The riders wore black, the men on foot, purple. If it's some nobleman's livery I don't know it."

In the ensuing silence Cynddl began to tug the arrows from their baggage. A wind hissed down the river, rippling the water and rustling leaves. Crows began calling madly from the trees.

"Well, at least we're past these men now," Fynnol said, still hunched on the floorboards. "Doesn't the road go off in a great loop from here? Or is there another path through the woods that they might take?"

"There are no paths but the road or the river," Cynddl said. "But we might not be free of them yet." He looked off down the river. "The party that turned into the woods near the Vale was larger than we saw at Willowwand. The main body likely went on from here days ago, toward the north bridge. I'm afraid we might meet them there— or some of them, at least." He paused, considering. "But at least these men we've just passed can't get to the bridge in time to warn their fellows. We'll have that to our advantage."

Baore cursed under his breath. "And what'll we do when we come to the bridge?"

Cynddl began to work again at the knot on his pouch. "We've only two choices. Abandon the river and your boat, or try to slip beneath the bridge at night."

"So we shall either burn or boil," Fynnol grunted.

Cynddl finally pulled the knot free and put the opened bag up to his nose, breathing in the aroma. "As soon as we think it safe we should get ashore for an hour," he said. "I need a fire so that I can make a poultice for Fynnol's wound."

The river carried them on, the boat spinning slowly in the current. The weak light of the sun cast thin shadows along the river's edge and beneath the trees where crows cried frantically.

They went a long way before they dared to go ashore, and then the three who were unharmed took turns at the oars the rest of that day. The land seemed unnaturally quiet that afternoon, as though the birds and beasts were as apprehensive as the travelers. High overhead the veil of watery cloud was still drawn across the sky, leaving Tam with the impression that he looked up toward the surface from beneath the sea.

The strange sadness of the land seemed to seep into Tam's heart at times, and he would find himself feeling as though he had lost something of inestimable value. The urge to weep came over him at such times and he had to struggle against these feelings that were not his own.

"Where has summer gone?" Fynnol asked.

As though in answer Cynddl began to sing.

> "As a leaf upon the wind
> With summer to mourn.
> As a boat upon the river
> You shall be borne.
> Though lands be harsh and summer cold
> You shall be safe upon her breast

Carried on the moving stream
Toward an endless rest."

The song ended softly.

"It has the melody of a lullaby," Fynnol said, surprised.

Cynddl, who was at the oars, nodded. "Well, really it's a sad song put in the form of a lullaby. We don't sing children to sleep with it. In my language it's longer, of course, but that's all I can remember in your tongue. It came to me as we went, borne upon the water."

"It's the sorrow of the place," Tam said. "It turns the mind toward such things. I find myself thinking of sad ballads and tragic stories." He shook his head, unable to say more, but the others nodded. For a while they rowed on in silence.

Tam was taking his turn to rest, Baore and Cynddl at the oars. At the ford he'd cut and bruised his feet, dashing them against stone, and the others had fared much the same, as they had all stored their boots away in an attempt to keep the leather dry. He looked down at the unnaturally white flesh, spotted with red scrapes and cuts, and his body seemed suddenly vulnerable. If stones could inflict such wounds what would steel do?

"I'm wondering," Cynddl said, interrupting Tam's morbid thoughts. "The river seems very flat here . . . Shouldn't we carry on by night, at least for a few hours? The moon will give us some light. If we're to pass the bridge it would be best if the men there had not been warned."

"But I thought you said we'd reach the bridge before any rider from the ford?" Fynnol said. He found their map and spread it over the baggage, all his movements stiff and tentative.

Cynddl and Baore shipped their oars and bent over the map with the others. Fynnol did a rough measurement of the distances. Cynddl had traveled the road and could guess how long it would take to ride. But none had traveled the river and their knowledge was incomplete.

"There's some difficult water ahead yet." Baore ran a calloused finger along the course of the river. "We're still in the hills, really. This is only a plateau before we begin to drop again."

Cynddl nodded. "Baore is right. The north bridge is quite a bit lower down than we are here. But it seems to me there should be some smooth water for a while. The plateau goes on for several leagues before it meets the hills again and begins its descent toward the lowlands. I think the risk would be small."

Fynnol measured the distances to the bridge again. "Our path might be shorter but we're not traveling at the speed of a man on horse. The river's broad and lazy here. I think we should row on through at least a few hours of darkness."

The others agreed, though Baore did so only reluctantly.

They ate a cold meal in the boat, missing Cynddl's cooking. As Tam and Baore took their turn at the oars, the story finder produced a small flute and played as they went. At first he gave them tunes that were quick and cheerful, but they didn't seem to do much to lift the mood or push back the oppressive day. In the end he played a soft, sad air in a minor key, which he abandoned before its end, as though it brought back some memory. He sat with his gaze cast down to the passing river.

The sun sank into the gray haze, lighting it briefly from within, like a stain upon the sky, and then darkness settled.

It was an exceptionally black night except for a faint, nebulous glow where the waning moon floated among the hidden stars. Between the trees, the river flowed like ink and Tam wondered if they'd chosen wisely to go on. How would they find a place to land their boat in this darkness? They might have no choice but to go on till morning.

Baore grew restless and positioned himself in the bow, staring ahead into the gloom. The others were quiet, listening intently for the sounds of fast water. If they were unlucky, Tam knew, even a small rapids could hole their boat, and out here in the wildlands any damage would be hard for even Baore to repair.

By unspoken agreement, they had stopped rowing at some point so that the creaking of oars would not mask the sound of rushing water.

"This wasn't a good plan," Cynddl said, speaking very quietly. "I should have listened to you, Baore."

Baore said nothing but kept his attention fixed on the rippling river.

"Has our pace increased?" Fynnol whispered.

Tam stared off toward the dark shore, trying to catch sight of the treetops against the sky. "I can't say for certain. Perhaps."

They all sat, unmoving, trying to still their breathing so that they might hear the slightest sound—the tiniest change in the voice of the river. Memories of the Lion's Maw came to them all. Was that wind in the trees, Tam wondered, or the sound of water whispering over stone?

"I hear fast water!" Fynnol said firmly.

Tam and Baore jumped to the oars, backing quickly, checking their speed, but the darkness was impenetrable and they didn't know what to do. Any course in the darkness could lead to disaster. For a second they stopped to listen.

"It isn't so loud," Baore said, "but I don't know if that means it's only a small rapid or if it's distant yet."

Tam kept his oars in the water, rowing slowly into the current while they all strained to hear. Suddenly, without warning, the boat came to a grinding halt, lurching to one side and tossing them all from their seats. And there they seemed to be stuck fast.

Baore and Fynnol cursed the darkness, dragging themselves up from the floorboards. Tam took an oar and sounded around the boat and found shallow water everywhere. They stepped out into the chill river.

"I don't know which way we should go," Baore said. Even a few feet off, the big Valeman was invisible in the darkness.

"There are trees here—look." Cynddl waded through the water. "We've run up on the shore, somehow."

"But weren't we in the center of the river . . .?"

The others scrambled up onto the rocky beach.

"It is an island," Fynnol said firmly. "I'm sure of it. There is water flowing to either side—rapidly flowing."

Tam stubbed his bruised toes on stone and wished for a torch. As though in answer to his request, the hunch-backed moon appeared, stooping over the dark shapes of trees. Across the western heavens haloed stars seemed to surface in the blear. Dimly, an island appeared—palest gray of a rocky shore, dark shadows of trees above. Water rippled between them and the banks of the river, and Tam could see their boat, heeled to one side, stranded on a rock.

"Well, I think we'll spend the night here and count ourselves lucky," Tam said. "Can we free the boat and beach it somewhere more hospitable?"

Baore bent over their boat, unfastening the ropes holding their cargo in place. "Yes, but we have to lighten the load before there's any more damage."

They unburdened their craft and lifted it from the rock, sliding it up onto the rough stone beach. By the faint and filtered moonlight they collected wood and Cynddl kindled a fire. He also brewed a sweet beverage he called tull, and they sat beneath the overhanging trees and talked about what a strange and frightening day it had been.

"I often wonder about Alaan," Fynnol said. "What was

he doing in the north? Searching for some beast who'd burned a village? Or was he a thief who thought he'd outrun his victims?"

Cynddl leaned forward, feeding some sticks to the flames, his face appearing as the fire flared: eyebrows and eyes like shadows. "Did Alaan say nothing of his destination or where he came from?"

"Only that he was going south. I recall nothing more." Tam looked at his cousin.

"He knew this man Truk of Inniseth." Fynnol shifted and winced, revealing the pain he was doing much to hide.

The river prattled and clattered like a crowd before a play. Baore had fallen asleep while patching arrow holes in the oiled tarp that covered their baggage. Tam could hear his rough, even breathing. Closing his eyes, Tam said a silent thanks to the river spirits that none of them had been seriously wounded that day.

Tam found he could not stay awake and his eyes closed of their own will. He slipped into dream. He stood alone in the center of the ford, riders attacking from all sides. The sun glistened ominously on the horse tails streaming from the riders' helms, and then he realized they were slick with blood. Just as he was about to be run through he heard a kind of keening, far off. Tam's chin hit his chest and he came awake. Cynddl had risen quietly and stood, unmoving, staring into the trees. Immediately Tam thought of the apparition they'd seen.

"Do you hear?" Cynddl whispered.

"Faintly. I thought I was dreaming. What is it?"

"I don't know, but I've never heard an animal make such a sound. It must be a man . . . or woman."

Fynnol roused from sleep and saw the other two standing, listening silently, and he scrambled up. "Have they found us again?"

Baore, too, woke and jumped up, thinking they were being attacked.

"Shh," Cynddl said. "It hardly seems likely they would be making such noise. I don't think it's a threat, but I can't guess what it might be."

Cynddl took up his bow and Tam found his sword. The four went creeping into the shadowed wood, the moon casting only a little light in pale patches beneath the trees. The strange sound, high and thin, drew them on. In fifty feet they found themselves on a path, and then a square of orange light appeared above. A window.

The island was rocky and steeply sloping. The path wound back and forth among the trees, roots delving in and out among the shattered rock, involved in the great labor of breaking the island to pieces.

In the darkness, Tam could hear the others breathing raggedly, afraid in spite of themselves. It appeared that someone dwelt on this island and the companions' experience of that day had made them wary and distrustful. They went forward slowly.

Finally, they came up to the crest of the island, and there among the trees stood a house—not a woodsman's cottage but a large, stone house with a walled courtyard or garden. The noise came from beyond the wall, a mewling, almost inhuman sound which wandered up and down the scale of tones in a random, unmusical manner.

The four companions hesitated, listening.

"I'll tell you," Baore whispered, "I'm sorely tempted to go back to the boat and never knock on this door. Whoever waits beyond is strange."

In the moonlight Tam could see Cynddl nod his agreement, but Fynnol stood with his head cocked, listening intently. Curiosity would be his undoing.

Before any decision could be made, the door opened and a woman stepped through carrying a wooden bucket in each hand. The keening ended abruptly, and she dropped the buckets in fright and bolted back through the door in a flutter of skirts and apron. She left the door ajar, however, and the four stood looking into a small, dark courtyard.

"Well, we can hardly disappear now," Tam said. "She did not look so very strange, Baore, though she was hardly polite."

A moment later they heard footsteps.

"What is it you want?" came a creaky voice: an old man, it seemed.

"We want nothing, grandfather," Tam said gently. "In the dark we ran our boat up on the shore of your island and wait only for sunrise to be on our way again. We are honest men, grandfather. You needn't fear us."

Tam thought he saw movement in the archway where the woman had disappeared.

"If you are honest men why do you carry arms?"

All of them hesitated to answer for a second.

"We were set upon by brigands at the ford at Willowwand. It's made us wary, for we're unused to such things. We're three young men from the Vale of Lakes and our Fáel companion, Cynddl——"

"Fáel?" the man said quickly. "Would good Cynddl walk out where he can be seen?"

Tam looked over at Cynddl.

"Good Cynddl . . .?" the story finder echoed. He stared into the dark for a moment. "I don't think he'll stick me full of arrows," he said and went a few steps into the courtyard, where the moonlight found him, silvering his hair.

An old man wearing a long robe emerged from the shadows, bowed, and to everyone's surprise, greeted Cynddl in his own language.

"Have we found Fáel dwelling here, on this isolated island?" Fynnol whispered.

"No," Tam said, "though for one of our own people, he seems to have a strange liking for black wanderers."

"Will you vouch for these others who accompany you?" the old man asked a bit anxiously. His voice rasped and creaked like iron wearing on iron. "I have always found the Fáel to be peace-loving people . . ."

"I will, grandfather. They mean you no harm." Cynddl could be seen leaning forward slightly in the poor light, staring at the old man. "How is it you know my language?"

"Oh, I do not know it," the old man said, smoothing

his robe. "Only the greeting and a few other polite phrases. I am an old man and have learned much in my years. Much that I've forgotten, I'm afraid. But I'm being a poor host. Welcome to my home. Come in, come in." He waved a hand at the dark doorway. "You will have to forgive Hannah. We get so few visitors here and you surprised her in the dark. She is not used to people, you see. Well, my son and I are people, I realize, but strangers— They seldom find us on this stretch of the river."

They followed the old man up a flight of stone stairs, poorly lit from above. Whoever held the candles at the stairhead was leery, hanging back, hoarding the light. As they reached the top they saw the woman, Hannah, back away, holding up a candlebranch like a bright shield.

The old man crossed to her, gesturing to the visitors and patting her reassuringly on the arm, then touching his heart. "They are friends, Hannah, you needn't be concerned." She nodded quickly but backed away, thrust the candles into the old man's hand, and then darted out a door.

"Ah, you see, she is terribly shy." The old man stroked his beard, staring at the door where Hannah had disappeared. Then he shook his head and turned back to his guests. "But I am a poor host. Did I say that already?" he asked but didn't wait for an answer. "Shall I offer you refreshment? I will tell you, we are so isolated here that we make do without many of the comforts of civilization, but we have wine and ale and the purest water that man has ever drunk."

Another man appeared then, a servant, younger than his master but not young. The old man sent him off for wine, water, and ale, not waiting to hear what anyone would chose. He stood stroking his beard again, looking terribly distracted. "Now I know I am forgetting something . . ." he muttered.

"I am Tamlyn Loell and this is my cousin, Fynnol Loell. Baore Talon is his cousin, and Cynddl's name you have heard."

The old man listened to this, nodding his head rhythmically. Still his blank look remained. "Cynddl . . ." he mused. "This is a derivative of the great navigator's name: Cynddlyn. You must be the heir of an important family."

"Not so important," Cynddl muttered.

They waited a moment more, then Tam spoke. "And you are, sir . . .?"

The man's face lit. "That's it! My name. Introductions!" He laughed gently at his own folly. "I am Eber son of Eiresit, and this house, like the island, is called Speaking Stone, for if you walk to the cliff edge you will hear the waters flowing among the rocks below and it will sound like speech to you. Often I have stood thinking I understood, or nearly understood, a few words, a phrase. One day it muttered, 'All your wisdom will be mine . . .' And yet another time I heard, 'Oh, my sons, my daughter . . .' And then one day it said my name— clear as clear.

"You might listen yourself and see what you hear, for if a river speaks to you . . . Well, it is one of the voices of the world, like the wind or the moving sea." He paused, looking toward the open window where the breeze could be heard in the trees. "Did you meet the mapmaker?" he asked suddenly. "Did he give you a map for this section of the river?"

The companions glanced at one another.

"We came here only through our own folly," Tam said, "attempting to travel the river by night."

Eber gazed at Tam a moment, then nodded. "Then come," he said. "Come up to my tower and I'll show you what has led me to live in such a remote place."

The old man held up the candelabra and led them to another flight of stairs which wound its way up into the darkness. The companions looked at one another, eyebrows raised, and then the curious Fynnol fell in behind the old man—with the others behind him.

They entered a large, square room lit by candles. In the center stood a great table littered with papers and open books, writing implements, dividers and rulers. On shelves stood strange devices of brass and polished wood and glass. Bunches of dried plants and flowers dangled on cords from the ceiling, and on the walls hung charts covered with lines and curves and calculations. To one side, doors stood open onto a balcony.

"Here I study the stars and listen to the river," the old man said. "I cultivate patience, for the river is not forthcoming and disdains the impetuous. It tests a man, waiting long years before revealing anything at all. Many have grown restless and abandoned their vigil before the river would offer up its secrets."

The servant came in then, bearing a tray of glasses and flagons of ale, wine, and water. The old man led them out onto the balcony to roughly made chairs with worn cushions. The travelers settled themselves, wondering what strange thing their host would reveal next.

Tam saw Baore and Fynnol glance at each other oddly, as though to say *See what peculiar folk dwell beyond the Vale.*

The old man poured himself a cup of "the purest water that man has ever drunk." The moon lit the balcony, and, below, the river flowed swiftly among rocks, muttering distractedly.

"This was once the house of Gwyar. Do you know this name? Gwyar of Alwa? He was said to be a sorcerer, though I cannot vouch for that. But he was a man of great learning, that is certain. As a young man I read several of his learned treatises—though they were difficult to procure even then and are nearly impossible to find now." Eber spoke as though they were not there, as though he were used to conversing with himself, justifying his life in this place.

"Gwyar was deeply learned in old lore, a student of the stars—their ways and influences. Healing was his special province, though he wrote about many things. He came here in his later years to chart the heavens— and in the end found himself listening to the river, trying to understand its speech." Eber son of Eiresit paused, listening intently. He raised a crooked hand, as though about to mark some sound of the water, but then let the hand fall.

"I came here because of my son, Llya, though it took me some time: Speaking Stone is not easily found." He looked down, his face suddenly very old and haggard. "I hoped that Gwyar would cure him, but I found Gwyar near to death, his knowledge lost, scattered like ragged clouds across the sky of his once-fine memory."

Tam listened intently, thinking the man's manner of speaking reminded him of old books.

"It is a sad tale, I fear. Sad, and for no one more than my son's poor mother. You see, I married her against the wishes and advice of many. Against her wishes, I fear, but her family gave her to me in marriage because I was a man of some position, and I thought her the fairest thing I had seen walk upon this world." He shook his head and began to pull a long strand of beard through his fingers, over and over. "She was a dutiful girl and tried, I think, to love me. I got her with child not long after our marriage, for though I was old she was young and the moon smiled upon her—or so I thought." He looked up at the sky. "Our son was born beneath that moon, full and bright . . ." He put a bony hand to his forehead. "An auspicious beginning, I thought, until the moon began to grow dark. As my young wife cried from the pain of her labor the whole face of the moon turned slowly black and a shadow crept into the room. And then, at the very moment the child came into this uncertain world, a raven landed upon the sill of the open casement. Thrice it croaked before I drove it away . . . but too late." His face was hidden behind his hand now.

"My bride did not survive the hour but bled out her short life upon our marriage bed. Died because of my desire and weakness . . . and love. I knew better—that is the hell of it." Eber drew a long breath, almost a sob. "So the young died, and the old lived on, as should never have been. But my son survived; as inauspicious a birth as I have ever known. One might expect such a child to be blind—the darkening of the moon—but this is not so. Llya has not the power of speech, nor can he hear—not the loudest report—but his sight is unblemished." Eber looked up at the young men around him. "So I came here to the house of Gwyar, who might have been a sorcerer, to seek the cure for my son's affliction, for certainly I brought it upon him, marrying his mother against the warnings of the stars." Tam thought the old man's mouth quivered a little. "The old should leave the young to marry among themselves, for in them life quickens and grows while in the old it shrinks and shrivels away. It was a cursed thing I did and now I would make amends. Gwyar, it is said, cured many ailments and infirmities. I hope one day I will do the same." He gestured toward the river. "After all, if a river can speak, then cannot a child of man learn to do the same?"

He looked at each of them in turn, as though they would have an answer to this question. It was then that Tam noticed a small boy had crept to the door behind them. He lurked there, dressed in a beautifully made velvet suit—like a little lord. He stared out at them evenly.

Eber's gaze followed Tam's and his sad face lit in a

smile. "Ah, there you are, my treasure." Eber beckoned, but the child stepped back behind the door so that only one eye could be seen. The old man looked at Tam and raised his hands in a helpless gesture.

"It is the curse of living so far from my fellow men. Like Hannah, he is timid with strangers, for he's seen so few. Perhaps you realized that Hannah, too, is deaf? I have sympathy for any with this affliction and took her on. Unlike Llya she has the ability to produce sound, but how can one learn speech who cannot hear it? Instead, she goes about making an odd, mewling noise. I am not sure she is even aware of it." He shook his head. "I search on. I have some of the writings of Gwyar: his beginnings of charts of the heavens, his musings about the voice of the river, some reflections upon the nature of magic and its uses in healing. But nothing that tells me how to give a voice to silence . . ."

He stopped then, looking at the child who hung back in the shadow. Tam watched the old man's face soften as he gazed at his child. What terrible guilt the old man suffered.

"But I have burdened you with my tale and have heard nothing of you. Did you say you were set upon by brigands? This is almost unheard of in these times in the wildlands."

Tam nodded. "We don't know why they attacked us, but it would seem they believe we are allies of a man we met briefly near our homeland. We think these same men killed him."

The old man shook his head, the sadness returning. "This is unsettling, here, on my river. Will they come after you?"

"They didn't have boats but were on horseback. We fear they'll race us to the north bridge."

"Ah, but you are on the river and it will flow swiftly now. It will carry you past the bridge before any man on horse can make the journey, for the road must skirt the hills going far east to a difficult pass. This man you say they murdered—who was he to them?"

"We don't know," Fynnol said. "He called himself Alaan. He was fair-spoken—a man of some learning, we think, and an inveterate traveler."

The old man looked up. "I know such a man, also named Alaan. Did he travel with a whist? A small, dark bird?"

They looked at the old man in surprise.

"You knew him?" Fynnol said quickly.

"Yes, yes, though I have not seen Alaan in several years." The old man sat up, suddenly troubled. "These men you say attacked you; they are dangerous men indeed if they caught Alaan out in the open. You're certain Alaan was killed . . .?"

"Yes, there's no doubt. These men caught him in the dark as he held Telanon Bridge so that we might escape."

The old man massaged his temple gently, his eyes glistening a little. "I warned Alaan long ago. Warned him that he must change his ways . . . 'Someone will catch you, one day,' I said, 'as fleet-footed as you are.' It is what befalls rogues, you see, but he did not listen."

"How did you know Alaan?" Cynddl asked.

"You called him a man of some learning, and indeed you were right—more than you know. Alaan came from a learned family. He found me here, as you have, and few who travel the river have managed that. He traveled as widely as any Fáel—perhaps more widely. And now you say he is dead. Perhaps he seduced the daughter of the wrong nobleman. No good comes of it, you see." His head lifted quickly, and Eber stared off toward the river. "Did you hear? Almost a word, but more like a muttered sigh. It is always thus, never speaking clearly . . ."

"But what manner of life did Alaan pursue?" Tam asked. "His presence in the north was a mystery to us. And it was not the first time he'd been there. A few years ago he came to the Vale and seemed to be looking for someone he thought might be hiding there."

Eber found a loose thread in his robe and tugged at it gently with pale, bony fingers. "Who knows what Alaan did. He was interested in all manner of things, some quite arcane, others very worldly: the politics of the nobles, the history of old Ayr; languages old and new; the races that once dwelt in the wildlands. The River Wynnd held a particular fascination for him, and he had a keen interest in the ladies of the courts." Eber's list petered out. He still worried the thread in his robe.

"You say he came from a learned family," Tam said. "We'd hoped to send word to his people so they would not be left wondering for years why he's not been seen or heard from. It seemed a small thing, considering what he did for us."

The old man shook his head, the long beard and hair swaying. "I'm afraid it's of no use. You'll not find any of Alaan's people. Not now." Eber rose stiffly and went to the railing, staring down into the darkness. He was silent for a long time, but then Tam saw his shoulders sag a little.

Fynnol, who sat favoring his injured side, gestured to the old man and rolled his eyes. Clearly he had spent too long in this lonely house, listening to his river, musing over what he believed to be his terrible transgression.

"Imagine a life without language," Eber said softly, still staring down into the river. "I might teach my son to read and certainly that is language, but not a spoken tongue. What beauty can there be to it without sound: the play of tone and syllable, assonance, rhythm, rhyme? I cannot think what a loss this would be. Imagine poetry without sound—meaning but no music." He shook his head. "It is a silent world I have consigned Llya to. Devoid of laughter, no song to touch the heart, no echo, no river's secret speech. Even his name he has never heard." He bowed his head, staring down at the flowing river. For a moment there was no speech but that of the water.

He looked up at them, surprised and embarrassed, as though he had been caught musing to himself. He turned so that he leaned against the rail. "I will tell you this one thing I learned of Alaan," Eber said. "He had the knack of hiding himself from others. Oh, you might think you knew all there was to know of Alaan, and I dare say there were some that did believe this, but they did not know the half of him. Alaan was secretive—like his bird—secretive and wary. But this was all hidden beneath a facade of immense charm. And yet he was not unaffected by the difficulties of others. He once brought me a gift, brought it to me out of story. I'll show you."

Eber walked stiffly inside and returned bearing a small box, long and narrow. He slid it open, for it fit together in two parts, and from inside removed a flute, once white but now yellowed with age.

"Alaan hoped I might read what is written on this, but it is too old a script for my meager knowledge—if it is a script at all. It is said to be an enchanted pipe, if you are inclined to believe such things. A pipe even the deaf might hear, but either it was only a story or I could not find the secret of it."

He passed the pipe to Cynddl.

"Have you ever seen its like?"

Cynddl took it gently, holding it up in the moonlight. "I haven't, but it's ancient, I think. I can't even say what it's made of. Is it bone?"

"It is the horn of a mystical beast—a whale-fish it is said—at least that was Alaan's story. The pipe is said to have belonged to a minstrel: Ruadan, by name."

"I've heard of him!" Cynddl said, looking up quickly. "There are songs. A minstrel who won the heart of a princess with an enchanted flute."

Eber nodded. "Yes, though when the pipe was stolen

the spell was broken, and the Princess had her father kill poor Ruadan for bespelling her and stealing her love unwarranted. But it was said that the deaf could hear his pipe and Alaan brought me this, not certain it was the flute of Ruadan, but hoping. He was fascinated by ancient things—artifacts and antiquities." The old man looked up at Cynddl, measuring him, it seemed.

"Alaan asked me to keep this here, safe, and tell no one of it. But now that he is gone . . . Perhaps there is someone—someone whom Alaan knew." Eber said this somewhat reluctantly. "Gilbert A'brgail is the man's name. Would you carry the flute to him? He should have it, I think. Ask for him at tournaments near the borders of the old kingdom. He was a friend of Alaan. The only one I know." The old man shook his head sadly. "The only one but me."

"My people range all across the land between the mountains," Cynddl said. "I'll send out word and we'll find Gilbert A'brgail and deliver your flute."

"But you must not . . . !" Eber's gaze darted about the terrace without settling on anyone. "It is a valuable object which many might want—because of the story attached to it. You should not go about the lands telling everyone what you carry. I tell you this for your own good."

Cynddl bobbed his head. "Then I'll say nothing of your pipe but ask only after Alaan's friend," he promised, and then raised the pipe to his mouth, sending a trill of notes into the night. Eber's son looked up suddenly from where he played, but then went back to his amusement, only attracted by the sudden movement of Cynddl's hands. The story finder played again but the boy did not hear.

"I've never heard a flute with such a sound," Cynddl said, holding the instrument out again to look at it.

"Nor has anyone, I think," Eber said softly. "But it grows late. You may stay the night in the house of Gwyar, if you wish. We have beds enough if you will consent to share rooms. Here we sleep by day and are alive by night so that I might study the stars, but you must be tired from your traveling."

They looked quickly at one another and then Cynddl said, "We have our camp on the tip of your island and our boat to watch. It's a kind offer, Eber, and we thank you, but our bed will be the riverbank tonight."

The old man nodded, perhaps a little relieved. "If you will lie by the river, then listen when it speaks. It has a secret, I tell you, for the man who can hear."

Tam made his bed in a place less rocky, and lay listening to the river murmur as it passed Speaking Stone. The entire meeting with Eber had been so unexpected and so peculiar that he almost wondered if it had happened at all. Perhaps he had been dreaming and just now awoke? The shadow of Alaan seemed to follow them. From Telanon Bridge, where they had escaped with their lives, down to the ford at Willowwand, where they had barely avoided disaster again.

And now they nearly wrecked their boat upon this

rocky island and what do they find? A half-mad old man and his poor son; and this man, too, knows Alaan. A rogue he called him, though not without some affection in his voice—more affection than Delgert Gallon had, that is certain. But now they had another name: A'brgail. Alaan's other friend, Eber said. How could a man of such charm have only two friends?

Tam lifted his head suddenly. What was that he heard? Almost a sigh, but a sigh that contained vowels and harder sounds—rocks shifting in the river, no doubt. Now the old man was infecting even him with his madness and obsession. Tam lay back, closed his eyes, and felt sleep drift over him like a dark, heavy mist.

He fell into a dream.

He walked in the wood, seeking the path to Eber's house but wandering among the trees, lost. Finally he found a steep, twisting way and on it was Eber's son, standing in the shadows, still and silent in his dark velvet clothes.

Llya beckoned to Tam and, taking his hand, drew him down so that Tam knelt upon one knee. The boy put his mouth close to Tam's ear but instead of speech he blew out through his moving lips, and manipulating his tongue, made a sound like the river murmuring among stones.

SIXTEEN

First light found them on the river again. They easily negotiated the rapids that surrounded Speaking Stone, for in daylight the waters weren't so formidable. Passing the island, Tam looked up to catch a last glimpse of the home of Gwyar, but no sign of it could be discerned. Only swaying trees and towering stone. Men who came down the river would never realize the house was there, their attention on the hazards of the river—but not its voice.

Overhead the sky remained thinly overcast; and a fine mist seemed to hang among the trees on the hillsides, reducing them to silhouettes, only Cynddl able to name them by such vague shapes.

It was at Speaking Stone that the landscape changed and they found themselves among steep, rugged hills, the river flowing swiftly between. It wound its way, sometimes tortuously, through the outcroppings of stone, and the occupants of the boat were ever on the alert for rapids and rocks.

The land seemed drier, the bare bones of it tearing through the covering of green, thrusting up to heights, cliff faces broken and sheer. Tam thought it looked an ancient land, sculpted and battered by the ages; but even so it was beautiful in an eerie way, for not only was it empty of the signs of men but one had the feeling that if men had ever dwelt here it had been a long age ago.

The haunting sorrow that pervaded the Greensprings still touched Tam at times, but he was wise to it now and when it welled up he knew immediately that it was not his own. This made it easier to bear, somehow.

High overhead the hunting eagles soared, banking and gliding, their golden feathers flashing in the weak sunlight. The ancient eagle perched, white headed, in trees along the river, watching for unwary fish; while on the shallow banks, cranes and herons stalked, staring down into the waters with meditative concentration.

Late in the morning, Fynnol pointed out two black swans swimming in the shadow of the bank. Cynddl sat up and begged Tam to row near. As they did so, the swans moved down the bank, twisting their elegant necks to keep the strangers in view. With their wings arched up and their feathers dark as a raven's they were a beautiful sight, Tam thought.

"We never see such swans in the Vale," Baore said.

"Such birds are not to be seen anywhere," Cynddl whispered, "or so I would have said. The black swan was more than rare when my people first set foot on the shore of the land between the mountains. Only a few years later their race was gone altogether, hunted by men who prized their feathers—or so we believed. But here are two, swimming out of story, it would seem. And look. See how they draw us downriver? I'll wager there is a nest hidden away, back among that stand of water-willow. That's a good sign." Cynddl waved them on, though he sat and watched the swans until the river carried them out of sight.

Twice they passed islands formed like Speaking Stone and Tam wondered if there were hidden dwellings on these as well—the homes of alleged sorcerers or half-mad old men—but they didn't stop to find out. The companions traveled in silence, watching the land slip by, heartened by Eber's assurance that no horseman could race them to the bridge.

Fynnol stood in the boat suddenly. "Tam!" he said.

A billowing cloud of fog washed up the river toward them, tumbling in a slow, toppling wave. Tam rose, trying for a moment to judge the speed of the advancing bank, but its edge was so nebulous it seemed to flow up the river and out from the banks all at once. The sun drowned in the sky, and before they could turn toward the shore, the wave broke over them, silent and cool. Suddenly it was neither day nor night, but some nether time with neither sun nor stars but only a diffuse gray—shadow-less and featureless. Cynddl found a cloak in his pack and pulled it on and the others did the same. It was suddenly clammy and chill, water beading and dripping in dull diamonds on the planks and frames.

Baore shipped a pair of oars which thudded dully into place. "Shall we try to make the shore at least?" he said, whispering for some reason. "Even if we don't find a place to land properly we might tie to the bank and wait." He began to row in the direction of the bank. After a moment he stopped, twisting around and staring into the gray. "Am I turned around already? Certainly the river isn't so broad."

"I can barely see Fynnol," Tam said from the stern. "We could be rowing along the bank and not know."

Cynddl stood, tugging his dark-red cloak close. He turned slowly, gazing into the fog. The sounds of birds carried to them but muffled and distant. "Row more to your left," the story finder said.

After ten minutes of this Baore stopped, staring over the side. "Which way does the current flow? I can no longer tell."

Fynnol spat over the side to see if they moved in relation to the waters, but the gray light and mist hid even this.

Cynddl dropped back into his seat. "I would say we were in a lake, but the river meets no lakes this far north."

Fynnol called out and his voice trailed off and faded into the fog. "When the banks are stone there's almost always a little echo," he said, turning where he sat and looking quickly in all directions. "Can the mist muffle that?"

No one knew.

Baore bent to his oars again, choosing a new direction, but still no embankment was found. They sat in silence, watching the slow swirl of mist, listening to the small lapping of water on wood.

"It's as though we've taken some turn in the river that we didn't see," Fynnol said. "And now where are we?" He waved a hand at the mist. "I have this terrible feeling that the fog will lift and there'll be no land in sight, only watery horizon in all directions."

The boat knocked against stone, causing them all to jump, and then a scraping sound came from below. Everyone bent over the side, heeling the boat until it almost tipped.

"Do you see anything?" Baore asked, the words coming out in a rush. He took up an oar and plunged the blade straight down, but found no bottom.

Cynddl hung over the side, staring down. Very hesitantly he reached out and touched the water, bringing his dripping hand up to his lips. Tam wondered if the story finder half expected it to taste of salt. As though they could have been washed out of the mouth of the river into the open sea.

"This isn't our river," Cynddl said.

Tam dipped his hand into the water and put it to his lips. It tasted the way rainwater would when it sat for a time in a stone basin. Drinking it left you with a dry, acrid taste—like sour wine and chalk.

"The taste of the Wynnd has changed as we've traveled away from the mountains," Tam said, "but you're right, Cynddl; it's never been like this."

"Rocks!" Baore cried.

Tam spun on the thwart, wet now from the fog, and saw a great column of stone looming up out of the mist. Fynnol fended off with his hands.

"But look at this, Tam!" Fynnol said. "I've never seen such rock. It looks like roots." Fynnol bent back and gazed up. "And this looks like the trunk of an enormous tree."

As the rock passed Tam reached out a hand to touch it—cold and coarse, like granite. And surely it did look like a tangle of thick roots, as though the earth had been washed away around them. He stared up. The rock was striated and irregular, like bark, and trunklike, its girth that of a small shed. It slipped into the fog astern and another loomed up before them, and then another.

"I've heard of trees turned to stone," Tam said, "but none so large as these."

Cynddl reached out and patted the stone as it came abeam. "But these were once trees, all the same," he said. "Ancient cedars, though of a massive kind. I can't begin to guess how this has happened to them."

"A forest of water and stone," Tam said. He felt incredibly small. The girth of the trees was enormous, their crowns lost in cloud. And here he was drifting among the roots like an insect on a leaf. The place was somber and still. No sound of wind, only a low swell, rising and falling and slapping on stone. Trees appeared out of the slowly curling gray, then fell astern, silent and lifeless.

"Have we died and don't know it?" Baore said.

Fynnol turned and looked at his cousin, his dark features taut and creased. "What are you saying?"

"If there is a land of the dead," Baore said flatly, "it would look like this."

There was a swirl in the water a few feet away and a flash of white, barely visible.

"What was that?" Fynnol said, starting back.

"At least the fish are alive," Cynddl said. Another tree drifted out of the fog.

"Where are we, Cynddl?" Fynnol asked softly. Tam heard no trace of humor in his cousin's voice now. Fynnol turned toward their Fáel companion. "This seems like a dream landscape to me. Not a real place. But it's a disturbing dream." Fynnol reached out and let his hand run over the stone of another tree—and then he struck it hard with his fist. "Where are we?" he shouted.

Cynddl stood in the center of the boat, his feet braced, an oar in hand. "I don't know, Fynnol," he said. "I've never heard of such a place."

"Could we have entered some lake that is undiscovered?" Baore asked.

"Does that seem likely to you?" Cynddl said.

Baore didn't answer. He ran one hand deep into his mow of hair and stared at the passing trees as though they were ghosts rising up to haunt him.

Some other shape took form in the murk, dark and long, like the hull of a ship: a fallen tree. The size of these cedars was clear now, for even lying half-covered in water it was taller than Baore. They all reached out and felt the stone bark.

"Look how long it is!" Baore said as they passed. "These trees must stand two hundred feet."

"It's as though a mad sculptor had been at work," Tam

said, "at work for a hundred years." The fallen tree ended in a massive tangle of stone roots. The gunwale of the boat bumped gently against stone as it floated past.

"Will this mist never lift?" Fynnol asked, his voice almost a whine. He was moving about in the bow, unable to keep still, looking this way and that as though he expected something to leap out of the fog. Baore had fallen silent, and slumped down in his seat.

He's met something his strength is no match for, Tam thought.

They passed a broken stump, like the base of a column that would hold up the sky, and then they were back in the featureless gray.

"If we have passed through the forest," Baore said, "I don't like to think what we'll meet next."

They drifted, unable to mark any progress in the oppressive gloom, the boat rocking gently over the low swell. The four sat silently, staring into the fog, each in a different direction, waiting—for what they weren't sure.

And then the drowned sun appeared, nebulous and faint, casting a muted, shadowless light into the color-less world. Tam had the impression that they were moving again—that a current carried them along through the mist, which seemed to grow thinner around them.

"Did you hear that sound?" Fynnol said. "Like some-one calling?"

"It was only a bird," Cynddl said.

"No. Listen . . . There it is again."

Tam heard it this time, but it seemed to him quiet

speech floating over the water. Then the knuckle knock of wood on wood.

"Don't . . ." Cynddl said, as Fynnol cupped his hands to his mouth to shout. "Let's see who it might be first."

"But they might know the way to land," Fynnol said.

"Only if they can see through cloud." Cynddl dipped the oar he held and began to paddle forward, still standing. The mumble of voices drew clearer, and the story finder set his oar down gently and strung his bow, tugging at his sword to make sure it would come easily free.

The boat drifted into a hole in the fog fifty feet broad. On its edge men appeared, dark silhouettes standing knee deep in swirling gray.

"There is your land, Fynnol," Baore said.

And then one of the men gave a shout and pointed at the companions in their boat, snatching up a bow as he did so.

Cynddl let fly an arrow. "It's a raft!" he shouted, and dropped down, letting fly another arrow.

"They've found us again!" Fynnol shouted.

Tam threw himself down hard on the slick floor-boards, searching for his bow. An arrow buried itself in the planking near his head.

Tam swore, strung his bow, and jumped up to his knees, an arrow ready. But there was no target, only a river awash in twisting cumulus.

"Where . . .?" he whispered.

"Gone into the fog." Cynddl hunched down, his eyes just over the gunwale. He pointed. "The current runs that way. Back the oars a little, Baore, and put some water between us."

They drifted into fog again, but it began to thin; and the silhouettes of treetops appeared, dark spires like arrows aimed at the sky.

"There is more current here," Baore said. "See how quickly the trees pass?"

They emerged from fog into a stretch of sunlit river, and there a raft floated, manned by men-at-arms dressed in both purple and black. Arrows began to fly again, and Cynddl and Tam sent a few away before Baore managed to pull them out of range. They drifted for a moment, the men on the raft shouting threats and curses, for some of their companions were down, wounded.

"They'll go back into the fog in a moment," Tam said. "I don't want to find ourselves within arrow range again. Can you carry us nearer the far bank, Baore?"

Baore nodded and began to work his oars. The mist from the shore stretched out over the river again, and the raft sank into it like a stone into water. For a moment they pressed on, gazing into the fog, listening intently. Muffled shouting could still be heard, but from where it came or what distance Tam couldn't guess. And then suddenly an arrow pierced the water nearby, bobbing to the surface.

"There!" Cynddl shouted and shot again.

The raft appeared out of the fog, nearer than they would have guessed. Fynnol scrambled into Tam's place at the stern oars. Arrows began dropping around them like hail and both Cynddl and Tam let fly arrow after arrow.

An island lifted up before them, rising out of the river, mantled in green. They could hear the water chattering and then white water and standing waves appeared.

"To the left!" Cynddl called. "Put the island between us."

With an effort Fynnol and Baore missed the head of the island. Tam braced himself to meet fast water, but before them the river stretched still and lazy, the fog thinning and a soft sunlight breaking through.

"How can this be?" Cynddl said, turning back to the others. "Where are the rapids?"

"This channel must be deep," Tam said, "while on the other side of the island it is shallow and strewn with rocks."

Cynddl gazed around at the river. "But I could see down the other side. Didn't you see a fall of several feet? This channel has no fall."

Tam, too, stared at the river, but there was no denying that it flowed easily on, not broken by a ripple. He looked back the way they'd come, and found Fynnol slumped over the oars.

"Fynnol? Are you hurt?"

His cousin shook his head. "My side," he whispered, and Tam realized Fynnol had been rowing too hard for his injured ribs.

"Out of there, Fynnol. Let me take up those oars."

But Fynnol shook his head. "I can't draw a bow. Stay as you are."

"Do you think that raft can ride the rapids?" Cynddl asked.

Baore shrugged. "If they're lucky. If they built it well. But they were men-at-arms not shipwrights—or rivermen, for that matter."

They came to the foot of the island then, but there was no raft to be seen. For a moment they all stared intently at the river. Tam pointed at the tip of the island. "There's a log and a tangle of line."

They gazed at the end of the island, which was gravel and rock with small poplars shimmering in the new sun. Behind this a thick forest arched up the spine of stone that formed the island.

"They could be in the trees, waiting to shoot us if we draw near," Fynnol said.

"Even if someone managed to get ashore," Tam said, "he won't have kept his bowstring dry—if he kept his bow at all. I think it's safe enough. I'd like to know what's become of our hunters. Unless you want to be constantly on the watch from here to the Wold of Kerns?"

"Tam is right," Cynddl said. "Can you man the oars, Fynnol, and let the three of us go ashore? Better if you keep the boat out in deep water in case we've made a terrible mistake."

Fynnol nodded, though the thin mask he managed hardly hid the pain he was feeling. His hair was plastered to his glistening forehead, black against white—too white, Tam thought—and the stillness of his eyes said everything. There was no mischief there today. No clever remark being fashioned. Fynnol had been lost in the forest of stone and water—the land of the dead, Baore had called it—and he would be a while finding his way out again.

Fynnol nosed the boat into the eddy, where the log washed back and forth against the shore, the tangle of rope swaying like lifeless tentacles.

Baore and Tam followed Cynddl, who splashed into the shallow water, bow in hand. A low gasp sounded, followed by a moan and a choking cough. Cynddl and Tam drew their swords, and Baore raised his staff. Lying half beneath the log, caught in the snarl of lines, lay a man in a purple surcoat. A thin crimson rivulet circled about him and streamed off down the river, and from his chest an arrow protruded. As Tam stepped over the log the wounded man's eyes flicked open.

"I am dying quickly enough," he said softly. "You've no need to hasten it."

Tam could see the man's hands in the water, empty of weapons, so he crouched down so that he could hear what the man said over the sound of the river. The stranger was perhaps in his third decade, his handsome face unnaturally white, dark hair drifting about it like kelp.

"We've no desire to kill you at all, but you've hunted us without reason."

"Without reason?" The man closed his eyes a second. "You're the allies of a demon. That's reason enough."

"A demon? Alaan? He was a stranger, a traveler we let share our fire out of kindness."

The man's eyes seemed to focus on Tam for the first time. "You're one of those who disturbed the battlefield by Telanon Bridge. For days we watched you, waiting. And then he came, just as that cursed captain predicted. You can't keep what you have. The black guards will have it. Better to live. That would be my choice."

"But we have nothing!" Tam protested. "Whatever Alaan thieved from your lord, he didn't give it to us."

The man moved a hand to his chest, cringing from pain. He stared up at Tam, his eyes wide with a terrible knowledge. His lids grew heavy, and Tam could see him struggle to keep them open—open to the light.

"Tam . . ." Fynnol said from his place in the boat. "We should not tarry. Perhaps there are others about."

"No . . ." The man reached up and placed a hand on Tam's arm, but there was no strength in the fingers. "Stay a moment more. I won't keep you long, I think. Already the world seems to be drifting away—or I am drifting. Here," he said, gesturing weakly, "take my sword. It's a good one. But stay a moment more."

"But that is my arrow in your heart," Tam said softly.

The man nodded. "Yes, but it might have been my sword in yours—and perhaps you tell the truth and we had no cause to be hunting you. If that's so, we've paid." He gestured to his sword, as though he would offer it again, but did not. "Flee the black guards," he said so softly Tam barely heard. "Flee them at all costs." The man pressed his eyes closed, then opened them, shaking his head weakly.

"I cannot hold," he said. "My life flows into the river." He clutched Tam's arm. "Drag me onto the shore," he whispered. "Let the crows have me. Don't leave me to the swimmers." He looked up at Tam, tears appearing: tears and hopeless fear. He gasped and seemed to relax, his eyes fluttering closed. A long sigh escaped him, and he lay still, the vein of red slowly coiling into the current.

The river chattered and muttered. For a moment wind rattled through the poplar leaves, and then was still.

"Good-bye, man-at-arms," Cynddl said. "You didn't even tell us your name so that we might send you properly on your way." He crouched down beside Tam. "He belongs to the river, now. Help me with him."

"No," Tam said. "He begged us not to do that. I'll drag him ashore myself."

"But, Tam, the river has claimed him," Cynddl said. "I wouldn't meddle in this. He would've killed you and left you to the river without a thought."

"Perhaps so, but I'm his murderer and my claim is great. The river won't have him. His grave ashore will be lonely enough." Tam pulled the man's sword from its ring and began cutting away the lines that bound him.

Baore took the man's feet and Tam the shoulders, and they carried him, heavy and lolling, up into the cedars above the high-water mark. With the spade from the boat they scraped out a shallow grave, mounding the earth over the body. All the while Fynnol waited nervously by the boat and Cynddl stood guard with his bow, pacing back and forth as he gazed into the shadows, and urging his companions to hurry. When they were done Tam drove the man's sword into the ground for a headstone. They stood around the grave, Baore and Tam breathing hard from their labor, their hands dark with dirt.

"Are you satisfied, Tam?" Cynddl whispered.

Tam shook his head. "His children will never know what became of him . . . or even where he lies. They will always wonder." Tam bent and wiped his hands on the spring grass.

Cynddl stared at him a moment, then said softly, "Let's look up the other channel before we go. I want to see these rapids again—if they're there at all."

They set out along the rocks, alert for other men who might lie hidden in the underwood. They climbed onto a finger of stone and looked up the length of the island. The water foamed and flashed in the sun, falling and swirling around rocks and along the shore.

Tam waited for Baore or Cynddl to say something, but the only explanation offered was the sound of the water rushing over stone. Even Eber could not translate it.

"It is a river with many branches," Cynddl said at last. "Isn't that what the man below the Lion's Maw told us?"

"Yes, and we thought he was mad," Tam said. "There have always been tales told in the Vale . . . of men lost on the river, traveling through lands they'd never seen, taking a fortnight for a seven-days journey. Old wives' tales we called them." He turned to the story finder. "How did we find our way onto this hidden river, Cynddl? And how do we get back?"

Cynddl picked up a rock and flung it out into the speeding waters, where it made barely a splash. "I don't know the answer to either question." He turned and looked down the broad, sunlit river. "Perhaps this is a place where the branches meet and ahead lies the Wynnd we know."

"Or perhaps there are stranger things awaiting us," Baore said. "But let's get away from this place, at least. There might still be men-at-arms about." He reached out and took hold of Tam's shoulder, gently turning him away. They climbed down from the vantage point and walked over the exposed gravel bar, feeling the heat from the sun-warmed stones. The aroma of the trees' new growth scented the air, sweet as new-cut hay.

As soon as Fynnol saw them he began to push the boat out into the moving stream. "I thought you'd spend all day in this place!" he said as the others clambered aboard.

Baore and Tam took up the oars and sent them speeding down the river. The island fell quickly astern, the water to one side white and broken, while the other side was calm and shadowed. They rowed on in silence, Tam working hard to match Baore's stroke.

For an hour they kept this up until Tam collapsed over his oars, gasping and heaving. He closed his eyes and saw the dark silhouette of a man clinging to the roots of a gray stone tree, fog weaving around him in ragged strands.

SEVEN†EEN

The castle had come to life as though a spell had been suddenly and mysteriously lifted. Elise could feel it in the excitement of the servants—the whispering and quick looks.

The Prince of Innes had come secretly to visit, bringing with him his son—the young man Menwyn hoped Elise would marry.

Marry.

Even the word had an unreal quality. As though it didn't quite have meaning—or its meaning was just beyond her grasp.

Elise's maid laced her into a gown for the reception and dinner, and as the servant struggled to make her charge presentable Elise's thoughts went back to her strange meeting with the minstrel that afternoon.

With him travels his handsome son. I will tell you honestly, lady, that if you are not made of stone you will find him much to your liking. But I have come to warn you.

A shiver ran through her and she colored a little.

Of course, the memory of the minstrel's dark, unsettling gaze disturbed her enough. Those world-weary eyes had looked upon her and she had almost blushed, for immediately she felt that he knew what she was feeling—and what she was often feeling it were better men did not know. His look had so plainly said *You are a young woman like many another and will hold no surprises for me*.

She shook her head just a little. It was the look of a man who had known too many women, she thought. A rogue. Gwyden Dore she had called him. A hero's name, not a scoundrel's, but she feared he was the latter. Then why should she listen to such a man?

. . . if you are not made of stone you will find him much to your liking. But I have come to warn you.

She was not made of stone. Elise was well aware of that. In truth, she wished she were made of sterner stuff.

For the first time since she had talked to the minstrel his final words registered. He had come to warn her— not set her afire with anticipation. To warn her.

Of course she had no intention of marrying the son of the Prince of Innes, no matter how much to her liking he might be. Menwyn wanted this alliance to further his own designs, and that was almost enough to harden her resistance: to thwart Menwyn. But there was more. She wanted no part of the Wills's madness or their arrogant ambitions.

She had never once heard a member of her family say that they wanted to rule to bring peace and order to the land or prosperity to the people. They wanted to rule out of some misguided belief that it was their right. That was the sad truth of her family, and she was sure the Renné were no different.

She dared a glance toward the mirror. Certainly no elegible young prince would be interested in her—in her name perhaps, but not in her. She tried to smile charmingly and failed completely, watching her face collapse into a frightened self-conscious look. Her face was too long, her eyes not large and doelike as men seemed to prefer them. Her brow was good, and her nose straight and regal enough, and her hair was . . . well it was almost flamboyant it was so splendid: thick and long and curly and corn-silk golden and—

"Ouch!"

"Well, don't hunch your shoulders so. Pull them back," her maid said. "Stand up straight as you should. You are the daughter of a nobleman."

No, Elise thought, *I am the niece of a usurper.*

She came down the stairs and into the rotunda. Braidon Castle was not large but it was a lovely building, she thought. The "candle stair," as it was called, tonight boasted a taper in every sconce; and there were half a hundred of these—two for each stair. The sconces paralleled the curving railing and the candles gave light to the entire rotunda so that the decorations in the white stone walls seemed almost aglow. If one flew down the stairs, which she had done as a child, one could put out most of the candles in one go.

Two footmen stood by the entrance to the reception hall, and they bowed and opened the doors for her. Of course, she should not enter unescorted, but it would annoy her uncle so she did it. She stopped inside the door. All the usual faces were there as well as the party of the Prince of Innes, dressed in more somber colors—no doubt the fashion this season in the old kingdom.

Musicians were playing quietly in the corner, which would be driving her father mad. He detested this treatment of music and its players. Music was meant to be listened to. Listened to in almost reverential silence and with all of one's attention. In fact, there was her father sitting in shadow near the players, listening attentively. Most minstrels would be more flattered by this than by an audience of ten thousand.

"Your Highness." It was Menwyn's vicious wife, Bette: the other person Elise hated utterly. She crossed quickly to her niece and took her arm, as though hoping to hide the fact that Elise had entered alone.

Bette was the most outwardly gracious woman in the castle, but well known to be quietly malicious and vindictive. Elise happened to know that the servants called her the "collie" after the herd dog that would only bite from behind.

The Lady Bette was not an unattractive woman—not that she was beautiful or even pretty—but she did much with what she had. Her long, thin face was made to look more full by careful arrangement of the hair and her small eyes were made larger by skillful use of makeup. Her mouth, her weapon of choice, was surprisingly full and promising—deceptively so.

"Our guests are so looking forward to meeting you," Lady Bette said, her manner expansive and overly merry.

The crowd parted as they crossed the room, men bowing and ladies curtseying to the only child of the Wills family heir—the man who sat alone in the shadows, ignored.

Menwyn bowed as they approached, then reached out to put a hand on her back, pressing her gently but firmly forward. "Your Highness," he said, "Prince Neit of Innes."

A large man, whose face and age were hidden behind a thick, black beard, bowed stiffly. "Your Highness," he said, kissing her offered hand.

She almost cringed at the touch of him, her immediate reaction was so strong.

Is it the man or his intent that fills me with such loathing? she wondered.

"Prince Michael," Menwyn said, introducing the son.

A young man seemed to appear out of the throng, and such a contrast between father and son she had seldom seen. The son, a youth about her own age, was all light and joy where the father was dark and dull. His boyish face seemed about to break into a grin of mischief, while gaiety and humor filled his eyes, already etched with lines from too much laughter. In form he was tall, thin waisted, and lithe—not yet having broadened to his full stature.

Immediately she liked him. Here was a fellow spirit, Elise thought. The nameless minstrel who had ridden out to warn her had not even begun to guess her response to this young man.

Prince Michael had said something that she did not catch and was kissing her hand.

She was not made of stone. Not one part of her.

More than anything she wanted to sit down. To catch her suddenly absent breath and regain control of herself. There was a cousin to whom she was introduced, though he was indistinguishable from the crowd, and then several other notables who had accompanied the Prince. Elise did not register their names.

It was clear that the young prince, Michael, was the joy of his father's circle. He had wit and charm and a mischievous streak that delighted ladies and men alike. He was appropriately respectful and hilariously disrespectful by turn, knowing just when and where to aim his wit and when to be still. But above all he was the brunt of his own jests, for he mocked himself less gently than any other.

It was more than a contrast of appearance between father and son, for whenever Prince Neit spoke he revealed his ponderous thinking, lack of originality, and utter absence of subtlety. He took himself completely seriously, listened poorly, and did not brook disagreement. Elise recognized him for an ass and detested him completely.

He was also a thick bodied man with no neck, and gave her the clear impression that he was actually an animal under a spell that allowed him to pass as human: not an ass but a bear dressed in the clothing of a nobleman. He lumbered through society and was thought merely dull, with only a few simple wants that he would go to any length to fulfill.

Very soon they were called to dinner and she found herself seated between Prince Michael and some cousin of the "Old Prince," as she had come to think of him. The cousin was clearly there to listen and report everything she said. Next to the young prince, her father sat at the table's head, quiet and a bit sullen, for the sham of his situation he found humiliating—even after all the years he had endured it.

To Carral's right the old prince took the place of honor, and beside him Lady Bette smiled and nodded ingratiatingly. Next to her sat Menwyn, of course, secure in his position, not needing to usurp the place at the table's head, too.

"I hope, Lord Carral, that we will have the honor of hearing you play," Prince Michael said to her father.

Elise noted that he was quite respectful as he said this, which won her approval.

Her father tilted his head to one side. "It is hardly an honor, Prince. Will you stay long?"

"A few days, I think. Not long enough. I—I have tried to play many of your pieces, for minstrels come to our doors claiming to have learned them from you. But I will tell you, they are too difficult for me."

"What instrument do you favor?" Carral asked, coming out of his shell a little at this talk of music and the sincerity of the Prince's voice.

"The Fáellute, sir, though after years of dedicated

effort and the best intentions of a dozen teachers, I have now attained a level of mediocrity that, after so great an effort, can only be achieved by the truly talentless. It is a sad thing, for I dearly love music."

"We are not all born to music," Carral said, smiling, "though many wish they were. No doubt you have another calling."

The mischievous grin flashed, then disappeared. "I don't think so, sir, to be completely honest. I seem to have come into this world without any native talent for anything useful. Oh, I am told I have some charm and excel at the art of conversation, but any society that values that would be impoverished indeed. No, I'm afraid I have no talent, though I enjoy nothing more than to hear those of true talent practice their art."

"Beware of him, Lord Carral," the old prince growled, "he has a talent for flattery, if nothing else."

Lady Bette laughed at this as though it were a clever jest, but there was no jesting in the old prince's tone.

"I shall gladly play for you, Prince," Lord Carral said, "and perhaps Elise will sing."

She could not refuse her father, though the thought of singing before this handsome young prince unnerved her terribly. She felt like such a country girl in his presence, for he was so at ease and always found the right thing to say. He was her age but seemed years older.

"You must spend your days here pining for the cities and great houses of the old kingdom," the cousin to Elise's left said. "Some others have been telling me they die of boredom here."

"I have always thought that only bores die of boredom," Elise said, feeling her anger rise, which made her speak before she thought.

Prince Michael laughed. "Well, that explains a number of previously mysterious deaths: Aunt Win, Lord Delddor."

Some of the ladies covered their mouths and tittered annoyingly.

Michael leaned forward so he could see the person to Elise's left. "And have you been well recently?" he asked with great sincerity.

His cousin colored but apparently felt there was no hope of gaining the upper hand here, and turned quietly to his food.

"But you should consider spending some time in the old kingdom, my dear," Lady Bette said softly. "You would gain so much from the experience."

Elise was suddenly very alarmed. She glanced quickly at her father, but as usual his face betrayed nothing. "I couldn't leave Father," Elise said quickly. "He depends on me so. Do you joust, Prince Michael?" she asked quickly. She had not the slightest interest in the tournament, but it seemed that she was the only person in the land between the mountains who was so afflicted. It was always a safe area of conversation.

"When forced to, Your Highness," he said smoothly, "but otherwise I do everything to avoid it. It doesn't hold any particular interest for me and it has the added disadvantage of offering the chance of becoming seriously injured."

"The Prince is accomplished with both lance and sword, my lady," the old prince said, "but his frivolous manner will not allow him to speak of it."

"I see," Elise said. "It is fortunate for us all, don't you think, that so few have talent for art and so many have a talent for killing their fellow men?"

"War is an art, Lady Elise," the old prince said, "and if not for sworn men-at-arms we should be at the mercy of brigands and warlords, always and forever."

Elise was about to answer that these brigands and warlords were, in fact, men-at-arms when Menwyn slipped into the conversation and led it off down a different path. Elise thought the Prince of Innes glowered at her for a moment before turning his attention to her uncle.

Lady Bette and Menwyn carefully guided the conversation after that, and Elise would have been annoyed if not for the feigned interest of Prince Michael, who made gentle mockery of Bette and Menwyn without their even noticing. It was all Elise could do not to laugh out loud.

Dinner ended and they returned to the reception hall where minstrels played. Some few of the guests listened, but most talked. Elise maneuvered herself, she feared rather shamelessly, into the group that included Prince Michael. Here she had the joy of his quick asides to her that included her in the joke while excluding all others.

She was flattered beyond caring that it was calculated to
have this very effect.

A servant came and fetched her to her father, and her
heart suddenly began to beat against her ribs. She had
foolishly agreed to sing.

"What will it be?" her father asked, deftly tuning his
lute. "'The Winter's Spring'?"

"Do you remember the old tune of Gwyden Dore?"

"We have not tried my hand at that in many a year,"
Carral said, "not since you were a girl."

"But you remember it, don't you?"

Her father seldom forgot a tune.

"I can manage if you can."

She took her place, standing by him and closed her
eyes as her father played the introductory phrases.

"Gwyden Dore was a man of lore,
A knight of battle true."

She faltered only over a line or two, and her father
did not falter at all, for it was a simple tune and did not
tax his talent. Around her melody he embroidered subtly,
never drawing attention from the song itself, as though
he put a frame around a picture—a beautiful frame,
certainly—but its purpose was only to enhance the
central theme. He was too generous a soul, Elise knew.

The song she sang bore the tragic ending, as she had
preferred as a young girl, not the ending her mysterious
minstrel had mentioned. But now that she was a little

older perhaps a happy ending would not be so unacceptable, though less romantic for all that. She glanced at the young prince and was bewildered to find him staring at her raptly. She almost stumbled over a line.

The song ended to applause and calls for another, but Elise slipped away as quickly as she could, knowing full well that the minstrels had with them a girl with a voice like an angel and that everyone really wanted to hear her father play. Even the minstrels who would be invited to perform with Carral would watch raptly as he played—minstrels who heard music every night of their lives.

Elise stepped into the shadow of a column for a moment, catching her breath and calming her heart. From her hiding place she surveyed the room, hoping that no one would notice how intently she searched and for whom. Just as she was about to resign herself to disappointment she found Prince Michael across the room. His back was to her and he was talking to another—a man, she was glad to see, and not one of her witless cousins. But there was something odd about this conversation, Elise thought, for the Prince seemed stiff, almost rigid, not his graceful self.

The man he spoke to moved so that she could see him a little. He was dressed in the long overrobe traditionally worn by knights and he was tall—as tall as Michael, but broader. The man shifted again and came into view. He was old, she thought immediately, though she was not sure why, for he was clearly strongly built—not bent or feeble. He stood before Michael with his great arms crossed over his chest, and he lectured the young prince. Elise was sure of it. Lectured him sternly.

The man caught sight of her just then and turned his head her way, giving her a withering look. In the candle-light his eyes were dark, set in a hard, square face. The Prince turned to see what the other looked at, then they both turned away. The conversation lasted only a moment more and then Michael turned and came directly toward her.

He crossed the room, his shoulders hunched, his whole manner changed. She could not read it. Could not tell what had transpired that had changed him so.

"My lady," he said formally as he came up.

"Who was that you just spoke with?" she asked.

The Prince glanced back over his shoulder, but the old man was gone. "That was Eremon," he said, his voice flat, devoid of all expression. "My father's counselor." He reached out suddenly and snatched up her hand, almost pushing her behind the column.

The Prince looked directly into her eyes, his manner desperate, all of his charm fallen away. "Do not agree to marry me," he said suddenly, his voice quavering a little. "You cannot know what it will mean. They have no care for you or me, but only for the son they dream they will place on the throne. The son that will be taken from you. Do not let your family press you into this union, Lady Elise. It will be your ruin." With that he let go her hand and swept off through the crowd toward the far doors.

She was left shaking, her hand hurting where he had squeezed it, her heart aching for this young man trapped in the designs of his father, any vision of a life of his own stolen from him. Stolen as her own family conspired to steal hers.

EIGHTEEN

Carral could not quite believe what he was doing, ascending to the tower hoping to have a conversation with a man who claimed to be a ghost. A stranger who professed to have knowledge about the intrigues of the noble families.

Had I allies, real allies, Carral thought, *I would not be driven to this.*

It was the beginning of the fortnight, and servants would have brought food and drink to the tower to placate the uneasy spirits who were believed to wander the old castle—were even seen to do so at times, or so people claimed.

Carral was no believer in such things, but there had been times over the years when a strange chill had crept over him and he had felt as though another were in the room—but no one answered when he spoke, nor did a door open letting anyone leave. But the feeling passed.

This ghost, however, spoke in the warm tones of a living man. His footsteps could be heard, his breathing. Carral had tried to find out who he was, but to no avail. So many came to Braidon Castle, some, like the Prince of Innes and his family, to plot with Menwyn, but most came to sit at the feet of Lord Carral Wills and hear him play. Too many came, lately, Carral thought, and it was impossible to find his ghost among them.

Minstrels ranged far across the land, and learned a great deal. Many were wellborn and not poor. They did not lower themselves to play for money but only for the adulation, the recognition of their skills. When they traveled they mingled with nobles at the highest level, even among the families which plotted with the allies of the Renné and Wills. His ghost would be one of these, but how he had avoided Carral's detection within the castle, Carral did not know.

The final tread creaked beneath his foot, and he opened the door to the tower room. The aroma of food and wine mixed with burning elm wood wafted out. For a moment he paused, listening, oddly apprehensive. But then he went in, not asking if any other were there, as he was tempted to do.

He found the chair by the fire, and as he reached out toward the table there was the sound of someone clearing his throat. "Is that my ghost?"

"I belong to no one, sir," a familiar voice said.

Carral almost sighed with relief. He was not sure why. "You will not tell me who you are?"

"Who I was is of little interest now," the ghost said, not without a smile in his voice.

Carral heard the soft splash of liquid into a glass.

"Hold out your hand," the other said, and a wineglass

was passed into his waiting fingers. Was that the heat of another's hand that he felt?

"You have met the Prince of Innes?"

"Yes, though it was not the first time."

"And his counselor?" The ghost eased up from its chair and crossed the room. The staccato of rain beating on slate came to him. Then, far off, a rumor of thunder.

"In the distance I see lightning," the other said. "A storm sweeping north from the old kingdom."

"My daughter says that thunder is the precise aural equivalent of lightning. Do you think that's true?"

"Your daughter is a perceptive young woman. They mean to send her to live with the Prince of Innes—'to complete her education.' Once in that house I don't think even her strong will can last long. You don't know Hafydd. I shouldn't like to be left to match wills with him."

"Was that a jest—to match 'wills' with him?"

The ghost shifted by the window, but did not move away. A deep stutter of thunder shuddered the glass.

"But then you are a ghost, what care you for the threats of men?"

"Hafydd has learned more than he should. I am not certain even I am safe from him now. Be wary; he has not begun to work his knavery yet. He bides his time, hoping to keep his knowledge secret. Better it were not known until the last. Until his army—the army of Lord Menwyn and the Prince of Innes—has flushed the Renné out into the open." The ghost pivoted where he stood and suddenly his voice was very clear——he faced Carral now. "Do not let your daughter go with the Prince."

"But what can I do?" Carral said. "I can forbid it certainly, but Menwyn has overruled me before and will do so again. I am powerless . . . My only daughter and I can do nothing to protect her."

"Then we must whisk her away," the ghost said.

Carral slumped back in his chair. "Unless you know some secret chamber within the castle . . . They would have her back in a day." *What foolishness was this man speaking?*

"There are several secret chambers, but that's not what I have in mind." The ghost turned back to the window—— Carral heard him move——and stood silently for a long moment. "We can spirit her away. I've thought it through. We'll need the aid of several of the minstrels who are guests of Braidon Castle, but that shouldn't be difficult. Just the right people are here. One would think that someone had planned it."

NINETEEN

Tam and the others bent over the map, the boat finding her own way on a stretch of broad river. "There is no island of Speaking Stone," Tam said, "nor any of the other islands we passed, let alone a lake of stone trees." He looked around him at the low limestone banks and the hills rising up out of the forest. "We could be anywhere on this map or not on it at all."

Fynnol leaned forward awkwardly and gazed at the creased paper. He hunched over his wound, protecting it. His stint at the oars had set the injury aflame again. At night he had difficulty sleeping, and he didn't take up the oars now or draw a bowstring. Tam often saw him stiffen and shut his eyes hard, remaining still for a moment or two. Then he would take a slow tentative breath and sigh as the spasm passed.

Baore sat whittling a tholepin to replace one that had been broken. His big hands moved with a sureness and grace, the astonishingly sharp knife deftly paring away what wasn't needed.

"Do you remember what Eber said?" Cynddl asked. "That Speaking Stone was not easily found? He also said that Alaan had found him, as we did, 'And few who travel the river have managed that.' I did not mark this as odd at the time, but it's taken on a different meaning now. Eber's island is on the secret river——maybe one of the 'many branches.'" Cynddl looked at the map again, his dark eyebrows knitting together. He tapped the paper with a fine-boned finger. "Somewhere in the darkness, below the ford at Willowwand, we left the River Wynnd."

"But where are we now?" Fynnol cried.

"I don't know, Fynnol. There seemed to have been signs that indicated we were on the secret river: trees I'd never seen before, animals either unheard of or long thought dead and gone. I've seen no signs of these today. But there really are no landmarks on the river now until we find the north bridge. Five days, it should be from the ford at Willowwand. Four days hence."

"Or three or nine," Fynnol said sharply, "or perhaps we won't see it at all. Can we miss sections of the Wynnd when we're on this other river? The Wyrr, I think it should be called, as the Wynnd once was."

No one spoke for a moment, the silence burdened with unspoken worries and fears. "I did not like the way that man-at-arms talked about the 'black guards,' and Alaan said something similar. I fear it's almost certain we'll find some waiting for us at the north bridge, and fearsome, murderous men they appear to be."

"Blackguards . . ." Fynnol said, forcing the jest out with a grimace. He touched his side gingerly. "We'd best prepare. These others were intent on killing us . . . and showed no interest in discussing the merits of this scheme. Get out your whetstone, Baore—we've weapons to edge."

Baore didn't smile. He stopped his whittling, knife held loosely in hand. "I'd hoped I wouldn't have to fight another man for whom I've neither name nor anger. I came to buy horses and have a bit of adventure, Fynnol. I didn't come to kill strangers . . . or to be killed by them either." He looked down at the knife in his hand, and Tam thought Baore caught sight of his own reflection in the blade. Suddenly the big Valeman turned away and busied himself fitting the tholepin in its place.

But the bridge did not appear on the fourth day or on the fifth or the sixth. Cynddl, Baore, and Tam took turns at the oars, and when not rowing kept their bows to hand. They watched the banks and river ahead with an intensity that only fear could breed.

Fog appeared at times, especially in the evenings and early mornings, and the occupants of the boat would fall silent and watchful. Nothing strange appeared out of the gloom this time, though a heron on a log caused them all to jump when it croaked almost in Fynnol's ear. It took noisily to flight, beating its wings along the gunwale, and the occupants of the boat laughed for the first time in days.

On the seventh evening Cynddl stood, gazing at the

shore. "Now here is land that looks familiar! The bridge can't be far now—a day's journey at most. Let's put ashore here in case we're closer than I think."

A low bank and narrow beach allowed them to land the boat and make a camp. Baore, self-appointed fire starter, kindled a small blaze while Tam and Fynnol set out to find fish. Cynddl unrolled his map and examined it closely by the failing light. But something about Baore tugged at his attention and he turned to find the big Valeman staring unhappily into the flames.

"Are you sorry you came, Baore?" Cynddl asked quietly.

Baore nodded, not looking up. "Yes." He almost whispered. "Yes. I've killed a man and nearly been killed myself. I'd no choice, I know, but what does that matter? If I'd stayed at home it would never have happened."

"But if you'd stayed at home the rest of us would likely have died at the ford. It was you who dragged the boat free and unhorsed the rider. We'd have been caught and murdered."

Baore added a few sticks to the fire, and it crackled and flared. "I know, but regrets don't care for reason, Cynddl. I've watched men turn wicked sons from their doors. They'd no choice, but even so, regrets all but devoured them. I've not chosen regret, Cynddl. It's chosen me."

Cynddl found himself looking at the big man anew, surprised to find him so thoughtful. "Perhaps that's so. But what will you do now? You can't go back alone—

not with these men who hunt you riding the roads."

"No, I can't go back, as you say. And I've my cousin and Tam to think of. I can't leave them. We go to the Wold of Kerns as planned. And then home. Home by autumn." He considered a moment. "And then we try to forget."

The others returned, bearing their catch of sun trout and silt bass.

"Well, here are two men too serious," Fynnol said. His injury was not paining him so and it showed in his spirits. "Come along, now. Cynddl will take us around the bridge by the secret river, and we'll be in the Wold of Kerns by noon. We'll have our pick of the best horses, not to mention the young ladies who'll be desperate to meet anyone so exotic as a Valeman."

Neither Cynddl nor Baore smiled, however, and supper became a subdued affair. Darkness fell and a small breeze from the north sprang up after a day of calm. Tam thought he could feel the mountain air in the wind, and it reminded him of the Vale, which seemed very distant suddenly.

Not so distant, he reminded himself. *A ride that can be measured in days.*

They settled down to sleep, keeping their usual watches, but sleep eluded Tam and the breathing of the others seemed to say that sleep was not much interested in any of them. Overhead, the stars were winter bright, and Tam lay, gazing at the heavens, wondering if they would find the bridge the next day, and if they did, what would happen. There was no going back now. Even pulling against the current to the ford at Willowwand would be almost impossible. They could take to the road and walk north but it was a long way by foot, and their attackers from the ford were undoubtedly riding south.

Cynddl offered their only hope—if he was right about where they were. Tomorrow they would look for the bridge perhaps from the bank, the boat following. There might be a way of slipping quietly by: after all, they had surprised the men at the ford. It was possible the men waiting didn't really believe their quarry would come down the river. Perhaps they thought no one would be so foolish.

The stars wavered and faded, and Tam slept. He dreamed that a man carrying a sword walked about the edge of their encampment, a dark faceless form in the shadows of the trees. And Tam couldn't tell if this man was their sentry or if he meant them harm.

Tam woke to a hand on his shoulder. Cynddl leaned close and whispered. "There are men nearby in the wood. Make no sound. Load everything into the boat. Quickly."

Tam rolled to his feet, snatching up his sword, staring into the darkness. Their fire was a glowing eye, staring upward, unblinking. He smelled the fragrance of it immediately.

It is like Telanon Bridge, Tam thought, and felt a dread creep over him. *Men died that night.*

Fynnol and Baore were gathering up their belongings. Though he strained, Tam could hear nothing but the furtive sounds of his companions and the breeze drifting through the wood.

In a moment they were aboard their boat, bobbing out into the night river. A low haze swelled up from the water, curling like vaporous moonlight. *Not thick enough to hide us,* Tam thought.

The moon waned into the west, but Tam feared they might still be seen. Baore shipped the oars but kept them still, letting the current carry the boat along in the shadow of the trees. The other three nocked arrows and waited, searching the night for movement, hearing a threat in every forest sound.

As silently as he could Baore moved them away from the riverbank, and Tam realized this was necessary— there were often rocks near the shore. The shadows of the trees clung to them a moment, then they were gliding through a patch of moonlight and a shout broke the silence.

Tam heard the arrows in the air but could not begin to guess their source. The boat rocked wildly as they all dropped below the gunwales. Overhead, arrows hissed and buried themselves in the hull with precise *thwacks*. For a moment the archers had their range and then the arrows were seemingly loosed at some other target. The boat had been lost in a shadow or a ripple in the water had drawn the archers' eyes.

No one made a sound. Cynddl raised his head, searching the dark river. Men shouted from the bank, and in the distance came faint answers.

"We're in a patch of fog," Cynddl whispered. "I can see the bridge, I think: there are torches waving. Ready your bows and keep your faces down. They're waiting for us."

Tam heard no sound but their quick breathing. The river carried them lazily forward. The smell of their fire was in the air, and Tam realized they'd been much nearer the bridge than they'd realized—just around the bend.

He risked a glance and saw the torches guttering in the gloom. The bridge was a black arc curving out of the mist and on it he could see men moving.

"Into the water," Tam whispered. He dropped his bow and slipped over the side as silent as an otter. "They'll see the boat."

Cynddl came over the stern with barely a ripple. Then Fynnol.

"Baore . . .?" Fynnol whispered.

The big Valeman appeared at the stern, wavered a second and then Cynddl and Tam had hold of him, lowering him into the water. Tam felt an arrow protruding from Baore's shoulder, and a wave of nausea and fear swept over him. *Baore was wounded!*

"We have to get away from the boat," Tam heard himself say. "Can you swim, Baore?"

"I don't know," he answered. The sound of his voice, so filled with dread, struck Tam.

"We'll bear you up, Baore," Fynnol whispered. "I'll take his head."

The four clung together, and treading water slowly,

separated themselves from the boat, watching it drift off on the current—their haven slipping away.

Tam felt Baore's weight dragging him down. "Baore?" he said close to his friend's ear. There was a hiss of breath, as though Baore tried to answer, but no sound.

Tam kept his legs pumping, sinking low in the water until it lapped over his chin. He laid his head back, and the quick sound of his own ragged breathing sounded in his ears.

A shout went up, and the air filled with arrows.

"Turn your faces away," Cynddl whispered. "They'll be seen in the moonlight."

Tam turned slowly in the water, expecting an arrow to thunder into the back of his skull at any moment. Men were shouting and running across the bridge. Arrows struck wood repeatedly and buried themselves in the Valemen's belongings with a soft sound eerily like steel burying in flesh.

What if they realize the boat is empty? Tam thought.

He risked a look. The bridge was drawing slowly near. The river narrowed between rising banks, though not so high as at Telanon Bridge. The course was wider here, too, and in the center of the span Tam could see a supporting pillar which the boat would pass to the right. Tam began to move them more to the left, and he felt Cynddl begin to do the same.

The men on the bridge were in a fury now, and the sound of arrows striking the boat filled the air. The boat passed into the shadow of the bridge, thudding dully once into stone. The men rushed to the other side, some few running off along the bank.

There was nothing the companions could do but remain still in the water, let the current carry them, and hope the feeble moonlight did not betray them. They leaned their heads close together, faces hidden from the heavens. Tam even closed his eyes, like a child who did not want to be seen. On the bridge men were calling to others on the western shore, and their voices were so close.

The shadow of the bridge passed over Tam like the wing of a great bird. For a moment the sounds of the river changed, echoing hollowly. Tam could hear their harsh breathing, then they were in the moonlit river again, floating among the stars.

There was no sudden shout of discovery, no arrows loosed toward them. Tam heard Fynnol let out a long-held breath. They floated on, moving their legs and arms only enough to bear up their companion. Baore was breathing shallowly, in pain, but he was conscious now.

"Tam?" Fynnol whispered so low Tam could almost have imagined it. "Go after the boat."

He hesitated only a second, then struck off as silently as he could, wondering how he would find their boat on the darkened river. The icy spring water seemed to seep into him, and he began to shiver.

Swim, he ordered himself. *Swim to bring the warmth back.*

Tam forced reluctant limbs to obey his commands.

Moving forward, searching the dark river for the more substantial shadow of their boat. Without it they were lost. No way to treat Baore's wound, no blankets to warm him, no food, not even the means to hunt. They'd be weaponless and easy prey for the men who pursued them. Tam tried to force these thoughts from his mind; it was enough to be weakened by cold.

The stars swirled around him as he parted the waters. They wavered on the surface, swinging wildly, and then shimmered to stillness.

I am swimming through the heavens, he thought. *What would Eber think of that?*

He had passed beyond the men crashing along the shore. Alone in his own ribbon of stars. If the river carried him up into the sky now, he would not be surprised. Tam turned about, searching the darkness. If Baore had only painted their boat white instead of such a deep blue . . . Would the currents carry the boat to the bank or into some small eddy? Or might it stay to the strongest current and continue south? Eventually it would go ashore, he decided. That's what his experience with lost boats told him. But which shore and when?

He kept moving his arms and legs, not so worried now about the noise he was making. For a moment he wondered if he should simply lie on his back and let the river take him where it would—carry him along as it carried the boat. Would they not end up in the same place?

Tam shook his head. He was falling into fancy.

He pushed himself to greater speed and began to angle across the current; then, when he neared the shore, he began to cross the other way. The boat was out here somewhere, adrift. He had to find it. Find it before he grew tired. Once he was forced ashore to rest, it would be over. The boat would be gone.

For a moment he rolled onto his back, moving only enough to stay afloat. Overhead the stars spread, sharply defined, across the dark vault of the sky. He felt as though he were staring down at them from a great height. So far to fall.

Tam rolled again, and swallowed a mouthful of water. He choked aloud, and nearby something moved, causing him to recoil. But it was only a bird. A small heron had been perched on a drifting log. Tam looked again: a dark shape, starlight faintly illuminating a long, regular curve.

In two strokes he had his hand on the gunwale. He hung there a moment, taking long deep breaths, water running from his hair and eyes, relief washing through him.

And then he realized the boat lay head to current, the broad river flowing by. He reached out and felt her painter running taut over the bow—caught on something on the river bottom. And then it went slack in his hand and the boat slewed slowly about.

It took two tries to climb aboard, as the chill of the river had sapped his strength. Finally Tam floundered aboard, collapsing for a moment to shiver on the floorboards. There were arrows everywhere—embedded in

wood, in their baggage, even lying loose in the bottom.
If they had been caught aboard . . .

There was no time to contemplate what might have
been. He stripped off his dripping clothes and dug out
something dry, staring back down the river into the darkness.

How would he find the others? He shipped a pair of
oars and slowed the progress of the boat, taking a
moment to think. With only two to keep Baore afloat,
they would need to get out of the river soon. They would
go ashore on the eastern bank, for the men from the
bridge had gone down the west. Tam struck out for the
shore as silently as he could, listening for sounds of their
pursuers or for his companions.

He thought about Baore's wound—an arrow deep in
his shoulder, it had seemed. If no major blood vessels
were severed he would likely survive, as long as the
wound didn't fester.

The shadow of the shoreline loomed over him, blot-
ting out the stars. Tam felt the hair on his neck bristling.
If any of their hunters had come down this shore . . .
He moved his oars even more carefully.

A bird called not far off, and then again.

The sorcerer thrush, he realized. Not a night bird at
all . . .

"Cynddl . . .?"

"Here," came the reply.

In a moment he'd found them, drawn up in a shallow.
Without a word they helped Baore aboard; and Tam was

striking out silently for the river's center, feeling safe for the first time since Cynddl had wakened him.

Morning stole the glitter from the stars and a gray tide flooded the sky. Then, mysteriously, it was blue.

Tam looked at Baore, who lay crumpled in the bottom of the boat, his good hand holding his shoulder. His eyes were closed and he lay utterly still, only his chest rising and falling, though gently, as though even breathing brought him pain.

"Baore . . .?"

The big man nodded, his eyes remaining closed.

"We've traveled far enough," Fynnol said. "We need to get Baore ashore and see to his wound."

"We're too close to the bridge yet," Cynddl said. "We have to go on for an hour or two at least."

Fynnol turned on the story finder. "We're taking Baore ashore the first place we find."

"Fynnol? Cynddl is right," Tam said softly. "We need to go on for an hour or two. We haven't come half a league or anywhere near it. We'd be foolish to stop."

Fynnol stared at Tam a moment, then he pushed Cynddl aside and took up a pair of oars. "Then let's put some distance between ourselves and the bridge." Ignoring his injury, he dug the blades deep into the river, and drove them forward. Tam took up a pair of oars and joined him, straining so that he felt the muscles in his back pull and his shoulders ache.

* * *

An hour later Cynddl found a place for them to land. They slid their boat up a small side stream curtained by willows, and moored against a grassy embankment. A fire was kindled in a small clearing and Baore's wound examined. The arrow had entered the mound of muscle below the shoulder, and though there was little blood seeping from the wound, the flesh was inflamed and swollen to a strange hardness.

As gently as he could, Cynddl probed the wound. The arrow in the skin looked so unnatural, the wooden shaft emerging from a small, red mouth. "I don't think it's in the bone but it's deep in the muscle, Baore."

The big Valeman nodded. He kept eyes averted from the wound, as though it were too awful to look at, and sweat dripped from his face, though the morning wasn't hot.

Tam and Cynddl examined the arrows bristling from the boat, trying to determine the shape of the head.

"I wish Aliel were here," Cynddl said. "We need a proper healer." He touched the head of an arrow. "It won't back out easily, nor was it meant to, but I don't think we can push it through. My knowledge is poor. There are vessels that, if severed, might bleed so badly we'd never stop them." The Fáel stared at the arrow, weighing it in his hand, then pressing the point gently against his palm.

Cynddl's uncertainty disturbed Tam. Men died of

lesser wounds than Baore's. A few years earlier a neighbor hadn't survived a gash accidentally inflicted by a scythe. The wound had corrupted and swelled with poisons. It was a slow death, ghastly and horrifying.

Cynddl took a long breath and looked at Tam, returning from whatever place he went to contemplate. "We'll have to cut around the wound enough to draw the arrow back, but carefully, so that we sever no blood vessels. I don't know what else to do."

Tam nodded. He knew less than Cynddl about such things, he was sure. "I'll help any way I can."

Cynddl produced a small, thin-bladed knife and tested the edge. Baore held out his good hand. "Give me that," he said. He had Fynnol find his whetstone and then, gritting his teeth, sat for half an hour with the stone held between his knees, meticulously honing Cynddl's blade.

"Here," Baore said as he finished. "It will cut glass now, so wield it with care."

Cynddl set the blade carefully aside and then probed the wound again. A shirt was torn for dressings, and Cynddl produced a poultice of yarrow and arnica that would help bind the skin together. The story finder began by cleaning around the wound, washing it with water from a nearby spring. "We'll have to keep the opening clear so that I'll see any vessels," Cynddl said. "Can I begin, Baore?"

The Valeman nodded, turning his head away. Cynddl took up the knife, his knuckles white, and broadened the opening in the skin, a thin red line following the glittering steel. It took a long time to go deep enough to free the head of the arrow, and Baore, despite his strength, cried out more than once at the pain. Finally the arrow was worked free and the wound closed. They bound it as best they could, applying the poultice Cynddl had made.

Baore lay on his side, head buried in his good arm, and moved very little the rest of that day. The fire was smothered—smoke had betrayed them twice already—and the three companions took it in turn to watch the river.

Baore didn't rest easily but muttered and thrashed in his sleep, waking occasionally, bathed in sweat. Eyes wide, he stared at the others in incomprehension, and then realized who they were and sank back down into his muddled blankets. His companions looked at one another in fear, knowing there was little they could do.

In the morning Cynddl removed Baore's dressing and found the wound still open. To Tam's horror it seemed to glow like a coal and was hot to the touch, oozing a milky yellow fluid. Baore couldn't move his shoulder for the pain, which had spread into the pit of his arm.

"I'm cold, Cynddl," Baore said, though there was a sheen of sweat on his face.

"We'll give you our blankets and kindle a fire." Cynddl renewed the poultice, but Tam thought the story finder's expression more grim than usual, which was saying a great deal. When Baore was resting beneath their blankets Cynddl drew the others aside.

"I don't like the turn that Baore's wound is taking. Keep him warm and make him drink water. He must pass the poisons through. I'm going to search nearby. There are other plants that might help bring down his fever and bind the wound." He put his hand on Fynnol's shoulder, for the Valeman was as white as Baore. "Try not to look so, Fynnol. It's better for Baore if he sees we believe he'll heal—and he will."

Cynddl went off into the forest and Tam and Fynnol sat quietly watching Baore, afraid to speak and disturb him. Baore complained of the cold for a time, then threw the blankets aside, saying that he was burning up. All the while sweat ran from him. The pain, Tam thought, was considerable, for the big Valeman would curl up like a child and hide his face, occasionally unable to suppress a moan. Fynnol kept bearing him water to drink, but Baore had little interest in it and took only a sip. Now and then he fell into sleep for a few moments and then he muttered and raved and thrashed about.

Tam tried to comfort Fynnol, who was ill with worry for his cousin. He wouldn't eat, and he sat still as stone watching his cousin. "He didn't want to come," he said to Tam in the afternoon, "but I wouldn't listen. I've never listened. What Baore might want has never meant much to me. No, he must always do what I wish, and now look what I've brought him to."

"Baore's not a child. He could have said no, but he didn't."

"You don't know the half of it. I know what to say to

make poor Baore do as I wish. I know how to shame him and praise him until he finally agrees. I put that arrow in his shoulder, Tam, as surely as if I'd shot it myself."

Cynddl returned, finally, bearing plants wrapped in bark.

"Bloodwood," he said, "to bind the wound. And bark from the waterwillow to bring down his fever."

Fire was rekindled so that a tea might be made of the waterwillow bark, and Cynddl soaked the leaves of the bloodwood in the boiling water and then, while still hot, bound them over Baore's wound. He was forced to drink the tea, and then covered again in all their blankets.

Night came with no sign of improvement, and the others divided up the watches, not to guard against attackers but to watch over Baore and to make more of the waterwillow tea for him to drink. They kept the fire burning, no longer caring who might see it. One death seemed so near that they would risk four without question.

The fog lay all around him, feathers of gray falling and swirling. Baore sat in the boat's stern, facing forward, oars in hand. He made his slow way through the murk, only the squeak of the oars moving between tholepins breaking the silence. The surface of the water was flat, opaque, as though he were afloat on a sea of unmoving mercury. Along the oars gray pearls of water formed, sliding up and down the shafts as he rowed. His shoulder pained him and he felt weak, almost unable to work the sweeps.

"Where am I?" he whispered. *Where were the others?*

And then a face broke the surface nearby, silver-gray drops rolling off pale cheeks. It was a woman's face, white as wax, eyes like moons, hair a tangle of kelp.

"Who are you?" Baore asked, his voice sounding unnaturally hollow in this place.

"Sianon," the water spirit answered.

"How have I come to this place?"

"You do not know?"

Baore shook his head.

"You have been pierced by an arrow, and now the wound spreads its poisons toward your heart."

Something loomed ahead, half hidden by mist, and then stone stairs appeared so close that Baore could not back the oars in time. The boat thudded heavily against them, throwing Baore to the floorboards.

"Here is your destination," the water spirit said. She was standing up to the neck in the water, moving neither hands nor legs.

Baore crawled forward, not sure why, and stumbled out onto the stone quay, falling to his knees. But even this he could not sustain and toppled, rolling onto his back, too weak to rise.

A woman knelt by him now, not a water spirit, but a woman dressed like a warrior. She wore a sword. Baore pressed his eyes tightly closed and then opened them again.

"Who are you?"

"Sianon."

"What is this place?"

"You are at Death's gate, Baore Talon, and it is about to open and you will pass inside, into that lightless place where all men's stories are lost. Once you have passed through that gate there is no way back to the world of life. Do you understand?"

Baore's eyes clouded, as though fog had drifted across them. He felt a cold hand take his own. Sianon bent over him, gazing at him, eyes as beautiful and dark as the night.

"Look at me, Baore Talon . . . Do you not feel love for me? Do you not?"

Baore thought he'd never seen such unworldly beauty. To look at her was to feel a blade in one's heart.

"I feel cold," he said.

A scraping sound seemed to emanate from the rocks. Sianon's eyes darted up, then back to Baore.

"Death's gate opens," she said quickly. "But I will save you. I will carry you back to the world of life, if you will do as I ask."

"What . . . what is it you want?"

"Part of that life I give you will be mine."

The scraping was louder now, as though the earth were being wrenched open.

"No . . ." Baore forced himself to say. "No. Better death than to give one's life to a ghoul. Better death." He shook his hand from hers and squirmed away. The scraping stopped and darkness was cast down on the stone like light spilling from a doorway.

He closed his eyes. He felt cold hands take hold of him and lift him up, and then he fell into darkness.

Late in the night Tam woke to find the fire burned down to coals and Cynddl, whose watch it was, slumped against a tree, snoring softly. Fynnol, too, was asleep, exhausted by worry.

Tam began to rise, but the smallest movement caught his eye. Something crouched over Baore: a woman, it seemed to Tam, lithe with long, copper-gold hair. But she was dressed as a man. And then he realized he could see the moonlit river through her! She wavered like air shimmering above rocks on a hot summer's day. She had risen and was moving, his eyes not quite able to follow, as though she flickered in and out of existence with each step. For an instant he could see her at the river's edge, and then she was gone.

Tam lay very still for some time, then rose gingerly, his eyes jumping from shadow to shadow. He wondered if some sprite had come to bear poor Baore's spirit away. But Baore slept quietly, neither muttering nor tossing as he'd done all day. Gently Tam put a hand to the big man's forehead, and found it neither warm nor cool.

Cynddl woke with a start. "How is Baore?" he whispered.

"Better. I think his fever has broken."

Cynddl let out a long sigh. "The waterwillow," he whispered. "Let's hope the bloodwood works as well."

Tam looked out over the river, where a low mist lay, lit by moon and starlight. "I woke a moment ago and saw a—an apparition. A ghostly woman bent over Baore. I couldn't see what she was doing. And then she went into the river, I think, though it was difficult for the eye to follow."

"Our apparition," Cynddl said, turning to look out over the river.

"But this was something else. I saw her shape. A woman without doubt, though she appeared to wear the clothing of a man."

"Yes, the apparition is taking form. I've seen her twice since that first night. In the stone forest she broke the surface by our boat—we thought it was a fish, remember? The second time was at the north bridge. I glimpsed her beneath the span as we floated by. Each time she's been more substantial."

"But who is she?" Tam said, rather plaintively. "*What* is she?"

Cynddl shook his head, looking out over the river. "I don't know, and I'm afraid to guess. I hope she doesn't mean us harm."

"I'd rather have men-at-arms following us than ghosts," Tam said.

"That might not be as foolish as it sounds," Cynddl said quickly. "Though I don't think this is a ghost at all. She's of the river, somehow, and like water, transparent, only reflecting the colors of the surroundings—the sky and shore."

"But what did she want with Baore?"

"To heal him, I would guess."

"But why?"

Cynddl crouched down by Baore and pulled the blankets up over his wounded shoulder, pausing to listen to him breathe. "I don't know, Tam. You ask me questions as though I know something about the Greensprings. I know almost nothing. I haven't found a story that explains our apparition. And somehow I don't think I will." Cynddl, too, felt Baore's forehead, then stood, staring down at the peacefully sleeping figure. "Why did we find our way onto the secret river? Why did we run aground on Speaking Stone in the dark and not go through the rapids where the current certainly should have taken us? There have always been strange stories of the Greensprings, Tam. We're not the first men to have seen a specter rise out of the river."

"But have you ever heard of a river spirit rising up and healing a man's wound?"

Cynddl looked at Tam, his eyes impenetrable shadows. "No, I haven't."

Tam looked down at Baore. "Perhaps we should merely count ourselves lucky and not worry." He looked at Cynddl again. "But you don't think so, do you?"

"We'll see where the river takes us," Cynddl said.

"That's one thing we can be sure of. There's no getting off the river now until we reach the Wold of Kerns. I don't think I should tell Baore or Fynnol what I saw tonight. Baore needs to recover and not worry, and Fynnol's world has been shaken enough."

"Fynnol's world . . .?" the story finder said. "He needs to learn that the world isn't defined by what he mocks and what he doesn't. But as you say—Baore doesn't need the worry—and Fynnol . . . The world will impose itself upon him soon enough."

Baore rolled over then and muttered softly, pushing his blankets aside. Tam bent down near him, pulling the coverings up over his shoulders.

Baore's eyes opened. "Where am I?" he asked in a dry whisper.

"You're here with us, on the bank of the River Wynnd," Tam said. "Your fever has broken. Do you feel it?"

"But I was at Death's gate," Baore moaned. "A ghostly maiden bargained with me, but I refused her. The gate ground open and I felt cold hands take me up."

Tam wondered if the fever had truly broken. Poor Baore was raving. "You're not at Death's gate, Baore. You're healing, in fact. Bloodwood and waterwillow do their work. But sleep and dream of home. Dream of sailing on the lakes. We'll watch over you and keep all ghosts away."

Baore nodded, his eyes closing of their own will. His breathing became deep and even, and his head rolled a little to one side.

Tam looked up at Cynddl, who made a quick warding sign toward the river. The story finder drew his sword from his baggage and knelt down by Baore. "I'll do my penance for falling asleep on my watch. You sleep, Tam; I will keep Baore safe. Death will not take him," he said and shifted his grip on his sword, as though such a weapon might keep death at bay.

TWENTY

The next day Baore was weak and still troubled by pain, but the wound had begun to bind and looked less corrupt. Fynnol thanked their Fáel companion over and over for his bloodwood and waterwillow bark, but Cynddl only shrugged and took no credit.

On the fourth day Baore rolled out of his blanket and sat up, blinking. "Can we not have some cooked fish, at least?" he said. "And, Cynddl, where are the greens and wild mushrooms the Fáel are famous for? I shall die of privation soon if we go on like this."

The companions looked at Baore, then at one another and smiled for the first time in days. A fire was kindled and fish lured from the river. Cynddl prowled through the wood and came back with fiddleheads, thimbleberries, fairy-caps, and the largest springmoon the Valemen had ever seen.

"I see the moon is full—at least beneath the trees!" Fynnol said when he saw the fungus.

A feast was held there on the bank of the River Wynnd to celebrate Baore's deliverance. His arm wouldn't be useful for some days, but that was a small price to pay.

Fynnol was almost recovered from his own injury and could take a short turn at the oars if needed.

They'd lost two pairs of oars over the last few days, and under Baore's tutelage Tam took up their axe and hewed a pair from a newly fallen spruce.

On the sixth day they took to the river, Baore with a mild glow on his face again, the wounded arm tied across his chest. The pain was not gone, but was near to bearable, at least for Baore, whom Tam thought could stand more pain than most. But despite his apparent return to health Baore's spirits remained downcast, or perhaps merely subdued. Tam was sure that standing before the gate of Death would have such an effect on anyone.

"I'll never look at a river the same way again," Fynnol said. "Imagine if the path from my house to Baore's suddenly began leading elsewhere—to Tam's, for instance, or out of the Vale in a short walk, though it isn't a short walk out of the Vale." Fynnol was trailing a fishing line over the side as they went, though he did it rather halfheartedly. "What kind of world is this that can't be relied on to be the same from one day to the next? Where roads could lead one morning to Dingle Shale and the next to Parth? We might be going north now, rather than south, and never know it."

"Once we reach the Wold of Kerns, Fynnol," Baore said, "we'll be off this cursed river and on a road that I've never heard of leading anywhere but north—to the Vale."

Fynnol looked up from his fishing, a quick motion like a startled crow. "Perhaps there are worse things than untrustworthy rivers," he muttered.

Cynddl had spread, over the sailcloth that covered their belongings, a number of leaves and flowers. He was comparing them carefully but looked up. "Did your parents tell you the story of the girl named Glass? No? Lucky you. No Fáel boy or girl was thought able to reach adult years without it.

"She was born with a crooked foot and a short leg and went unnoticed by the boys, and later by the young men. In bitterness she took to calling herself Glass for the way that everyone looked through her. One spring morning she gazed out her window and found that the swallows had returned and were gliding and turning in the sunlight. 'How I wish I could be one of them;' she said, 'and be free of this burdensome form!' And, of course, as such stories go, she awoke the next day and found she had wings and feathers, and her crooked foot was gone. Glass was perfect, but she was no longer Glass. Immediately she took to the air, gliding and soaring with the grace and freedom she'd only known in dreams. But within the hour a falcon had her. Glass was unwary and new to the dangers of the air, for she had never been noticed before." Cynddl shrugged. "It's a good lesson for young children, I guess." He nodded toward the north. "Do you think the men at the north bridge believe we're dead? Or will they build a raft and come after us as the others did?"

"If they were going to come after us they would have passed us where we camped while Baore was ill," Tam said. "It can't take a day to build a raft and we were only a few hours downriver from the bridge."

"They'd have passed us if they were on the same branch of the river," Cynddl said. He looked back to his leaves and flowers. "But I think they believe we're dead. At least that's my hope. Even so, we should keep our watches." Cynddl held up a twig bearing leaves and a small, white flower. "This is stoneberry and I'm beginning to suspect it grows only on the known branch of the river." Cynddl stood up suddenly, rocking the boat. He shaded his eyes and gazed at a large island in the distance.

"Cooling Keep," the story finder said, "the last stronghold of the Knights of the Vow. I want to stop there and spend a few days. Have a care with the oars, Tam. If we're carried past we'll have to fight back against the current, and the River Dyrr adds its waters to the Wynnd just below the island so the flow is sped."

Tam gazed up at the ruined fortress perched high atop a rugged island. "It seems strange that the Knights of the Vow had a keep here," he said. "Aren't we still leagues from the borders of the One Kingdom?"

"Many, many leagues," Cynddl said. "Cooling Keep was said to be unassailable—perhaps that's why they built it here. This was the home of the grand master of the order. From here he would direct his marshals and grand marshals, and a constant stream of boats would go to and fro carrying orders and reports. At their zenith the

Knights were as powerful as any prince or duke—second only to the King, perhaps. But in the end the Renné trapped them here and collapsed a wall of their 'impregnable' fortress. No Knights were spared, and the great towers of the keep were toppled and what was left put to the torch." He lowered his hand but still stared off at the island, which now boasted trees for towers. "The Knights recorded that when they first came here they found the foundations of a more ancient fortress, which makes this a place of interest to me."

Tam stood up so that he could see past their Fáel companion. A tall island, carved out by the relentless river, stood at the joining of the two waters, the Wynnd and the River Dyrr. It was not unlike the island of Eber but larger and more imposing.

"Céile A'gnnel was the grand master of the Knights," Cynddl said, "and with him stood many of the great warriors of that time: Hallen Gann and Bregan of Dirrth. They thought their position unassailable, but they'd underestimated the cunning of the Renné. When the wall fell, a great battle was fought, the Knights terribly outnumbered. It's said that Gann and Céile A'gnnel stood in the breach and sang 'Bloodwing' as they fought, until all their men took up the terrible song, throwing back assault after assault until at last they fell. After the final Knight had been slain there was an awful silence. No shouts of joy or triumph, only the knowledge that the Renné had never met such foes before. Men they would never have defeated without vastly greater numbers. The

Renné, it is said, were ashamed of their victory. Something I'm sure they had never felt before—or since."

"Wasn't Céile A'gnnel known as the 'Oath Breaker'?"

"He came to be known as that, but he was still one of the great knights of his day. Breaking his oath didn't make him weak."

"But there was a curse, wasn't there?" Fynnol said. "The King who gave the Knights their charter said the order would be lost if they broke their vow."

"King Thynne, it was. And, yes, that's the story, though I don't know if it's true. Certainly A'gnnel came to a terrible end here, and all the last Knights with him."

Fynnol looked up at their Fáel companion. "How do you know so much history of our people?"

Cynddl laughed. "How is it you know so little?"

Fynnol's head snapped up. "Our families never spoke of it," he said with great precision, "even when asked. People came north escaping their pasts. And there isn't some great storehouse of books in the Vale set aside for the curious."

"No. No, I'm sure that's true," Cynddl said softly. "I'm a story finder, Fynnol. Without history, much of what I'd find would seem even more fragmentary than it already does. History is like . . . well, it is like Cooling Keep: a fortress collapsed. My stories are the stones that once made it. As I find them I search for their place in the larger structure. Without the ruin of the keep I'd be collecting stones but building nothing. So I study history."

At a crumbling stone quay they landed before the ancient gate. For a moment they stood in awe of the massive opening cut into the cliff. The gates were gone and the iron of the hinges rusted away, but the sheer scale of it was beyond the experience of the Valemen.

Around the gate the stone had been carved with the devices of the Knights—the swan and the lion, the leaves of the silveroak. Clinging vines overran the gate now, creeping among the heraldic devices. The shadows beyond gave the place an ominous feel and no one stepped forward to lead the way.

Beyond, Tam could see a stairway, as wide as the gate, climbing up into the stone heart of the island. It turned to the right where a soft, filtered light fell in ghostly shafts. Here the roots of trees and the waving fronds of ferns could be seen clinging to the rock.

"I don't like the feel of this place," Baore said. He stood with his large frame slightly bent, the injured arm still hanging in its sling, tucked tight against his chest like a broken wing. Tam hadn't realized how much flesh had been stripped of Baore's frame while he lay shivering with fever and infection. All of the soft roundness of his face had been pared away and he was almost gaunt, his face all hard surfaces and sharp angles.

"I don't much like the feel of it either," Cynddl said. "Too many battles fought here. Too many men lost. But I will spend a few days here all the same." He fetched his sword and bow from the boat, and the others took up their weapons as well—they went nowhere without them now—and they mounted the stair. Cynddl, Tam, and Fynnol went up three abreast, but Baore lingered, following only reluctantly.

On the rock walls they could see the lists of the brethren of the Knights of the Vow—column upon column of names, many famous, cut into the stained white stone. As they went they read, and, though most of the names meant nothing to them, there was a certain majesty to the roll all the same.

"It's like reading a poem," Fynnol said. "A long, sad poem in a forgotten language: halbert a'dair, gildon d'or, abril wills, tor'on norr. The names themselves seem almost to be the words of a story—the tale of the Knights of the Vow and their tragedy of betrayal."

Tam stopped to look at his cousin, who was not commonly so solemn or philosophical. "I know what you mean," Tam said. "I can almost see the Knights riding beneath their banners, silhouetted by failing light. It must have been a time of great glory."

Fynnol laughed. "How *glorious* to have been slaughtered at Cooling Keep! Don't you wish it had been us?"

Tam laughed as well. He should have known better than to have taken Fynnol seriously—not that he wasn't, but one wasn't allowed to notice it.

In a few moments they left the ghostly roll behind, reached the stair head, and found themselves among the fallen stones of the ancient citadel. Some of the walls still stood. The massive outer curtain wall was largely intact but for the eastern side that had plunged into the river where it had been undermined by the Renné. Moss and vines covered the crumbling walls, flowers nodding in the breeze. Even trees had taken root on the battlements.

"It puts the tower at Telanon Bridge to shame," Baore muttered. He shuffled where he stood, still looking as though he might retreat to the boat at any moment.

"Yes, and this was not their greatest fortress by any means," Cynddl said. "In the south they built two of the greatest fortresses of their time: Cloudloft and Eagle Crag. Cloudloft still stands, as formidable as it was centuries ago. I've walked its walls and looked out over the plain. You feel there as though you could never be harmed. What arrow could even reach the top of such walls? But history has taught us that any stronghold can fall. Cooling Keep fell, and it sits high atop an island deep in the wildlands. The Renné couldn't even carry their siege engines here."

They found themselves at the crest of a slope, looking down at the rubble of the fallen walls that lay in the river below. "A'gnnel and Gann stood here, holding the gap against the Renné. The rocks below were said to be slick with blood, the *crimson cliff*, though it is hardly a cliff. A great part of the citadel must have plunged into the river."

The day was waning when they climbed back down to their boat. They hauled it up into a stand of shrubs that would hide it from any men who happened to pass by on the river, took what they needed to make a camp, and climbed back up to the gap where the wall had fallen away. Here they built a fire and watched the shadows lengthen across the still forest. They could see the River Wynnd wending south, the waters of the Dyrr swelling and hastening it. In the south and east, a dark band of cloud charcoaled the horizon.

Tam thought Baore surprisingly still. True, his injury left him with only one arm at the moment, but even so Tam would have expected him to gather wood and take over the feeding of the fire—to do whatever could be done one-handed. But instead Baore remained idle. Tam had thought the river more likely to halt in its course.

"What made the Renné so treacherous, do you think?" Fynnol asked Cynddl.

The story finder was turning a pair of spitted hare over the coals. "What made them so? Indifference toward anyone who wasn't Renné." Cynddl rescued a rabbit leg that was about to fall away and be lost in the coals. "And even that isn't true. The Renné fought among themselves as often as they fought the Wills, I think. Perhaps it was indifference to ideals like honor. Somehow being born Renné made you above such things. You could do as you pleased. Laws and codes were for lesser men." Cynddl passed the cooked leg to Baore. "In the south they say, 'He'd trust a Renné.' Which means either a fool or someone far too innocent. Of course the Wills were no better, but somehow they escaped the reputation of the Renné.

"The current heir to the Renné name, Toren Renné, seeks to keep the peace. There is even talk that he'll return the Isle of Battle to the Wills, though I can't imagine his family will allow that. We'll see what this Renné does over the years. He's young yet, and the idealism of youth usually doesn't survive into the middle years."

Their supper was cooked, and they sat with their backs against walls or fallen rocks and watched the first stars appear in the deepening blue. The conversation seemed to meander, like the river running below.

"This reminds me of the night we met Alaan, in the old keep by the bridge," Baore said, breaking his silence. He ate sparingly, and not with his usual enthusiasm.

"'You can't keep what you have.' Isn't that what the man-at-arms said?" Cynddl bent over the fire and began slicing off more meat. "I wonder what Alaan had that they wanted?"

"Whatever it was they didn't find it, or they wouldn't be chasing after us still," Fynnol said. He sat up and looked through the gap in the wall, onto the rubble of stone below. "What was this you said, Cynddl?" he asked. "The Knights sang 'Bloodwing'? What was that?"

"Bloodwing was the sword of Prince Deedd. I'm surprised you've not heard of it. There is a song that tells its story: a long list of carnage, really. 'From his steed the dire knight fell. Bloodwing, Bloodwing, gate to hell.' I don't know enough to sing it for you, but it's a gruesome song, and artless as well. Armies would take it up as they went into battle."

"And what happened to it? The sword."

"Bloodwing? I don't remember if the song tells, but

it was sung here, in this very place, as the Renné attacked."

Tam reached out a hand and patted the wall he leaned against. "This seems a likely place for a story finder, Cynddl," he said. "I can almost hear the stories of this place myself."

Fynnol laughed. "Maybe you should start listening to the river, Tam—like Eber. Perhaps it will whisper your name as well."

Cynddl ignored Fynnol. "There is sorrow here, Tam, and deeper sorrow beneath that—like an underground river. There was tragedy in this place, even before the Knights fell to the Renné. That's what I think."

"I feel the sorrow as well," Baore said, a little defensively. "I can't explain it. But even more strongly, I feel a hatred and bitterness that's not mine own. An ache for vengeance . . . against whom I can't say, but I feel it." The big Valeman looked quickly back to his food, his face coloring a little.

No one spoke for a moment, even Fynnol keeping his tongue in check.

"Here is a truth I have learned while finding stories," Cynddl said. "We are alive, though briefly. Then we are memory, for the lives of those who knew us. And then we are story. Story lasts longest of all—if there is any story to tell.

"Some write their story across a single field or the walls of a cottage. Some write them across an entire land, an entire age." Cynddl looked out the gap where the battle had been fought. He held a small stone in his hand and tapped it on another as though marking time. "One day a story finder might come to this place and find the tale of three northerners and a Fáel who journeyed down the river. What will he make of us, I wonder? Four men whose stories went nowhere at all? Or will we make stories worth finding? Will we scratch the stories of your lives upon the wall of a cottage or across the sky?"

Fynnol laughed suddenly. "If we had a chisel we could carve our names into the roll of the Knights of the Vow. Who would know any different?"

This made even Cynddl laugh.

A wind came sweeping up the river then. Tam could see it brush the water back and bow the trees. The hiss of fluttering leaves reached them, and then a cool breeze curled over the fallen wall, luffing their clothes like sails.

"A storm is coming," Cynddl said, standing and staring up at the sky. A thin dark haze streaked the sky overhead, and all around the horizon black clouds gathered. "We'd best find some shelter."

Supper went down in a trice and the four gathered up their belongings. The only shelter they could find was on the stair to the main gate, which had been carved through the rock of the island and was protected by a roof of stone all the way to the first landing. Very quickly their belongings were shifted there, and then they returned to the top of the crimson cliff to watch the storm sweeping in from the south.

"Look at these clouds!" Fynnol said. "Like the smoke from a great fire. As though the lands to the south have all been set aflame."

But Tam thought it looked like a bruise, overspreading the world from a terrible wound on the far horizon. They stood a moment more, feeling the wind press against them, piercing their clothes to send its chill into the flesh. And then the surface of the river appeared to erupt, as though a thousand fish had all touched the surface at once.

"Hail!" Tam said, and they ran for the shelter of the stairs.

The hailstones, however, were quicker and caught them at the stair head, pelting the companions and rolling treacherously under foot. In a moment they were all under the canopy of stone, staring out at a river riddled with driving hail. Occasional stones bounced and rolled down the steps, coming to rest near them and melting quickly away. And then, as swiftly as it had come, the hail turned to rain. The sky was black now, and the failing evening light was snuffed like a candle. Far off, thunder drummed, and then lightning flashed so close Tam was blinded for a moment. Thunder seemed to reverberate from the rock around them, shaking the keep as though the earth trembled in fear.

The Valemen threw themselves down on their belongings and pulled blankets around their shoulders. They sat gazing out at the river, which appeared in the flickers of lightning. Above the wildly swaying trees, distant lightning forked, and sent peals of thunder crashing and echoing among the hills. Conversation was impossible and the companions fell quiet.

Baore tucked up his knees and buried his face there, pulling his wounded arm free and covering his ears with his hands. Cynddl wandered down to the foot of the stair and stood gazing at the chaos.

Here we make our story, Tam thought, *though I'm no story-teller and haven't the skill of it. Nor have I the understanding of our tale so far. Why were these men lying in wait for Alaan? And why do they continue to pursue us? It is all well and good for Cynddl to talk about making one's story, but I can't even begin to understand the story I've fallen into.*

It was true, though, as Cynddl said: life was short, memory limited to the lives of others, but stories lasted. It seemed to Tam just then, with the storm raging around him, that men flickered into being like lightning, cut a single stroke into the earth, and were gone; but the single stroke they made might last for hundreds of years. A brief instant to find one's place in the larger story, and then darkness.

He heard the murmurs, the whispers and cries masked by the thunder. All around him Cynddl could feel the stirrings, feel them growing like desire long denied. Lightning flashed and he saw boats on the river—a small armada sailing beneath waving banners, moonlight glittering dully on helms and armor. And then it was dark and there was only the image in the mind. *Who were these men and when had they come here?*

The lightning fell again, and thunder rumbled around the walls of the keep like falling stone. Seven men stood atop the wall, illuminated by lightning, and when the light faded, they leapt. Seven men, tumbling through darkness. Men he knew . . . from somewhere.

Without realizing, Cynddl had wandered out onto the quay and into the teeming rain. The cold water streamed down his neck and streaked his back. He felt his clothes plastered against his skin—but there were too many whispers and murmurs to care about cold and rain.

A man stood nearby, draped in a long black surcoat. He stared up at the gate. And then he was gone into the darkness, swept off on the screaming wind.

"Find me at Death's gate," a voice whispered in the thunder. "Find me . . ."

Cynddl had been driven down onto the stone, or perhaps he'd slipped. But he crouched there, buffeted by the gusts, blinding rain slatting down around him like dripping darkness. His knuckles were bleeding and one knee throbbed. The river had risen and swept past, gurgling and hissing.

"What is it you say?" Cynddl asked aloud, but his words were drowned in the chaos.

"At Death's gate . . ."

He is a man reborn, Cynddl thought. *Reborn. But who . . .?*

In a bright burst of lightning he saw the seven plummet into the black river, but only six surfaced. Only six struggling with the speeding current.

Lightning fell so close that Cynddl covered his ears to shut out the thunder. Closing his eyes he saw the wall give way and crumble into the river, and then it swarmed with men. In the harsh moonlight the rocks ran crimson.

There was burning, and men feeding the blaze in a frenzy. Cynddl could see the silhouettes running, adding fuel to the flame, and then he realized: books! They were burning books in the courtyard above. Knights of the Vow bore armfuls of books and scrolls and threw them on the pyre.

Cynddl looked up and saw the man in the black surcoat going stiffly up the stairs, as though injured. The sky burst open, and in the blaze of light Cynddl saw a face at the edge of the quay. It gazed at him with eyes pale as the moon, hair streaming like kelp, a white arm laid along the wet stone. And then darkness returned, and he blinked the rain from his eyes. A hand clutched him under the arm.

"Cynddl . . . Are you hurt?" It was Tam, standing over him, raising him up.

"He came here!" Cynddl said, not rising.

"Who?" Tam called, but a peal of thunder rolled over his words.

"He journeyed here, to Cooling Keep . . ." Cynddl shouted, "the man reborn. To loose the hatred!"

"Tell me this story under shelter," Tam shouted over the din. "Can you stand?"

"I've twisted my knee."

"Come, I'll help you," Tam yelled.

With the Valeman supporting him, Cynddl hobbled in under the roof of stone, going painfully up the steps. Tam lowered him onto a bag of clothing and found a blanket to wrap him. Water was seeping down the stairs now, and the Valemen inhabited a small island, a patch of steps that remained dry. They huddled here while around them the sky made war on the earth.

Tam pulled the blanket closer and sat watching as the night was torn apart over and over. In the flashes of lightning he could see Cynddl, who gazed fixedly at the river, his dark eyes glittering in the bursts of brilliance.

As each spear of light struck the earth, shadows fled across the walls and beneath the trees, as though some god hunted them for sport. The names of the Knights of the Vow, etched into the wall, appeared and disappeared: *Dallan A'dair, Ashen Korr . . . Gilbert A'brgail, Simll D'or.* Each time the darkness returned Tam lost his place reading the ghostly roll, and he would find his gaze running over the same name again and again until finally he gave it up and closed his eyes. The explosions of light, however, could not be shut out so easily and registered on the eye all the same.

Tam awoke to silence, or so it seemed after the tumult of the storm. The world was still, the air fragrant. In the darkness, water dripped and trickled. Moonlight dappled down through the trees beyond the gate and silvered the river. For a while Tam listened to the sounds of the night: the water murmuring, a nighthawk's call, the staccato songs of insects.

Someone stood on the quay, Tam realized: the Fáel story finder, he was sure. Tam rose from his blanket, damp and chill, and his shadow hurried down the stair before him.

"Are you well, Cynddl?"

The story finder looked over his shoulder and nodded. He flexed one leg. "My knee is stiff, but no more."

In the north Tam could see dull flashes in the clouds, and the distant, muffled rumble of thunder reached him. Overhead the sky was bright with stars. "The storm passed quickly."

Cynddl nodded.

"What were you doing out here in the rain?" Tam said. "You looked . . . well, when I came to help you up, you looked at me as though I were a stranger."

"I don't know what happened," Cynddl said. He lowered himself stiffly to the bottom step and shivered visibly. "It was as though the storm released the stories that had been fading here for so long. Or perhaps they came flooding down the river with the rain. I don't know. But they swept over me in waves until I was reeling. I saw strange things. I don't quite know what they mean, yet." He pointed up at the towering walls. "Seven men plunged from the battlements into the river. Seven men, but only six survived. Six men who fled north, pursued by the Renné.

"And up in the high courtyard Knights burned all the books and scrolls, even as Céile A'gnnel and Hallen Gann stood in the gap and sang their terrible dirge and threw the Renné back, and threw them back again."

"Six knights . . . but you talked of six knights who crossed over Telanon Bridge?"

Cynddl nodded. "Yes. Stories are always thus. I find fragments here and there, but every part has a place if you can only find it." Tam could see Cynddl move in the faint light, like a man unsure whether he would stand or sit or do something else altogether. His hands went from his knees to the stone step, to his forehead, and then he rubbed his eyes as though they still burned from the things he'd seen.

"The Renné didn't destroy the Knights of the Vow simply because disloyalty and betrayal were in their nature," Cynddl went on. "There was another reason, though I don't yet know what it was: perhaps they wanted the books and scrolls that were destroyed." He tilted his head toward the stair. "But another has been here before us . . ." He closed his eyes and put a hand to the side of his head, as though it pained him. "But I don't know what he sought," he said bleakly.

"Was this the man reborn you spoke of?"

Cynddl nodded distractedly. "I need to go south now, Tam. South with all speed."

"Then this is why you've come here," Tam said, "to learn the story of the Knights?"

Cynddl became very still for a moment, and then he shook his head. "No, Tam. I came to this place because the Fáel who study such things believe that a sorcerer once made his home here—when people still dwelt in the Greensprings. Long before the Knights built Cooling Keep. I have come to find his story. To learn the manner of his death and discover what became of his knowledge."

This silenced Tam. He could not have been more surprised, and not just by what the Fáel had said but by the fact that he had answered at all. "And what happened to this sorcerer?" he asked quietly.

"Caibre was his name and he was defeated—defeated in a long war by his most bitter enemy—and then banished . . . into a dream, perhaps. I can't really say. Perhaps to the land of death. And though he might have stood before the gate, Tam, he didn't pass through. That's what I think."

"Like Baore's dream . . ." Tam said. "Why do the Fáel want to know this?"

Cynddl shrugged. "Some of my people you don't question, Tam. When they ask that you perform a task, you accept it as an honor." He pointed toward the river, his fine-boned hand frost white in the moonlight. "I saw our apparition again, as well—there, watching me in the midst of the storm. And in the thunder I heard a voice that said, 'At Death's gate you will find me.'"

This silenced Tam, and he shivered from the cold and damp.

"I don't know what it all means, Tam. I have only

fragments of stories. It might be months before I've found enough to make sense of them—"

Baore screamed in his sleep, scrambling up where he stood, swaying. Neither Tam nor Cynddl could move for a moment, so chilling was the scream; and when they went up the steps Fynnol was already by his cousin, speaking soothingly.

"What is it, Baore?" Tam said.

The big Valeman stood shaking, bent double and breathing in short, quick gasps. Fynnol kept a hand on his shoulder, clearly not sure what to do.

"I don't know," Baore said at last. "A dream . . . a dream of battle, here. All around me men were slain by lightning. I stood alone at the end, before some other, and we fought, and I was pierced by lightning. I screamed and found Fynnol shaking me." He looked up, barely visible in the shadows. "I was there, on the quay, shattering the gate with a hammer, each blow louder than thunder." He collapsed back down on the step. "Can't we get off this terrible river?" he cried. "It's seeping into us, drop by drop, and will drown us in the end."

Tam woke to a still morning, hardly a sound. Baore lay tossing and muttering nearby as though his fever had returned. The mound of blankets surmounted by a cloak concealed Fynnol, unmoving; and Cynddl was not to be found. Tam lay still a moment, tired from the tumultuous night. His eyes wandered down the step to the rain-swollen river. It swept by, bearing branches and leaves and whole trees washed free of the banks. A litter of torn leaves and small debris spread over the stairs and across the coverings and baggage of the travelers.

Tam's eyes climbed up to the roll of the Knights carved into stone, and he realized that his confusion of the night before was not caused by losing his place in the dark—the same names repeated often.

Alaan, he thought. He'd asked old Gallon about given names repeating in families. And Cynddl claimed that six Knights had escaped the Renné siege of Cooling Keep and fled north to eventually cross Telanon Bridge. Alaan was searching for survivors of the Knights of the Vow among the families of the Vale.

Tam tossed his covers aside and rose, going down to the water to wash his face and hands in the flooding river. It lapped at the top of the quay now. Then he went up the stair and into the sunlight streaming into the ruin through gaps in the walls. He found Cynddl standing at the crest of the crimson cliff, gazing down toward the river below. He looked up as Tam came near.

"Ah, Tam. Have the others risen as well? We should be off as soon as we can be." He gestured toward the river. "We should take advantage of this flood, which has sped the river. It won't last long, I would imagine."

"I'll rouse them as I go down," Tam said. "They'll be eager to travel as well. At least Baore will be. I think he's seen enough of the outside world. The Vale of Lakes is calling to him."

Cynddl loosened a stone with his foot and sent it tumbling down the slope. It bounced and shattered and bounced again, and then plunged into the water in the center of a white star. "And what about you, Tam? Have you found what you were looking for? Have you seen the world your father saw? And has it brought him nearer, somehow?"

Tam looked down at the slope of fallen stone and the river snaking off into the secret south. "I'm not a story finder, Cynddl," he said softly. "Perhaps my father's spirit lies beyond the gate, but I haven't found it. All I've learned of my father is how it feels to be hunted by men-at-arms you don't know and to whom you wish no harm. I often think of that man we found on the island. He was so afraid to die that he would try to make peace with his killer just so he wouldn't face the end alone." Tam shook his head. "My poor father . . ." he whispered.

Cynddl said nothing for a moment. The river muttered in its flight.

"Even if you were a story finder, Tam, I think you'd quickly learn that your father's story lies in the Vale with his wife and child. You search for him in the wrong place."

TWENTY-ONE

Carral Wills loved to sit in the garden his late wife had created. The smell and sound of the place brought back memories that filled him with a delicate and exquisite sadness. More than anything it was the sounds that touched him, though the scents worked their magic as well.

Water trickled through rocks into a pool and brought back the many things said, the promises, the affirmations of love. Today the promises returned to haunt him, ghost-like.

He had made a promise to protect Elise . . . He thought of the man in the tower, the "ghost" and his suggestion that she could be whisked away. Foolishness.

Carral had spoken to many of his relations, pleaded with them, in truth, but to no avail. All were determined that this alliance should take place—especially now that they had met Prince Michael. A more likeable young man it would be hard to find. But they blinded themselves, as always, to the harsher truths. It was a proclivity of the Wills.

The situation was so hopeless that Carral could hardly bear to think of it.

The wind stepped over the wall, causing the trees to whisper in their different voices. Carral thought he might be the only man in the world who could distinguish the sound of wind through a willow from the sound of a breeze in a beech or an oak. He often wondered if a sound garden could be created—broad-leaved plants to bring out the sound of rain, water running in a stream, the careful placement of walls and standing stones to funnel winds through the trees and shrubs, all chosen for the beauty and variety of their sound. Plantings to attract certain species of songbirds; whippoorwill, winter wren, and sorcerer thrush. A garden for a blind man. But who else would appreciate it?

If only the intentions of men rang so clear to him. But men were a mystery, living as they did in the sighted world—as though he lived beneath the water and they swam upon its surface, like carp and swans.

Oh, men's voices revealed a great deal, but there was always something missing, some part of the conversation that was lost to him.

Other men want such different things from you, Elise had once said when he'd tried to explain his confusion to her. And that was no doubt true. Men preferred the hunt and the tournament to music, to contemplation. Certainly there were a few who appreciated music as well, more than a few, perhaps; but even so, they would give up music before the arts of war.

Carral had attended a tournament, listening carefully to the crowds, to the gallop of horses, the crash of knights meeting, the splintering of lances. He remembered the silence that sometimes ensued. The moans and cries of the fallen and their loved ones.

No, those who swam upon the surface in the light of the sun were different in some fundamental way—they did not realize how blessed they were, and wasted their time in vain pursuits.

The breeze abated suddenly, and the garden hushed, like the crowd at a tournament when the hero falls. Footsteps came to him, the dull sound of leather boots on a dirt path. Carral could usually recognize the sound of different men walking—those he encountered frequently, at least—but this was a stranger.

My ghost, he thought. But no, he remembered the sound of the ghost's footsteps—most distinct.

"Lord Carral . . ." It was not a pleasant voice, though educated and refined in its own way. It reminded Carral of iron scraping over stone—razor-sharp iron.

"Who is that?"

"Eremon," the voice said. The footsteps had stopped some few paces away.

"But you sound so much like another . . ." Carral said. "Someone known to the Wills long ago . . . Hafydd I believe he called himself then."

He could hear the man's breathing change, quicken. Was that anger? Some gravel scuffed as the man shifted from one foot to the other.

"Do not think to joust words with me," the voice said slowly. Carral had never heard a voice bear such menace.

"I do not joust but merely wish to know with whom I speak. What is it you want of me, Sir Hafydd?"

Carral heard the folds of clothing move as the man settled on the stone bench opposite. "You are not old enough to have ever heard the voice of Hafydd," the voice said. "How could you know it?"

"The blind have exceptional hearing. Did you not know?"

Carral heard the sounds of the man rising from his bench, two quick strides, fabric moving, and then the side of Carral's face exploded and he was driven from his bench. He sprawled, dazed, upon the ground, the bitterness of blood in his mouth.

"*How—how dare you! How . . .!*"

"Dare!? Oh, you would be surprised what I would dare."

A hand grasped Carral by the back of his collar and jerked him up, depositing him roughly back on his bench. Carral, hand to his face, leaned away from the man, wondering if he would be hit again.

"You—you struck a blind man," Carral heard himself say, not quite able to believe what had happened.

"But only with an open hand. You have not felt my fist yet."

Carral could sense the man standing over him.

"Wars have been fought for less."

"Go to war against the Prince of Innes and that will bring an end to the Wills's family pride, for it is only in pride that you are still great, Lord Carral." Hafydd said his name with particular disdain. "I have no need of your inbred family, you in particular who can bear neither lance nor child, but the Prince will have an heir with Wills blood. That is his wish and I will see that it is done."

Carral felt the man lean down closer to him so that he could smell his breath, his age.

"You cannot fight me, minstrel. Do not even dream that you might, for you see, I care nothing for honor or chivalry or vows or so-called civilized conduct. I am unlike any man you have ever met, in this. Your daughter will marry Prince Michael and bear him a son, and if you interfere I shall throw you from the tower where you visit your ghosts. Do not imagine that my threats are idle."

The man straightened. "Do we understand each other?" the voice said softly.

"I understand you," Carral said.

There was a very brief, dry laugh, sand in the wind. "I will allow you that," Hafydd said, turned, and strode off.

Carral sat very still, holding a hand to his throbbing face. He still could not believe what had occurred. But what would happen if he told Menwyn? Even Menwyn could not allow such an insult. They would go to war . . . with the result that Hafydd predicted. The man was no fool. He knew that Carral could tell no one. He even knew that Carral was smart enough to realize it.

"What a monster," Carral said aloud. And this man wanted his daughter. Wanted her for a broodmare. The thought of Elise trapped in the same house with such a man was a horror beyond enduring.

He heard footsteps again, tentative this time, light. They approached almost as though not wishing to be noticed.

"Who is that?"

"Prince Michael, Lord Carral."

"Ah." Carral could not think what to say. He was bleeding from the mouth and must seem terribly shaken. "I— I fell."

"I saw what happened," the young prince said. "I watch Eremon whenever I can."

"That . . . that seems a dangerous pastime."

"Perhaps, but he cares little that I know what he does. He doesn't think me a threat to his purpose. Why did he do that to you?"

Carral hesitated. This young man was the son of the Prince of Innes — Eremon/Hafydd's ally. Yet . . .

"I oppose your marriage to my daughter—no, that is not precisely true. I oppose my daughter being used only to create an heir with Wills blood. I do not presume to judge you, of whom I know so little."

"You are wise to oppose this marriage." He paused. "Sir, you are bleeding on your clothes. May I . . .?" Without awaiting an answer the young man stepped near, and Carral felt a cloth begin to dab about his mouth and chin. "Can you hold this to the wound for a moment?"

Carral pressed the cloth to his face, and the Prince rose. Two steps and he settled on the bench where Eremon/Hafydd had been.

"I wish I knew what to do to ease this situation," the young man blurted out. "Sometimes I think I should——" But he stopped in mid-sentence.

"You think you should what?"

"Run away, I suppose, though they would track me down in a trice."

Carral might not be able to see the young man's face, but even so he knew that what he had begun to say was not, in the end, what was said. "Have a care where you let your thinking go, Prince Michael. More dangers lie there than you might guess."

No response was offered to this and the two sat in silence, the garden whispering around them.

"What are we to do?" the young man said, his tone flat.

"I don't know. I have just had my life threatened if I dare to interfere in the plans of Eremon."

"He is not subtle. Eremon is a mace, not a dagger, and will bludgeon any who stand in his way. Men fear him——I fear him——but none dare refuse him. But there is more to him than that might indicate. He has a confidence, a knowledge of what others are doing and what they intend . . . I can't explain it. He must have the greatest network of spies ever created. It is uncanny."

If you interfere I shall throw you from the tower where you visit your ghosts, Hafydd had said.

Hafydd knows of my ghost, Carral thought. Or did he merely know that Carral went to the tower when the offerings were left? It made him wonder again about this man who claimed to be a ghost. What was his involvement in all of this? And could the son of the Prince of Innes really be trusted?

"You know Eremon better than I; what do you suggest we do?"

He heard Prince Michael shifting on his bench, the moment stretched out, and Carral's hopes grew thinner.

"I don't know, sir. Your family will not refuse, nor would my father allow it. His army is strong and he is anxious to see it in the field." Carral could almost feel the despair. The young prince's voice grew smaller with each word. "Marry her to another, that is all you can do. Is there not some suitable young man? It could be done in secret—tonight if possible. I don't know what else can be done."

"What else indeed," Carral muttered. Suddenly he was leery of sharing any plans with the son of the Prince of Innes, no matter how the lad felt about his own father. "But I know of no such young man."

Again the silence, like darkness to the sighted, Carral thought, and then the Prince stood.

"Good luck to you, sir. If . . . if the marriage cannot be avoided I will do all I can to protect her, but I will tell you honestly, that is very little. She doesn't deserve this, Lord Carral. Lady Elise is . . . an admirable young lady."

"Yes, I think she is," Carral said, "and I believe you would try to protect her. I'm sorry you are caught up in this."

"I'm sorry we're all caught up in it. Good day to you, sir."

Carral gave a slight bow, but as he heard the Prince turn, spoke again. "Do you realize that Eremon is not who he claims? He was once known as Hafydd and was an enemy of my family."

"It is a rumor my father has heard but does not believe. Do you think it true?"

Carral considered Eremon's reaction to his accusation. "I think it very likely."

The Prince walked off, his footfall so light upon the earth that Carral thought he might float into the air at any moment.

†wen†y-†wo

The town of Inniseth appeared around a bend in the river, and Tam had to look twice to be sure of what he saw. The houses lay beneath a massive shoulder of stone which overhung the little town and pressed it close to the river.

The buildings seemed to have grown out of rock and blended into the surroundings so well that they were difficult to see. Streets and houses followed the contours of the land, roofs and walls jutting off at unexpected angles and on odd levels. There was nothing even remotely like it in the Vale.

The roofs appeared to be of the same stone as the walls and the surrounding countryside, though split to roof-tile thickness. The town was all of a color and all of a piece but for bright flowers in pots by doorways and on window ledges. They had drawn fairly close before Tam realized the town was well defended by natural cliffs and walls cleverly connected to make any assault difficult.

We are in the wildlands yet, he reminded himself.

"You have to wonder if there's a stick of wood in the entire town," Fynnol said, staring. "Look at it! I expect the people to be made of stone themselves, getting about like living statues."

"Yes, but are our hunters among them?" Tam wondered.

Cynddl shook his head. "I don't think it likely. This is a village whose road is the river, and I don't think the men who pursued us came down the river. Our pursuers believe us dead, or so I hope, and if they don't they wouldn't likely come here looking for us. They want to catch us alone in the wilds: that's their way."

Across the river from the town lay the fields of the townsfolk. Here a level valley lay on either side of a tributary, and the travelers could see new oats waving in the sunshine, as well as green fields of sprouting corn and long mounds of potato plantings. Thick hedges set one field off from another, and there men and women were at work, bent to their toil beneath the late spring sun.

Tam could see two small stone wharfs along the tributary where boats were moored or pulled up onto the grass. Odd, many-sided barns dotted the landscape, and in the pastures livestock wandered.

As they rowed near to the town, an old man stood up from behind an overturned boat, a caulking mallet in hand. He removed a shapeless hat and wiped his brow with the back of a shirt cuff, staring at the Valemen and their companion as though he'd never seen strangers before. And then he hobbled, stiff-legged but quick, through a nearby gate.

"We don't look that unkempt, surely," Fynnol said.

Tam brought them gently alongside the stone quay.

"Hello!" Fynnol called, for he could see the old man staring out at them, the gate open a crack. "We mean no harm, grandfather. You can come out."

But the old man stayed where he was, gazing out anxiously. "And where you be coming from?" he demanded.

"From the Vale of Lakes," Fynnol said, and then added, "far north."

"I not be such an old straw as not to have heard of the Vale. And what is it you want in Inniseth?"

Tam glanced at Cynddl, who did not look quite so perplexed as the Valemen.

"We thought we might see a little of your town," Tam said, "and there is a man here with whom we'd like to speak."

"And who might that be?"

"Morgan Truk."

There was the slightest pause. "Truk lives down the way. The last house to the south." And then the gate creaked shut and they heard a heavy bar fall into place.

"Well, there is a welcome for you!" Fynnol said. "Perhaps we should cross the river and speak with the people in the fields."

"I fear your reception there will be little different," Cynddl said. "Inniseth doesn't welcome strangers— especially when one of them is a black wanderer." He reached out and shoved the boat back out into the river.

"Let's try this man Truk, then," Fynnol said. "Perhaps

he doesn't believe that strangers will eat his children."

The last house to the south was separate from the others, as though it had been pushed out of the town and its enclosing wall. A small, walled garden shaded by plane trees grew off one side of the house, and from within they could hear the sound of scraping. In a moment they found a gate, and to their surprise the top half was open.

Sitting on a bench in the shade was an old man with a pipe jutting out from between clenched teeth. He was absorbed in the task of cleaning a latch mechanism. Tam cleared his throat and the man looked up, his eyes narrowing shrewdly.

Morgan Truk was a square-built man, not tall but strong looking with powerful arms and legs that appeared to have been attached to his torso by an indifferent craftsman. "'Day to you," he said, nodding, still clenching his pipe. He kept at his work.

"And to you," Cynddl answered a bit truculently.

Truk raised an eyebrow in response, but kept his attention on his latch, which he held up close to his face as though the light were poor, which it was not. Around the man the little garden seemed to have had all its flowers replaced by oddities and other people's castoffs and throwaways: trunks and bed frames; bellows and forge; broken-down furniture, grindstones, and doorknobs.

"And what have you need of this day?" Truk asked.

"Nothing," Tam said, but was suddenly unsure what to

say. "We bring you news of a friend . . ." Tam hesitated a second. "It isn't good news."

The man set his latch mechanism down on the bench and took the pipe from between stained teeth. He motioned them to come in.

"We met a man named Alaan . . ." Tam began, finding his way among the debris in Morgan Truk's garden.

"Alaan A'bert?" Truk asked, thick eyebrows lifting a little.

"We never knew his family name, but he traveled with a bird. A whist . . ."

"That is A'bert," Truk said softly. He looked like a man receiving the final news of a relative long ill. "What has befallen him at last?"

"We were set upon by men-at-arms and he was killed helping us escape."

Truk put his unlit pipe back in his mouth and drew on it loudly. He looked down at the ground and shook his head—a small, sad motion. "Where did this happen?" Truk asked quietly.

"By Telanon Bridge," Tam said.

"But that is to the north," the man said, glancing up sharply. "When was this?"

Tam looked at Fynnol. "About a month ago, more or less."

Truk snorted and shook his head, a small smile appearing around his pipe stem.

"Then he has risen from the river, for I've seen him quite alive since then. Quite alive. He came down the river in a nice new boat bearing a cargo of old odds and ends, as he has before. Sold a few things to me, and then went on his way south."

The Valemen looked from one to the other, unable to voice their surprise.

"He sold you our artifacts!" Fynnol said in outrage.

Truk looked up quickly. "He sold me artifacts, but said nothing about them belonging to others."

"Then he's not dead . . .?" Baore said.

Truk laughed and shook his head. "Rogues like Alaan will outlive the likes of you or me." But then something about the faces of the young men stopped him. "But you'd best tell me your story. I see you've a need to."

The visitors sat down heavily on trunks and decrepit chairs and slowly told Morgan Truk of their encounter with Alaan at Telanon Bridge, the midnight attack, and how they had then been hunted as they came down the river.

Truk sucked on his pipe as the story was spun, his large eyes on the strangers. Tam thought he looked a sympathetic old man, but then he remembered that Alaan had called him an "old crook," or words to that effect. And what had Truk called Alaan?—"a rogue," as had everyone else who knew him. It seemed to Tam that this title was well earned and, if anything, too generous. Alaan had robbed them, as sure as Tam was sitting there. *Robbed them!*

At the story's end the old man took the pipe from between his teeth and tapped it on the edge of his bench, spilling the contents on the ground. "Well, it is a tale and then some besides," he said after a moment. "And I don't know what to do about it. You see, Alaan has come to me with old objects before; some older than old— ancient. And at other times he has purchased or traded for things I'd come by over the years. It is a passion of his, and he knows the value of such things like few others. It is how we struck up what passes for friendship among men who covet and collect the same things. But in all the years, I've never known him to be dishonest; oh, shrewd, certainly, and willing to stretch a point or two to find a bargain, but in the main he was upstanding in his dealings with me." The old man found a pouch in his vest and began slowly tamping tobacco into the bowl of his pipe. "Now see the position I'm in . . .? I have deal-ings with a man for years, tolerably fair dealings, and then some strangers come along and tell me this same man robbed them and sold me their goods. Now, if I am any judge of character, I would say these strangers are as upstanding and true as any you will find.

"Now what is true in this, and can't be denied, is that I bought these goods from Alaan, believing fully that he had come by them in a fair manner. Eh? I paid good money for them and, though I've feeling for you in your plight, I'm not of a mind, nor am I honor bound, to pay for these goods twice. Do you see my point?" He looked at each of them in turn until Baore nodded.

"Now, it seems to an old man that your quarrel is with A'bert. He is the one you need to speak with. Now, normally I wouldn't tell anyone what I am about to tell you, but . . ." he paused for a moment, jamming his unlit pipe between his teeth, "but this is a peculiar predicament I'm in. You see, I know where Alaan was going." He looked from face to face to see the reaction this caused. He took the pipe from his mouth again. "He was planning to attend the tournament at Westbrook."

"But that is not until first summer's day," Cynddl said.

Truk nodded once.

The Valemen looked at one another, faces as confused as stormy mornings. "But Westbrook is far to the south," Fynnol said.

"Not so far, as the river flows, as we say in Inniseth."

"But we are to be home before the snows," Fynnol said, looking to Tam with real distress.

Truk shrugged. "Be that as it may, Alaan has gone south to Westbrook and taken your goods with him."

"And my boat," Baore growled.

Truk took up his latch mechanism again. "Luck to you, whatever you might decide," he said.

Cynddl rose to his feet, but Tam and the others remained where they were, as though too confused to make even the simplest decision.

"Close the gate as you go, if you will," Truk said, and began again to scrape away the layer of rust coating the iron.

Tam tapped Fynnol on the shoulder as he stood, and Baore followed. They picked their way through the debris, but at the gate Truk called to them.

"If there is anything you need from within the village best come see me. The villagers are nervous these days. Some say they've seen swimmers in the water by evening: strange creatures watching with pale eyes. Everyone's locking their windows by night and no one will cross to the fields in darkness or alone. Even men, such as you clearly are, might find a cold reception up in the town, for in Inniseth we have no village fool—but a village of fools, instead. Treat them kindly, for they've no more reason than children."

The companions returned to their boat in silence, and once there Fynnol drew Tam's sword and, with great energy, thrashed a bush that stood nearby, sending leaves and branches arcing through the air to scatter over the ground like severed limbs. Finally, red in the face and gasping he threw himself down on the ground, sword held loosely in his hands.

"How is it possible that Alaan escaped those raiders, let alone thieved our boat!" He slashed at the stump of a branch from where he sat. "All of the hours we spent digging through the earth—and finding almost nothing. And the few things we did discover some fair-spoken thief makes off with!" He raised the blade as though he would cut the ground. "If I had him here I'd cut him a mouth that wouldn't be so fair."

"We'll not see Alaan again," Tam said. "You can be sure of that. Unless he's stopped to practice some roguery in the Wold of Kerns."

"The Wold?" Fynnol said. "I say we go to Westbrook and find this lowborn thief."

"I'm not going on to Westbrook," Baore said, breaking into the conversation, "but to the Wold of Kerns and then home by the north road." He touched his wounded shoulder gently. "I've seen enough of the world beyond the gate. Let Alaan take the things we found. No matter what their price, they aren't worth staying on this cursed river for." The big man got to his feet deliberately, took hold of the bow of the boat, and pushed it back out into the river with his knee. "Whoever will come best jump aboard now. The Wold of Kerns is where we are going and the way this river changes and stretches we best make time."

In the end they crossed the river and made their camp in a copse of trees within sight of the river-rock town. Just before sunset, the people working in the fields boarded a fleet of small boats and crossed silently over to Inniseth, pulling their craft up onto the quay behind them.

"I wonder what they think of us, sleeping the night here, beside the river?" Tam wondered aloud.

"Likely they think us in league with the river spirits," Fynnol said. "We are a strange-looking lot, after all."

Fynnol cast a glance at his cousin, but Baore would not meet his eye. Tam had seen this many a time before, though he was not so certain Fynnol would win the contest this time. Baore was determined that his journey south would end at the Wold of Kerns, and not a league further on.

Tam, however, was worried that they might meet the men-at-arms from Willowwand upon the road. But he was not sure he was ready to journey all the way to Westbrook, even to find the rogue who'd robbed them. Somehow getting Baore back to the Vale seemed the most important thing—he was not sure why.

"Might I see your map, Cynddl?" Fynnol asked.

The Fáel found the rolled paper and Fynnol spread it out by the fire.

"Where is the city of Westbrook?" Fynnol asked after a moment.

"It's hardly a city," Cynddl said. He leaned over and pointed with a small stick. "There is the Westbrook itself. The village of the same name is near the place where the two rivers join."

"But that is not so far south!" Fynnol said. "I thought it was near to the sea."

Cynddl shook his head, a small smile appearing. "How can you know so little of the world?" He tapped the paper again. "You do know there were thirteen duchies and principalities that made up the One Kingdom? Each was situated in a valley of a tributary of the Wynnd. And each was divided from the other by low, rugged hills. These valleys were called wolds in ancient times and all but one was named for the river which made it.

"If you count from the sea you will find the Westbrook

is the twelfth tributary—on the edge of the old kingdom, really. The thirteenth was the Dimml, sometimes called the Eastnook; the home of the Wills family. The Renné dwelt, and still dwell, near the Westbrook."

"That is all well and good, Cynddl, but you miss my point. Can a man not ride from the Westbrook to the Vale before the snows arrive?"

"Do you know when the snows will come this year?"

Fynnol looked at the Fáel, a little exasperation flickering across his face in the firelight.

"Perhaps you can," Cynddl said, "if the snows don't fall early, but the river is broad and in no hurry further south. We will not be to the Westbrook for some time yet. And the fair does not begin until first summer's day."

"But can a man ride from there to the Vale of Lakes before the snows or not?"

"It would be a close-run thing. The Fáel leave for the far north early in spring, the snows retreating before them. But riders travel more quickly than a train of carts. It's possible, Fynnol, though the road does not follow even as straight a course as the river, and climbs many hills even before it goes up into the highlands. If you are caught in the snows before you get home to the Vale . . ." Cynddl tilted his head, gray eyebrows lifting. "You are resourceful young men, you might survive, but you would almost certainly lose your mounts."

Fynnol cast his eye toward Baore again, but the big Valeman kept his gaze fixed on the fire.

"Well, I for one will go south with Cynddl," Fynnol

announced. "I cannot bear the thought of this rogue Alaan profiting from all our efforts. And if we have our artifacts, or the proceeds from them, added to what Cynddl has offered, we might find very good mounts indeed. And we will see more of the world, for I will tell you, Inniseth has been something of a disappointment to me."

Neither Baore nor Tam responded. Only the fire crackled, sending a sudden shower of sparks up among the stars.

They stood watches that night, the fears of the villagers infecting them, perhaps. Baore insisted he was well enough to take his turn, and stood the watch after Tam.

Cynddl woke in the darkness, as he often did, hearing the whisperings of women and men, tales surfacing from the dark pool that lay within his thoughts. He gazed into this pool, for hours sometimes, seeing only the surface. Or walked about it waiting patiently. It was an eerie place, and not made less so by familiarity. The stories of men seemed to burble up from the ground in the Greensprings and find their way into the river, where they ran together in confusion. But somehow they surfaced in this quiet pool, connected to the greater river in some mysterious way. And Cynddl waited.

He rose from his blankets, hearing the river run and cattle lowing in the distant barns. Insects sang their love songs and goatsuckers jeered in the air above.

It was Baore's watch but the big Valeman was nowhere

to be seen. Cynddl took himself down to the river to check their boat, suddenly fearing that Baore had gone off on his own, crossing the river to find his way back to the Vale on foot.

Baore was sitting on the bank, his knees drawn up like a child. Cynddl wondered if he should approach at all or leave the young man to his thoughts. But the sadness of the Valeman was unbearable and Cynddl drew near.

"Baore? Are you well?"

The big man glanced back and then returned his attention to the river. "No," he whispered, "I'm not well."

Cynddl came and sat on the bank nearby. "Does your wound trouble you still?"

"My wound? No. It heals as it should." He said nothing more for a long moment and Cynddl waited, as he was used to doing.

Baore shifted where he sat. "When I lay fevered and raving, Cynddl, I thought I heard voices. They whispered and muttered like Eber's river, hissing things . . . I don't know. I didn't really understand—though almost I could. I thought I heard threats and promises." He shook his head. "Of what I don't know. And when I sleep now, I hear them still. Like voices from another room, the words hard to distinguish, but even so, you know when people argue or whisper secrets. You know, somehow. It is like that, and I dread to sleep, now. I——I dread it."

Cynddl shifted on the grass, wondering what he should say. Certainly he should tell Baore what Tam and he had seen that night, but there was some part of him that sensed Baore would not do well with such knowledge. The largest and strongest of them, he seemed to Cynddl the most fragile as well. Baore needed firm earth beneath his feet and familiarity all around. How unlike Fynnol he was in this. Yet Fynnol dragged him along on all his adventures. Poor Baore that he had such a cousin. And yet what a tiny world he would inhabit without Fynnol.

"I suppose you will say they are only dreams," Baore said, "and that I should not let them trouble me."

"I would never say that," Cynddl said quickly. "The dreams of men cause all the troubles in the world. All the troubles, and all that is beautiful and glorious."

TWENTY-THREE

No offering had been left for the castle ghosts that night, but Carral mounted the steps to the tower anyway. He wanted to speak to this man, this phantom, and find out how he proposed to whisk his daughter away when the castle was filled with supporters of the Prince of Innes—and he knew no other way to contact him. They had met nowhere but in the tower upon the offering nights.

Carral hurried as quickly as he dared up the winding stair, treads rising, uneven and worn, beneath his feet. The door at the stair head was closed and he pressed it open, his senses alert.

There was no fire and he felt the dampness of the place. A breeze stirred as the door swung open. Carral felt his disappointment and frustration well up, and then a throat was cleared.

"I thought you might come this night," a voice said, causing Carral to sigh with relief. It was his ghost and not Eremon as he'd feared.

"I have no more time for this charade," Carral snapped, shutting the door behind him. "Who are you and why should I trust you at all?"

A small laugh came from the vicinity of the window. "My name would mean nothing to you, and who I was, even less."

Carral stamped his foot on the floor. "I haven't patience for it! You ask me to entrust my daughter to you and give me no reason for doing so."

"The alternative to trusting me is reason enough, Lord Carral. I do not need to say what that is. You have met Hafydd now, and know what you deal with. If all I wanted was to whisk your daughter away for some purpose of my own I would hardly need your permission. I would simply abduct her. Yet here I am, discussing the matter with you, hoping for your aid . . ." He paused and said softly, "Will you aid me in this?"

Carral closed his eyes to stop the sudden burning. He had never been left so little choice. Trust a nameless stranger who played at being a ghost or surrender his daughter to that monster Hafydd.

"What would you have me do?" Carral said softly.

The ghost took a long breath and was about to speak when the sound of men upon the stairs reached him.

For a second he listened, hoping it was not true. "They've trapped us," Carral said, hearing the despair in his voice.

"She must come this night," the ghost said quickly. "Tell her only to dress for travel. Any other preparation will alert Menwyn and Hafydd. Arrange for her to come down the servants' stair three hours after midnight."

The men pounding up the stair were almost at the door.

"But you will be in the clutches of Hafydd, my ghost. How will you proceed then?"

Soft laughter lit the eternal darkness. "And what manacles will they find to chain a ghost?"

The door burst open and an indeterminate number of men streamed in, voices and footsteps all ajumble. Carral was pushed back into the room, and sat down when a chair pressed against the back of his knees. Men milled about in confusion, cursing.

And then they fell silent and still. Footsteps came into the room. Footsteps Carral recognized now.

"Sir Hafydd," Carral said before thinking, and cringed in spite of himself.

"We heard voices as we came up the stair," a youngish man said quickly, "but when we came into the room, he was alone."

Carral could feel Hafydd staring at him.

"I was speaking to myself. The habit of a man who spends too much time alone."

Hafydd said nothing for a moment. Carral half expected to feel the side of his face explode again, and tried to maintain an appearance of calm and dignity.

But nothing happened at all. Hafydd's footsteps sounded. Carral heard the scuff of boots as they turned and went deliberately down the stairs. Immediately the others followed and Carral remained in his chair.

When he was sure they were all gone he stood.

"Hello?" he said tentatively. "Am I alone?"

There was no response, only the soft whisper of a night breeze. Suddenly the door creaked, then slammed shut. Carral jumped.

He put a hand over his heart and slumped back down in his chair. Only the wind. No one but he remained in the tower. No one.

For a few moments Carral sat in his chair, heart racing, the damp, night air coming reluctantly into his lungs. His thoughts were a whirl of confusion and disbelief.

Where has my ghost gone?

Carral began to wonder if he were going mad. He had been speaking to a man who breathed and coughed, walked solidly upon the floor, drank wine, even poured some into Carral's glass and put it into his hand. For three years Carral himself had been coming up here to partake in the offerings left for the ghosts—ever since Ancel had died. *He* had been the ghost.

And now some man claiming to be a ghost had disappeared into the night. Disappeared from a high tower from which Carral knew there was only one exit. The room, after all, was round, the walls made of the curving stonework of the tower itself. There could be no secret passage, no bolt-hole. The only way out of this room was through the door . . . or out the window.

He rose and carefully crossed the room to the open window. A bit embarrassed by what he was about to do, Carral reached out and felt along the wet sill, assuring himself that no one clung there.

"Foolish," he said aloud.

For a moment he stood there, leaning upon the sill, letting the damp breeze touch his face like a daughter's kiss. Somewhere in the night, a bird called.

TWENTY-FOUR

E lise opened the door to her room with such care that it made not a sound. She put her eye to the crack, gazing out into the candlelit hall. Yes, they were there—guards in the midnight-blue livery of the Wills, and one in the dark purple of the Prince of Innes. She pushed the door to silently, and crept back to her bed, slipping beneath the covers.

There had been a ruckus the night before—a thief was seen skulking the halls it was said, and guards had been posted everywhere. Everyone seemed to believe it was one of the minstrels who'd come with the Prince of Innes—a jewel thief perhaps, posing as a player, or an assassin, others whispered. This had made Elise laugh. Such was the Wills family sense of self-importance— who would want to assassinate one of them and why? If there was one, she hoped he would assassinate Menwyn and his vicious wife. She picked up her book and opened it gently.

Elise read in bed. It was frowned upon as being bad for one's character and was said to incite strange dreams that somehow led to daydreaming and idleness. She thought some of the wisdom of her elders was so stupendously foolish that it defied all reason.

Well, it was true that she was somewhat prone to daydreaming and idleness, but she was quite sure it was not caused by reading before she fell asleep. No, her idleness and daydreaming, she had come to believe, were a secret and silent rebellion against the life she was forced to live.

But then she rather liked being idle—and daydreaming, too. It was how she kept her imagination alive, for without her imagination she would certainly go mad. If life could never be anything more than living in this stifling castle dominated by Menwyn and Bette . . . She pressed her eyes closed for a second to drive out the thought.

Only her flights of fancy allowed her to escape. How much time she spent constructing a future in which she was free of her meddling relations, their stupid feuds and constant intrigue. How hateful they all were!

For perhaps the tenth time she realized she had finished the page and not comprehended a single word. She began again at the top, but then laid the heavy book down in her lap. Her mind kept returning again and again to the anguished warning she had received from Prince Michael.

How had he appeared so charming and at ease earlier in the evening and then so forlorn and desperate later? Was the "engaging young man" only an act? Or, more unsettling, was his later mood the act?

She remembered that she had noticed him in conversation with that forbidding-looking knight—Eremon, she believed—a counselor of the Prince of Innes. A little shiver of revulsion ran through her at the thought of the man. Had that conversation precipitated the change?

There was no way to know. All she knew was that her heart went out to him. His own situation must be a thousand times worse than her own to prompt such unhappiness.

She wondered if he read at night before he went to sleep, if he imagined a day when he would be free of his family's demands. Perhaps he felt such despair because he could never imagine such a day. Perhaps he had no imagination at all.

The softest knock sounded on her door. For a second she could neither answer nor move, imagining it to be the young prince. Her heart began to beat as quickly as a bird's.

But then the handle turned and the door opened and she heard her name whispered in her father's unmistakable voice.

"Come in," she whispered in return, not sure why they were whispering.

Carral scurried in, closing the door after him with such care she did not even hear the tick of the lock. As he turned away from the door, she was shocked by his face, which was dark and haggard.

"What has happened?" she said, thrusting aside her book and sitting up.

Carral crossed the room, sounding before him with his cane. She took his hand as he reached the bedside and lowered himself to the edge. One eye lay within a stain of dusky blue, and a bright, jagged bruise blossomed over his cheek.

"What has happened to your face?" she said.

He brushed her hand away from the injury. " 'Tis nothing," he said quickly. "The Prince will ask for your hand in marriage tomorrow." He seemed a little out of breath. "I have just spoken to Menwyn, who has already given consent, not bothering to speak to me until it was done. 'Knowing I would agree,' he said." He clutched her hand tightly, his own hand uncharacteristically cold. "But, Elise"—he took a deep involuntary breath—"you cannot marry him." He swallowed suddenly, running out of words, as if not sure what to say. But then he plunged on. "The Prince's counselor, a man calling himself Eremon, is actually a knight once known as Hafydd. He was our enemy in the past and is, I can assure you, as base a man as I have ever encountered. You do not want to fall into the clutches of Hafydd and the Prince whom he serves. I know that Prince Michael is handsome and has all the wit and charm you could ever desire, but, Elise, his father wants only a child with Wills blood so that he might attempt to unite the old kingdom and put his grandson upon the throne." He stopped, suddenly breathless, and she thought he looked unwell, pallid and tired.

"Yes," she said, " Prince . . . Prince Michael warned

me not to marry him. He seemed so wretchedly unhappy." She felt her eyes grow damp.

Hearing the tears in her voice, Carral touched a hand to her cheek. "You must worry about yourself, now," he said softly. "No one else. You must away. Tonight."

A tear escaped at the words and she felt him stroke it gently away.

"But there are guards in the hallway . . ."

"The guards will be distracted."

"But they will have me back within a day; two at the most." She almost burst into tears as she said this.

"No," her father said, his voice warm and soothing—as she remembered it from her childhood. "Arrange-ments have been made . . ." He hesitated—she felt it. "A friend will guide you. You'll not be caught by any man, you can be sure of that."

"But what of you?" she said. "What will become of you without me?"

"Oh, I shall waste away and die, most likely." His smile was forced, but it took some of the darkness from his bruised face and made him look less ill.

"You're saying that you can exist without me?"

"I shall not be as happy and will miss you more than I can begin to say, but don't worry about your father. I have my music and all the minstrels who come to visit. I won't perish." He traced her eyebrow very gently, as though afraid he would forget it. "I must go. Come down the servants' stair three hours after midnight. Dress for travel but don't spend any effort on packing, for if the servants see they might alert Menwyn."

"Go with nothing? Not even a change of clothing?"

"Nothing. If you're found carrying a bag in the hall it will all be over. Take nothing but this." He pressed a small bag into her hands.

Elise squeezed it and felt its weight. Coins and likely jewels as well: the currency most easily carried.

"But how long shall I be away?"

"Not long, I hope. A few months. We'll see. I'll send word when you can safely return."

"But what will the Prince of Innes do to us, to the family?"

"Elise, flee while you may and stop making arguments. Menwyn created this situation, let Menwyn deal with it. It is his problem not yours. You must go. And so must I."

He leaned forward and kissed both her cheeks, then she did the same to him. For a moment they embraced. She could feel his reluctance as he rose from the edge of the bed. He released her hand last.

And then he was crossing the room and out the door. Blind from birth, her father could never look back.

She carried a single candle and her embroidery bag, which contained only toiletries and her journal. The servants' stair was narrow, airless, and creaked terribly. Fortunately, Elise had learned a little trick from listening to the servant girls talk—walk on the very outer edge of the tread, near the wall, and the stairs would creak less. But even less seemed far too much in the silence of the sleeping castle.

The candle flame wobbled as she went, light and shadow wrestling back and forth along the walls and down the well of winding stairs.

Elise was scared. She was stealing through the castle at night to meet a person whose name she did not even know. Why had her father not given her a name? As things stood she could meet a servant of the Prince of Innes and not know if he was the friend who was to take her away. A tread complained loudly beneath her foot, as though she had stepped upon a sleeping cat. She paused to still her racing heart.

Elise trusted her father—that was not in question— but even so, a little more information would not have been out of place. Another stair creaked, and Elise froze in place. The sound had not come from beneath her feet but had echoed up the stairwell. And then her name seemed to chase the echo, as though she had whispered it herself and now it came back to her.

"Who is that?" she said. It was a woman's voice, she was relieved to hear.

Footsteps came quickly up the stairs, the light of a candle chasing the misshapen shadows ahead. A vaguely familiar woman appeared—a singer, Elise was certain. She remembered the soft face beneath auburn curls and the large, observant eyes. The woman had come with one of the minstrels, a well-known man, but Elise could not remember his name let alone this singer's.

"I am to guide you out," she said quickly. "Put this on." Across her extended arm lay a hooded cloak of fine fabric. Elise realized it was her own.

"We took the liberty of packing a few of your things," the woman said, her alert gaze on Elise.

Elise shrugged the cloak on when she realized the woman did not mean to assist her—she was her savior, after all, not her servant. The singer put a finger to her lips and they set out down the creaking stair. Certainly servants used the stair at night and it wouldn't do to meet one of them. But the sound of someone on the stair at this hour should not raise suspicions if any of the Prince's people were about.

In a moment they were in a narrow hall, and then down another long stair and into the kitchens. Servants would be in to light the fires shortly, but for the time being kitchens and scullery were empty. Elise's worst fear was to come upon two servants in a tryst—it had happened once when she was younger. And though she had been told to report seeing any such behavior, her embarrassment had been so great she had said not a word. For this she had long been a favorite of the young maids and kitchen girls.

They slipped out a large set of doors through which stores were brought, up an open flight of stairs, and into a courtyard behind the stables. From the shadow by the stable door Elise caught the sound of horses shifting, a bridle's rattle.

She looked around the open courtyard into which at least two dozen windows opened. They could hardly expect to slip out of here unseen. *This is foolish,* she thought, and felt her hopes fall. This was the plan she had submitted to? She could have done better herself.

In the shadows a man waited with two horses, one of them her own Morn. Without a word the man led her mare to a mounting step, and she was up and settling herself in the saddle in an instant. He swung up to the back of his own horse and without a word led them quickly across the courtyard, beneath an arch, and out the small gate. There was someone there in the darkness, who closed the gate behind them. He wished them luck in a southern accent.

And then they were trotting along the track that ran around the high wall, moonlight tossed down like coins beneath the trees. In a moment they were on the long bridge, crossing toward the shore, challenged by no guard.

They turned onto the grass that ran along the eastern shore, cantering through the still, dark morning. The waning moon drifted down toward the hilltops and cast faint shadows of the two riders. In half an hour, before the sky grayed, the open grass turned to a wood and a road took shape, bending away from the water. They followed this up, bringing their horses to a walk beneath the shadows of the trees.

The wood was all dark shapes and bits of broken moonlight—a spooky place, unrecognizable as the lovely wood she walked in during the day. Elise caught a glimpse of water through the branches. A small breeze swept down the lake, shattering the moonlit surface, and the shards began a dazzling dance.

At the crest of the hill her guide brought his horse up and signaled for her to do the same. "We must have light to go farther," he said. "I don't want to risk breaking a horse's leg if we don't have to."

"Is it Gwyden Dore?" Elise said. "I thought as much. Ever since my father came to me this night I've thought you must be the friend who would take me away."

"How very clever of you," her guide said.

"You know they will be after us by daylight. And anywhere along the way they will have fresh horses."

"Not on the ways that I will take." He rode over near the bluff's edge so that he might look down at the lake and the dark castle on its island. "They must have daylight, too, if they are to find our track. Can you keep the saddle for a few hours yet?"

"I will ride all day and night if that is what's required." She saw him turn toward her—a silhouette against the star-filled sky.

"I might hold you to that, yet," he said.

They dismounted and let their horses browse along the bluff top. Elise watched the moonlight make patterns on the water, patterns that were never repeated—like the lives of men. Similar but never the same. And now the pattern of her life had been broken and she was cast out into the world. Like the bird that had tried to steal her ring, flying out over the waters and into the world beyond with only a branch for a bed, for a country the vault of the open sky.

As soon as the sky paled they were riding again, though not so fast now, her guide choosing to preserve their horses as though expecting a long day—or saving them for a sprint should their pursuers appear, which she was convinced they would. She wondered why she went along with this at all. The countryside hereabout was well known and all the valleys given over to open farmland, each with a small village or two. They couldn't stay to the trees forever. The valleys would have to be crossed, and the first soon.

Gwyden Dore led her off the road and along a narrow path into dense wood. She rode behind, branches whipping at her face and spoiling her fine cloak. The day grew warm, and the wood was soon filled with birdsong and the buzzing of insects. They crossed a small swift brook, and then another. Elise found herself looking about constantly, as though she expected men-at-arms to leap out of the underwood.

Conversation was impossible, for she stayed far enough behind Dore that the branches he pushed aside did not sweep back and strike her, but she longed to ask him how he thought they would escape. Certainly the huntsmen from the castle would find their tracks easily and follow them into this wood. And they were traveling so slowly here. When they came down into the valley she was certain that Menwyn and the Prince would be waiting, for any fool would have this wood encircled in a trice.

They began to descend, the path snaking back and forth across the slope. An hour and this charade would be over, Elise thought. And foolish Gwyden Dore would find that his tale had the tragic ending after all—at least for him. She would merely suffer a lecture from Menwyn —unpleasant enough—but her guide . . . She did not like to think what would befall him.

For an hour they meandered down the hillside, following the narrow way, and then the land leveled and they came upon another small stream hidden among the trees. Gwyden Dore jumped down to water his horse and to drink himself. Elise stayed in the saddle.

"I am turned around," she said, gazing about. "I thought we descended into the Cloffen Wold. Where are the open fields and the village of Kadre?"

"We have come a different way," her guide said.

She could see him now for the first time since the sun had risen. He balanced on a rock at the stream edge, crouched over the running water, his dark beard slick and wet. She thought him handsome, still—his face strong featured, his lips soft and promising.

He rose and took two drinking skins from his saddle. "You should drink and let your horse do the same. It will be a warm day and long. You will be glad of the refreshment."

He made no move to help her down, and Elise had to slip from the saddle on her own.

"It is a foolish saddle for traveling," he said, as he bent down again, filling the skins with water. "But I thought you might object to a man's saddle."

"A sidesaddle will suit me well enough," she said, and led her horse upstream from him, waiting until he filled the skins before letting her horse wade a few steps into the stream. When it had drunk enough—too much would not be good—she led it out and wrapped the reins around a branch so that she might drink herself.

Her guide had taken a seat on a rock, and was slicing cheese and bread with a dagger. He waved a hand at the food. "Eat a little, and then we must be away again."

Elise came and sat near him, finding shade beneath the trees. It was a crude meal, but her stomach was not as offended as she thought it should have been.

"You might tell me your name, now," she said. "I feel a bit foolish calling you Gwyden Dore."

He had laid his head back against a tree, but opened his eyes and looked at her. "It is a good name, and one I am flattered to bear."

She gave him a look of calculated, mild exasperation.

"You may call me Alaan," he conceded.

"Not your real name, I assume . . .?"

He let his head rest against the tree again. "Oddly enough, it is my real name. And was my father's before me."

"Where is it we are going, Alaan?"

He opened his eyes and rose to his feet suddenly. "I will be on my way to a small cell and worse if we sit here any longer." He gathered up the makings of their meal, and they set off again, into the warm, green afternoon.

They rode along the streambed beneath white-barked trees that leaned out over the water, surprisingly large yellow flowers hanging down from the branches like elongated bells. Sun sparkled down through the leaves and shimmered on the water.

Elise brought her horse up beside Alaan's. "What are these trees?" she asked.

He glanced at the bank. "Morning trumpet."

"But I've never seen them before."

"They're common enough here," he said, and spurred his horse forward so that her own fell in behind.

They kept beside the streambed for a few hours, yet didn't emerge from the wood, which Elise would have said was impossible. She tried to recall their course: they'd crossed the bridge and gone west along the north shore of the lake, then turned north up Halbert's Hill, over the crest, and down into what should have been the Cloffen Wold. But now they were in a valley traveling west again through open wood. Even if she had become turned around in the trees, they would have had to emerge into open fields, for that was all that surrounded Halbert's Hill: fields on three sides and lake on the other. Yet here they were in trees—and such trees they were! How could she have never heard of morning trumpet?

"Where are we?" she asked, spurring her horse up beside Alaan's again.

"On a path that few know," he said. "We're not lost. Don't worry."

"But where are the fields? I have ridden all the way around that hill—and more than once—and fields surround it."

"Not completely, no." He glanced over at her, forcing the worried, thoughtful look from his face. He smiled. "If we traveled the common roads we would soon be caught. Don't you agree?"

"Yes, but—"

"So I have taken you another way." He pointed up the stream before them. "We leave the river here."

He paused a moment to let the horses drink, then led the way up a bare slope of rock. Immediately the path narrowed again and went up, forcing her to follow behind—alone with all of her unanswered questions.

Late in the afternoon Alaan took out a bow and shot a partridge, leaving his saddle only to retrieve the unlucky bird from the ground. At dusk they crested a hill, and just beneath, on the other side, made a fire in the shelter of a stooping shoulder of rock. To Elise's surprise Alaan retrieved a bag hanging by a rope from a tree, and from this he took food for them and grain for the horses.

Elise was put to work plucking the feathers from their main course, a task she had never performed before. She was surprised at how much labor it took to get all the small quills. Alaan worked about their makeshift camp, surprisingly at home in the wilds for a minstrel, she thought. He performed all of his tasks with an unhurried ease, suggesting that he'd done them many times before. She watched him surreptitiously, taking guilty pleasure in the sureness of his movements, the strength and manly grace that he displayed in everything.

She could tell that he thought her young and believed he knew better than she—but unlike that ass the Prince of Innes, who clearly had held the same opinion—she was a little worried that Alaan was not wrong. At least not entirely. She'd become afraid to say anything lest she appear foolish, though why she should care for the opinion of a minstrel she didn't know. For his part, Alaan did nothing to encourage conversation with anyone so young and lacking wisdom.

When they'd met before she'd thought him a rogue, but now that they were alone here in the wilds he seemed unaware that she was a young woman traveling without proper escort. His attention was clearly taken up with other matters.

Alaan applied himself to the preparation of dinner with the same unhurried competence. It was dark when the meal was done, and they sat by the fading coals, stars filling the gaps between the leaves overhead. An owl hooted from its branch of the night, and Alaan looked up, a tiny flare of apprehension appearing on his face.

"Will the men sent to find us be able to follow these secret paths we've taken?" Elise asked. She was not used to being in another's company in silence and could bear it no more.

Alaan had stored bottles of wine in the sack he'd left here, and drank rather too freely, she thought.

"If they're close behind us they'll find them, but if not . . . not."

"You don't seem too worried that they'll catch us here." She nodded toward the fire.

"No, they're not so close behind. It takes some time to prepare twenty or thirty men for a pursuit. And two who know the way will always travel faster than a greater number who've never seen the land before. There are places where they'll lose our tracks—where we crossed rock or where we made our way up the river for a time— and they'll have to search until the tracks are found again. They won't be foolish enough to ride at night beneath the trees. So we're quite safe this night. You may sleep as though you were secure in your own bed."

She shifted a little at this assertion. "I have a feather bed," she said, trying to find a position of comfort on the hard ground. "Have you one of those hidden in your sack?"

Alaan laughed. "Did you not save the feathers from our bird? I'll make you a mattress of green bows and you'll think feathers as hard as wood ever after." He poured more wine into his crude cup, but she shook her head when he offered more to her. She thought his hand was growing unsteady. And did he appear to be looking at her differently, now that the first bottle had been emptied?

"So tell me, Alaan . . ." she said, her mouth suddenly dry. "Are you a sorcerer?"

He smiled and raised his cup to his lips. "Women commonly save such flattery until the morning."

"I'm not jesting. I'm not quite as young and foolish as you seem to think. There is no path through the wood that leads from Halbert's Hill. We have traveled today along streams that flow *toward* the hills, not away from them. And I have seen both trees and flowers that have never grown within a day's ride of Braidon Castle. Where have you taken me, sir?"

Alaan opened his mouth to speak, but a small dark bird fluttered down out of the night and landed a few feet from Alaan.

"Jac!" he said, and grinned in slightly drunken delight.

"I know this bird!" Elise said. "It tried to steal my ring right from my finger!"

"Any bright thing Jac covets." Alaan found some nuts in his sack and spread them over the ground. The bird fell upon them greedily, glancing warily up at Elise every few seconds.

"Is this your familiar, then?"

Alaan laughed. "Jac thinks I am *his* familiar. No, he is not even a pet. A sometime traveling companion, for we have certain things in common—a liking for walnuts— and we both go about the countryside warning people of coming troubles. No one heeds either of us, however."

"You've not answered my question . . . Are you a sorcerer, Alaan?"

Jac sprang back up into the night; a flutter of wings and he was gone. Alaan didn't look to see him go but sat holding his cup on a raised knee, looking at Elise a bit too boldly. "No, Lady Elise, I am not a sorcerer. I have no unnatural abilities save this one you have witnessed: I can find the hidden paths that others cannot. It must seem a strange thing to you, but it is no more strange than your father's ability to play music: a gift that some are given."

"It is quite a bit more strange than that. But where are we?"

"How can I tell you? We are on a path that leads from Halbert's Hill to—well, it has several branchings and leads many places."

"How do you do it? How do you find these paths?"

Alaan shrugged and drank from his cup, pausing to fill it again—too soon, she thought. "Can you raise your hand and touch your nose with a finger?"

"More readily than you," she said, eyeing the bottle.

"Do it," he said. "I'm quite serious."

She lifted a hand and quickly touched the tip of her nose.

"How did you do that?" he asked.

"Well, I don't know—"

"That is exactly how I find the paths that others can't."

"It isn't much of an answer."

"It is the only answer possible."

Elise fell silent a moment, sipping at her own wine. Alaan seemed suddenly rather forthcoming, after a day of near silence. She was not sure how she felt about that. Some part of her worried that she was entering into an unspoken bargain——he would answer her questions, and in return . . . Yet, she kept asking questions.

"Why are you involved in this matter between my family and the Renné?"

"Oh, I'm not really. The Wills and the Renné could massacre each other for all it matters to me. I sometimes think the world would be better for it. I've met and spoken with members of both your clans, and I'll tell you: all that distinguishes a Wills from a Renné is the object of their hatred——otherwise the lot of you are much the same."

Elise took a sip of her wine, surprised to feel a little flare of resentment. "Then why have you gone to the trouble of rescuing me?"

"I regret to tell you, Lady Elise, it has almost nothing to do with you. It is the poor innocent people who will die if your families go to war again. But even more than that, it is Hafydd."

"Who?"

"Hafydd," he said again, with just the slightest trace of a slur. "But of course, you know him as Eremon, the Prince of Innes's counselor."

"The knight in the black robe?"

"Yes, that's him."

"My father warned me of him."

"And well he should. I've helped you escape to foil the plans of Hafydd and to humiliate him before his allies, the Prince of Innes and your uncle, Lord Menwyn. I wish to sow the seeds of doubt in their minds."

"Well, I'm glad to learn that your concern for me is so great."

"Yes, I'm sure it is difficult to be a Wills and be told that you're not, in the end, the center of all things."

"I live under no such delusion, and I am as cynical of the Wills as anyone—even you, perhaps. I come from a family schooled in hatred, Alaan, but I do not hate the Renné, for all that they've done to us."

"And all that your family has done to them," Alaan said. "The hatred of the Renné and the Wills is not really such a great thing. It is barely an echo of hatreds that existed in the past." He leaned forward a little. "Have you ever noticed how the minstrels and storytellers go about the countryside singing of all the wrongs that have been done? The same minstrels, who come to Braidon Castle and sing of the evils done you by the Renné, will then travel to Castle Renné and sing of the injuries the Wills have done to them. And have you watched the hatred kindle as people listen to these songs? The minstrels are like carriers of disease, going from place to place, bearing the plague of hatred with them, spreading it from one village to the next to the next until the whole land is infected." His cup traveled a fairly steady course to his lips again, and when it descended a few jewels of wine hung in his beard.

"But you are a minstrel, or you pose as one."

"Oh, I am at times, but I'm not a minstrel of hatred,

as I call them. I sing of love, most often, and mystery. Sometimes my songs tell stories with strange twists and odd endings. But I never sing of the wrongs done by men."

"What of all the wrongs done in love?"

He looked very directly at her. "You are, on occasion, surprisingly sage for one so young. What is your age?"

"I am twenty years."

"Going on thirty-seven."

This near-compliment made her feel awkward suddenly. "Why does this knight call himself Eremon?" she asked quickly, "if his name is Hafydd?"

"Because he was reborn, or so he believes." Alaan set his empty cup down on the ground and stood, more steadily than she would have predicted. "It is time for sleep. We rise with the sun, and tomorrow will be a more difficult day."

†WENTY-FIVE

Menwyn was in a rage. Carral could tell by the way he opened the door. Carral had always enjoyed his brother's furies, for there was nothing Menwyn could do but rant. Unlike Hafydd, Menwyn would never strike a blind man—he had some twisted sense of honor, or perhaps it was merely good manners he could not give up.

"Where has she gone, Carral?" Menwyn said, his voice low and flat and deadly serious. "The Prince and his villainous counselor, Eremon, are demanding to speak with you. Better to tell me."

Carral swallowed. He touched a hand to his bruised cheek. "I do not know. Eremon—who is Hafydd, by the way—may strike me again at his pleasure, but I truly do not know."

This stopped Menwyn a moment. "He did not strike you," he said firmly. "You fell. You told everyone you fell."

"So I did, but it was Hafydd's hand that drove me to my knees."

"I don't believe you, Carral. I don't."

"That is your privilege, but what I tell you is true,

nonetheless. Hafydd struck me savagely, as you see, because I dared to oppose the marriage of my daughter to the son of his master——though who is master in that house is open to dispute, I think. And it is also true that I don't know where Elise has gone, luckily, for if Hafydd treats me as he did before I would surely tell. But I have nothing to tell. So by all means, set the dogs on me again. They may savage me all they like. I can tell them nothing."

Footsteps sounded in the hallway and then turned into the room.

"Prince Neit, Sir Hafydd," Carral said and bowed from his chair.

"You did not strike my brother," Menwyn said, his voice filled with repressed outrage.

"Are you suggesting that I would strike a blind man?" Hafydd said.

"You say that as though you had honor that could be offended," Carral said, fear drying his mouth suddenly.

"Have a care what you say, minstrel," Hafydd said quickly. "There are limits to what I will tolerate, even from a blind man."

"But what was it you said to me, the day you gave me this?" Carral touched his bruise. "That you cared nothing for honor or chivalry or vows or so-called civilized conduct. 'I am unlike any man you have ever met, in this,' I believe were your words. I do not know where my daughter has gone, Sir Hafydd. You could tear off my limbs and I would not tell you because I cannot.

"She has gone off with a man I met in the tower. He claimed to be a ghost and would never give me a name. Of course, I did not believe him; but then, remember that night you came up to the tower and heard me speaking with another? I was talking with this very man, and when you entered the room . . . he was gone." Carral paused, still overwhelmed by what had happened. "Of course, you will not believe me, but that is often the case with the truth."

This confession was met by silence. Carral waited for the men to protest that he was treating them like fools.

"We know him, our whist," Hafydd said, his voice very quiet, almost still. "Twice he has escaped us, but he cannot hope to do so again."

Without a word the men began to file out, but Hafydd stopped in the door. Carral could hear the scuff of his boots as he turned back. The silence extended a moment, and then he walked out, leaving the door open.

TWENTY-SIX

The muttering began as soon as they descended into the valley. Prince Michael had no idea what it was about, and finally sought out Lord Menwyn Wills, whose men-at-arms were doing the whispering.

Menwyn was a cold little man who looked down on everyone with such a pained indifference that one wondered if there was anyone whose company he did not disdain. But this seemed to be something of a Wills family trait. Only Lord Carral and his daughter appeared to be free of it.

"Your men-at-arms seem unsettled by something," the Prince said.

Menwyn gazed at the Prince a moment, as though trying to remember his name, or perhaps hoping the Prince would realize he shouldn't ask questions of one so far above his station. "We've descended into the Cloffen Wold," he said slowly and gestured to the trees. "So this should be a wide valley of open fields, not forest. In the Cloffen valley there isn't a stand of trees so wide that you can't shoot an arrow over it." He looked oddly at Prince Michael, as though he might have an explanation.

"Perhaps the fields lay just beyond the streambed."

Menwyn began to tug at the riding gloves that he wore despite the warmth of the day. "Riders have gone off in all directions to look. We are, they tell me, in a forested valley with no fields in sight—which, I will tell you, is impossible. I know the lands around Braidon Castle as well as anyone. We are not on those lands." The Wills lord let his horse go forward into the stream to drink, leaving Prince Michael to ponder. Certainly these men were turned around somehow.

Michael gazed up the creek bed. Thirty mounted men milled about in the small stream, no one quite knowing where to go. The huntsmen had gone off both up- and downstream looking for signs of Elise and her "abductor," as he was being called—although Prince Michael was sure no one actually believed she'd been abducted. The huntsmen hadn't yet returned. Hafydd, surrounded by half a dozen of his guards, sat on his horse slightly apart from everyone else—and no one approached him.

All around, the Prince heard men quietly offering opinions on which direction their quarry had taken or how they'd ended up in this river bottom, shaded by strange trees that no one had ever seen before. But Hafydd was silent, waiting, brooding perhaps. Certainly he was in the grip of a slow-boiling rage that everyone else seemed to feel.

Why is everyone so afraid of him? the Prince wondered. *He is an old man, still hale, perhaps, but not the equal of a young knight. He's not from a powerful family, has no allies but my father. Yet everyone fears him. I fear him.*

It made no sense, yet the Prince found himself inching back from Hafydd, putting other men between himself and the black-robed knight.

When the huntsmen had not returned in an hour, Hafydd's patience expired in a sudden exhalation of oaths. He swung down from his saddle, guards scrambling to snatch his horse's bridle. With every eye on him, Hafydd splashed through the shallow water; drew his sword; and in the shattered, dancing light, struck the flat of the blade upon a rock so that the sword shivered and rang. He raised the weapon, still ringing, and closed his eyes. The sound faded but sustained, its note dropping to a dull drone. But it did not die.

Hafydd held the blade aloft and turned in a slow circle, his eyes still pressed tightly shut. Suddenly Michael found himself nearest Hafydd, as everyone else retreated around him. Hafydd stopped, his blade pointing upstream.

He opened his eyes. "He has gone this way, my whist," he said, and motioned for his horse. Sheathing the sword silenced it, though the Prince still heard a faint ringing in his ears. Hafydd mounted quickly and sent three of his black-clad guard splashing up the stream before him.

No rider moved to follow. All the horses stood rigidly still, ears up, as though they might bolt at any moment. The riders looked no more confident. And then Prince Michael's father urged his horse forward. It waded unsteadily up the slippery streambed, and the others followed reluctantly behind.

They rose before the sun and broke their fast with haste. Alaan kindled no fire, and Elise washed in cold water, and dressed in the same clothing she had worn the previous day. Her saddle seemed to have grown uncomfortable overnight, but that passed within an hour. They found their way down the hillside beneath tall pines and firs through a sparse underbrush. The ground was overrun in places by tangles of spreading green spattered with small blue flowers. Here and there clusters of large ferns clung to the shade, but these bore a deep crimson blush that overspread the green near the base of the fronds. She had never seen either of these plants before.

But other than the trees and plants and the lack of fields or familiar landmarks, the landscape was surprisingly like that around Braidon Castle: a succession of hills and ridges, separated by deep valleys through which streams ran.

The stream that lay at the foot of this slope could have been the same one they had met the day before. The same white-barked trees leaned over it, their pendulous trumpets swaying in the breeze.

Elise alighted from her mare, and it nuzzled her, looking for treats she did not carry. "Do no people live here?" she asked Alaan, who filled their drinking skins from a pool.

"Very few. Most who discover a path here quickly find themselves on familiar ways again, though not quite where they expect, and they can never find the path back again, search as they might. But even that is uncommon. Further north, in the wildlands, the paths are more easily found—especially upon the River Wynnd. But here few ever find them."

"Well, it is a wonderful place for thieves to hide," she observed. She let her gray drink, holding the reins and trying to keep her feet dry.

"Better yet, for fugitives from injustice." He smiled at her—or perhaps at his own attempt at wit. He slung the skins over his saddle. "We'll go up again. In places it will grow very steep and will be better for the horses that we walk. Are you frightened of heights?"

"No more than most," she said, twisting the leather reins in her hands. She moved to look up through a gap in the trees. She could see stone cliffs standing out starkly against the sky. Certainly there were no cliffs this close to Braidon Castle.

"Don't look so frightened," Alaan said. "The way we go will appear more dangerous than it really is."

She shook her head, tugging her mare's head up from the water and pulling it near. "It isn't that. It's this place. That I am here at all . . . A day's ride from my home but somewhere no one has been before."

"I've been here," Alaan said. "And is it not a beautiful place I've led you?"

"It is more than beautiful. But it is strange, all the

same. What if we're lost here and can never find our way back?" Her mare jostled her, and she almost lost her balance on the slippery bank.

"We're not lost, and finding our way back is easily done. If I were to leave you here and let you go on alone you would be back on known paths in a few hours, perhaps less." Alaan tethered his horse to a branch and sat down in the shade. "We can rest awhile," he said.

Elise glanced back over her shoulder. "What of our pursuers? What of this knight Hafydd?"

"I don't want to outdistance them quite yet. Let them follow us a little farther. Hafydd is nowhere near as angry as I wish to make him."

"How do you know that?"

"Oh, I have known him many a year."

Her mare struggled a little to pull its head free, but she would not let it drink again. "Do you not fear him— as others do?"

"Not as others do, but I fear him." Alaan went up the stream a few steps to a place half screened by leaves and pulled his shirt over his head. The white flesh contrasted with his darkly tanned hands and face and seemed softer somehow, though there was little sign of softness in Alaan's physique.

Elise knew she should look away, but did not. As he bent to wash himself she saw a small scar on his back— a thin horizontal line beneath his shoulder blade. She didn't know what to think of a man who'd been stabbed in the back, for only a blade made such a scar.

When he stood and turned to retrieve his shirt from a branch, she saw a matching scar, though longer, over his heart. She pulled her eyes away, as he emerged from behind the bush.

Certainly no one survived being run through, she thought, so they were separate wounds: two attempts to stab Alaan in the heart, from before and behind.

Elise tethered her horse to a tree, and she and Alaan made a meal by the streamside, saying little. The slow-running water made a small pool of silence before them, and the light sprinkled down through shimmering leaves, drenching them in gold. Morn flashed her tail to chase the flies, and a bird broke the silence with a hoarse half-whispered call.

Alaan sat up with a quickness that startled her. And then the call came again. *"Whist, whist."*

Alaan sprang to his feet, scooping up their luncheon in one motion. "They're closer than I hoped," he said and pulled her up. He tightened her mare's girth, and boosted her up into her saddle. He was on his own horse immediately, and they set off up the streambed, too quickly, for the rocks were slick and dangerous.

Both horses slithered and slid, snorting and breaking into sweat. They shook their bridles in protest, but Alaan drove them on. After a time they climbed a steep bank and cantered beneath the trees. Too soon the floor of the wood sloped up and they were forced to slow, picking their way around rock faces that broke through the soft surface of the land. These were not large—fifty feet high,

perhaps, never more than a hundred feet in breadth—
but they grew more numerous as they climbed.

They rounded one of these and Alaan led them to the
top, where they could gaze down over the treetops
below.

"There," he said, pointing.

"I don't see . . ."

"Where the trees break. Can you see the stream glittering?"

"Yes!"

A column of mounted men crossed the water, sun
glinting off helms. They disappeared beneath the trees,
like ants in the grass. Elise stared a moment, unable to
look away.

They will not hurt you, she thought. *Only Alaan need fear.
They will only take you back. Back.*

She tore her gaze away. "We'd better hurry," she said.

They angled up the slope now, for it was too steep to
approach directly. Alaan had an uncanny knack for finding game paths that led where he wished to go—or
perhaps he merely went with the paths, she wasn't sure.

It was an arduous climb for the poor horses, and Elise
found that she suffered as well. Her back was stiff and
sore, and the muscles of her stomach had begun to cramp,
as did her legs. Though she rode often she'd never ridden
such rugged terrain, or for so many hours without proper
rest. She began to regret her boast now that she could
keep to the saddle night and day.

Suddenly they came out from under the trees but were

met by a steep slope of fallen stone. Above this a massive cliff face lifted up, so steep it seemed to lean over them.

"Where will we go now?" she cried.

Alaan had leapt down from his horse and shook the reins over its head. "Up," he said, "but on foot for a while."

Elise slid out of her saddle and pulled the reins over Morn's head. She glanced up the scree slope once more, and hitched up her skirts to climb.

The rock was loose and slipped and slid beneath their feet. The poor horses had the worst of it, and Elise was sure her mare would never have gone on if Alaan's sorrel hadn't led the way. After a few moments they stopped to catch their breath.

Elise looked down the stone slope and thought that if poor Morn ever really slid she might not stop until the bottom. She glanced up again.

"Where are you taking me? Surely they'll trap us here against this cliff."

"There is a path," Alaan said. "It's narrow and high but passable. Your mare is of calm disposition, and Briss has been along it once, and many another strange place with me. He won't falter." Alaan patted the sorrel's nose, and with his first step set off a small slide of rock. An elongated circle of stone was suddenly in motion, rumbling down the slope for fifty feet before it came to rest again. A few pieces of rock rolled on, gathering speed as they spun until they crashed into the trees below, the sound of shattering branches clear in the quiet afternoon.

Three more times they stopped before they came up under the cliff itself. There was a break in the rock above, as though a massive piece of it had fallen away, leaving a sort of stone roof. For a while this hung over them, but the slope angled upward; and soon they could almost touch this overhang and then emerged from beneath it. Two hundred feet farther along Alaan stopped. He bent over to catch his breath and pointed at a stone ledge sloping slightly up. It broke the cliff face for as far as Elise could see before disappearing around a corner.

"We are not going up there!"

"Our choice is to give ourselves up to Hafydd. Not so frightening for you, perhaps, but death for me. I'll go on."

Elise stared at the ledge in disbelief. "But we can't take horses along that!"

"Yes, we can. They're less afraid of heights than we— it's one of the benefits of having no imagination. They don't imagine falling, as we do."

Elise was at a loss for words.

"It is wider than it looks," Alaan said. "Once you are on it you'll see. And it's not so long."

"Is there no other way?"

"Only one, half a league away."

A shout came from below, and Elise looked back. Men and horses were milling about where she and Alaan had emerged from the trees.

"It's a good thing I appear to have no other choice," she said, a tight voice betraying her a little.

Alaan tried to smile, but his face was grave, his hair plastered to his forehead by sweat. "Listen to me a moment," he said. "If your mare startles or begins to dance about, don't hold tight to the reins. She might throw you off. The same if she slips. Let go the reins, or she might take you with her. If she looks as though she will lunge ahead, throw yourself down against the cliff."

"But she might trample me!"

"Better that than knock you off." He reached out and squeezed her hand. "It looks much worse than it is. You'll see."

Alaan turned and led the way out onto the ledge. Elise couldn't quite believe that she followed, but she found herself falling in behind. To her surprise, Morn came along easily.

I am no better than a mare, she thought, following stupidly along.

But Alaan was right. It was not as narrow as it had looked. There was a dirt track of sorts; and stunted, hardy shrubs and other plants found purchase here. The ledge was the height of a man in width and sloped gently up; and it was surprisingly smooth. After a hundred feet Elise began to breathe more easily.

And then she looked down.

While the ledge was sloping up, the base of the cliff had been sloping down, so that suddenly she was very high up, and getting higher with each step. If she were to fall even now, it would likely mean her end.

"River take me . . ." she heard herself say.

Morn's soft nose nudged her arm, and she looked up to see Alaan now far ahead. She went on, afraid to hurry, but just as afraid of being left behind. She kept her eyes fixed ahead, watching her footing, looking neither left nor right—nor down. Alaan slowed to wait for her.

"Are you all right?" he called over Briss's head.

"No, but I'm coming along all the same. Keep moving. Let's be done with this." She glanced right and almost stumbled. The valley spread out below, the great trees diminutive from her eagle's view. If fear had not already done so, the view would have taken her breath away.

Alaan had disappeared around a corner, and she pressed on, not quite sure how she went forward. A strange thought went through her mind: *I would like to see one of my witless cousins do this!* This heartened her, somehow, and she pressed forward.

Around a corner she found Alaan and his gelding waiting among trees. The ledge had widened out to twenty feet, and here there was a little oasis of green in the vast desert of stone. He was untethering his bow and quiver from the saddle.

"You'll have to take both horses on," he said. "Morn will follow if you lead Briss."

"And what will you do?"

Alaan sprung his bow and slipped the string into its notch. She didn't like the look on his face.

"I'll teach Hafydd to be so foolish as to follow me along a narrow ledge." He handed her the reins of his horse. "Don't look so dismayed. When you fled you should have realized there would be consequences."

Before she could protest, he stepped past her and set out along the ledge at a trot. For a moment Elise stood utterly still, watching him go. She looked around at the little island of safety in the hard world they traveled. The soft green of leaves and ferns made her want to cry suddenly. And then Briss perked up his ears and whickered.

There were other horses near.

She pulled the reins over Morn's head and fastened them loosely to the saddle—she didn't want her mare tripping on her own tack—and led Briss on, leaving Morn to follow. She hesitated only a second before stepping back onto the narrow track, the world opening up to one side, cold stone to the other. The wind ghosted up the bluff, and a hawk broke the silence with a shrill, plaintive cry. The cliff was in shadow, but beyond the world was green and russet brocade thrown down upon the sunlit hills. The horizon seemed impossibly distant, the far hills fading to hazy blue.

Briss pricked up his ears again, suddenly alert. Elise stopped to listen but heard only the wind licking dryly over stone.

The path turned up in broken steps and ramps, and she clambered over stone, trying to stay clear of Briss, who made small jumps at each rise. The wall curved slowly inward and Elise found herself in a narrow draw that went steeply up. The path, which she was sure only wild goats could have made, snaked among fallen stone, worn smooth by the wind and rain. A tiny brook, barely a trickle, tripped and tumbled down the draw in small falls and clear pools. She let the horses drink for a moment, hoping Alaan would appear on the path below.

The whole endeavor had taken an ugly turn suddenly. She wanted to escape this marriage and the ambitions of Menwyn and the Prince of Innes, but she wouldn't have anyone *die* so that she might accomplish this. Part of her felt like a spoiled child, petulantly running from duties she did not care to face; and now this mad minstrel was killing men to aid her.

A wind came up the draw, hissing in reproach.

Prince Michael kept his shoulder against the coarse stone, not caring if he wore holes in his clothing or if he were the object of teasing on the morrow. He cast his eyes down a little now and then, catching just a glimpse of the valley far below. The horse before him knocked a stone free; and it spun through the air, taking longer than he would have thought possible to strike the scree below. The Prince took a deep breath, pressed his shoulder hard to the wall, and walked stiffly along.

Ahead of him the column of men and horses made their halting way forward, few of the men more comfortable than he. The Prince could hardly believe that Lady Elise had gone willingly along this ledge. Perhaps she *had* been abducted.

A horse screamed and reared up some ways ahead of him, and the horse right before him started back, hammering the Prince's shin with a hard hoof. For a second he was caught between his own horse and the one before, and then he squeezed back against the wall and let the two horses jostle each other. Another horse reared, and men began shouting. Then an arrow sparked off the wall three feet away.

Arrows! Someone was shooting arrows at them.

Horses lumbered into him, their weight crushing him against the wall. He kept moving his feet, trying to save them from being broken. A roiling sea of horses rose up before him like a sudden storm. One horse slipped, its forequarters going down, and another horse had turned and was knocked forward half over it. For a moment they scrambled like that. Michael struggled to get clear, pressing his back against the wall, jiggling his own mount's bit. And then both horses toppled and were gone.

The Prince heard himself cursing over and over. And then something like calm returned, horses frightened but under control. He heard men moaning, injured by their own horses, he guessed, or shot with arrows. Near the head of the column Hafydd was giving orders, then they began to move forward again, the Prince wondering if an arrow would suddenly find him.

The ledge seemed to go on forever, hugging the undulating cliff face. Prince Michael thought the experience a perfect vision of death: suspended between the earth and the sky; gazing down onto sunlit hills that were always out of reach; nowhere to go but forward on this narrow, endless ledge.

And then he was among trees. He reached out to take hold of a thick branch, as though assuring himself that it was real. The Prince found his father, who stood gazing along the cliff, where to his horror Prince Michael saw that the ledge continued.

"Why are we stopping?" Prince Michael asked.

"We've sent men forward to cut down this archer."

Prince Michael nodded. He didn't believe for a moment that they would succeed. Hafydd's whist would elude them. Only a fool would have taken to this ledge without knowing where it led: Hafydd's whist was no fool.

Prince Michael sat down upon a rock, twisting the reins of his horse around a nearby branch.

"Don't become too contented," his father said. "We'll go on in a moment."

"Oh, I don't think so, Father," Prince Michael said. "This man we chase has made a fool of Hafydd before. I'll wager he'll do it again."

His father did not answer but only cleared his throat. Prince Michael glanced left to find Hafydd staring coldly down on him. The Prince tried to smile, but mocking Hafydd to his face took more nerve than he could muster. The smile wavered and disappeared, and the Prince looked quickly away.

Elise forced herself to go up, the walls of the draw closing in as she went. What if Alaan did not appear below, but only Hafydd and men-at-arms? Would she run or give herself up? But where would she go? She had no plan of her own but followed Alaan blindly.

"Bloody fool!" she cursed.

She heard a sound and wheeled around, her heart stuttering against the wall of her chest. But it was Alaan, bounding over rocks as he ran. She was both relieved and frightened.

"What did you do?" she demanded as he came up, gasping.

"Sent them back . . . for a time," he panted. He bent over, plunged his hands into a pool, and threw water on his face. He looked up. "I don't know if I managed to shoot any men, but I certainly hit horses, which caused some chaos on the ledge."

Elise raised a hand to her mouth. "Will they go back?"

"Back? No. They'll send armed men with shields ahead on foot. They think they'll brave my arrows that way, but I have no intention of shooting more arrows." He took the reins of the horses and tethered them to low bushes, and led Elise fifty feet back down the draw. They stood atop a little rise of stone, staring out over the vast world.

There was a mound of broken stone here, as though much of the rock that tumbled down the draw had collected against this outcropping. Alaan took up a rock, twice the size of a man's head and balanced it at shoulder height.

"Take up a stone," he said, "as large as you can lift. They will be along in a moment."

Elise stared at him. "You don't expect me to—"

"Take up a rock," he said, "or I will leave you here for Hafydd! And I'm not sure your uncle has come along to protect you."

Two black-clad men appeared below, swords in hand, shields raised—and then a third and a fourth. They came sprinting up the draw, hollering when they saw Alaan.

"Wait a moment . . . Now!" Alaan sent his rock spinning down the draw, careening wildly off mounds and boulders. Elise waited and then sent her own rock, hardly tossing it. But even so it quickly gathered speed and went crashing and bouncing toward the men. Alaan grabbed up another stone and flung it down the slope and another. Elise did the same and the next time she looked the men were in retreat, running for their lives.

"Crouch down," Alaan ordered, pulling on her arm. "We don't want them to be able to see us. Let them wonder if we're still here or if we've gone on."

"What will we do now? Are we trapped?" She looked desperately around.

"I would never lead us into a blind end. No, the path leads to the top from here, but I don't want these others following too quickly behind. They'll try to overrun us again—more of them this time—but we've the advantage here. I'm sure the two of us could keep them at bay the entire day. They might make their way up under cover of darkness, but we'll be gone before then. Here they are!"

There were more men this time. Elise hadn't time to count. She hurled stone after stone down the slope, and

Alaan worked in a fury. The men came farther up the draw this time, until several of them were hit by flying rocks, and then they retreated.

"That will do," Alaan said, taking her hand.

He pulled her, running, up the twisting path. They took up the leads of their mounts and pressed on without a rest. Elise was out of breath in a moment, her shoulders weak from her efforts; but she drove herself on, stumbling, forcing one foot in front of the other.

A massive fissure in the rock appeared before them, ten times the height of a man, though narrow. Alaan led them in, slowing his pace. Inside the walls were sculpted and curved strangely in and out. The passage would only allow one through at a time, and she followed behind, stepping carefully over the narrow watercourse that trickled and twisted along the floor.

"We have no torch," she said, as the light from the opening grew dim.

"We won't need one," Alaan said, not looking back, his voice sounding deep and hollow against the stone.

As the light faded from behind, a pale gray appeared before them. After a moment, the walls suddenly flared out, and they entered a chamber perhaps a hundred feet across but with a narrow slit open to the sky high overhead. Small trees and flowers grew among the rocks, and the stream pooled and fell and pooled again, as it found its course among the debris. Leaves and old dried branches littered the floor, and here and there graying logs lay at odd angles among the stones.

Elise stopped she was so surprised. As though they had found another world inside the world. Muted light angled down in rays so sharply defined that she thought she might reach out and feel their substance. Against the coarse gray walls, trees and ferns waved gently on a breeze from above, and water tinkled, echoing softly.

"What an astonishing place," she whispered, barely able to take her eyes from the scene. But Alaan did not wait.

He led them along one wall, finding his way surely among rocks and logs. At the chamber's far end the passage began again. Elise stopped to look back once.

"Elise? You'll have to admire it in memory," Alaan said, and she turned away.

They emerged onto the cliff top into bright sun, and Elise blinked, wondering if what she had just seen could have been real. In every direction the world seemed to retreat from them, hills rising up like waves and stretching to a far horizon. Alaan was on Briss. He paused to take water from a drinking skin, handing it to Elise as she climbed awkwardly into her saddle.

"We go along the ridge and then down. The way is easier now, but we'll have to make speed."

She handed him the skin, and he heeled away, setting his horse off at a fast walk along the bare cliff top. In half an hour they were traveling down, over a high meadow and then into trees. Elise was exhausted, hungry, and still frightened. Her head had begun to ache, and she felt a growing resentment and anger toward Alaan. She had never meant for anyone to be harmed!

Alaan, however, seemed unaware of how she felt. He guided them among the trees with barely a glance in her direction—and even then only to see that she had not fallen too far behind.

When finally he did stop, it was out of concern for the horses. He let them drink from a small creek, then browse on the grasses while he lifted each of their hooves in turn.

"They've come through that well enough," he pronounced. He seemed to have noticed Elise for the first time in several hours. "But what of you?" he asked. "Have you recovered from the heights?"

"I am bearing up," she said, not meeting his gaze, hating herself for acting so childishly.

"Let's make a small meal," he said, his voice warming a little. "By the evening we'll have left Hafydd and the others behind—or so I hope. A few more hours and we can rest."

"But are they not close behind?"

"I don't think they'll chance that draw again until after dark." Alaan pointed up the hill. "And if they have braved it, I can see the cliff top from here. They'll not catch us unaware."

The trees were thinner, the slope covered in grass and bright flowers. The sun shone brightly on this side of the cliff, and the place seemed cheerful and welcoming. She could hardly believe that they were being pursued by armed men. An image of them coming up the draw, swords raised, came to her. This running away had seemed such a lark, so romantic, in a way. But that had changed when they'd sent the rocks flying down the draw. She'd seen one man struck, and he lay still and lifeless afterward.

She turned her mind away, gazing at her sturdy little mare. Morn was game for this life, that was certain. She didn't complain.

Stale bread, old cheese, and cold meat were not Elise's idea of a meal, but at least she felt her hunger abating, and her mood lifted a little as well. She sat on the soft grass, dressed in clothes that were both dirty and torn, eating peasant food, and was thankful for it. Anything to be out of the saddle—and off that ledge!

Alaan kept his eye fixed on the ridge above while they ate and said little. He might have talked confidently about what Hafydd and these others might do, but his vigilance said otherwise.

He rose much too soon. Elise felt terribly weary and found her feet stiffly. For a moment she stared at her saddle, hesitating, and then Alaan came to help her up.

"Only a few more hours. Tomorrow will be an easier day," he said. He stood staring up at her a moment, his manner very serious. "We don't do this for amusement, Lady Elise," he said softly. "If Menwyn and the Prince of Innes make an alliance, the Renné will respond. Among the noble houses there will be a scramble to take sides— they know the consequences of trying to remain neutral. War will come." He reached out and stroked Morn's nose. "You're concerned about those men who perished today. A battle will leave a thousand times that many dead. A thousand times!" He looked up at Elise again. "You are doing this to escape a marriage, but I am doing it to avoid a war, or at least delay one."

"I am not running away, like some spoiled child, to avoid an unwanted marriage," she said coldly. "I would marry Prince Michael tomorrow, but I refuse to aid my family's desire to rekindle their feud. As a Wills I suppose I should not have been so shocked to see you set off to kill those men—or even to attempt to kill some myself— but I have lived a sheltered life. It might come as a surprise to you, but not every Wills is taught to slit throats on their fifth birthday."

Alaan made a small bowing motion. "Of course. I apologize, Lady Elise. Occasionally I forget whose daughter you are." He bobbed his head again and stepped fluidly up into his saddle.

They continued their descent, the trees changing as they went. Crossing a small meadow Elise turned to look back and was certain the hill did not appear so lofty. Where was the stone ridge? Was it hidden behind trees somewhere?

In the late afternoon they emerged from the forest onto the shore of a calm lake. They dismounted and watered their horses. Elise threw herself down on the grass.

"Tell me we're making our camp here this night. . . ."

"You're asking me to lie." Alaan pointed down the lake to the opposite shore. "There is a small house in the trees. It is hard to see from the lake. We'll spend the night there."

"Beneath a roof?"

"Yes, but there are no feather beds."

"And what of Hafydd and the others?"

"No feather beds for them either." He smiled at her. "I think we're safe from them, now, but just to be sure, I have a final trick to play. Can you swim?"

"I cannot."

"Not taught to slit throats. Not taught to swim. What did your family teach you?"

"I was taught hatred of our enemies, and from my father I learned to play the lute and sing. I have wonderful manners, and I can ride all day over any terrain. Oh, and I am a decent archer, though I've never shot at a target that had a beating heart."

Alaan bowed his head. "It is an impressive enough education, I suppose. With a little luck, swimming won't be necessary."

He led the way down a long beach above the lake and then down the slope to the water again. Here there was a small sandbar, and upon it a raft of logs was beached. Elise looked at this, and then out at the lake, which looked very deep and cold to her.

"Will we abandon our horses?"

"No. They will have to come aboard."

"They will not!"

"Briss has done it before. Not happily perhaps, but without complaint." Alaan looked over at Elise's gray mare. "She has followed Briss everywhere else, let's hope she's not grown suddenly independent."

"Or suddenly wise." Alaan had dismounted, but Elise would not leave her saddle. "The horses will upset the raft, surely, and then I'll drown!"

Alaan met her eye and smiled, which seemed to have the same effect on her no matter what the danger. She felt her will soften a little.

"If we founder I'll rescue you," he said. "I swear it."

"And what of Morn?"

"Horses can swim, though they might not know it. Don't worry about her."

Alaan took a pole and levered the raft free of the beach, pushing it out a few feet into the water. He led Briss aboard. Elise did not like the way the raft rocked as the gelding surged aboard but she dismounted anyway. Morn whickered anxiously.

Alaan took the mare's head and coaxed her forward, but though she walked to the raft, she wouldn't step aboard. For some reason, Elise felt enormous satisfaction at this. But Alaan was not to be made a fool of by a horse. He brought Briss near, then banished him to the raft's far side. Morn surged aboard, then stood, bracing her feet, too frightened to move. Alaan pulled Elise aboard and pushed them off.

They were gliding swiftly out across the lake, the bottom falling quickly away. Elise looked down into the dark green waters, thinking of the great height of the ledge she had traversed. If she slipped here she would fall so slowly but just as far, down through the green slanting light, toward the inky waters that lay near the bottom. There she would sleep the dreamless sleep.

But somehow she felt this would not be the end. She would be reborn in some way—the water would give her new life. Elise looked up and shook her head. If she survived this day, it would be a miracle.

✝WEN✝Y-SEVEN

A laan had lit a fire in the hearth to cook their meal. Tapers burned on the broken mantelpiece, on dusty tabletops, and sideboards. It was a rough little stone house, one great room and a single bedchamber. The walls had been crudely plastered and long ago washed over a chalky white. The roof beams lay exposed overhead, darkened by smoke, and these supported a tile shed roof visible from inside.

Elise stood at the door, gazing out toward the lake that was just visible through the trees—a pool of melted black glass. Stars and moon and opalescent clouds vied for the sky.

"This hidden land is a beautiful place," she said, not looking back at Alaan. She hugged herself against the cool air of the night.

"This land is not hidden. We're at the head of the Sweetwater Valley and will be riding through farmlands before noon tomorrow."

Elise became still by the door. "The Sweetwater Valley is five days' ride from Braidon Castle."

"Five days as others would ride it."

She closed her eyes and listened to the sounds of the night, the small lapping of waves below, the house creaking as it warmed to the fire. Elise wondered if the lake would even be there when she woke in the morning.

Suddenly she saw a vision of a man lying still, high up above the valley, and his fellows running for their lives. Had that been her stone that had felled him? Had she killed someone to manage her escape?

She remembered what Alaan had said: a thousand times that many would die in a battle. If the feud began again . . .

Menwyn had been right, curse him. *Childhood has run its course,* he'd said.

It seemed that she had escaped her uncle but not his pronouncement. Childhood *had* run its course. She was a girl no more, and if she did not make decisions for herself, others would make them for her. She must write her own story, or it would go terribly awry: an unwanted marriage, isolation in the house of Innes, a broken, melancholy man for a husband. It was not the story she would choose.

A hand came gently to rest upon her shoulder and neck, causing her to shiver.

"My gratitude for what you've done has limits, Alaan," she said, fighting to catch her breath. "Don't presume too much."

"Always better than presuming too little," he said, his voice touching her so that she shivered again.

The hand didn't go away, and when she did not move,

began to softly caress her neck. Elise didn't open her
eyes. It seemed that every fiber of her being was concentrated on the touch of Alaan's hand. She felt herself lean
back and make contact with his chest. His other hand
came to rest on her waist, the fingers splayed over the
softness of her belly. He gently drew back her hair and
she felt soft lips touch the skin of her neck. She wanted
to let herself fall back, to let herself be overwhelmed by
the wave of pleasure that surged through her.

But instead she stepped forward, breathless, out onto
the dark terrace where the light from the candles threw
Alaan's shadow down on the stone floor. She wondered
how long she would have to remain there to make her
point, and how much she would regret it when she did.

In the morning they made their way down, all those who
had survived. They'd spent the night in a narrow draw,
unable to find the path Hafydd's whist had used to escape.
The morning had revealed no more. Unless Elise and
her abductor had climbed the sheer stone walls and
pulled their horses up behind them there was nowhere
that they could have gone. Yet they were gone.

Prince Michael found the ledge no less daunting for
having traversed it once—in fact it was worse, in some
way. He knew what happened now if horses were spooked,
as did the others. He could see that in their faces.

When he stepped back on the scree slope he tried to
hide his relief. Down the loose rock and they would be

in the trees again. Another half an hour. He was sure his nerve could last that long.

One horse did take a fall and a long slide, though not to the bottom, and it found its feet again. Otherwise, man and beast arrived at the bottom largely unscathed. They'd lost four men and three horses on the ledge, and had nothing to show for it but Hafydd in a silent, murderous rage.

He had climbed up the draw the previous night, pulled his sword from its sheath, and set it ringing once again, but this time his lodestone had pointed to solid rock— there was no passage, only the towering gray cliff. The Prince had never heard a man curse so, and Hafydd's own guards had scurried out of reach as their master took down a stunted tree with his blade.

Now the company rode under the trees in silence— hungry, tired, and unsettled. They had ridden through lands no one had ever seen, chasing a man who disappeared into stone. And that was not the end of it. When they came down into the valley bottom they emerged from beneath the trees onto cultivated fields, the land opening up, houses and barns scattered over the green.

"The Cloffen Wold!" a man near Prince Michael said, and then he swung down from his horse and touched the ground as though to be sure it was real.

The Prince spurred his horse out into the pasture and turned to look back up the hillside. The hill was forested to its crest. No cliff rose up, cold and forbidding, and no ledge snaked across the open sky.

Hafydd took out his sword again, to the consterna-
tion of all but his own guard. He stood on the grass, the
company about him, and turned a slow circle, his blade
extended and pointing slightly upward, his eyes closed.
The sword began its high-pitched ringing again and
Hafydd stopped, the sword pointing back toward the hill
they had just descended.

"He is there. Farther off, but there," he said, and
motioned for his horse.

"You cannot catch this man," the Prince of Innes said.
"He is a sorcerer." He pointed up at the hill. "Look, Sir
Eremon. Where are the cliffs we climbed this night? No,
you will never catch this one."

"You may come with me or no, your grace," Hafydd
said, his jaw so tight that it was a wonder he could talk.
"But I will have this man, and this girl, back. And when
I catch him I will limb him myself and burn what's left.
He will only escape me as smoke."

The Prince of Innes was a man used to having his
slightest suggestion taken as an order, but he remained
remarkably civil, his son thought. "Our horses require
feed; the men have not eaten since yesterday noon. We
came unprepared for a long chase. We cannot start now
for a few hours. Let's ride down to these houses and see
what they can provide us."

Beneath the skin, the muscles of Hafydd's jaw
twitched. For a moment Michael was certain he would
refuse—refuse the Prince of Innes. "Let us be as quick,"
the knight said at last. "Our whist is flying as we speak."

* * *

The path from the lake twisted down among rocks and trees, and in this way was like much of the land they'd ridden over the past two days—but these trees Elise knew. A falls plummeted over the cliff at the lake's foot, and after a glorious moment of flight, was transformed into a steeply flowing stream which dodged this way and that among the trees. They were a few hours descending, and then suddenly emerged at the head of a broad valley of irregularly shaped fields.

"We've not far to go, now," Alaan said.

Elise nodded, and then wondered what he meant. Is this where he'd brought her to hide? So near her home?

A path followed the stream, which broadened and flowed sedately. Weeping willows and poplars overshadowed the path, wending along the watercourse. Elise swept through a curtain of branches and there found a man and woman lounging by the riverbank. Alaan greeted them warmly.

Traveling minstrels, Elise realized immediately. Her father's fame meant she had associated with such people all her life. Had envied them, in truth.

Since Menwyn had pushed her father aside, minstrels had been Lord Carral's only subjects. But then, few rulers were so loved by their followers as her father was by his eccentric, wandering people.

"This is Lady Elise, daughter of Lord Carral Wills," Alaan said as he helped her down, something he had done

only once or twice the entire journey. "You will be joining this small troupe of minstrels," Alaan said to her, and
smiled. "They'll take you south. This is Elffen, who will
be your companion, and Gartnn who will be your boat-
man when he is not forced to play his Fáellute." He
reached out and lightly touched Elffen's hand, and her
gaze flicked up to meet his, then turned quickly away.
She blushed with pleasure.

Rogue! Elise thought, and was, for the first time that
day, pleased she hadn't succumbed to Alaan's advances
the previous night.

Gartnn was a slightly scruffy man of middle years,
who looked like he'd been squared off with an adze. He
was gray haired with a thick beard that seemed to radi-
ate out from his mouth in wiggling lines of black, white,
and gray. The smile that appeared at the center of this
was a masterpiece of perfect white teeth and heavy pink
lips.

"Any daughter of Lord Carral Wills is welcome with
us," he said. "We deem it an honor to serve him in any
way we can." Elise thought Gartnn had the most musical
voice she'd ever heard—rich and warm and resonant. If
she had tried to imagine a man whom women would
find irresistible, Gartnn was not the man she would have
described, but she was quite sure Gartnn was well loved
by all the women minstrels, and quite a few noblemen's
wives and daughters as well.

Elffen was Elise's opposite in color and shape. Dark
haired and voluptuous, she had a hint of the Fáel about

her, and Elise wondered if this were not actually the case: a grandfather, perhaps, who'd been a black wanderer. She curtsied to Elise, though she didn't quite bend the knee enough and the act was too quickly performed.

Elise wanted to ask Alaan where these minstrels would take her, but she was suddenly embarrassed to ask this question. The minstrels would think her a fool, coming along with Alaan, never knowing where she was going. Minstrels thought the nobility were weak-minded from intermarriage to begin with. Somehow she couldn't bear them thinking this of her—the daughter of Carral Wills.

"Is *this* the best boat you could find?" Alaan asked, stopping to gaze at the craft pulled up on the grassy bank.

Gartnn nodded seriously. "Boats are not so easily bought here. Most are needed for their purpose, and no boatwright could build us one in time."

"Does she leak?"

"A little, though she's taken up since she was launched and we've had to bail a little less each hour."

Alaan stared at the boat a moment more, then turned to Gartnn. "Lady Elise carries a pouch of gold and jewels. If need be she can buy you another boat."

Elise hadn't told Alaan about her father's parting gift!

Alaan turned to her, then bowed and took her hand, raising it to his lips. He lingered too long over that kiss, and met her eye too boldly when it was done.

"Every moment has been a pleasure, Lady Elise," he said. "Perhaps we'll visit the grotto together again, when we have leisure."

Her bag was taken from Morn, and set beside the boat. Alaan was on Briss in a moment, his strong hands on the reins calming him. He looked from one to the other of them. "May the river bear you swift and straight. Luck to you, Gartnn."

"And where will you go?" Elise demanded, suddenly unwilling to be left with these strangers.

"I shall torment Hafydd a little longer, then I have some errands in the south. Don't be concerned: you are in good hands." There was the slightest smirk as he glanced at Gartnn, and then he turned his horse, took up Morn's reins, and went back the way they'd come. She listened to the sound of the horses passing along the bank and then they were suddenly gone, along some secret path, leaving her in the company of minstrels, as she had been all her life.

†WEN†Y-EİGH†

T am walked through the dew-dampened morning, following a footpath along the river. He could see the town of Inniseth still, clinging to the embankment, the shutters all tightly closed, the superstitious inhabitants hiding inside. It was a strange world beyond the Vale of Lakes, that was certain.

He thought of the mad old man they'd met below the Lion's Maw, and his eye followed the river north to where it disappeared into low-rising hills. Far off, the Vale lay beneath the shoulder of the mountains. Tam had realized a truth on this journey—a truth he had never been able to admit to himself before. He did not feel at home in the Vale.

He couldn't explain why, but he'd always felt like a visitor there. Not that he was treated in any way differently by the people of the Vale: he was not. But it didn't matter, he wasn't at home there. He'd never admitted this to himself before, for the obvious reason . . . if he wasn't at home in the Vale he had no home. Not a good feeling.

"It is being an orphan," he whispered to the river. But he sensed that was only partly true. There was more to it.

And now that he was out in the larger world he didn't feel any sense of belonging here either. If one judged by the reaction of the people of Inniseth, he would not find welcome in the world beyond the Vale.

He remembered Alaan saying something about traveling and not being able to find a home. Perhaps this was why Tam had felt a liking for the man almost immediately—before he robbed them!

Again he glanced toward the town of Inniseth. Villages were all much the same. You belonged there because your father and mother were born in that place, and likely their parents before them. You did not walk into a new village and suddenly realize that here was your home, for it took years to make your place, to establish who you were in the minds of others, and to find the people who saw the world "through the same window," as his grandfather put it.

He turned and set off back toward their camp, looking at the river passing by, always toward the sea, never resting, even its course changing over time. It seemed a cold, relentless god that morning, utterly unconcerned with the few paltry beings who clung to its shores.

The Vale did not seem such an unwelcoming place at the moment, as though all his melancholy thoughts were but a passing mood. Perhaps no one ever felt perfectly at home anywhere.

He brushed aside some willow tendrils and found Baore stowing their belongings in the boat. He glanced up from beneath his mow of hair as Tam approached.

"She was down a bit by the bow the past two days," Baore said. "We need some weight aft."

Tam nodded. For a moment he watched Baore at work, gauging the movement his friend's shoulder had regained. He was recovering nicely, Tam guessed. Baore's big hands made and unmade knots with a quickness and ease that belied their size. Out over the river, terns called and dove, whirling in the air like leaves on the wind.

"Baore?" Tam said on impulse. "I will go back with you from the Wold of Kerns."

Baore paused in his efforts, then pulled a bag into place and ran a line over it, tying it securely to the floorboards.

"But if we both go back, Tam, Fynnol will not go on. He won't face the ride home alone. I hate to think how angry he will be."

"We weren't born into this world to please Fynnol," Tam said.

"Perhaps *you* weren't," Baore muttered, "but Fynnol believes otherwise of me."

Tam heard himself sigh. He couldn't help it. "Fynnol may do as pleases him, but I will return from the Wold as we planned . . . if that is what you want."

"And what of these men-at-arms who seek us? Certainly they are riding down the old road."

Tam looked out at the wheeling terns. "I don't know, Baore. All we can do is wait awhile for them to pass south. And then make our way north."

* * *

As Baore predicted, Fynnol was not pleased by this news, though he still held that he would continue on with Cynddl. He sat in the bow, sullen and silent while the river bore them gently south.

Tam took up his place in the stern and gazed into the river, sunlight knifing down into its green depths. Ever since they had passed the island with a falls to one side and smooth water to the other, Tam had looked at the river differently. It seemed to him to be a dark vein of mystery running through the hills. A vessel bearing the souls of a lost race. Had they offered their dead to the river? Tam wondered. Were these countless generations confined to the sunless depths, all drifting south toward the endless sea?

Inniseth disappeared behind a bend in the river, and the Valemen found themselves in the wildlands again, the deep forest stretching back from the banks into the hills. Tam thought their visit to the town of Inniseth seemed like a dream. How could such a place exist here, in the middle of the wilds?

But Inniseth existed for the same reason as the Vale—men came there seeking an escape from the wars in the south. It was a place of refuge—though no longer a welcoming one it seemed.

Tam looked off toward the banks, where massive trees leaned out over the water as though they gazed at their reflections on the surface. A single, gray gull followed the boat, gliding in aimless circles. It peered hopelessly down into the waters and uttered its forlorn cry.

This is not a land of men, Tam thought. *We seem out of place here.*

The morning passed like the countryside, quietly and without haste. Just after noon Fynnol stood up in the bow and then, forgetting his mood, turned to the others.

"There is the Eye of the Wynnd!" he said, pointing downriver.

In the distance Tam could see the banks drawing up into vertical walls and, arcing over the river, a natural stone bridge. Beneath this, an almost perfectly round opening could be seen: the Eye of the Wynnd. The gorge was said to be without rocks or obstructions, but the water ran through it with fearsome speed—and fastest through the Eye itself.

The current picked up its pace, as though suddenly in a rush, and the voice of the river rose in anticipation. Tam took up the oars to keep the boat pointed downriver and in the center of the gathering flow.

In a moment the walls of the gorge closed in around them, and along the foot of the cliffs the water gurgled and spun, lashing them with sudden spray. Tam struggled with his oars, for turning broadside to the current could be disastrous. The great arch of stone hung over the gorge, massive and imposing, the opening beneath almost a hundred feet round, Tam was sure. He could see the distant river through it and, as they drew near, a piece of the sky.

The roar of the water echoed off the walls, and the boat flashed forward at impossible speed. Beneath the arch, the water appeared to bend upward, sunlight illuminating this standing wave of green and white. They shot through like an arrow, yawing first to the right and then left before Tam had their boat back under control.

In a moment the gorge was past and the river fell quickly back to sleep, muttering and sighing where it lay. Fynnol let out a whoop, turning to grin at the others.

"Shall we go back and do that again?" he asked.

Tam twisted about to look back at the opening, which did indeed look like an eye, though weeping a torrent of tears.

"I don't think we can do it again," Cynddl said, "but we can climb up and walk over the bridge, or so I understand. It is said to be good luck to cross the bridge, though you must do it at least three times."

At the end of the gorge they beached their boat on gravel and ran it up under overhanging trees where its dark hull faded into the shadows. Taking up their bows and other weapons they started back along the bank and were soon walking along the cliff edge, staring down into the speeding green waters of the gorge.

Fynnol ranged ahead, still working his will on Baore, reproaching him with silence. Tam shook his head. How quickly grown men fell back into their childish ways with members of their own families.

It was an hour's scramble to reach the Eye, where they walked out onto the natural bridge of stone. Tam set his feet gingerly at first, not sure why. Clearly the bridge was stronger than any man-made structure and had stood since the river carved its channel here. It just seemed so very strange and unlikely to him.

Below them, the river ran like a cord of clear green glass being drawn through the gorge. For a long while they stood staring down. Tam felt a strange pull from the speeding water, and then Fynnol voiced his thought.

"Has anyone ever jumped from here? It seems you would be shot to the surface in the Eye and carried quickly out of the gorge. There are no whirlpools or eddies, so you would likely escape unharmed. And what a feeling that would be! Can you imagine going through the Eye without aid of a boat?"

Cynddl looked up at him, somewhat alarmed. "Now, let us not become foolhardy," the story finder said quickly. "There is danger enough on the river without seeking it out."

The Valemen all laughed.

"We have not taken leave of our senses completely." Fynnol laughed. "But don't you wonder? There is a narrow little gorge in the Vale where you can leap into the water and be carried over a falls. Below, it is quite deep, but in an instant you shoot to the surface without even the slightest effort. I imagine that this would be like that."

Just then Baore gave a startled cry and pointed at the river. For a second Tam stared, seeing nothing, but then a wavering white form appeared beneath the surface, flickering like a candle flame. It came toward them at the speed of the river, but appeared to swim like a fish.

"It is a *woman*!" Fynnol said.

And so it seemed to be: white as foam and sleek as an otter. But if a woman, she had no need of air, for she never once broke the surface.

Tam glanced quickly at Cynddl, who crouched down to stare intently over the edge of stone. In a moment the figure was beneath them, hard to follow with the eye, like a fish prowling beneath the surface. And then it was lost in the shadow of the bridge.

They all bolted across the stone arch to stare down on the other side, but Tam only caught a glimpse of white there in the sun-sparkled water, and then the creature was gone.

"Well, what in the world was that?" Fynnol asked.

Both Baore and Cynddl stood staring down into the depths of the speeding Wynnd.

"Was it a body committed to the river?" Fynnol asked. "Have we seen one of the dead of Inniseth?"

"The people of Inniseth commit only the ashes of their dead to the river," Cynddl said, not taking his eyes from the running water.

"Then what was this creature, so like a woman but which never surfaced to breathe?"

Cynddl looked up at the others and shrugged. "A river spirit," he said. "Isn't that what the people of Inniseth saw? Some strange sprite that made them afraid to cross the river alone or by night."

Tam glanced over at Baore, who said nothing but only stared at the river, his face pale in the warm sunlight. Then he turned away, crossing over the bridge once, and then back, then again, and once more.

†WEN†Y-NINE

Morning found them sailing across an open lake, reaching between round islands and rocks scattered and bleached like bone. Elise could see sails in the distance, their sharp angles bright against the blue. It was going to be a beautiful day, already windy and warm, and she was free! Her family and all their folly left far behind.

Elise braced herself against the motion of the boat and wondered why she did not feel a great sense of relief. She'd escaped, or at least it appeared so. She tried to force herself to feel elation but could not. All she felt was flat and empty and strangely out of place.

I am a daughter of the Wills, she thought. *What am I doing here pretending to be a traveling singer?* But here she was, living her oft-repeated daydream, and she felt oddly close to tears, and not tears of joy.

She turned her mind away from this and focused on her companions, who bent low, trying to avoid the dollops of spray that occasionally found their way over the bow.

Gartnn sat at the helm looking far older than Elise

suspected he was. The "early frost" of his gray beard and hair and the lines cut in his face by the knife of the sun gave the impression of age, but his motions were all strong and youthful and his voice could not have belonged to a man much over thirty-five.

He sat with a hood pulled up over his head, his big sun-browned hands gripping the tiller. With enormous intensity he watched the water, the wind sign, the passing islands. His eyes were a startling blue set in a burnished face and a frame of coarse, gray hair. When he noticed that she was gazing at him he smiled and Elise looked quickly away.

For a moment she concentrated on the passing scene. The boat dipped and a sheet of spray came over the bow, soaking them all and slapping with surprising solidity against the planks opposite.

"How long will we have to put up with this discomfort and wet?" Elffen asked.

Gartnn looked solemnly around. He glanced up at the clouds. "An hour or two more," he announced, the sound of his voice rasping slightly like sand whispering over stone. "If the wind holds."

Elffen rolled her eyes in disgust. She was pretty enough. That's what Aunt Bette would have said. Pretty enough for what? Elise had always wondered. Pretty enough that men noticed her, that was what she had come to believe. Pretty enough but not beautiful, not striking.

Elise herself had always been pretty enough—at least according to the judgment of her aunt. But to her it really meant just that—it was enough. She didn't dream of being one of those women who caused all the men to become wide-eyed when she entered a room, wide-eyed and then suddenly animated and loud. There were a few women like that around—one of her cousins among them—and they were terribly uninteresting, she thought. Prisoners of their beauty, as Elise had been a prisoner of her name. They could never walk unnoticed into a room. They were always observed, never the observer.

But now I am the observer, Elise thought, *my name stripped away, like a woman might lose her beauty to age or disfigurement. There is nothing now that makes me stand out, nothing that makes me different.*

She found this thought affected her profoundly. If you took away her name she was like anybody else, as though she herself were nothing—nothing but a sound, air passing over the lips.

Elise was surprised at how leisurely their flight had become. As often as opportunity allowed they stopped to perform in villages and at the castles of knights and other landholders.

We must appear to be minstrels, not fugitives, Gartnn had said, and Elise hadn't argued. Despite all her flights of fancy she had no experience of escaping into the real world.

This night they lodged in the guest rooms of a castle

that was property of Lord A'denné, a man Elise thought she might have met once, though fortunately he was not in residence, nor was he often. He left a trustworthy knight as steward of the castle and surrounding estates.

Over their meal the knight had told stories of chasing down and destroying a particularly brutish band of brigands—hardly delicate table talk, but he had not really been bragging. It almost seemed more an interest in the minds of these men—renegade men-at-arms.

"They had lost their places and had nowhere to turn. No craft but war. Bitterness and loss of knightly dignity brought them to ruin. But pity though I felt for them, we showed them none upon the field, for it must be known that such crimes as they committed are punished more harshly when undertaken by men who have forsaken their vows."

It was a harsh world beyond the confines of the Wills household. Harsh and brutal. And she felt very alone in it.

Elffen did not seem to be preparing for bed that evening but paced back and forth, more animated than usual, laughing often, though with a certain hint of nervousness.

"Will you pace the whole night, Elffen?" Elise asked finally, "or do you think you might sleep?"

Elffen seemed to find great amusement in this, though she tried hard to suppress her laughter. "Sleep is the one thing I plan not to do this evening."

Elise realized, finally, what was afoot.

"Oh, do not look so shocked," Elffen said. "Certainly there are affairs enough amongst the nobility. Are the Wills family so pure that these things are unknown?"

"No," Elise said. "No. The Wills aren't so pure. I . . . I don't judge, Elffen. It is only that I have been sheltered by my family."

"Well, your family shelter you no more," Elffen said, unable to hide her excitement. "But what you do with this sudden freedom is not my affair." In her heightened state this accidental, and not terribly clever, play on words amused her terribly.

Elise sat down on the edge of her bed, staring down at the floor.

"Oh, Lady Elise, have I distressed you?"

"No . . ." Elise was not sure what she felt—a common state of affairs these days. "I have dreamed since I was a child of being free of my family, but now that I find myself free I don't know what to do." She looked up at her companion, who grew serious for the first time this evening. "Perhaps I don't yet believe we have escaped. I have this terrible foreboding that we shall be found out yet."

Elffen dropped down in a chair, her mood suddenly grave. "It is possible that we won't escape. I've known Gartnn many years now—since I was a girl—and I've never known him to worry so. This knight Eremon . . ." She swallowed hard. "Gartnn fears him. And if Gartnn fears him then I am terrified." She looked up at Elise. "You know this knight: what is it that Gartnn fears?"

"I don't know. He is a forbidding man, brooding and sure of himself. But there is something more . . . Those around him fear him—those who are closest to him. He seems to inspire this. As though the more you know of him, the more reason you find to be afraid. I have never encountered such a man before."

Elffen gazed at her a moment, though clearly she was lost in thought, perhaps trying to picture such a man.

"Why is Gartnn helping me? Why are *you* helping me?"

Elffen gazed at her, blinking, as though so deep in her own thoughts that the question had barely registered. "You're the daughter of Lord Carral Wills: that is reason enough. But also because Alaan asked us, and Gartnn would do anything that Alaan asked."

"I find that strange enough. So that explains Gartnn's involvement, but what of you? It seems to me there is more than a little danger in this endeavor. Couldn't Gartnn and I travel alone?"

"Oh, Alaan would not have you traveling without a companion," she said. "I'm sure he made promises to your father that he would protect you."

Elise remembered his hand touching her shoulder that night, his lips. It seemed to her that he'd not been so concerned about protecting her then.

Suddenly Elffen seemed to remember herself and jumped up, her face lighting again, a faint blush discoloring her neck. "But tonight we remain free, and I, for one, intend to make the most of it." She wrapped a shawl about her shoulders, stood before a looking glass, her excitement wavering through an instant of doubt. But then she smiled coyly at her reflection, planted a kiss on Elise's cheek, and swept out the door.

Elise sat upon her bed, feeling suddenly very still—as though around her the whole world were in motion. People kept assignations, were swept up in storms of passion, bore children, won tournaments, died upon fields of battle. But Elise did nothing. She played her lute and wrote in her journal. She daydreamed.

Not true, she reminded herself. She had run away, posed as a traveling minstrel, escaped a prince and his evil counselor. This was the stuff of stories—and yet she did not feel as though she were the heroine of a story. Heroines did not sit in their rooms alone each night. They went to balls, slipped out windows to escape over rooftops by moonlight. Were courted by handsome nobles and roguish knights. They moved within the dance of life.

But she was motionless.

"I am a wallflower in the dance of life," she said aloud, and smiled at the image. But she didn't know what to do. To throw herself into some affair for no other reason than to do something seemed foolish to her.

"Perhaps I'm too sensible." But she longed to be in motion. To be part of the movement of the world.

Sounds from her open window drew her. The shutters were still in their half-closed position against the heat of the day, and in the slit between them she could see horsemen dismounting: men-at-arms, more than a dozen of them.

"She's in her room alone," someone said. "Shall we fetch her down, Lord A'denné?"

"No, I will go up."

Lord A'denné!

What a fool she'd been to come here—though she hadn't known until it was too late. Some servant must have been with Lord A'denné when she met him and she'd been recognized!

What was she to do now? She dashed to the door, thinking to warn Gartnn, but then realized that if they knew where she was they were likely watching her door. She collapsed back against the wall, feeling tears well up. In a moment they would be at the door. She threw the bolt, and then stopped. What profit was there in making a prisoner of herself?

Quietly she pulled the bolt back again. She tossed a few belongings into a bag, slung it over her shoulder, then snuffed the candles. Going to the window she looked down again into the courtyard. The men-at-arms were gone, and only the stable boys were left, leading horses off to the stable.

Fearing it made a terrible noise, she pushed back the squeaky shutters. In a moment she was out onto the roof that sloped down from her window, the slate still warm from the day.

The roof was perfectly dry and not too steep, but where would she go now? It was unlikely they would imagine she had gone out onto the roof, for ladies didn't do such things—except perhaps in stories. No, more likely they would believe she'd slipped past the man watching her door. Servants commonly took bribes to look the other way.

Other windows were lit, and she crouched to crawl quickly past them. Before one she slipped and slithered half a dozen feet before recovering, crawling on all fours. Someone had poured their wash water out the window— she hoped it was only wash water. She gazed down into the courtyard and realized that if she fell that would likely be the end of her story. For a moment she knelt, trying to catch her breath, but then she went forward more carefully, making sure the slate before her was dry.

Elise traversed the length of the roof until it met a wall of stone that jutted up among the stars. How in the world would she ever get down from here, and where would she go?

Unsure of what to do, she retraced her steps, crouching outside the first window to listen. The shutters here had been thrown back, and the windows lay open. Curtains stirred fitfully to the inconstant breeze.

Elise stilled her breathing a moment, listening, but no sounds came from within. Steeling her nerve, she drew the curtain aside and looked in. Candles burned but she could see no one. The bed lay undisturbed, as though servants had lit the room but its occupant had not yet arrived.

Elise tried to think where this room would be. Down the hall from her own, obviously. She counted the windows. Five rooms—near the end of the hallway. There was a servant's stair very close by. Could she slip out and down the stair? To go where?

She didn't know. Out. That was all she could think. Out into the night. Their boat lay to a dock not far off. If she could reach that she could slip away, though how far she'd get if pursued she didn't know. Not far, she feared. But she'd worry which road to take when she reached the fork and not before.

Grasping the sill Elise crawled awkwardly in, almost stumbling as she tried to turn around in the frame. And as she sorted herself out, still crouched with her back to the window, a movement caught her eye.

A young man sat in the corner, book in hand, gazing at her with an odd half smile.

"Of course, I am dreaming," he said. "Beautiful women never crawl in my window when I'm awake."

"Don't let me interrupt your sleep," Elise said, trying to regain some of her composure. "I shan't be staying."

"What kind of dream is that?" he said, setting the book aside and rising to his feet. "At the very least you should stay for a glass of wine and a chat."

Elise couldn't remember seeing this young man before. Certainly he was a nobleman's son; no more than twenty, she thought. She wondered what he would do——but then he looked quite delighted with the situation, and somehow she didn't feel threatened by him.

"In this dream I cannot tarry. Perhaps another time."

"This is a very disappointing dream. Too much like

life, in fact. Dream girls are supposed to arrive and fulfill one's fantasies."

She raised a finger. "We are under no such obligation," Elise said, backing toward the door. He followed her but kept his distance.

The young man shook his head. "Even in my dreams the girls run away."

"I hardly think that women are running from you, sir," she said.

"Spoken like a true dream girl, but, alas, you're wrong. I set them to flight like flocks of birds, no matter how gently I approach, it seems."

"They must suspect your intentions," Elise said quickly, almost to the door now.

"I thought all men's intentions were suspect?"

Elise laughed. "Well, then, perhaps it is your cynicism."

"You do me an injustice. I am a romantic. No one more so." He gestured to her. "I dream of exquisitely mysterious women climbing in my window by night. What can they be up to? From whom do they flee? Someone very evil, I think."

"More evil than you know. What is your name?" she asked.

"I have the honor to be Lord Carl. This is my father's castle."

"Your father has just arrived," she said.

"Has he indeed? He was to have been in Dunharrow, a day's ride away. I was sent no word."

"Nevertheless, he is here."

He looked at her more seriously now, his youthful face growing thoughtful. "It cannot be my father whom you flee. He is not in the least evil. His justice is celebrated, in fact."

"We are sometimes, unknowingly, agents of others." Her back came up against the door.

"Then it *is* my father you flee. Now you have placed me in an odd predicament. So this is one of those dreams where you must make difficult choices. To keep faith with my father and betray the trust of a beautiful woman, or to ally myself with the dream girl who claims her innocence. May I ask your name?" he said.

"How mysterious would I be if I told my name? Now, before you wake, I must say good night."

She opened the door a crack, looked out, and found the hallway filled with men, almost all before her door. Immediately she closed the crack, turning back to the young man who had drawn closer now, two paces distant.

"Perhaps a glass of wine and a chat would not be untoward," she said, trying to smile.

"Is that my father outside?" he asked.

"It seems likely," she said, her voice small.

"What have you done that he seeks you?"

"I spoke the truth. I am fleeing an evil man. I've done nothing immoral or dishonorable. I swear."

He looked into her eyes a moment, then nodded. "If it is a dream, what harm can there be in letting you escape?"

"None, I should think."

"Where will you go?"

"Down the servants' stair."

"And then?"

She shook her head. "There is a boat at the dock."

He nodded. "Let me look out into the hall."

"You give your word?" she whispered.

"I'll not betray you," he said.

On impulse, Elise kissed him on the cheek and stepped aside, feeling her heart pounding.

Lord Carl opened the door and stepped out.

In an instant he pushed the door wide. "Quickly," he whispered, taking her arm. They almost leapt across the hall and into the servants' stair, which was unlit and they bore no candle.

"My dream is turning very dark," he said, as he felt his way down, leading Elise by the hand.

"Our faith is tested in darkness," she said, "but we must not falter."

"You talk just like a woman in a dream," he said.

Elise did not answer, for she missed a step and stumbled, recovering with aid from her savior. "Not so quickly," she said. "Let's arrive at the bottom intact."

There was a sudden noise in the stairwell above, and light cascaded down, splashing from step to step.

"*Run,*" her companion whispered.

The light illuminated the way and they flew down, barely touching foot to tread. From above them the sound of boots thundered in the well. In a moment they were in another hallway, lit by candles in sconces. They fled hand in hand, already out of breath, and as they turned a corner they ran headlong into a band of men-at-arms.

"Ah, just in time," Carl said quickly, stepping aside. "There is some confusion in the hallway outside my rooms. He waved the men on, but no one moved.

"Lord Carl?" one of the men ventured. "It is this woman that is the cause of the confusion."

"I can hardly credit that——"

But it was too late. The men who had chased them down the stair rounded the corner then, and all ways were blocked. Elise did not think wit could save them now. If only she were a woman in a dream, and could disappear.

A moment later an imposing man appeared, the others giving way to him. He was like enough to Carl to be his father, and in tow he had Gartnn between two burly men.

"What goes on here? Carl?"

They were still holding hands, Elise realized, and relaxed her grip, but Carl did not do the same. He kept her hand within his own.

"I don't know, Father. We were merely having a tour of the castle when these men assaulted us."

"That is the woman, your grace," a servant said. "I saw her in the house of Lord Menwyn Wills. Daughter of Lord Carral, your grace, I am sure."

Lord A'denné gazed at her solemnly. "Are you the daughter of Lord Carral Wills?" he asked.

Elise did not know what to answer, and even if she did, the power of speech seemed to have fled.

"She certainly is not," Gartnn spoke up.

"I did not ask you, minstrel," Lord A'denné said darkly.

"I . . . I am not, sir," Elise managed, thinking her denial sounded particularly unconvincing.

The lord continued to gaze at her a moment more. "No, I don't think you are either."

"But, your grace!" the servant spluttered.

The nobleman turned and cuffed the servant across the head. "You've caused trouble enough!" he said sternly. "Making false accusations against my guests. Causing me to ride most of a day for nothing. You will apologize immediately."

The man cowered now, hanging his head. "Certainly. I apologize most humbly. Most humbly."

"And not a word more of this or you will be the new stable boy." The lord turned back to Elise and shook his head. "And your name, my dear?"

"Angeline. Angeline A'drent."

"A noble name," the lord said, performing a graceful bow.

Gartnn had given her the name. Many minstrels took noble names; and there actually were highborn minstrels, though few of these were women. But even so, it was a custom that a player claiming a noble name was treated, if not as a noble, then with a certain deference. Very few could carry it off, though, and those who couldn't play the part were quickly the butt of jokes.

Elise, however, would have no difficulty "carrying it off."

"You are a gracious lord," Elise said, curtseying. "Your son said you were renowned for your fairness, and now I see he did not exaggerate, as sons sometimes will."

"No, he is not prone to exaggeration." The lord turned to the guards detaining Gartnn. "Free him. Please accept my apologies, good minstrel." He turned back to Elise. "Would you join me a moment?" He gestured down the hallway.

Elise nodded her assent, and squeezing the Prince's hand once, she followed, paying no attention to any they left behind, as a noble woman should.

Lord A'denné opened a door into a large study lined with books and allowed her to precede him in. He gestured to a chair, and Elise lowered herself into it. She still carried the bag she had quickly packed for her escape. And after slipping on the roof she must look a sight.

He went to a sideboard and found a decanter of wine, which she accepted with a nod. Passing her a glass, Lord A'denné took a seat opposite.

"Do you think you can actually escape the Prince of Innes and his counselor?" he asked.

For a second she did not respond. "Whatever do you mean?" she said.

"You need not continue the farce. I've no intention of returning you. You see, if you marry Prince Michael I will be forced into a war I don't wish to enter." He tasted his wine. "And yet, if it is learned that I let you slip away——or worse, that I knew you for who you were and aided you on your way . . . Well, the Prince has long wanted to try his army in the field, and what forces I can muster cannot hope to stand against them. So you see, I should return you, yet I won't. If I'm to take such risks, then at least you might reward them by trusting me. It's all I ask."

Elise stared into his eyes for a moment. "You have a remarkable son, I think," she said evenly. "Perhaps I should marry him and then I wouldn't have to be concerned about other suitors."

Lord A'denné smiled. "He is remarkable and you would be a good match, but I would eventually have to pay for so insulting the Prince of Innes, which I'm not prepared to do. But, of course, you jest. Were you serious I couldn't refuse."

Elise merely shrugged and sipped her wine.

"Now that we've established that you are not the Lady Elise Wills, daughter of the famous Lord Carral——how fares him, by the way?"

"Well, thank you."

"I'm glad to hear it. Now that we have established that you are not that lady, how might I aid you? Certainly I owe you something for the distress you've suffered this night."

"I don't know that there is anything you can do, though it's kind of you to offer. May I ask my companion Gartnn? If there is any boon we might ask, he would know."

"You may indeed." The lord gazed at her as though

there were something about her he could not quite fathom. "Why would the Lady Elise choose to flee, do you think?"

Elise shrugged. "Perhaps she will not be a broodmare for the Prince of Innes and his counselor. Perhaps she sees an alliance leading to war, and there has been enough war."

"I think her a wise and courageous woman. If she were serious about marrying my son I would almost be willing to take the risk."

"But then the war you hope to avoid would come to you. I think it would be an unwise union, though a happy one, perhaps." She set her wine on a small table. "May I speak with my companion?"

He nodded his consent, and Elise rose, thinking that it had turned out like a dream after all: like a story, with wise compassionate lords, handsome sons, and escapes over rooftops.

She expected to wake at any moment.

The sky pearled toward light as they untied their lines. They had interrupted Elffen's tryst, for which she hadn't forgiven them, and still sulked ominously. Along the riverbank, the gray forms of the daylit world began to emerge. And the river lay like mercury: inert, viscous, impenetrable.

Carl accompanied them to the dock. "I shall never again have so fair a dream," he said.

"Oh, I think you shall have many dreams, and fairer," Elise answered, trying to make the moment light for reasons she didn't understand.

"If ever you pass by again, I want you to know, my window is always open."

Elise laughed. She looked over to the boat to find both Gartnn and Elffen watching. They looked quickly away.

I am protected by my family no longer, she reminded herself, stood up on the tips of her toes, and kissed Carl softly. For a moment more her hands lingered within his, and then she was crossing to the boat, a blush warming her cheek.

Gartnn pushed them off, taking up the oars. "I wish you would both stop smiling so," Gartnn growled. "We are in grave danger, you realize. If we are caught . . . Well, it will not be you, Lady Elise, who pays the price."

Elise felt her smile evaporate.

You don't know, Gartnn, she thought. *You don't know what price I would pay.*

THIRTY

The apparition they had seen pass through the Eye of the Wynnd did not appear again that day, though they watched the river almost constantly. Fynnol kept returning to the subject again and again, seemingly unaware of the others' reluctance to speak of it. Even Baore seemed to shy away from the subject, but then the big man liked to dwell in a solid, familiar world. Not one where phantoms swam just beneath the surface.

They stood their usual watches as darkness fell, but this night Fynnol and Baore were not just on the lookout for men-at-arms who might still be pursuing them. Tam thought they all looked in need of more rest when they set out in the morning.

The leisurely pace of the river soon lulled Baore and Fynnol to sleep, but, as always, Cynddl watched the banks, ever intent and curious.

And he has come looking for the stories of long-dead sorcerers, Tam thought. He wondered if it were true that Cynddl didn't know why his people had sent him.

In the late morning the Fáel whispered Tam's name

and then stretched out a hand, pointing at the bank. And there Tam saw a hart, its pelt white as cloud. The beast raised its head from drinking and regarded the boat and its occupants regally.

"See the spread of antlers!" Cynddl whispered.

"All the beasts of legend seem to live along the river," Tam said softly. He reached forward to rouse Baore, but the motion caused the beast to start, and it gazed only an instant more and then was gone up the bank and into the shadows of the trees. For a moment Tam followed its flight, the unnatural white appearing here and there in the dark-forested hillside.

Cynddl looked to him and smiled. "Men who say they've seen the white hart are branded liars, so perhaps we shouldn't admit to it, but we'll always know what we saw, Tam. Black swans and white hart. If you were a man of old you might think these were omens and take them for your coat of arms."

Tam stared off at the bank as though the hart might appear again. "In the Vale they say if you can take the skin and antlers of a white hart, men of the lowland will pay you a fortune for them."

"That's true," Cynddl said. "Do you wish you'd drawn an arrow?"

Tam shook his head. "No. The life of such a creature was not meant to profit me. But it is a good thing Fynnol slept. He might not've felt the same way."

* * *

Later that day they drew the boat up at a sharp elbow in the river, and climbed a high, steep bank. It was one of Cynddl's mysterious way points—a place where a sorcerer once dwelt and where his story perhaps still echoed. After what he had found at Cooling Keep, Cynddl had not planned to stop here, but once within sight he couldn't resist a brief visit.

"There was a city here?" Fynnol said, looking around at the underwood and trees. His mood had changed a little since they had seen the swimmer in the gorge. When he realized the others would not speculate as to its nature, he had become uncommonly pensive.

"I don't know if it would be a city, Fynnol, but certainly the race that lived in the Greensprings built a place of dwelling here. On my map it's marked as Aullioc, which in the Fáel language means 'Overlook.'" He gestured to the views both up and down the river.

Tam found himself staring down the sparkling south-running stream. He could almost imagine strange craft plying these waters, bearing the lost race of the Greensprings: maidens fair as summer nights and chieftains wearing the skin of the white hart over their shoulders, antlers decorating their helms.

As he stared at the glittering waters, a dark silhouette appeared from the shadow of the bank—a man standing in a small boat, a pole in hand. For a moment Tam was so surprised that he didn't speak, and then the shape was lost in the shimmering ribbon of river. He glanced at the others, but all of them were looking elsewhere and none had seen.

Perhaps it had been only a fallen tree, afloat with a branch pointing skyward. It was so far off . . .

"I think we should dig here," Fynnol said, "and see what we find. If this were once a village, then something should lie beneath the surface."

"You'd dig very deep before you'd find anything here, Fynnol," Cynddl said. "Men haven't lived here in many, many centuries."

Tam found a seat of moss, his back against the bole of an oak, and stared off down the river, which seemed much more distant than reason told him it could be. Cynddl went quietly off into the wood—listening for the voices that only he heard. Baore had brought his shod staff, as though expecting wild beasts, and he and Fynnol went off into the wood to explore, Fynnol waving his bow and promising to bring back dinner.

Tam sat for a time, staring at the gleaming river, and then he nodded and fell into a dream. A river of silver coins spread before him, glittering in the sunlight. Tam stood high upon a hill, dazzled by the sight, the distant tinkling of silver like leaves fluttering in the wind.

And then he awoke, and found himself lying on the moss looking up at the leaves moving in the breeze, sunlight dancing across his arms and face.

Someone cleared his throat and Tam propped himself up, expecting to find Cynddl or one of the others. But instead a stranger stood a few feet away, a staff in one hand and bag over his shoulder.

"Ah, you return to this world," the man said, offering a smile like sunlight through the leaves.

"And who are you?" Tam said, surprise turning his question into an accusation.

"I am Theason Hollyoak," the man said, making something of a bow.

"Did I see you on the river"—Tam motioned south—"standing in a boat?"

"Yes. That was Theason. He chanced to look back and saw silhouettes moving on the hilltop." He bent his thin neck forward a little and narrowed his eyes to gaze at Tam. "I am looking for three young men from the Vale and a Fáel story finder."

Tam scrambled up, brushing dead leaves and detritus from his clothes. "You need look no further. I'm Tamlyn Loell. Tam, my friends call me."

"Then I will call you Tamlyn, for I know you not," the stranger said, and did not seem to be jesting.

He was slight of form and the height of Fynnol, perhaps. His thin hair was pulled back into a tail. Tam thought the man should be a minstrel, for he had delicate hands and fine bones. Not the heft and muscle of a man who wandered the wildlands. His face was serious and long, with three parallel scars running from above one eye down to the chin opposite.

Seeing where Tam's gaze went Theason waved a hand at his face. "A mountain lion took exception to Theason's curiosity in her cubs," he said, "though it was perfectly innocent curiosity, I assure you." He touched a long finger to his scar. "I have teeth marks in my shoulder that set these scratches off rather finely. Like marks of punctuation scrawled over my skin. Thank the river for bloodwood and widow's bloom."

There was an awkward silence for a moment—at least Tam felt awkward. Theason didn't seem to notice.

"I have just woken," Tam said, "and my brain is all wool and dust balls. Did you say you looked for us?"

The man nodded. "I am a friend and messenger of Eber son of Eiresit—" But just then the voice of Fynnol came through the trees, followed by Cynddl's laughter. In a moment the two appeared, Fynnol holding up a brace of hare. They paused in surprise.

"This is Theason. He's been seeking us." Tam introduced his cousin and Cynddl, and the odd silence fell again.

"You began to tell me of Eber," Tam prompted.

"Oh, yes," the stranger said, blinking as though he looked into the sun. "When you left Speaking Stone, Eber had a visitor," he said very quietly, and looked at each of them in turn. "A nagar appeared upon his island."

"A what?" Fynnol asked.

"I've heard that word," Cynddl said. "A spirit you mean? Or a ghost?"

"No, not really," the man answered. "No one can say what they are, but Eber believes they are the remnants of a people long dead. The people who made their kingdoms in the north. They were strong in magic, if that is the proper word. And the strongest did not die but merely faded, dissipated, perhaps. At times they take form, coalesce, around a place or an object. Sometimes around a person or an animal. At times they can be quite substantial—almost as you or I. At others they are fainter than moonlight or like a mist on the river.

"Eber saw one upon his island, after you left—a fair woman, searching among tree and stone. Even into his house, she came, and went silently from room to room. To his horror, she found his son and spoke with him, but harmed him not. It was then that she went down to the shore where you had made your camp. There she searched again. Not finding what she sought, she went into the waters and the speaking river swallowed her up." The man looked at each of them in turn. "I see you are not surprised by this."

"We saw something in the water at the Eye of the Wynnd," Fynnol said. "It appeared to be a woman, but we couldn't be sure."

Theason nodded solemnly. "That will be the nagar Eber saw," he said. "He sent me to tell you: hurry south. Do not tarry. The sooner you leave the wildlands the sooner you will be free of this creature, for they're seldom seen below the Greensprings. I would add my own warning: you would be foolish to ignore the counsel of Eber son of Eiresit. He dwells in the heart of the ancient kingdoms and knows more of the lost people than any other. And *he* fears the nagar."

"But why should we fear it?" Fynnol said "Cynddl and Tam believe it healed my cousin Baore when he lay dying of a wound gone septic." Fynnol glanced at Tam. "You've not been as secretive as you think," he said, "whispering among yourselves at night."

Theason sat down upon a hummock, as though tired from his efforts to find them. For a moment he was very still. "Tell Theason how it healed your cousin."

"I saw it," Tam said after a moment, "as Baore lay suffering from a wound—"

"But how was he wounded?" Theason asked.

Tam glanced to Cynddl and then shrugged. "If you're in no hurry, it's a long story."

Theason settled himself on his hummock. "I will hear it," he said.

And so Tam told their story from the chance meeting of Alaan at Telanon Bridge, down to the sighting of the nagar at the Eye. He left out only Cynddl's true purpose for traveling the river and the things he'd found—everything else he told, and he was not sure why. There was something about Theason—a kind of innocence, not unlike Eber's—that made Tam trust him.

When he was done Theason lifted the strap of the bag over his head and sat it at his feet, rummaging inside. He found a thin, gray stick of some shrub and split it, gouging out the dry, brown core with his fingernail. This he put in his mouth and began to chew thoughtfully.

"Theason," he began, softly, "hasn't the knowledge to advise you in this, but it is the worst news you give me. Your kinsman is in greater danger than you know. Better to face any number of men-at-arms than be indebted to a nagar. Better death, some would say. Among the people of the wildlands the nagar is the thing most feared."

"But why?" Fynnol said.

"The nagar, Fynnol Loell, are creatures of story and myth," Theason said. "None have been seen in many generations, and if anyone but Eber had told me one had appeared I would not have believed it.

"There are many stories and songs of the nagar. Theason can't tell you which are true and which are fancy, but here is one I offer for your judgment." He split his stick further, digging out the soft core and laying it on his tongue. "A man named Tannl dwelt by the River Wynnd, though in those days it was called the Wyrr— 'the strange.' Tannl lived in a house of log and stone that he had built with his own hands. Here he and his wife settled, far from the villages of men.

"The long winter set in and snow fell in unusual abundance that first year, but the river flowed swiftly there and did not freeze. The first full moon of winter rose crimson in the east, and then the next was white as frost: Tannl's wife was with child. Their joy pressed back the cold and loneliness they felt in that far-off place.

"One night, in the calm and silence of the snows, they heard, far off, high voices crying. And as they listened these cruel voices drew near: wolves, driven down from the skirts of the mountains by the harsh winter.

"Soon the voices were all about them, howling eerily, and wolves began tearing at the doors and shutters. All night this went on, Tannl and his wife huddled by the fire, he with axe at hand for fear the doors would be breached. When light came the wolves fell silent and withdrew into the forest. Tannl ventured forth to fill a bucket with snow so that they might drink, but all about the house the wolves had fouled the snow, and Tannl was forced to go to the river. As he bent over the flowing water the wolves leapt out from among the trees, snarling and howling, some going to the house and others to Tannl.

"He had only his axe to defend himself and in a moment was driven into the winter river. The cold poured into him and he sank down into the icy green waters. Here he floated, his life leaching out, carried away on the current. But then he realized a face stared at him—a woman's face, sad and pale. In the sounds of the river running among stones he heard a voice and it said to him, 'Your wife and unborn child are doomed, and you are drifting now toward death, but I will save you all if you will do my bidding.'

"'Yes,' he said. 'Save us and I will do whatever you ask.' The nagar nodded and took hold of his hair, dragging him out of the river onto a narrow ledge of ice formed along the bank. In a moment the wolves found him and came bounding down onto the ice. But where they put their paws the ice broke away and they floundered into the swift-flowing river, and were swept to their deaths.

"Tannl saw the wolves tearing at the door to his home, and from within heard the screams of his wife. He rose up, caked in ice like a candle dripping wax, but as he clambered onto the bank, a scream split the air. A great, white eagle, the ghost king of legend, dropped out of the sky and dug its talons into the chieftain of the wolves, carrying him up into the sky. The rest of the pack fled in terror.

"So Tannl was delivered and heard the howls of the wolves no more. In the early autumn the child was born, but before its time—a baby girl tiny and frail, too weak even to nurse. It lay on its mother's breast, suffering to breathe, the life seeping out of it by the hour. Finally Tannl's wife fell asleep, too exhausted by her ordeal to stay awake. Tannl took the dying babe and wrapped it in a blanket, then, clutching it close to his breast, went out into the night.

"He walked to the bank of the river, where he stood in the shallows and whispered, 'You said you would save my child, but here she lies, near to death.' The surface broke and the creature that had saved him rose, walking up into the shallows, its eyes like moons, flesh white as fish skin. 'I will save her,' the nagar said, 'but she is mine now. That is the price of your deliverance.' Tannl could not bear to give up the child, but the nagar reached out and, turning back the folds of the blanket, lifted the barely breathing child. She went back into the river, disappearing into the green depths, the child cradled in arms white as snow.

"Tannl wept then, for a time, on the bank of the cruel Wyrr. Then he went back to his woodpile and built a pyre. He wrapped sticks in the blanket he had used for the child, and tucked this deep within the pyre. He woke his wife and told her their daughter had died as she slept and took her out to the pyre. She fell on her knees and wept, begging to see the child once more, to hold it close once before he lit the flame. But Tannl fired the wood, and the flames soon consumed the blankets and what was hidden beneath.

"For years after, his sad wife would say that she saw a small girl peering at her, sometimes from the river, sometimes from among the branches of trees. Finally Tannl took his wife away, though she did not want to leave the place, as though she could sense that her daughter lived, somehow. But they went south, back to the inhabited lands, and lived out their days, childless and haunted by sorrow."

Theason looked at the companions seated before him. "The stories of the nagar are always thus—bargains that go awry, promises broken. The nagar have purposes of their own and no loyalty to living men. Did the nagar speak with your kinsmen?"

Fynnol looked at the others quickly, then shook his head. "Not that we know. In truth we don't believe Baore knows that she came to him that night at all. But he's been haunted by nightmares and has slept poorly ever since."

Theason rocked back and forth a little where he sat, like a child. "Perhaps it's better that he knows nothing more. Get south of the wildlands, that is your best course."

"If the river will carry us there," Fynnol said. "Who knows where the Wynnd will take us next?"

Theason opened his bag again, taking out a small sack of nuts. This he offered to the others, and then took some himself. "The Wynnd will always bear you south, though you might find yourself upon some other branch for a time. In the end all branches lead to the sea."

"You've found yourself on the hidden river, then?" Tam said.

"Many times. Indeed, I seek it." He patted his bag. "The plants I gather are found nowhere else. I carry them to healers in the south. But the secret river isn't easily found. One can spend years on the Wynnd and never vary from its course, though I have traveled the secret branches more often than most. I've never seen or heard tell of this drowned forest of stone, though."

"Speaking Stone is not on the normal course of the Wynnd, is it?" Tam said.

"No, Eber is one of the few who lives on a branch of the hidden river, though there are others. I've met them now and then. I am one of the few men I know of who travels back and forth a purpose. Most are like you—finding their way onto the hidden river unknowing, and wishing never to see it again. But I am an explorer of sorts. I do not make maps of my travels, for how can one map a river that appears and disappears and never in the same place twice." He reached into his pack and took out a small book. "But I keep a record of my travels. Perhaps I will make sense of it one day, piece it all together." He opened the book and paged through it slowly. "So far there is no rhyme or reason to it, but I have been at it only a dozen years." Theason glanced up at Cynddl. "What stories you must have found as you've traveled. How I envy you your calling."

"You shouldn't envy me," Cynddl said. "The stories of this river are disturbing—sometimes brutal and horrifying."

Theason nodded, reaching up a hand to gently trace the scars above his eyes. "That does not surprise me. There is a pool of hatred deep within the Greensprings. It seeps and trickles south, infecting the people there, though they know it not." He looked up at the others, and took his hand quickly away from his scars. He stood, lifting his bag and slinging it over a shoulder. "But I have fulfilled my promise to Eber, and now must be about my own errands." He patted his bag. "I have widow's bloom and heartleaf to gather."

"But where are we now?" Tam asked quickly, as Theason bowed and turned to go. "Are we on the hidden river?"

"Can you not tell?" Theason said, staring at him oddly. "Surely you have noted that the trees change. The underwood is different, plant by plant. It is unmistakable. You have only to open your eyes. Luck to you," he said, took up his staff, and set off into the trees, silent as sunlight.

Baore stepped out of the bush then, surprising them all. He said nothing, but looked coldly from one to the next, his gaze finally falling on Fynnol. "Then it was not a dream at all," he said, his voice and manner very subdued. "This creature came to me, this nagar, and offered me a way back to life." He paused. "And you said nothing . . ."

Fynnol cast his gaze down, his head twitching back and forth, as though he searched for an explanation.

"We thought you needed peace of mind to recover, Baore," Tam said after a moment. "We . . . we were concerned for your well-being."

Baore didn't even look at Tam. "Or Fynnol wanted me to go on to Westbrook, to stay on this cursed river."

"That's not true!" Fynnol said looking up.

Tam thought he might have to step between the cousins, such was the look Baore gave Fynnol.

"Isn't it? What care you if I'm haunted by a ghoul, as long as you have your way." Baore continued to glare at his cousin, and then his look of outrage wavered and snuffed out like a flame. He collapsed onto an outcropping of stone, covering his face, his great chest heaving. "This . . . *thing*," he almost sobbed. "It wants some part of my life. That's what it said. But I refused its offer, and here I am all the same. Did it carry me back to the world of life? And if it did what will it want of me in return?" He turned his head up, gazing at Cynddl.

The story finder crouched down so that his head was on the same level as Baore's. "I don't know, Baore. What happened to you is beyond my knowledge. Nagar, Theason called this apparition, but the nagar are a mystery. Among my people only Rath might have answers for your questions, but Rath is far away."

"I shall go no further than the Wold of Kerns, no matter what anyone else chooses to do. From there I will go north—home, by road, alone if need be. But I shall travel no further on this haunted river."

"We will reach the Wold in a few days," Cynddl said. "There I will keep my bargain and buy horses for all who wish them. Let me have just this one night in this place, and we can be on our way in the morning. Three days or so to the Wold of Kerns, Baore, and your part of our bargain is done."

Baore looked up sharply at Cynddl as he said this. "I've heard enough of bargains," he said. "There is no profit in them for me, but only sorrow. Sorrow and nightmares. Nightmares that remain when the morning dawns."

THIRTY-ONE

They saw him first on a ridge high above open farmland. Hafydd's bewitched sword had begun sounding madly, like an angry wasp. It was the first sighting they'd had of Hafydd's whist since he'd eluded them on the cliff.

The huntsman soon had his trail, but there was only one horse now. Elise was no longer with him. Lord Menwyn and his men-at-arms gave up the chase then, the Wills lord saying it was clear they could never catch this man who was obviously a sorcerer. He'd glanced at Hafydd's sheathed sword as he said this, his mouth turning down a little.

Prince Michael's father decided to join Lord Menwyn, but Hafydd would not hear of giving up the chase. He and his guards would go on. And to his own surprise, Michael chose to ride on with them.

"This pursuit is vain," his father had said to him. "Will you not ride back with me?"

"No, Father, I will go on and learn something of this sorcerer you've taken as your counselor—this man who has bespelled you."

And so he had ridden on, following Hafydd, who ignored him, the two of them in the center of a circle of voiceless, black-clad men-at-arms—Hafydd's revenant honor guard.

They had no need of huntsmen now and used only Hafydd's blade to guide them. The Prince had never ridden a horse so hard and felt pangs of guilt over this. Twice more that day they sighted Hafydd's whist, but they never seemed to draw nearer.

He led them down through one of the thousand river valleys that made up the land between the mountains. People they met had seen him pass. One young woman had actually spoken with him. Michael got the distinct impression that their quarry was in no hurry. He was toying with them, as though he knew that Hafydd could never give up the chase. He was taunting Hafydd.

For his part, Hafydd said nothing, but only followed his lodestone wherever it indicated: over fields, once through a marsh, up steep hills, through dense wood. By night they led their horses and went forward in the darkness, Hafydd claiming that their whist would rest, but they would not.

They had found a campfire burning and had approached it stealthily, with swords drawn, but there was no one there. Hafydd had taken his ringing blade and attacked the fire, sending sparks and burning chunks of wood everywhere. He had stood there in the center of a small clearing, Prince Michael and his guards having drawn back to the shadow's edge.

The knight glanced quickly around at the others, his face mostly shadow, scattered bits of fire burning around him. "We shall find him yet," Hafydd said. "He'll not make a fool of me."

"He already has," Prince Michael heard himself say. "I have only ridden with you to witness it." His breath caught then, and he could say no more. The night seemed to have fallen silent, and Hafydd's guards became suddenly still. Prince Michael was almost unable to keep to his feet, his fear was so great.

Someone must stand before him, he thought. *Someone must.*

But when Hafydd strode across to him, the Prince stepped back, then held his place. The old knight stared at him, and Prince Michael was not able to meet that gaze long. He looked away, hanging his head and hating himself for doing it.

"You talk like a brave man," Hafydd said, standing before him a moment more; and then he stepped away, holding up his humming sword and turning in a small circle, the shattered fire burning in shards about his feet.

THIRTY-TWO

Baore took them ashore at the mouth of a small creek that whispered into the larger river. It had been four days since their meeting with Theason Hollyoak, and the Wold of Kerns had not yet appeared. Baore had grown more restive and silent as the days passed, and now put them ashore so that Cynddl might walk in the wood and try to determine if they were on the Wynnd or the secret river.

The four went single file up the edge of the creek and very soon found themselves walking beneath trees with bark white as birch. The leaves shivered in the breeze, and large, pendulous flowers hung down like narrow, yellow bells. Cynddl stopped, reaching up to pluck a flower from its branch. A bee landed clumsily on the lip of this blossom, wiggling into the throat, its small legs working furiously.

"I think this will answer our question," Cynddl said, watching the bee do its work. "We hardly need look any further."

Baore slumped down on the rocks of the embankment, his arms limp, as though he'd lost control of them. Tam didn't know what to say.

"We'll reach the Wold," Cynddl said. "It is only a matter of time."

"Yes, and our heron man once thought he'd passed through the Lion's Maw," Baore said, his voice bitter and soft.

But the Wold of Kerns did not appear that day or the next, and they were still on a branch of the hidden river, as far as they could tell. On the evening of the sixth day they made a camp on a gravel beach, and Fynnol fished their dinner from the river.

They lounged about the fire in the long evening hours, the sun hidden by trees and hills, the eastern shore still bathed in golden light. Baore sat as far from the river as the beach would allow, his eyes fixed on the moving water as though it were a snake that might turn on them at any moment. He and Fynnol continued their joust of silence, and though Cynddl and Tam tried to make conversation it could not stand against the silence and was overwhelmed.

Baore rose suddenly, and stared out at the river. Tam spun around, thinking their apparition had appeared again, but there, in the river's center, two men stood in a crudely built barge, staring at the Valemen and their Fáel companion. One of them raised an arm and waved tentatively.

"Well, we aren't the only ones lost on the river," Fynnol said.

Baore cupped his hands to his mouth. "How far to the Wold of Kerns?" he called.

"We left the Wold three days past," the man's voice echoed over the water, "but it'll take you six days, maybe seven, pulling against the flow."

"But the Wold of Kerns is to the south . . .!" Baore shouted, pointing.

The man looked very darkly at the big Valeman, shook his head, and extended a hand to the north.

Baore stood for a moment, watching the men pass by, the slanting light illuminating their shoulders and heads. After they had disappeared, Baore stood for a moment more, gazing at the river. Then he turned quickly and disappeared into the wood, leaving the others silent in his wake.

The shadows stretched into darkness and Baore found himself on an outcropping of stone not far behind their encampment. The river lay below him, and the moon floated up from behind distant hills. The voice of the river was soft here as though it slept peacefully, but Baore had learned that it was never to be trusted, not even in its most tranquil mood.

"It'll never set me free," he said aloud, looking over the moonlit river to the hills beyond. Somewhere, leagues away, the road meandered south, but the forest was thick and the hills rugged. To walk out might take more woodcraft than Baore possessed, and certainly the others would never go with him. They still believed they could get off this river, that their journey would have an end, but Baore was not so sure. He was beginning to think that the river could keep them from ever reaching civilized lands, from ever seeing a road again. Perhaps the Lion's Maw awaited them yet.

"Why do you look so sad, Baore Talon? I returned you to the land of the living—and you made no bargains with 'ghouls.'"

Baore whirled around, and there in the fading light, on the edge of deeper shadow, stood the fair woman he had seen before. The woman from his dream of Death's gate.

She came out into the moonlight, and Baore felt himself shrink away, yet he also wanted to stay. She wasn't quite substantial, like a reflection in the twilit river. Her eyes were the shadows of overhanging leaves, her hair dark clouds. Even as insubstantial as she was he could see her long, thick lashes, her exquisite youth. She appeared hardly more than a girl of twenty. A girl abandoned in the wildlands, craving the warmth of others.

"What is it you want of me?" he whispered.

She took a step nearer, and he could see that she dressed as a man-at-arms, a sword on her hip. "I have watched you, Baore Talon. I watched as you carried the man-at-arms ashore—the man who had tried to kill you—and buried him in the ground, as he wanted. You are good and kind and incapable of hatred—even hatred of your enemies. In what I must do, you cannot help me, but you can journey south into the inhabited lands. That is all I ask. Let the river bear you south."

She had drawn closer now, and with each step she seemed to become more real, like a reflection appearing as the water calmed. Baore had a terror that she might touch him, and yet he longed for her to touch him.

"You think I am something terrible, don't you? A ghoul, you called me before—before I carried you back here to the world of life and human warmth."

"I . . . I don't know what to think," Baore said. "I even wonder if I'm going mad."

She shook her head, a small smile appearing, but then pushed aside by sorrow. "No, you are not mad, and I *am* terrible. More terrible than you know. But I am also lost and despairing and lonely and cold. If you knew how much I longed to touch you, you would be frightened, I think." She reached out a hand, but stopped. "It would be no more than the softest breeze to you—perhaps not even that. But I am tied to you all the same. It is you who keeps me near this world—the living world—as though we were tethered by an invisible cord. But if you carry me south, I will find another who will do what I need, and I will release you."

She stood close before him now, looking up. She was so small and slender, almost a child beside Baore. Her eyes were as dark and deep as an empty night sky. "Will you take me south, Baore Talon?"

"What if I refuse?" he said breathlessly.

She gazed at him a moment. "Will you refuse me?" she asked quietly.

Baore shook his head. "No," he said, "you carried me back from Death's gate. I will bear you south in return. But nothing more. I fear death, but I fear other things are worse. That is the only bargain I will make."

"It is enough," she said. For a moment more she stood, gazing up at him, then turned and went back into the shadows of the trees, like a drop of rain disappearing into the river.

THIRTY-THREE

L lyn walked in her garden, accompanied by uneasy wind. It sighed and shifted, uncomfortable in the branches of one tree, then another. It fell among the peonies that tumbled over the path, stirring them from their perfect rest. As Llyn stepped among the blossoms a gust swept up to twist her hair, then scurried off along the path, flowers swaying in its wake.

Her thoughts would not leave her in peace this night, and yet she couldn't give them voice.

Perhaps it was this vague suspicion of Beld that would not let her be. She knew his hatred for Toren had not healed miraculously, as a septic wound sometimes would. Beldor's lacerations were too deep to heal. They had cut into his heart and had festered there since childhood.

Beld had never been the golden-haired boy, as he had wished. That was the simple truth of it. All his life Toren had been the light of everyone's heart, while Beld had been big and awkward and petulant and jealous from his earliest days. The earliest days Llyn could remember, at least. And that had not changed, she was sure of it.

Dease did not seem to believe her—or perhaps would

not allow himself to believe her. He was too honorable, Llyn thought. He couldn't accept that a member of his own family might be traitorous: even Beld. Llyn, however, had studied the history of the Renné—the real history. She knew Dease's naïveté would not stand against the truth.

She stopped by the pool with its small falls. The moon was hidden and the starlight faint, but Llyn had the knack of perceiving an entire scene from only suggestions: the starlight on the bordering rocks and glittering off the crest of the falls, the dark pool at the center.

She spent so much time alone in this place that it had become too large in her life. Llyn knew its every flower, and almost mourned as each blossom passed, as each tree lost its leaves in autumn, as though these were a part of her. So an elderly person must mourn the loss of beauty or vigor or the luster of the hair.

She looked at her hands, turning them over in the faint light. They were no more familiar to her than the ferns that grew in the shade of the south wall, the wisteria that had twined itself high up into the branches of the birch, as though it longed to look out over the wall.

Llyn sometimes wondered if there really was a world there to be seen.

The latches on the balcony doors clattered free, causing her to start. A hinge creaked dryly. At the same time a small bird alighted on the garden wall and called out, *whist*. A sound like a whisper. A threat.

Llyn found she could suddenly neither breathe nor

move. Who was about to step out onto her balcony? Whose death did the whist foretell? Tears blurred her vision, and then a man emerged. Llyn had barely the presence of mind to step beneath a branch. Her vision did not clear, and the silhouette on the balcony seemed unfamiliar to her. Was it Dease?

"Who is that?" she said, her voice trembling audibly.

"You don't know me, Lady Llyn," a man said, "but I know much of you, and even more of the Renné and the Wills: but it is your knowledge of your family and its history that has brought me here."

Llyn was so relieved that it wasn't one of her cousins on the balcony she almost didn't care that this man had breached her solitude.

"I . . . I dreamed that a whist would come," she said, her voice still shaking a little. "I've thought all along that it was a prophetic dream, and that whoever emerged onto my balcony, after the whist called, would be marked for death."

"It's not me he's marked," the man said, "for Jac is mine. But he will sing his song many times more before this year is done if you don't help me. War is imminent, once again, in the land between the mountains. I don't know if it can be stopped, but I've not given up all hope. Will you help me?"

Llyn hardly knew what to say. Her dream had come true. A whist had lit upon the garden wall, and then a man unknown to her had walked out onto her balcony. And now he asked for her help in averting a war. She should call her maid and have guards summoned.

"Why would I help you?" she asked instead. "You are a stranger who disturbs my privacy. Are you even a guest at Castle Renné?"

"In truth, I'm not. And it isn't likely I would be welcomed, for, like my bird, I am a harbinger of bad tidings. I have come to warn you . . . and seek your counsel, as your cousins do. Menwyn Wills and the Prince of Innes hope to form an alliance, and though this has been delayed I don't think I've managed to stop it." He hesitated.

Llyn could just make him out in the faint light. A dark-haired man, richly dressed. Certainly he was fair-spoken; a nobleman.

"Somewhere in the archives of your family," he went on, "there must be a document—a journal or a memoir—that will tell me what I want to know. Did any Knights of the Vow escape the fall of Cooling Keep, and, if so, what became of them?"

"That is what you wish to know!?" And then Llyn laughed. "Oh, you are seeking their treasure!"

"No. That is not what I seek."

"Well, I can tell you that no Knights escaped. There, now you can leave me in peace." But she did not want him to go. When you dream a dream that comes true there is a reason. Who was marked for death?

"I believe that some did. The descendant of a Renné retainer—a trusted knight—claims that his ancestor rode with a company that pursued the last Knights of the Vow, six who escaped the slaughter of Cooling Keep."

"And what does he say befell these six Knights?"

"He doesn't know. They were pursued up the north road into the wildlands, and though I've journeyed there more than once, I haven't learned what befell them." Llyn saw him lift his hands and shrug.

"And why do you want to know this?"

"If I told you that this knowledge might save many lives, would that be enough?"

"It would if I knew you well enough to believe it."

"This is a situation where a lie would be more readily believed than the truth . . ."

"I am a seeker of truth. Its disappointments and implausibilities are known to me."

The man shifted from one foot to the other, then back again. "I believe the Knights who escaped carried with them knowledge that is dangerous—especially so if discovered by the enemies of the Renné."

"Well, that is cryptic enough."

He bowed his head as though he'd been paid a compliment. Llyn smiled in spite of herself.

"You realize," she said, "that what you ask is not easily done. There were several thousand men at the fall of Cooling Keep."

"Yes, but some commander must have sent the men north. And perhaps he even listed who they were . . . But then, you have no need of my instructions in these matters, I suspect."

Llyn said nothing. She didn't know what to do.

Certainly she shouldn't help this stranger . . . The whist hopped through the branches of a nearby ash, and Llyn shrank back, almost stepping out into starlight.

"Will you help me, Lady Llyn?"

"I will consider it," she said.

"Then may I call on you again?"

"I will allow it, though leave your bird behind. And I promise nothing."

"Jac does as pleases him, but I'll do my best to come alone." She could see the man place his hands on the balcony. "Thank you, Lady Llyn. It was an honor to have met you." He bowed toward the garden, and she heard the doors close, the latches fall into place.

The whist cried twice.

THIRTY-FOUR

Arden rode along the grassy lane beside his cousin Toren. He didn't like to admit that every movement of his horse sent great waves of pain to all corners of his being. Perhaps this was the pride of youth his father talked about—or the pride of men, of which his mother spoke.

They had spent this day and the last at a contest of courtesy; not a tournament proper but a meeting of men-at-arms. That afternoon they'd fought a mock battle—a melee—and Arden had been courteously battered to a mass of bruises and swollen joints. He was certain he creaked audibly when he walked.

And this had been after a day of jousting, which had left him with pain enough. Toren had unseated him yet again, and as he lay on the ground he thought he should never catch his breath, that surely the shattered stump of a lance must protrude from his chest. But only the wind had been knocked from him, and eventually he did breathe again—painfully.

Toren had come riding up on his great horse, gazing down on his poor cousin as he lay with tiny lights sparking around the edge of his vision. He had looked like a knight out of an old tale, stern and noble.

It had been a day of Renné fighting Renné, for all others had been swept aside. Dease had unhorsed Beldor, and for the first time, Arden had bested Dease. But Toren had triumphed yet again. It didn't matter that he gave up much in weight to several others, he was strong and skilled—supremely skilled.

Arden looked out across the river, seeing the twilight gather beneath its banks, as though it rose up from the river like a dark mist.

"You are being rather mysterious," Arden said.

"Not so, Cousin. I merely have someone whom I wish you to meet, and it turns out he would like to meet you also. Which is surprising for he is a man of excellent judgment."

Arden tried to rise to the bait. "And how is it then that he is a friend of yours, this man of excellent judgment?"

Toren laughed. "If only you were so quick with a riposte in a melee, Cousin."

"And if you had not fallen so gracefully upon your ass, I should not be sporting a rainbow across most of my rib cage."

Toren had slipped in the melee and, without thinking, Arden had put himself between his cousin and a vicious sword blow. If it had been an edged weapon he would have been cut in two.

"'A knight is modest in his manner, performing his deeds without need of praise,'" Toren quoted.

Arden didn't respond. He was too sore, and the false-ness of this banter struck him hard, knocking the words from him.

Where were they going?

Toren was being very close. Arden half expected that his cousin had arranged an assignation with some comely young women—at least that was his hope. But even this thought could not change his mood. He found it diffi-cult to be around Toren now. And yet he found he sought his cousin out, and was overly solicitous and helpful to him. He had never known such a conflict of feelings, and it confused him terribly.

They crossed the narrow river on a stone bridge that arced up to allow boats passage beneath. The River Wynnd and its tributaries were more important than the roads in many ways, and all manner of commerce traveled the waterways.

Toren pulled his horse up at the crest of the bridge and gazed down the curve of the river, lined by tall poplars and weeping birch. White flowers spread across the new grass of the banks, like a skiff of snow drifting here and there beneath the trees.

The remains of the sunset washed across the western sky, golden-orange and pale blue. A few elongated clouds glowed like molten copper, reflecting off the river.

"I can't tell you how much I love this land," Toren said, his voice suddenly deep and rich with feeling. He turned to his cousin. "Isn't it beautiful? Isn't it a miracle, the great-est of all good fortune that we are alive in such a world?"

Arden looked past his cousin and nodded. It was this that set his cousin apart from others: he was so vividly alive and so appreciative of the fact. Arden closed his eyes and a vision of Toren lying on the grass with an arrow in his heart came to him. Dease's arrow.

Arden opened his eyes and forced his mind to go elsewhere.

He, too, loved this land, the land their family had once ruled. Even the bridge they were on was raised to a designated height set by one of their illustrious ancestors to allow the passage of river traffic. And the same story was repeated all across the old kingdom. Castles and palaces in which they had lived, roads they had ordered built. Forests planted. Canals dug. Fields upon which famous battles had been won or lost, ancestors victorious or fallen.

He felt that Ayr, the land between the mountains, ran in his blood the way spring rivers ran brown with the earth's rich soil.

He looked up at the changing sky. A misshapen moon, a few days from full, floated free of the eastern wood. Such moons were invariably called "gibbous" in books, Arden had noticed, though he didn't know why. Dease would know, or perhaps Llyn. They were the scholars of the generation, but he didn't ask. He didn't want to break this mood of sadness and loss and beauty. Perhaps the last time he and Toren would be alone together.

Toren spurred his horse on, remembering his errand, and Arden reluctantly followed. They proceeded along the opposite bank of the river, riding slowly into evening. Five furlongs later they turned down a laneway between overarching trees, reducing their pace as they lost the light.

Arden fell into a silent revery, the meeting on Summer's Hill coming back to him unbidden. Most of the time he managed not to think of it, as though it were merely a daydream, a moment's flight of fancy, not something real. The Westbrook Fair had seemed so far off then. Certainly Toren would come to his senses before then. Dease would convince him.

But yesterday's joust had reminded him that spring fled quickly by and the tournament at Westbrook would soon be upon them. And Toren still planned to return the Isle of Battle to the Wills, against the wishes of almost his entire family.

Arden looked over at his cousin, reduced to near silhouette by the dusk. Toren seemed to be lost in thought, though his gaze came up every few seconds and searched among the shadows of the trees—they were, after all, two Renné lords out riding without guards. Arden didn't pretend to understand his cousin—in truth, he felt Toren's intellect too subtle for him—but he also felt that too many of Toren's decisions were made out of idealism and were not in the least pragmatic. Returning the Isle of Battle to the Wills was the prime example. It was a rich land and, rather than making the Wills grateful and placing them in the Renné's debt, it would merely give them the means to raise armies again.

Toren expected the Wills to be guided by his own idealism and sense of honor. He even expected this of the Renné!

Sometime later—Arden was not sure how long—a light appeared, then a second. As they approached he realized that he was seeing torches, and then a door materialized between them in an expanse of stone wall. Lights glowed in high windows, and as they came into the small clearing Arden could make out the structure's shape against the stars.

"What is this? A shrine?" It seemed to be a small keep. A castle in miniature.

"I don't know its origins," Toren said, dismounting. "It's a house of some charm and craft, but who built it or for what purpose I can't say."

The door was opened by a tall man bearing a candlebranch. He held it away from him so that he could see the callers clearly, and then opened the door wide, bowing them in silently.

Toren unbuckled his scabbard. "Leave your sword here," he instructed his cousin.

They fell in behind the man, who was not a servant, Arden was sure. He recognized the manner and bearing of a knight despite the long, gray mantle that did much to disguise his shape.

The high-ceilinged hall was lined with mounted lances, many broken, set in sockets and supported so that they leaned out at an angle. Even in the poor light Arden could see that these lances were very old. From each, a banner hung—tokens of battles won or lost.

They climbed a stair and entered a long chamber also hung with ancient banners. Along the walls beneath the banners, rough benches were set, and at the end of the hall was a dais upon which stood a large, elaborately carved chair. In the center of the room a long, wooden table stood. Here the man left them in the light of a few large tapers and disappeared through a door.

Arden turned in a slow circle, looking up. It was an odd room. Responds set against the wall were carved in the shape of tree trunks, and the rafters that supported the roof were shaped like the branches of stylized trees— oaks, Arden thought. He had the feeling that he stared up into the shaded reaches of a living forest.

From these branches more banners hung. Many of the coats of arms Arden recognized, for they were of noble families, most having fallen into obscurity or having been eradicated during the long years of war.

"I am beginning to think that my guess is wrong, Toren. We are not here to meet young women of great beauty and 'uncommon' virtue."

Toren did him the honor of smiling, but no more.

The door near the dais opened and a man entered wearing the same gray mantle, but instead of a candle-branch he carried a two-handed sword. It was a ceremonial weapon with an intricate handle and damasking upon the blade, but Arden could see that it was perfectly sharp. In the hands of a master it would be a formidable weapon. This man, who appeared utterly capable of wielding such a sword, looked the two cousins over and then said something softly to another waiting in the shadow of the door.

A second man entered, tall with graying hair, short cropped, and a neatly trimmed beard. He wore the same mantle of gray. Arden thought him an impressive man, regal and strong, yet without arrogance, almost without pride. There was a certain . . . *stillness* about him that struck Arden strongly. The world could fall to chaos and this man would not be affected.

"My lords," he greeted them, bowing slightly, a small smile enlivening a serious face. In the candlelight his eyes were too dark for their color to be distinguished, but they appeared black and thoughtful.

A third man entered the room, carrying a matching two-handed sword. He took up a position from which he could intercept either of the guests if they threatened his master, yet far enough off that he would not offer insult to the visiting nobles. Arden didn't know who this nobleman might be, but clearly he was unwilling to take risks with the Renné. Was this man one of the Wills? But gray was not the color of their livery.

"My cousin Lord Arden Renné," Toren said, his manner surprisingly deferential.

"My lord," the man responded. "Gilbert A'brgail."

Arden gave a slight bow, unsure quite how to respond to this man with his noble name and bearing, yet who was unknown to Arden.

"I had the pleasure of watching you at the contest

these last days," A'brgail said to Arden. "You acquitted yourself well."

"Though not so well as my cousin," Arden said, nodding to Toren.

A'brgail blew out through his lips. "But that depends on what is being judged. Toren won the tournament, though he would have been felled in the melee but for you. It was Lord Arden Renné who put himself between his cousin and another's sword." A'brgail glanced at Toren—an unspoken question.

Toren returned the slightest nod. "I've brought you here, Arden, to discuss a matter of grave import to our family—indeed, to all of old Ayr."

Arden said nothing, waiting. This A'brgail must be an emissary of the Wills.

"But before we speak further, Sir Gilbert needs assurances that you will not repeat this conversation to anyone —not even members of our own family."

Involuntarily Arden took half a step back. "Perhaps you might give me some notion of what it is I am swearing to keep secret . . . ?"

"Nothing that could harm the Renné in any way," Toren said quickly. "I give you my word."

Arden shrugged. "Then I will not repeat what I hear in this hall."

A'brgail beckoned one of his guards, who brought him a folded robe, gray like the one he wore himself. This garment was carefully laid out on the table.

"You have no doubt seen paintings of knights wearing

such robes," A'brgail said, "though none have worn them in many a year."

Arden was not sure what he was to make of this. What family livery was gray? Was this some claimant to the A'brgail name? If so, it was a name that meant nothing to Arden, who would admit his knowledge of history was poor.

A'brgail motioned Arden forward, and he leaned over the robe, which seemed to be without devices, and then on the left breast he noticed a fan of leaves, silver-gray. Silveroak!

"It is a robe of the Knights of the Vow," Arden said, "but perfectly preserved." His eye darted from A'brgail to his guards: none of their robes bore devices of any kind.

"It is not preserved," A'brgail said. "This robe was made new only a week ago. It was woven to fit Arden Renné, and no other."

Arden did step back then, turning his gaze on Toren—almost an accusation. "What goes on here, Cousin?" he said.

Toren walked over to a chair set against the wall and sat down, looking up at Arden. "Gilbert A'brgail," he said evenly, "is the descendant of a Knight who avoided the slaughter at Cooling Keep. This Knight and a few others were not present and they escaped the notice of our ancestors, who certainly would have murdered them. Much of the lore and ritual and purpose of the Knights of the Vow have been kept alive by the descendants of these few men."

"Unfortunately," A'brgail said, "little of the lore and ritual has been retained. Most of it was lost, for of the Knights who escaped only two ranked as high as first marshal. The rest were merely brother Knights. The secrets and lore of the Order were known only in the higher ranks, but the purpose of the Knights . . . well, even that is not quite the same."

Arden looked down at the robe spread over the table. "Are you telling me that the Knights of the Vow have hidden themselves all these generations?"

A'brgail shook his head. "No. The secret was kept, but the knightly order failed—until now. It is only I and a few others who have dreamed of the Knights' revival."

"And now you would welcome a Renné amongst you? Why? And why would I choose to do this?"

"It was my idea, Arden," Toren said, rising from his chair. The banners hanging from the stone branches above seemed to catch his attention. "It is a way of assuring our family that the reborn Knights of the Vow intend no revenge against the Renné. It is also a way of assuring the Knights of the same thing: the Renné will not betray them again." He combed a hand through his hair. "But there is something more." Toren's gaze met Arden's. "I would have you out of this feud, Cousin, before it does to you what it has done to so many."

"The Renné cause is mine, Toren. You know that. My family's war is my war."

Toren answered this by closing his eyes tight for a second. "It is a war without purpose, and certainly without honor. Here is a way you can still serve the Renné and remove yourself from this senseless feud that destroys the best of each generation."

Toren's display of emotion touched Arden. "But certainly there is as much danger in joining the Knights— if they again take up the duties they once held."

"Physical danger, yes—that we can't avoid—but your honor would remain unsullied no matter what might befall you."

Arden glanced over at the robe lying on the table. So drab, as though made for men who lacked all passion, who were only alive to half of what men felt. "I have the honor of a Renné, Toren. I aspire to nothing more. I will do what is necessary to preserve my family. I could no more join the Knights of the Vow and abandon my family than could you."

"I would gladly join them, Arden, but it is my lot to try to make some rapprochement between the Renné and the Wills. I can't easily give up my duties."

"Nor can I." Arden waved a hand at the robe. "I am not so pure of heart, Toren. That is the truth of it. I am Renné. Find some other to be your envoy to the Knights. My fortunes lie with my family, for good or ill." Arden was speaking as though A'brgail weren't there, but he glanced toward him now. "I don't want to be present when the rest of the Renné learn that you have sanctioned this reestablishment of the Order of the Knights of the Vow. They will think you've lost your reason altogether."

"Perhaps I have," Toren said softly, "but my actions were not taken without sober thought—many hours of it. There are enemies we cannot resist alone."

"The roads are safe," Arden said quietly. "Villages are seldom attacked by brigands, even in the outer reaches of old Ayr. What purpose would the Knights serve now?"

A'brgail looked up at Arden.

"We have a purpose, as noble as we had in the past." He turned his head, looking at Arden from the corner of his eye. "But of that I can say nothing yet. Before you make your decision, tell me of this feud with the Wills: do you support it?"

"Not willingly," Arden said quickly, "but they would destroy us if they could. That is the truth of it." Arden broke away from the man's gaze, shaking his head. "The Wills can never be trusted. We know that beyond a doubt. I wish I could believe peace were possible, but the hatred is too deep." He looked up at the Knight who still regarded him closely. Arden felt oddly close to tears. "In some families madness runs, Brother A'brgail. In the Renné and the Wills it is this blood feud that is the madness. Sometimes it skips a generation, but it always appears again in both families." He shook his head. "No, if we lower our shield the madness will take them and they will fall upon us. We cannot . . . We can never give it up, for they will not.

"I like this feud no more than Toren. No more than any man. I despise what it does to us, to the Renné, for it consumes us, generation after generation. But it is unavoidable, as I have said. Some place in our minds and our hearts there is this madness, this darkness.

"The feud should never have been started, for once begun there is no going back, no resolution but the destruction of one family or the other. We keep the Wills isolated, set their allies against each other, and there is a kind of peace, but it will not last. War will come again. And again. And again, until one side has triumphed utterly."

"Until you have regained the throne—is that it?"

Arden looked at the man in surprise. "Throne! We shall never see the throne again. Only fools dream of that. If Ayr is ever reunited it will not be by Renné or Wills, be sure of that. No, the feud has a life of its own. The cause is buried, almost forgotten."

A'brgail shook his head. "But could you give it up, Lord Arden Renné? Could you give up this petty feud for a larger purpose? I will tell you that I see a greater goodness in your heart, an honor and nobility that this feud will debase. Is this not so, Lord Toren?"

"It is so." He turned to Arden then, putting a hand tenderly on his shoulder. "Do not take lightly what is being offered, Cousin. You could escape the family madness. Renounce it. Replace it with a greater purpose. Consider carefully, Arden. I would see you, at least, unsullied by this Renné obsession."

Toren fixed him with such a look of compassion that Arden could hardly bear it. Here was a measure of the nobility of Toren, and of the love he bore Arden.

"Cousin—" Arden started, hearing his voice break. "It is too late for me." Arden wanted to drop to his knee and confess his betrayal. Beg his cousin's forgiveness. "It is too late."

He turned away from the two men and placed both his hands upon the table, hearing the heavy silence behind him. Taking a long breath, he forced himself to face his cousin and this knight. "I shall await you outside, Toren." And he walked the length of the room, feeling every step of the way that these walls were a sanctuary offered to him—to him and what remained pure in his heart.

THIRTY-FIVE

The circle of silveroak lay hidden within a shallow draw between two wooded hillsides. Gilbert A'brgail walked among the trees, lost in thought. His attending knights stayed beyond the ring of ancient oaks—four strong men with their great swords unsheathed—and gave their master time and silence in which to contemplate.

A'brgail paced back and forth across the grass, barely aware of the guards. It was his habit to walk beneath the silveroaks when troubles beset him, but usually he attained peace and clarity. This night it escaped him.

A bird lit in the branches overhead, the leaves bobbing and shivering where it moved. And then a soft whispered *whist, whist.*

A'brgail almost lost his footing. For a moment he didn't even dare to look up, and when he did the bird seemed to be gone. He looked about quickly, gazing into the shadowed wood where the moon and starlight could not penetrate.

"I am here, brother," said a voice, and the guards were in motion, swords raised.

But A'brgail lifted a hand and ordered them to be at peace.

"Alaan?"

A silhouette appeared between the gnarled trunks of two silveroaks. "Who else?"

"Yes, who else's arrival is proclaimed by the harbinger of death." A'brgail pressed the fingertips of his hands together and took a long breath to calm himself. "Why have you come, Alaan?"

"Did you not promise our mother that you would watch over me and protect me from harm? You have not been doing your duty, Gilbert, not for one who takes his vows so seriously."

Alaan crouched down between the trees, and the moving moonlight touched him lightly. He took up some small object from the ground, turning it in his fingers.

"I have done what I could to keep my word, but you would thwart me at every turn. None of my warnings would you take."

"Ah yes, your constant warnings. Worse than Jac by half, I would say."

"I will ask you again what you want," A'brgail said, embarrassed by the emotion in his voice. His half brother always brought out such passions in him, such anger.

"It is odd, for I have come to warn you, this time." Alaan paused, taking a quick breath. "Your worst fears have come to pass. Hafydd hadn't the strength to resist, just as you feared. Caibre is among us. Hafydd is become a monster."

A'brgail shook his head numbly. "Yes," he said. "Yes. I know." He looked down at his hands, rubbing his fingers over the badly healed joints. He looked up at Alaan suddenly. "And what of you, Brother? What have you become?"

Alaan didn't answer for a moment. He still toyed with whatever it was he had retrieved from the ground. But then he too looked up at his half brother. "What I've done was necessary, Gilbert. You couldn't have done it."

"No! No, even if I could have broken my vow, I would not. You are not even Alaan. Why do you come to visit me?"

"Because I am still Alaan, only changed, as though I had been away for twenty years and only just now returned. I am that different—perhaps more so—but I am Alaan, all the same."

"So you would say, but I know more of this than most. What you have done is utterly wrong, and it will not be just you who pays the price for this." A'brgail could see the cold look come over Alaan's face—that, at least, was familiar.

"What choice had I after your blunder with Hafydd?"

"Hafydd was a great knight," A'brgail said quickly.

"He was a great liar. And look what has become of him . . ."

"Hafydd was my mistake, and I will set things aright. I swear it."

Alaan shook his head. "You swear to too many things, Gilbert. It is a strange weakness."

"It is not a time for jests, Alaan, as you well know."

"No, it isn't. And you're right; Hafydd was your mistake, but you can't set that aright now. Only I can do that. You see, Brother, I am Alaan yet, for I will not stand by and watch Hafydd bring ruin to the land between the mountains. I will trap him if I can, and do what must be done."

A'brgail gazed at the dark form of his half brother, too much like the father, he thought. Reckless and insolent—incapable of hard discipline. These traits remained, no matter what he'd become.

"If you were a Knight of the Vow you would be burned," A'brgail said, his voice coming out like a hiss.

Alaan fumbled the object he held—a small stone—and then retrieved it, dropping it from one hand into the other, over and over. "I did not take your vows, Brother," he said softly.

"No, you took other things."

"As much mine as yours." He looked up, his face shadowed but appearing sad in the pale light. "I came hoping there might be peace between us, that I might forewarn you. Hafydd's knowledge has grown. He might even be able to find you, to find this place. Guard yourself, Brother. Death's gate is a frightening place."

"I shall welcome my end when it comes, Alaan, but what of you? What of you, whose herald is the foreteller of death?"

"No one seems to understand my bird," Alaan said softly. "It foretells nothing. The whist is a bird of warning.

But Jac will not sing my name for a good while yet. You should know me, Gilbert—I made a shrewder bargain than that."

Alaan stood and turned back into the dark wood. When he was almost lost to shadow A'brgail spoke quickly. "There can be no water, either running or standing—not even a trickle. And you must burn the corpse. Burn it immediately and spread the ashes to the wind, not over water. Do you hear?"

Alaan nodded once and was gone.

THIRTY-SIX

The river swept them south without rest or hesitation. If the men they'd met the previous day had been telling the truth, the Wold of Kerns was falling astern, and every hour that passed added many, many strokes of the oars to the return journey.

"If we stay near to the bank where the current is slower, and there are eddies to aid us, it won't be quite so hard," Cynddl said. It had been the story finder who'd broached the subject. Baore had said nothing the entire day and lounged in the boat, eyes closed—pretending to sleep, Tam suspected. Fynnol's silence was of a different character—it was aimed at Baore.

"I'll go back, if that is what Baore wants to do," Tam offered, earning him a quick, sullen glance from Fynnol.

"No," Baore said, rousing up and looking at the passing riverbank. "The river takes us south. It'll never let us go back now." Without looking at anyone, he lay back, draping an arm over his eyes.

Fynnol sat up, trying to suppress a smile of satisfaction, but Cynddl met Tam's eye, his look troubled and full of questions.

Two hours before dusk they drew their boat up to the riverbank, and Tam and Cynddl took their yaka bows and went quietly out beneath the trees.

"I didn't expect Baore to change his mind," Cynddl said as they walked. "He's been swearing for days that he'd not go beyond the Wold of Kerns, and I believed him."

"So did I," said Tam.

They walked through a sparse underwood beneath ancient hornbeams and maples, shafts of sunlight angling like arrows through the leaves. Cynddl stopped, listening to some faint rustling in the bush. He took a soft step forward and a hare leapt out of the ferns. It hadn't gone a yard before an arrow pinned it to the ground. Quickly Cynddl put the poor beast out of its misery.

"Perhaps what he said is true, though," Tam said. "We can't go back. The river won't let us."

"You talk as though the river possessed reason," Cynddl said. "I suspect the times we've found ourselves on the secret river were as random as raindrops. It was just luck—or ill luck—nothing more." He stopped again to listen, his narrow face fixed in concentration, the cloud of gray hair illuminated by a ray of the day's last light. "But even if the river possesses no reason, it does seem unlikely to me that we would reach the Wold of Kerns."

"The nagar . . .?" Tam said, pitching his voice low.

Cynddl stopped to listen again, drawing his arrow back, his yaka wood bow resisting. The story finder nodded. "That is my fear."

"Then we should keep Baore in view, and stand watches at night."

Cynddl looked down his arrow, nocked and ready. "We should, though I'm not sure such precautions will matter."

Something broke from the bush and took to the sky. Two arrows pierced the air, and the flight ended in a fluttering of wings and floating feathers.

Within the hour they returned with a brace of rabbits and a cock pheasant. Fynnol had taken over Baore's post of chief fire maker, and the aroma of Fáel cooking soon spread along the riverbank. Dinner was served just as the sun cast its last light over the river. For a few moments no one spoke but to make appreciative sounds in the direction of the cook.

"Tell us about this fair at Westbrook, Cynddl," Fynnol said, gesturing south with a leg of pheasant.

Cynddl's attention lifted from his food for a moment and he looked off down the river. "Westbrook is the seat of the Renné family, who are the patrons of the tournament. Traditionally, it has been one of the two great contests of the season, the other being at Dallynhoe, the capital of the One Kingdom. Dallynhoe has only ruins that indicate its former glory, and the tournament has been reduced to insignificance. Westbrook is preeminent now, and is really a great country fair as much as a contest of courtesy. The best minstrels in the land will gather, as will acrobats and conjurers, pickpockets and thieves. There will be plays and puppetry, singing contests, and everyone shall bring their wares to sell. Even the Fáel come, both to play music and offer their crafts. There will be country dances in the evenings, and the night of the last day of the tournament, a costume ball the likes of which you have never seen. As the nobles arrive for the ball, all of the people gather to see the costumes, many of which are labored upon for an entire year.

"The tournament itself will draw the strongest knights, the finest archers, and the most skilled swordsmen. There is a contest of horsemanship, a judging of armor, and if all that is not enough, there will even be a running of sheep dogs." Cynddl laughed. "There is something at the Westbrook Fair for one and all."

"As long as Alaan is there," Fynnol said between mouthfuls.

Tam laughed, and cast his gaze out over the waters. He was on his feet, a curse dying on his lips.

A boat crossed the stream, its bow aimed unmistakably for their camp. Cynddl, never far from his weapons, had bow in hand and an arrow nocked before the others had put down their food.

Tam fetched his bow and climbed quickly up onto a rock. The last light of the evening cast long shadows out over the river, but as the boat emerged from one band of darkness, Tam could see it sat low in the water and two of three occupants sent regular arcs of spray out over the rail. Tam relaxed a little.

"They don't appear to be men-at-arms," he called down to his companions. "If I'm not mistaken, two of them are women, and they are bailing to save their lives."

The four companions emerged from the trees onto the shadowed riverbank, watching the boat approach; and indeed the two bailing were women, with a large, gray-haired man madly pumping the oars.

He ran the boat up on the shingle beach and collapsed, none of them with enough breath to utter a word. Water sloshed about beneath the thwarts, and even as the people sat recovering, the stern of the boat settled until it rested on the bottom.

Tam and Cynddl helped one of the women out onto the bank where she collapsed, and then the other did the same. The man managed to make it on his own, though he was red faced and all but breathless. He made to retrieve their instruments from the encroaching water but Cynddl was ahead of him.

"Minstrels," Fynnol mouthed to Tam, who nodded.

The companions quickly had the boat emptied of its belongings and with some effort dragged it around and tipped the water out. Baore, who'd been silent and list-less for days, bent over it, rapping on planks with a knuckle, tearing up the floorboards.

"My cousin, Baore, is a skilled shipwright," Fynnol said to the strangers, though this was really an attempt to bridge the silence that flowed between him and Baore—now that they were going south to Westbrook.

Baore turned the boat over and continued his

inspection. "She'll need to be recaulked," Baore said, standing and running a hand back into his mow of hair. "You've a soft plank or two and some cracked frames. You can't sail her hard, which I guess you've been doing. She's too old and weakened in her structure. You're lucky she didn't sink from under you."

"Can you mend her?" the man asked. "We've not much money but we might pay you something . . ."

Baore gazed at the boat a moment more. "She needs rebuilding, is what she needs. New frames, new planks. You can't do that out here on the riverbank without proper tools and seasoned wood. I can try to recaulk her. That might take you some distance if you go easily. But don't sail her at all, just let the current take you."

"We'd be grateful for any help," the man said. "What would be your price for such a job?"

Baore shook his head. "Keep your coins. We won't leave you stranded." He looked up at the sky. "Too late to do anything tonight. We've a fire and some supper. Join us and we'll see better how things stand in the morning."

The man offered his hand to Baore. "It is luck to meet with kindly strangers. The river brought us to you, it seems. I'm Gartnn," he said. "Let me introduce Angeline A'drent. And Elffen N'Orr. We are minstrels, as you've likely guessed, traveling south to Westbrook for the fair."

"As do we," said Fynnol, stepping to the fore. He had a weakness for pretty young women, which these two certainly were. He made a graceful bow, and introduced himself and then the others, though Tam thought he was rather perfunctory in naming his companions.

It had been too long since they'd enjoyed the company of women, Tam was certain of that, and suddenly the river had cast these up on the shore. Although Tam had a feeling that one should beware the gifts of the river, he was willing to ignore this feeling for the moment.

The two women sat and dried their skirts by the fire, while Fynnol and Cynddl served food. Darkness coaxed the stars out, their reflections wavering on the smooth surface of the river. To Tam the river had the depths of the night sky. A watery world of infinite darkness.

Elise had never heard of the Vale of Lakes and wondered if these young men teased her—but that didn't seem to be their nature. At least it didn't seem to be the nature of two of them: Tam and Baore. Fynnol had a silver tongue and she guessed would tell any lie if it served his purpose. He was a rogue in the making, that one.

"What takes you to Westbrook?" Gartnn asked. He was partaking of the offered food with great relish, but Elise knew him a little now. She knew how shrewd he was. It was the Fáel who were traveling with these young men that interested Gartnn. Black wanderers didn't commonly mingle with any but their own kind, yet here was one traveling the length of the river with three young men from the wildlands. Peculiar, to say the least.

Elise examined these strangers surreptitiously. The leader was the one named Tam—the good-looking one.

He didn't say much, glad to let others talk and answer questions, but when he did speak, his words were chosen with great care. He was a smart one, she thought, and a little wary.

The shipwright was a veritable giant. After his pronouncements on their boat, he had lapsed into silence and seemed often to be unaware of the conversation, his mind elsewhere. He also didn't seem to care much that two comely young women had been cast ashore by the river. He was unlike the other two in this. Elise thought Baore looked like a man in mourning, and perhaps he was. Perhaps he'd lost someone dear to him and had come on this journey in hopes of forgetting—of escaping his grief.

Fynnol was the charmer. She had met him before, though he was usually better dressed and groomed, and often better looking as well. They were not nearly so coarse as she expected, these Valemen, which made her wonder if they were really from this place they'd named in the wildlands. Certainly men from the wildlands would hardly be so fair-spoken.

Gartnn was suspicious of them, too, she could tell. He was using all his guile to coax their story from them, but there were things that they weren't telling. Elise hoped she hadn't fallen in with dangerous company.

The last of the four was the Fáel. Fynnol had let it slip that he was a story finder—which hadn't pleased Cynddl, she'd noticed. Story finders, she knew, were greatly revered among the wanderers. Perhaps it was not so odd that he traveled down the river seeking the stories of the ancient kingdoms. The Fáel were little understood, though if there were any among her people who could claim some kinship with the black wanderers it was the minstrels. They too were wanderers, and lovers of music. Minstrels coveted the Fáel-made instruments, and the most famous of them owned nothing else. Her father had three Fáellutes, all of them gifts from admirers. But even minstrels were not entirely welcomed into the world of the Fáel. Yet these three young men from some unheard-of village in the north traveled with this story finder—a person of some consequence in his own world—and he treated them as friends.

Cynddl was older—in his thirties, she guessed—and gray before his time. He had the manner she expected of a story finder, remote and thoughtful. Not near as silent as Baore, but like Tam, he wasn't forthcoming, nor was he willingly talking about their journey. He was watching the strangers, weighing everything they said, just as Gartnn watched him.

"We'd only planned to go as far as the Wold of Kerns," Fynnol said, "but the river had its own ideas."

"What do you mean?" Gartnn asked innocently, but Elise saw his eyes narrow a little.

"We never laid eyes on the Wold," Fynnol said. "No, we were lost on some other branch of the river and never passed the Wold at all."

Gartnn's fork paused in its regular journeys to his mouth. "Some other branch of the river . . .?"

Cynddl laughed. "If you listen to Fynnol you'll hear tales of three-eyed men and the elusive white hart. I only wish I had so many stories to tell." The story finder laughed again, and Fynnol glanced over at him, suddenly uncomfortable.

There was an awkward silence for a moment.

"Did you stop in the Wold of Kerns yourselves?" Tam asked.

Gartnn shook his head. "No, we were never so far north. Never beyond the borders of the old kingdom. We've come down the Sweetwater and then into the Wynnd."

"The Sweetwater . . ." Cynddl said.

"Yes," Gartnn said and then, "you look surprised?"

Cynddl blew out through his lips and speared a piece of pheasant from his plate. "None of us have been down the river before. We thought we were further north, yet."

"Ah." Gartnn glanced at Elffen, his bushy brows rising just perceptibly.

The two women made up beds to one side of the fire—more comfortable with this than Tam expected—and Gartnn laid his own blankets between Fynnol and the women.

"We stand watches, yet," Cynddl said to Gartnn. "Not far back we had some trouble with thieves."

Gartnn reached over and drew his lute near, which earned him a look of wrath from Elffen. "I'll be happy to stand a watch," the minstrel said.

"We've our routine established," Tam said. "Perhaps

tomorrow night, if we're still camped together."

Elise lay by the dying fire, trying to sleep, but her eyes kept opening of their own accord. And there, in the ruddy glow of the embers, she would see the one called Tam sitting with his back to a tree, his sword laid near to hand. He didn't seem a bad man—none of them did— but then her experience of the world beyond the walls of Braidon Castle was small. She was trusting Gartnn, and *he* didn't look overly pleased with their company. She would wager the minstrel was awake yet.

If this giant could mend their boat, the next day they could be on their way. Perhaps they would find a village with an inn. They were traveling minstrels, after all; didn't someone want their services?

Sleep found her before moonrise, and she lay breathing softly beneath a coverlet of starlight.

Elise wasn't sure what woke her. A strange sense that something was wrong, that someone near her woke or moved. She lay utterly still, only her eyes flicking open. The fire had died away to ashes, and the moon had drifted too far into the west to offer light.

She could hear the river muttering along the bank and the emerald frogs singing in the trees. The easy, even breathing of her sleeping companions was only a little reassuring. Who was on watch? It was too dark to see much, certainly too dark to tell who might lie in their blankets and who might not.

And then she saw movement below her feet.

Some wild animal, she thought, and became suddenly stiff. But it was a person, she realized——or so it seemed——there in the faint starlight.

And then there was a great shout, and someone leapt across the camp, brandishing a sword. Elise recoiled in fear, but the sword wasn't aimed at her.

Whoever leapt over her was suddenly thrown back, his sword spinning into the bush. Elise scrambled up, crouching low to the ground, trying to see, wondering which way lay safety. A figure appeared in the starlight by the river——a woman it seemed to Elise——and then she went into the water, looking back once. But when she looked back her eyes were pale as moons, her hair glistening like kelp.

Elise thought she must have blinked, for suddenly this woman seemed not to be wearing a stitch, the white of her skin appearing through the long strands of hair. Then she was gone into the river without a ripple.

Everyone else was on his feet, the strangers and Gartnn with weapons, wary of each other in the poor light.

"It's me," she heard herself saying. "Don't hurt me. It's Elise."

"Where is Angeline?" one of the strangers asked.

"Here," Elise said, her heart trying to beat its way out of her chest. "I'm Angeline."

Figures were milling about and someone was moaning in pain.

"Fynnol! Are you hurt?" It was Tam speaking, she was sure.

Men gathered around a figure lying on the ground, while Cynddl stirred the ashes of the fire looking for embers to rekindle the flame.

"What was that thing?" Gartnn asked, an edge of panic in his voice.

"A nagar," Fynnol moaned.

Kindling crackled madly, and light leapt up to throw itself upon the leaves and faces.

"Bring him near the fire," Cynddl ordered; and Baore, Gartnn, and Tam lifted Fynnol gently and placed him on blankets near the flame.

"Are you hurt, Fynnol?" Tam asked. Elise could hear the edge of fear in his voice.

"I don't know . . . I don't know what happened. The nagar appeared, here among us, and was bending over Baore. I went at it with Tam's sword, but I was thrust back . . . I can't explain it. It was as though a wall had been thrown at me. And now I feel cold and sore, but when I concentrate on any one part of my body it seems whole."

"You can't fight a nagar with a sword, Fynnol," Cynddl said. "What in the world did you think you were doing?"

"I was protecting Baore," Fynnol said. "He thinks I do not love him, but he's wrong. I would fight a lion to protect him." And then his eyes closed and he fell into a deep sleep.

THIRTY-SEVEN

The ghosts of Eremon/Hafydd haunted his father's castle, drifting silently up and down the stairways and through rooms, apparently unaware of the presence of the living.

Of course they were not really ghosts. That was merely how Prince Michael thought of them, for they seemed so completely isolated from the normal life of the castle—as though they existed in some netherworld and but cast shadows into this one.

They never laughed or joked with the other men-at-arms, drank only when a toast was required, paid no heed to the various women, and cultivated no one's goodwill. They were like spirits brought back to life, though devoid of their human appetites. Brought back to life like their master, Hafydd, who was now Eremon.

They did, however, practice the arts of war, and this with a single-minded determination that put all of the Prince's men-at-arms to shame.

Prince Michael found their presence disturbing, chilling, even. They had no human compassion, or passions at all, and they owed allegiance to no one but Hafydd.

Two of them swept past, bowing to the Prince, who stood on the high parapet staring down into the practice yard below. He was a bit embarrassed, for he had thought his presence undetected by the men in the practice yard. In truth he was watching Hafydd, as he did whenever possible, and had hidden himself away up here where he would not likely be seen by anyone from below.

Hafydd's ghosts swept past, silent and enigmatic like shadows, one indistinguishable from the next, for they had not enough personality for one to be separated from another.

In the practice yard Hafydd—the Prince no longer thought of him as Eremon—was practicing with his sword. The same sword that had shuddered and sung as they pursued the man Hafydd always named the whist.

For a man of not insubstantial years the knight was still formidable, not so much for his speed—in this at least time's effects could not be denied—or his strength, which was less than the younger men, but for his cunning. He seemed to have countless dodges and tricks. Just when one thought he could not possibly avoid a blow, he employed some new deception that one had not seen before. It was the one thing about the man that Prince Michael was forced to admire. The depth of his cunning was apparently immeasurable.

The two ghosts appeared in the practice yard below. Hafydd broke off to converse with them. From his aerie Prince Michael could hear nothing, and guess even less.

It seemed somehow appropriate that they moved their lips and no sound came forth.

Hafydd suddenly turned and looked directly up at the Prince, then he waved a hand and smiled in invitation. There was little Prince Michael could do but come down. If he merely skulked away he would look craven and . . . well, skulking. He nodded to the men in the yard below and walked leisurely toward the stair.

Despite that fact that he was clearly immune to the cruelties of Hafydd, the Prince felt sweat slick on his palms and his pulse pounding down his arms. Hafydd was unpredictable, that was certain. He was like a mad dog in that way.

His meetings with Hafydd always left him unnerved, yet he continued to watch the man and make his presence felt. He was not sure why. Perhaps only to make it known to the knight that he did not accept his presence, that he did not trust him or his motives. That someone in the Prince's house was not under his spell. And yet doing this frightened him, not because he was fainthearted but because he knew what he did was dangerous.

He forced himself not to hurry down the steps, arriving at the bottom and into the yard.

"My Prince," Hafydd said, making only the slightest bow.

Prince Michael felt his jaw tighten. "Sir Eremon," he managed.

"You have been watching our training? I hope you found it instructive."

"It is always good to see how others waste their time so that one can avoid that particular snare."

Hafydd glared at him a moment. "I have often wondered why irony is considered a mark of sophistication. You see, I think you a young pup who has, as yet, no knowledge of the workings of the world. I'm surprised your father lets you out alone. I'm not a sophisticated man, but I've learned much in a lifetime of war, while you have learned little in a lifetime of aimless leisure. Allow me to demonstrate." He turned to the two armed men he had been training with. "Kill him," he said to them casually.

The Prince felt a smile flicker across his face, and then looked into the eyes of the two men raising their swords. His eyes went to Hafydd, who looked on impassively; but just as the two men came within sword's reach, Hafydd threw the Prince his own blade.

Prince Michael caught it by the pommel and ducked as a sword swung viciously at his head. The two men came at him, and the Prince backed away, raising his sword two handed. What was behind him? A wall without doors. A corner where the stair descended, but one of Hafydd's guards had circled that way already. There was no easy escape.

If he backed into the corner he would be trapped, but at least his attackers could not come at him from two sides or from behind. He dared not look at Hafydd to see if he appeared intent on this murder, for the men before him were not playing. One thrust at his shoulder while the other swept a blade low at his knee.

The Prince leapt up and turned, trying to cut the arm of the man who thrust at his shoulder, but he wasn't quick enough.

For a few moments he managed to keep the two men at bay with his speed and desperation, but then he realized he was tiring and they were not. In a moment they would cut him down, here in the practice yard of his father's castle. There was nowhere he could go, no ploy he could think of to escape.

A blade nicked his free arm, and he felt blood soak into his shirt. His hair was plastered wet to his forehead and sweat ran into his eyes, burning them, but he hardly dared blink. The two men kept coming at him, feinting, dodging. One would attack first to create an opening for the other, or the feint would be the attack and the second man a decoy. He could never know and only avoided ruin by leaping and twisting, suddenly thrusting forward when they did not expect it; but they were wary and did not expose themselves overly.

Suddenly one caught his blade and threw it up and the other leapt forward blade raised to cut him diagonally from shoulder to waist.

"*Enough!*" Hafydd called, and the man stopped with his blade a hand's length away from ending the Prince's life.

Hafydd came forward then, gazing at the Prince, who was doubled over gasping for breath, his arms screaming from the effort.

"I would have killed these two men in a moment had I been in your position. That is why I will accomplish what I wish in this life, and you will never be anything more than a drawing-room ornament. Good day to you, my Prince."

Hafydd turned and walked across the yard, not looking back, seemingly unconcerned that he had just ordered his men to kill the son of his master. The Prince watched him go, still shaking, and shaken. But there was something else he felt at that moment: Hafydd had spoken the truth, and he could not deny it.

Prince Michael was lying in his room, sore and weakened and disturbed. The small wound on his arm stung where he'd wrapped it clumsily with cotton—unwilling to go to the healer, not wanting anyone to know what had happened.

Hafydd had been right. That was the hell of it. Prince Michael felt the humiliation strongly, but he could not deny it.

I would have killed these two men in a moment had I been in your position. That is why I will accomplish what I wish in this life, and you will never be anything more than a drawing-room ornament.

The truth hurt more than the wound he'd received. He was no match for Hafydd. He pressed his eyes closed. All the time he had watched his father's counselor he had always had the same assumption: he was smarter than the knight. Eventually he would find the man's weakness. But all of his pretenses had been stripped away that afternoon in the practice yard. Hafydd could kill him at any time—and if it were not inconvenient, would do so without the slightest twinge of conscience.

He is ruthless, while I am . . . weak.

Weak.

The Prince let his eyes wander around his beautifully appointed rooms, at the books he had collected, the paintings and tapestries. Nowhere was there any weapon displayed, and intentionally so.

I am the son of the Prince of Innes, he thought, *the heir of my family. I cannot afford weakness. I have demanded all of the liberties of manhood, but accepted none of the burdens. That must change.*

The Prince had thought he'd discovered Hafydd's deficiency when they'd pursued the man he called his whist across the unknown landscape. Hafydd was consumed by his desire for revenge. It overwhelmed all else, including his powers of reason. Certainly this should be a fatal flaw, but somehow Prince Michael could not see a way to exploit it. In the Prince's position, he was sure, Hafydd would have found a way in a moment, but Prince Michael's mind simply did not work that way.

A soft knock at his door interrupted his self-flagellation. He rose from his bed and crossed the room stiffly. To his surprise, it was one of Hafydd's guards who stood in the hall. The man bowed to him.

"Sir Eremon requests your presence."

The Prince stood for a moment with his hand on the door, unsure how to respond. A gust of fear passed through him.

"I will be but a moment," the Prince said, and closed the door, going quickly to a wardrobe for clothes. His eye fell on a sword he kept there, and before he went out he buckled the scabbard about his waist. Hafydd wouldn't catch him unarmed again.

The silent sentinel led him through the halls of his father's castle, his obvious knowledge of the place distressing Prince Michael.

I'll wager he knows the whole of it better than I do myself, the Prince thought. *Drawing-room ornaments seldom worry about such things. The night Hafydd comes to kill me it might be my knowledge of the castle that saves my life.*

They went outside by a small door that let into an alley, and to the Prince's surprise, this emptied into the main courtyard. Another guard awaited them by the main gate, holding aloft a torch that seemed to be hissing at the stars. His father's guard let them out, and the Prince made certain to catch the man's eye, speaking to him briefly. At least his father would know that he'd left the castle in the company of Hafydd's guards—in case he didn't return.

They followed the cobblestoned way down to the river and the wharf that served his father's castle. The night was dark, wind gusting out of the north, then dropping to sudden eerie silence. Overhead a few stars appeared among ragged, fast-sailing clouds. A line of poplars were just visible against the sky, bending like longbows toward the south.

"There is a storm coming," Prince Michael said, but neither of Hafydd's guards answered.

The weak can never bear silence, Prince Michael thought, and hated himself for speaking.

In a moment the torch picked out of the murk the hard shape of the wharf, but here the guards turned and followed the path along the riverbank. The Prince desperately wanted to ask where they were going but refused to speak again, as difficult as that was for one who proved his worth with words.

The path sloped up, a steep, treed embankment falling off to their right. They went single file, the torchbearer before him, the second guard behind.

So prisoners are escorted, the Prince thought.

The torchbearer turned off and found a path angling down among the trees. Between gusts, the soft sound of the river could be heard clearly. The Prince had to keep his attention on the path lest he trip and go tumbling into the man carrying the torch. Another torch appeared through the trees. In a moment they were down to the lip of the river.

Hafydd was waiting there with two other black-robed guards, all of them silent as the darkness. Michael could see the river, its waves and currents weaving together into a single strand, speeding as though swollen by sudden rains.

Hafydd nodded to Prince Michael, then drew his

sword from its scabbard and waded into the water. "Now we shall find your bride," he said.

The blade looked like molten metal in the torchlight. Hafydd thrust the point into the moving water, and the Prince half expected to see steam rise. The knight mumbled something under his breath and then made a series of precise cuts with the blade. He bent and with his free hand cupped a palm full of water. This he brought to his lips and tasted. For a long while he stood, eyes closed, the torchlight playing madly over his face, his molten sword deep in the river's back.

Slowly, and without opening his eyes, Hafydd lifted a hand and pointed. "She is carried down the Wynnd," he said. "South, toward Westbrook."

"I could have guessed that myself," Prince Michael heard himself say, the slightest sneer in his voice. "How else would one travel if one wished to escape?"

Hafydd's eyes flicked open and his face contorted, not in a look of rage but in distaste—or so it appeared. "One would never travel by the Wynnd if one wanted to escape me. My whist knows that well." Hafydd thrust a large finger at the Prince's heart, which caused him to stumble back. "And you would do well to heed that . . . for the day I come hunting you."

"I forget nothing you say." Prince Michael snatched a torch from a surprised guard and went slowly back up the embankment, trying not to look like he was running.

THIRTY-EIGHT

Arden opened the doors onto the balcony and the scent of lavender enveloped him like a soft, tumbling wave. He closed his eyes and drew a breath. It was the fragrance he always associated with Llyn—Llyn and her garden—and it had lost its sweetness in recent years.

Llyn had, for most of Arden's youth, been one of his favorite aunts, though she was in fact some variety of second or third cousin. He was fascinated by her and found he could talk to her like no other. There was something so safe about her garden, the fact that there was never anyone else present, that Llyn saw so few others and never gossiped. She also seemed to have a startling insight into his very soul. Llyn had often seemed to know what he was thinking, what distressed him. During the storms and droughts of youth and adolescence, Llyn had been his pilot, guiding him surely between the many hazards.

But Arden was no longer a boy, and had made choices of which Llyn would never approve. He could not pretend he was a child just to satisfy her, to make her feel needed, locked away here in her garden. Arden was a man now, and made the hard decisions forced upon Renné men.

He had seen less of Llyn these last two years, and had avoided her altogether since the spring. He told himself it was because he now found her prying annoying and her wit oddly unfathomable—she was forever laughing when he did not—but it was more than that.

Llyn had always guessed his secrets in his youth, and he was desperately afraid that she might do so now. He wondered why she had called for him.

"How like your cousin you look, there in the moonlight." It was Llyn's lovely warm voice floating up from the darkness below.

"Toren?" Arden said, still not able to accept this comparison.

"No, Beldor." Llyn laughed. "Who else?" She laughed again and he felt vaguely foolish. "Of course Toren. How fare you, Cousin?"

"Well enough," he said, wondering again why she had requested he visit.

"I am happy to see you," she said warmly.

Arden hardly knew what to say. He could not tell the truth and a lie would sound so false. He chose the lie all the same. "And I am happy to hear you sounding so well," he said.

"Are you indeed?" she said, the laughter returning to her tone. "Well, I have very little of which to complain."

He could see her moving beneath the branches of a willow. Her dress was pale, perhaps yellow, and her beautiful hair swayed as she moved gracefully among the tendril boughs. A breeze shivered the leaves as though a thrill ran through the garden.

"You have done well at the tournaments this season, I am told."

"You don't care for tournaments," Arden said, his impatience coming to the fore.

"No, but I care for my cousins and wish them success in their endeavors."

"However misguided they might be," Arden said.

Llyn was by the small pool now, her shadow cast down upon the damask of moonlight that rippled across the surface. He leaned a little to one side and gazed into the garden for a glimpse, wondering if she were truly so hideous.

Neither spoke for a moment, and then Llyn said, "I'm sorry, Cousin; has my request that you visit inconvenienced you?"

Arden looked down at his hands laid on the balustrade. He felt a terrible guilt suddenly. What a selfish brute he was! Too busy to visit Llyn—Llyn, who was locked up here with few visitors.

"Not at all. I just feel . . . guilty that I have not visited you more often."

"Ah, is that it?" She didn't sound convinced of this lie. "Well, do not feel badly. I am rather too pleased with my own company, and I have my garden, my books, and my history of the Renné. I do host the odd visitor other than yourself. There are a few, in truth, whom I see too often. But that is not the case with you."

Arden bowed his head at this, as though accepting a compliment.

Llyn moved again, dodging among the branches and the patches of cold moonlight. "The truth is, I feel badly for asking you to come here . . ." She saw that he was about to protest and said, "No, it is true. I have requested your presence with an ulterior motive: I have a favor to ask of you."

"Anything at all," Arden said quickly, trying to make amends for hurting her feelings, which he was certain he'd done.

"There is someone I need murdered . . ." She laughed at his stunned silence. "You were supposed to laugh, Cousin," she teased.

He did laugh now, but out of relief. "With our history such things are not to be made jests." He could see her head nod in agreement.

"One of your mother's ancestors fought at the battle of Cooling Keep . . ."

"I believe that is so," Arden answered, and then was suddenly wary. He thought of his strange meeting with Gilbert A'brgail, who had appeared like a ghost come back to haunt them. Had Toren told her about A'brgail?

"Did he keep a diary of his war years, do you know?" Llyn asked. "And who would have such a book, if it existed at all?"

"I would have to ask Mother. She might know."

"Would you do that? I'm looking into the destruction

of the Knights of the Vow and your mother's kin Ajean A'ville was a commander of a wing of the army."

"I will put the question to Mother tomorrow," Arden said, wondering at the timing of this request. Was this merely part of Llyn's study of Renné history?

Llyn appeared to bend over some flowers, screened from his view by the branches of a tree. "You've traveled with your cousins a great deal this summer, have you not?" she said, and Arden felt his fingers take hold of the railing.

"It has been my good fortune to do so."

"Have you noticed anything . . . untoward among them?"

"I'm not sure what you mean," Arden said, feeling his mouth go dry.

"Dease came to visit me, and I thought him . . . I don't know, strangely unlike himself . . ."

Arden closed his eyes, casting about desperately for some answer.

"Cousin Dease is in love with you, Llyn," he said softly. "I'm sure he is never quite himself in your presence."

He could see that Llyn was suddenly very still. "I hardly think that is the case," she said, though it was not a very strong protest.

"Oh, it is well known within the family. It is why he has never married—or so everyone says."

"Is that what everyone says?" She laughed. "Well, everyone has been wrong before."

The sound of water falling into the pool was all that could be heard for a moment. Llyn stood so still that

Arden lost sight of her. Had she moved? Slipped silently away without his realizing?

"Llyn?" He saw her move then, where she had stood beneath the lace maple. "I didn't mean to distress you."

"Kind of you," Llyn said softly. Her fingers appeared, reaching up to caress the leaves, like a hand breaking the water's surface.

"Llyn? Do you think that Toren is making a mistake—returning the Isle of Battle to the Wills?"

The hand disappeared back into the depths of the garden. "I am an authority on the past, Arden. What will happen in the future I cannot say. Perhaps returning the Isle of Battle will prove a disaster. Perhaps it will be the gesture that ends our feud. I cannot say. All I know is it has taken unprecedented courage to do this—to bare his breast to the daggers."

"But the Wills have never hesitated to use the knife against us."

"Oh, I was not talking about the Wills, though that took courage enough. I meant the Renné."

Arden could see Llyn moving through her garden, too much like a ghost, he thought, living half a life.

"Good night, Arden Renné," she said. "Luck in all of your endeavors."

"Good night, Llyn." And then, "Llyn?"

She stopped. "Yes?"

Arden didn't know what it was he had suddenly wanted to say. "Luck to you as well."

"Thank you."

He heard her footsteps on stone and then a door closed. For a moment he stood staring down into the garden, all that was unsaid trying to tear its way out of his heart, and then he turned and went in, pulling the double doors to behind him.

Dease appeared to be waiting at the foot of the long stair, standing before a painting, hands clasped behind his back. He wore his habitual dark clothing and, as always, was perfectly groomed. He turned toward Arden as he descended the stair, a small smile appearing on his handsome, serious face.

He looks like a man in mourning, Arden thought suddenly. It had never occurred to him before, but Dease looked like a mourner. His Renné-blue eyes were always attentive and solicitous, his manner concerned and subdued as though out of respect for the dead.

"And how fares young Arden Renné this evening?" Dease asked quietly, as though Arden had lost a mother or brother.

"Well enough, Lord Dease. Kind of you to inquire."

Dease fell into step beside him. "You've been for an audience, I understand . . . ?"

"The castle rumor mill appears to be well greased this evening."

"No more slippery than usual. How fares our cousin?"

"I wish I could say," Arden said seriously. "Llyn is a mystery to me."

"And to me," Dease said softly.

"She is searching for some journals my mother's family might have: part of her history, I take it." He knew this was why Dease had waylaid him—to find out what Llyn wanted. At least that was part of the reason.

They emerged from the castle into a large quadrangle that Toren's mother, Lady Beatrice, had ordered made into a garden. Gravel paths meandered through the beds of flowers and among the small trees—Castle Renné was not famed for its beauty without reason. A watercourse whispered through the garden from one corner to another, for the castle was built over the Elbe, a tributary of the Westbrook.

Arden glanced up to the brightly lit windows of Lord Halbert's rooms. Toren's father was stalked nightly by madness, by battles and phantom assassins; thus the many candles, all swung up out of reach on chandeliers. There was no screaming this night—not yet.

Moonlight fell into the quadrangle, and torches guttered in sconces at the corners of paths. It was a garden of shadows and shapes, of faint light, cool and lustrous, warm and shimmering.

"How goes your argument with Toren, Dease? Is he at all nearer seeing the folly of his ways?"

Dease didn't answer for a moment, then shook his head. "No, he will not listen to me. No, that is not true. He listens but does not agree. Any number of times I have come close to warning him: saying that his own family might be forced to extremes if he continues with his plans, but I haven't said it yet. I don't know why."

Arden looked up again at the brightly lit windows. "I know what you mean . . . I have been tempted to do the same: to warn him in some general way, but it would only put him on his guard. It wouldn't change his mind. Though putting him on his guard has occurred to me as well."

"Careful what you say, Cousin. Lovers hide in the garden's shadows." They passed over a small stone bridge, moonlight flowing beneath. "What else did Llyn say?" Dease asked casually.

"Oh, I don't know. It was polite conversation. She asked after you."

"How kind of her," Dease said. "But no doubt she asked after many."

"Not so many, but you in particular." In this one area Dease didn't hide his feelings well: he was in love with Llyn and all of Castle Renné knew it. Arden wondered if Dease suspected, as Arden did, that Llyn was in love with Toren? But then Llyn hid her feelings much better than Dease.

They stepped out into a crossing of paths, the moonlight falling on the gravel. Dease stopped to look up at the moon floating overhead. As they stood there, staring up, a small feather floated down from the sky and fell at their feet. Arden bent and picked it up. It was delicate and dark, almost black.

"I saw no bird," Arden said. "Perhaps the night is molting?"

Dease laughed. "Perhaps so."

They walked on, gravel grinding beneath their feet like broken bones and teeth.

THIRTY-NINE

"**I**t wasn't near Baore," Gartnn said. "It hovered over you. That was clear when I awoke."

Elise felt a shudder that seemed to begin in her heart and pass out of her body through its extremities. She had woken just before Fynnol attacked the nagar, woken with a strange feeling of another's presence. "But what was this thing?" she asked.

"I can't really answer that," Gartnn said. "The nagar are like half-breeds—both river spirit and ghost, or so the old songs would lead you to believe."

"That was not some creature out of song," Elise said. "It was real, and utterly terrifying. I tremble yet when I think of it."

Elffen nodded, though Elise was not sure which part of her statement she was agreeing with. The three of them had taken a walk along the riverbank, though they could still hear the ringing of Baore's caulking iron with each hammer blow. It was morning, and the light of day had shone harshly on the ruin of their boat. To Elise's inexperienced eye it looked like it should be broken up for kindling. The caulking was coming out in thick, dark cords, planks were soft, and frames broken—but this Valeman said he could make it float, and Gartnn seemed to believe him. Elise only hoped they would stay close to shore, if the boat ever floated again.

"Why was this nagar near Elise?" Elffen asked. "And did you hear the way these strangers talked? Last night wasn't the first time they'd seen it!"

Gartnn nodded gravely, his gray beard like a bow wave before his out-thrust chin. "I haven't felt good about these strangers since we landed among them: a Fáel story finder traveling with men who claim to be from some innocent little village in the far north. Did you see . . .? The one called Tam carries a Fáel yaka bow and a sword that only a man-at-arms might bear. The moment Baore has our boat afloat we will set out, though I fear that won't be until late tomorrow." He looked up at Elise. "Keep your purse close, and try to remember your name is Angeline, not Elise."

FORTY

The moment Baore had pronounced their craft seaworthy the minstrels had loaded their belongings aboard and pushed out into the south-going current. They'd hardly waved good-bye, such was their haste. Before leaving, Gartnn had pressed a few small coins on Baore—almost an insult for all that he'd done. Better to have accepted the shipwright's efforts as a gift than pay him a tenth what his efforts were worth, but Gartnn wouldn't take no for an answer.

The companions watched the boat go, the low light of late afternoon glistening on the freshly painted planks. Tam could see the boat rock gently as the minstrels settled themselves and Gartnn took up the oars.

"It was the women," Fynnol pronounced. "Gartnn was jealous of them."

"It was the nagar," Cynddl said. "Who would choose to travel with men who are haunted by such a creature? I wouldn't. I only hope they don't spread this news down the river before us."

This killed the conversation, and the companions turned back to their small tasks, leaving the minstrels' boat to dwindle and disappear down the uncertain river.

Fynnol seemed much recovered from his encounter with the nagar, though the hand that held Tam's sword still tingled and occasionally felt a little numb. But even this seemed to be healing fast. This act of bravado had its effect, however, and Fynnol and Baore seemed almost to be on speaking terms again.

Tam cut open the white belly of a fish that Cynddl had caught not half an hour before, but then he remembered something and looked up. "Did you notice," he said, "when Fynnol attacked the nagar, the one named Angeline called herself 'Elise'?"

Cynddl turned his gaze upward a moment. "I hadn't noticed. But then minstrels often give themselves noble names, no matter how humble their own name or beginnings."

Tam scooped out the pink and white guts and dipped the fish in the water, splashing it around to clean it. "Perhaps that's the answer. I'm just suspicious of anyone the river brings us. That is the truth of it. I'm beginning to feel like Baore. The sooner we are off this river the happier I'll be."

Over the next few days the rejuvenated boat of the minstrels would appear now and then, for the river carried them all toward the sea at the same pace. In the distance Tam would see the large parasol of the women, and then suddenly oars would flash out and the boat would pull away, making Tam feel like some kind of scoundrel to be avoided at all costs.

Despite their travels on the secret river, Tam and the others could not quite believe that they were so far south. It appeared that they had traveled leagues and leagues in half a fortnight.

It is as though we have fallen asleep and drifted on, unknowing, Cynddl had said, *carried by the current, only to wake, days later, far down the river.*

The wildlands seemed very distant here; though in truth, there were still large expanses of forest separating the inhabited valleys. Between villages on opposite shores, ferries plied the river, too wide to span with bridges, and Tam and his companions would wave as they passed these decrepit craft, cattle lowing in return. The land was more populous; and the towns, though not too close together, swelled beyond their original protective walls as though they had no fear of brigands or war.

Farm boys in leaky skiffs would row out to sell new potatoes and poultry, fresh bread and parsnips. Cynddl's skills as a fisherman and Tam's archery were less in use, though their purses grew lighter for it.

At the joining of the river with a good-sized tributary they stopped at a village, partly to supplement their food, but also from boredom and the need for the company of others. Tam was at the oars and ran the boat up on a low, grassy embankment where many other craft lay. As they slid their boat over the grass, Fynnol pointed at a newly painted craft.

"Well, here are our fugitive minstrels! Ungrateful wretches that they are. Perhaps we shall have an explanation for their rudeness yet."

"I don't think that's likely," Tam said. "Not unless they need their boat repaired again. They probably feel they are above the likes of us—men from the wilds, after all. 'Wildmen' they likely call us."

"Well, let's find what we need in this town and be on our way," Baore said. He bent over their belongings, fiddling with some lines. "I don't need any accounting from Gartnn and the others. The way they've treated us is explanation enough."

Though the village was not large the minstrels were nowhere to be seen. Tam began to wonder if they'd found a better boat here and bought it, leaving their leaky old tub behind—but then they'd claimed to have little money and had certainly paid Baore as if that were true.

Fynnol quickly found the one inn the town boasted and they retreated there for ale, the one item all but Cynddl claimed to miss on their journey. The story finder did not join them.

"Come from far?" the tapsman asked as he delivered their foaming mugs. He was a balding man with a torso not unlike a beer barrel in shape and size.

"From the Vale of Lakes," Fynnol said.

The man knit his brows. "Now there's a place I've never heard of. Is it beyond the Sweetwater, then?"

"It is beyond the Wold of Kerns," Fynnol said jovially. "In fact it is beyond Inniseth, and even the Lion's Maw.

Beyond Telanon Bridge, nigh up under the shoulder of the great mountains."

The man looked at Fynnol, clearly saying that the price of a mug of beer allowed one certain license, but there were limits. "Enjoy your beer, then," he said. "So far north you've likely only heard tell of it." The man went back to his labors.

Fynnol smiled at the others and lifted his glass. "To our first ale," he said, and took a long drink. "Ahhh! Its legend was not overstated." Fynnol turned to two men sitting at the nearest table. "And what do young men do for diversion in this town?"

The two looked up at him as though this were perhaps the stupidest question they had ever been asked. "They leave," one of the men said, with a hint of bitterness in his voice.

"Well, perhaps we shall follow this example," Fynnol said quickly.

The tapsman looked up from his labors. "There are three minstrels here this night—quite renowned, if you believe them. Two of them comely ladies. They'll play beneath the trees on the riverbank."

The Valemen looked at one another.

"I wonder," Tam said, "if the money Gartnn paid Baore will equal entrance to their performance?"

The townsfolk collected beneath a stand of shaggy chestnut trees where colored lanterns glittered in the boughs.

Just beyond lazed the river, the voice heard at Speaking
Stone having fallen to a whisper. Blankets were spread
upon the grass where families lounged, children nestled
in their parents' arms.

Few musicians of Gartnn's stature stopped here, and
the townsfolk showed their respect by listening intently.
The Valeman were forced to admit that Gartnn, Angeline,
and Elffen were as skilled players as they'd ever heard—
as skilled as the Fáel who'd wintered in the Vale.

Some movement in the shadows beyond the lanterns
caught Tam's eye and, as he stared, a tall man leading a
magnificent horse emerged from the darkness. In the
poor light Tam recognized the garb of a woodsman—a
traveler: a leather vest over cotton shirt, sandy hair bound
back with a band of cloth about the forehead. The man's
thin face had the largest features: a long nose, big eyes,
and an outsized mouth. In some peculiar way he was an
impressive man.

Rather than sit, the traveler lingered at the edge of
the crowd, rocking from one foot to the other, his gaze
darting about as though he were afraid of being seen
listening to minstrels.

The singing of the two women called for Tam's attention again, and he turned away. Elffen had the finer voice
of the two women, Tam concluded, but Angeline's
displayed more emotion, and her playing was better,
though not so good as Gartnn's.

The recital came to an end, the townsfolk showing
their appreciation with enthusiastic applause. Blankets

were gathered up from the grass and sleeping children gently lifted by whispering parents. The crowd funneled back onto the path that led into the village, which had been built above the spring flood line.

Tam was surprised to find Angeline blocking his way, her face flushed from the success of their performance. He bowed quickly, not knowing what to say.

"Will you walk with me a moment?" she said.

"Are you sure you want to be seen with—" He couldn't think of a word, and said, "someone to be avoided?"

Angeline drew a breath and released a sigh. She crinkled up her eyes as though in slight pain. "Just for a moment, if you will?"

Tam allowed himself to be led through the throng, people paying Angeline compliments as they went. Near the riverbank they stopped, not far from where the boats were drawn up and just beyond hearing of anyone else.

"I know Gartnn paid Baore insultingly little: far less than he deserved. It was chary of him and unnecessary as well. Let me make it up. What would be a fair price for such labor?"

"I should not name a price for Baore's labor," Tam said. "He offered to do it out of kindness, anyway, expecting nothing in return."

Elise nodded, her eyes crinkling up again. "That is why I've asked you. I know Baore was insulted. He wouldn't name a price to make it right now."

"Nor will I," Tam said. He gave the smallest bow and turned to go, not sure why he was spurning this attempt at rapprochement. Was he so proud?

"Tam . . ." she said as he turned. "I've seen that thing again. That wraith that came from the river. What is it? What could it want of me?"

Tam stopped, looking at Angeline in the colored light from the lanterns. Her pretty face was garish—red and orange—and contorted in fear and pain.

"I don't know what it is or what it wants," Tam said. "It saved Baore's life far up the river, and has followed us ever since as though it has some claim on him now. He swears it spoke to him in his delirium, and whispers in his dreams even yet. But we'll be free of the river soon, and then it can't follow us, or so we believe. The nagar is a creature of the Wynnd."

Tam noticed Gartnn walking under the trees, looking about as though he'd lost something. Then he spotted Angeline and set out toward her with a determined gait, Elffen in tow. The riverbank was all but deserted now. Only a few boys remained to climb up into the trees and fetch the lanterns down.

"Your keeper is coming," Tam said, nodding to the minstrel.

"Tam . . .?" Cynddl appeared a few feet away, Fynnol and Baore at his shoulder.

They met on that same patch of grass—the minstrels and the companions—all of them hesitating for a moment.

"We should let these gentlemen be on their way," Gartnn said firmly.

Angeline looked in his direction, her gaze sliding off Gartnn and back to the ground before her feet. A small brittle smile appeared, then faded.

"You are Gartnn," a man said.

Tam looked up to find the traveler, the man who'd been leading the magnificent horse, standing a few feet away, still holding his mount by its bridle.

"And who are you that asks?" Gartnn said, though it had not seemed like a question to Tam. Gartnn stepped back, clearly a bit apprehensive.

"I am Pwyll, a friend of . . ." He cast an uncertain glance at the Valemen.

"These are friends," Angeline said firmly, causing Gartnn to look at her oddly. But he did not gainsay her.

"I am a friend of your traveling friend," Pwyll said. "He had sent me to search you out to tell you that you must leave the river, but it is too late for that." He glanced over his shoulder up toward the town. "You've been found. There is no time for discussion. The river is your only hope, now." He glanced back toward the shadows that lay beneath the trees, and Tam's eyes followed.

The last few stragglers disappeared toward the village, taking the colored lamps with them. Tam could see other movement there: men keeping to the shadows, advancing silently toward them.

"Into your boat now," the stranger said quietly, drawing his sword.

Tam looked up toward the village once more and saw a glint of starlight on steel. "Men-at-arms," he hissed.

Cynddl and the Valemen had seen enough of armed men that they acted immediately. In a heartbeat they were pushing their boat out into the river, even as they found their weapons. The minstrels stood, mutely staring into the shadows. Tam abandoned his companions and grabbed the bow of the minstrel's craft.

"Help me!" he called Gartnn.

Elise came to her senses, and grabbed hold of the boat, desperately heaving the heavily loaded craft toward the river. Finally Gartnn and Elffen recovered from their moment of shock and lent a hand.

Tam glanced back as he pushed the minstrels' boat out into the river, then splashed through the water to leap into the stern of his own. He could see the silhouette of the stranger, upon his horse now, gliding into a shadow.

Cynddl tapped him on the shoulder with a bow and Tam felt the yaka wood passed into his hands. Baore was at the oars, pulling toward the center of the broad river. In the other boat Gartnn did the same, though not with such speed.

Suddenly there was a shout and Tam could see dark figures running beneath the trees. A horseman appeared—the man called Pwyll—and Tam struggled to make out what was going on. There was movement where the moonlight filtered through the trees. Movement that flickered like dying flames. A scream echoed over the river, and then the sound of steel ringing. Tam could just make out Pwyll, whose horse spun and kicked and bit, as chargers were trained to do. Straining, Tam could see men lurking in the broken moonlight, looking for a chance to hamstring the charger or take the rider from his saddle.

"Baore! Hold up a moment." Tam nocked an arrow and let it fly at the armed men, knowing it would be only luck if he hit anything but moonlight. Three more arrows he sent toward the men, causing shouting and confusion. Suddenly Pwyll cut down a man and then galloped through a gap in the circle, disappearing into the night.

"Row on," Tam said, sinking back down.

A crack sounded to his left. Gartnn had broken an oar and leapt to his feet, shipping his remaining oar in the sculling notch in the stern. This slowed the mintrels' boat even more.

Tam nocked another arrow, gazing at the riverbank. Moonlight found its way down among the trees, illuminating patches of gray. Across these, shadows would dash, too quick for Tam's arrows. Men called out, and along the bank others answered. Three men appeared in a pool of moonlight.

"They're wearing black surcoats!" Cynddl said. "Look!"

Tam stared at the men, but it was hard to be sure. Certainly their robes were dark.

"They've found us again!" Fynnol said, not the least bit uncertain.

An arrow glanced off the moving oar and passed Tam so closely that the feathers brushed his shoulder. He dropped down in the boat, peering over the gunwale.

"Get down, Baore!" Fynnol said. He too had collapsed into the bottom of the boat.

"Just a few more strokes." The big man grunted, pulling hard on the oars.

An arrow buried itself in the planking with a terrible *thwack!* A great splash sounded and a small wave rocked them: someone had fallen into the river. One of the women in the other boat screamed.

Tam raised his head, searching the darkness desperately, expecting an arrow to find him at any moment. Water lapped against the hull; the river smell was strong in his nostrils. Elffen was leaning out over the water screaming. He could just make her out in the darkness, and it was Gartnn's name that she was calling, over and over.

Baore dove into the river, leaving the oars to thud about drunkenly between the tholepins until Fynnol took hold of them. Tam could still hear Elffen sobbing when three arrows buried themselves in the stern a foot from his head.

"They're in a boat!" Cynddl cried, and the story finder leapt up, letting arrow after arrow fly. Tam did the same, though he took a moment to find the boat in the darkness. Whoever manned the oars stopped suddenly and the boat lost steerage, wandering off its course, rolling over its own wake, and then it tipped as the men inside scrambled around; and they were all in the water flailing, some wounded.

Tam heard Baore surface, draw in a lungful of air, and then dive again. He seemed to be down a long time, and when he came up again Tam could hear him gasping for air.

Fynnol shipped the oars and brought their boat alongside the minstrel's. Baore clung with one arm to the transom, fighting to pull air into his lungs.

"I can't find him," the big man managed, and then let go of the stern and dove once more.

"Tam, take my place," Fynnol whispered, "and I'll man the oars in the other boat. We must away from here." He stepped over the side into Gartnn's place, taking their spare oar with him.

Elffen was sobbing now, though into her hands, trying to drown the noise of it. The noise that endangered them all. Fortunately the current had moved them out of bowshot of the shore.

Baore surfaced again, flailing the few strokes to the boat.

"Come aboard," Cynddl said softly. "We won't find him now. Not in the dark."

Tam saw Baore's head shake, his long hair plastered down around his face. The big Valeman looked infinitely pitiable to Tam at that moment: trying desperately to save the life of some other, and failing. There was no thought of the cost to himself or of the insult Gartnn had paid him.

He dove one last time, but was on the surface again almost immediately. Tam and Cynddl took hold of him under the arms and dragged him aboard, limp from his efforts. Without a word Tam took his place at the oars.

Elffen continued her soft sobbing. Angeline held her close, but Elffen suddenly pulled away from the other woman, crying so that she all but collapsed from her sorrow. "Why did we ever agree to aid you?" she sobbed. "He was worth ten of you!—you and your inbred family! The river take you!" And she struck out ineffectually at Angeline, but her anger was swept away by the storm of sorrow, and she fell forward over the sail that protected their belongings. Her cries sounded over the night river, and echoed back off the bank, and then echoed again and again, like the cries of a hundred women in mourning.

FOR†Y-OΠE

"**T**hey've hunted us down the length of the Wynnd," Fynnol said, "through the wildlands and even down the secret branches of the river. We'll never be free of them."

Tam saw an odd glance pass between Elffen and Angeline. The two boats were lying side by side, the current sweeping them slowly south. No one had recovered their nerve after the attack the evening before, and they had stayed to the river all through the night, pressing south, taking turns at the oars.

Tam had remained awake, listening to the night sounds, staring up at the moon and thinking what a pale, cold light it was—wondering if this is what the sun looked like deep beneath the river.

By morning they were all exhausted, and yet they'd dared only the briefest trip ashore for the convenience of the ladies. Otherwise they rested in the boats, letting the river take them, eating the bread and cheese and apples they'd bought in the town the day before. The day had passed this way, and night was drawing near—yet no one seemed inclined to go ashore.

"But why have they chased you?" Angeline asked. She and Elffen did not seem to be at all estranged this morning—as though Elffen's outburst after Gartnn's death had never happened.

Fynnol shrugged, bobbing his dark head. "A stranger came to share our campfire one night, and these same black-clad men-at-arms fell upon us in the dark. We thought the stranger had been killed, but later we learned he had escaped, stealing our boat in the bargain. We've come down the river looking for him, for we kept valuables in our boat," Fynnol said quietly, as though afraid someone would hear of this fortune. "Ever since that unlucky meeting we've been pursued. These men must think us allies of Alaan."

"Alaan?" Angeline said, reacting in surprise.

"Yes, that was the name of the rogue who shared our fire, then robbed us."

Angeline and Elffen glanced at each other again. "And where do you expect to find this rogue?"

"At the Westbrook Fair," Fynnol said.

"Perhaps we might be able to help you," Elffen said, smiling at Fynnol. "Tell us about Alaan."

"Perhaps you can tell us about Pwyll," Tam said abruptly. "He said he was a friend of Gartnn's friend and that you were to leave the river, and he would be your guide and protector." He stared at Angeline. "And your real name is Elise, not Angeline, and Gartnn and Elffen have been aiding you, though she cursed you for it; 'you and your inbred family.'"

The two women looked about uncomfortably for a moment, and then Elffen drew herself up and met Tam's eye. "I don't think we need tolerate accusations from men who are pursued down the river by men-at-arms and keep company with a river spirit. You have your secrets and we have ours—and I'll wager ours are far more innocent than yours." She looked pointedly at Cynddl. "Perhaps you'd like to tell us about the stories you've found along the river," she sneered.

"I've found your story, now," Cynddl said quickly. "Two young women on their way to Westbrook posing as minstrels . . . But why did you curse Angeline for Gartnn's death and not us, for those men-at-arms were after us—or were they? Perhaps they were after you— or after Elise in particular?"

Elffen appeared angry now, and her eyes glistened. "What do you know of us or our purpose?" she said, but faltered. Angeline spoke in her place.

"You don't trust us enough to tell us your secrets—" she straightened her skirt "—and we don't know you very well either. It is true, we are in danger, and it might be safer for you to leave us to make our way to Westbrook on our own. We will manage."

Tam spoke before anyone else could. "We're all traveling to the fair, Lady Angeline or Elise, if that is your name. Unless you can swim you'd better stay with us so that Baore can keep your boat afloat and we can rescue you at need. Keep your secrets. Whatever they are I don't think your intentions are wicked, but you might think about this: the men-at-arms who murdered poor Gartnn wore the same black surcoats as the men who've hunted us." He glanced from one woman to the other. "If they were really after you we might share an enemy, and perhaps you know more of him than we do. Alliances have been built on less."

They decided to travel by night and hide by day. The river was broad and lazy and hazards rare. Baore fashioned rope fenders to drop between the craft, and lashed the two boats together so that they drifted side by side. All four men could row then; one in the bow and one in the stern of each boat, but they tended to let the river carry them, trusting to darkness for protection.

Tam was on watch and steered them down the path of moonlight that shimmered on the river, almost unbroken the surface was so calm. He thought the summer nights beautiful here in the south, without the cool air slipping down the mountains as the sun set. Here the nights could be warm and languid, with only the slightest breeze to trouble the trees. The river, too, was strangely silent, as though it drowsed between its banks, lulled by its slow, steady progress toward the sea.

A fish jumped, dark rings rippling over the moonglow.

"Tam . . .?"

"Angeline?"

Tam could just make her out, her head cradled on her

arm, a blanket neatly wedged against the gunwale for a pillow.

"You may call me Elise," she whispered. "Are the others asleep?"

Tam cast his gaze over the still, dark forms and listened to their soft breathing. "So I would guess."

She reached up and tugged him closer, so that she could almost whisper in his ear. "I will tell you my secrets if you will tell me yours."

Tam felt his body react to her breath on his face, the nearness of her. "The secrets of the others aren't mine to tell. But such secrets as I have I'll trade with you."

"That is fair." She hesitated, and a nighthawk cried overhead. "I am Lady Elise Wills," she whispered, the words coming out in a rush, "and I am escaping a marriage that might see our feud with the Renné rekindled." She let out a long breath.

The nighthawk called again.

"You might say something," she whispered.

Tam was too dumbfounded to speak. Here was someone who claimed to be a member of the notorious Wills family, and she did not seem at all malevolent. "Were those men-at-arms after you?" Tam managed.

"That's what I assumed, until I heard your story." She shook her head, a strand of hair wafting down over her face. Tam closed his eyes without meaning to. "You see, it was a man named Alaan that helped me escape. And he and I were pursued by men-at-arms in black surcoats—they serve a man named Hafydd. No, that is not quite right: he calls himself Eremon now."

"Alaan was the friend Pwyll spoke of?"

"So I would guess, but we'll likely never know now."

Elise's eyes looked dark, dark and as mysterious as the river in this light.

"And did he travel with a small bird," Tam asked, "a whist?"

"He called it Jac."

Tam drew a breath. "This man seems to be known by everyone on the river, and he's everywhere at once."

"He is some kind of sorcerer, Tam."

Tam peered into her eyes, wondering if she jested.

"He is, or so I believe." She shifted a little and a wave of golden hair broke over his cheek, soft and cool. "You met him somewhere in the wildlands? Are you really from the wildlands?"

"Yes. Our home is at the headwaters of the Wynnd. We met Alaan not far from there, and, as Fynnol said, black-clad men-at-arms attacked us by night. They found us again at the ford at Willowwand, though there were others with them, then—men-at-arms in purple livery."

"Those serve the Prince of Innes. Hafydd is his counselor. But why are you on the river?"

"We came to carry Cynddl to the Wold of Kerns, but never found it. The river played us some strange trick and the Wold never appeared." He could see her nod in the dark, not surprised at all.

"And now you go to Westbrook, looking for Alaan because he stole your valuables?"

"Yes, though they are not really so valuable as Fynnol would have you believe."

She considered this, then shifted so that she could see him in the faint light. "Tam? Listen to me. This man Alaan, and this other Hafydd: they are dangerous men, each in his own way. Don't trifle with them. If you are innocent young men, as I believe you are, set out for your homes at once. Don't become involved in this matter. Men have died already, and more will do so, I fear; but this matter does not involve you. Go north with all speed."

"But then I should have to cut your boat loose and let you fend for yourself . . ."

She searched his eyes in the dark. "Yes, you should."

"But I can't. We're all going to Westbrook."

"Leave me there, Tam. I'm not jesting. I will not have your deaths on my hands. There are enough already."

Just then there was a ripple and a hiss, and Tam sat up in time to see the nagar, not two feet away, its pale eyes staring at him in the moonlight. In a flash it was gone beneath the waves, but not before Elise had seen it and gasped so loud she woke the others.

"What? What is it?" Fynnol muttered, shaking his head.

"The nagar," Tam said. "It was following us again. Theason said it wouldn't venture so far from the Greensprings, but it's with us still, and I don't know how we'll get free of it now."

"I say we take to the land, Cousin," Fynnol said.

"No!" Baore said quickly, and then more calmly, "the men-at-arms seek us there."

"Baore is right," Cynddl said, an edge of resignation in his voice. "We go where the river goes. There is no choice."

"Yes," Fynnol said softly, "river take us."

FORTY-TWO

Tuath could see Rath riding in the cart before her. He sat up in a chair that had been secured into place, like a king of old riding in state. He was the greatest living story finder of the Fáel; almost a man out of legend himself. Nann rode beside the driver, twisting around constantly to smile anxiously at her charge, to give Rath water, or arrange the rug over his legs.

Tuath had been torn from her work on the tapestry to accompany Rath and Nann to the River Wynnd, and she was not even sure why. *He will taste the waters,* Nann had said, and it was not in Nann's nature to jest.

The line of carts rolled through the shadows of wood now, and Tuath removed her hood and veil, noting the strange looks of the Fáel around her. Here among the black wanderers she was an outsider—waxen white, like some being who'd floated down from the moon. And yet she was Fáel, having even less in common with the fair-skinned people than did others of her race. She was a vision weaver, a rare and distrusted calling among her own people. If she had been born among the fair-skinned peoples she would have been burned for exhibiting such a talent. Among her own people she was merely shunned.

I am the pale wanderer among the dark, she thought.

The path they followed joined another, its course paralleling that of a small river.

"The Westbrook," the man beside her said. He didn't speak with her much, but he was not unkind—or at least not cruel. "Won't be long now. We camp not far from here. Will you go to the fair?"

"What fair?" she asked, surprised by this sudden display of interest. They had been traveling together some days and he'd hardly said so much in that entire time.

He gave her a sour look. "The Westbrook Fair, as you well know."

"I . . . I've never heard of it."

The man shook his head and flicked the reins, urging his horse on. "Then why have you come?"

"Rath commanded it."

The man did not have an answer for that. He might not respect her, but he respected Rath and wouldn't be rude to anyone accompanying the story finder. All the same, the conversation, such as it was, ended.

It was near dusk when the procession reached the joining of the Westbrook and the Wynnd. There were already Fáel camped in that place, and word spread quickly among the tents: Rath had come. Perhaps they might see him so that they could tell their grandchildren.

The leaders of the different trains gathered to be introduced to the renowned story finder, but Rath would have

none of that. He called for Tuath and, with Nann supporting him on one side and Tuath on the other, made his
way to the River Wynnd. Without thought for clothing
or footwear he waded directly into the water, bending
stiffly, one hard hand clutching Tuath's shoulder. Rath
cupped some water and brought it to his lips.

He straightened, closing his eyes in the failing light.
Tuath gazed out over the still river, a calm night, stars
just surfacing on the water and in the sky. She could see
boats traveling on the current, their occupants silent as
though the stillness and beauty of the place had stolen
all their words away.

Sometimes the world appears that way, Tuath thought; *there
are no words that don't diminish it.*

"They are free," Rath whispered suddenly, leaning all
his weight on the two women. Tuath thought he might
slip into the river and be gone, such was the burden.
"Caibre and Sainth . . . but Sianon, not yet." His head
hung suddenly down, and he drew his breath raggedly.

"Take him to shore." Nann grunted, and then said,
"Help us!" to the people who stood watching.

Rath was borne up into the camp and a bed made for
him. Nann and Tuath stripped him like a sleeping child
and laid the blankets gently over him. For a long time
neither of them spoke but only watched the wisp of an
old man as he lay, awaiting the breeze that would take
him away.

Finally Tuath could bear it no more. "Why did he ask
me to come?" she whispered. "What am I to do?"

The old man's eyes flicked open, though they didn't seem to focus. "Taste the waters," he said. "Someone must find them. Someone must find Sianon and stop her before it all begins again." His eyes closed. "I haven't the strength to tell you their stories," he whispered hoarsely. "But Caibre and Sianon lived to make war. Only war satisfied their greed for glory. There was nothing else, and once their father had passed into the river they warred with each other. The ancient kingdom of Wyrr, the land we call the Greensprings, was split in two and brought to ruin, for they cared nothing for land, nor for the people who dwelt there. Their subjects were only useful as conscripts. The land was denuded to feed the beast of war. The bravest and strongest warriors were raised up, given lands, which they in turn brought to ruin to build their armies to please their lord or lady." Rath opened his eyes, glancing at the two women. "The damage wrought by the Renné and the Wills in our time is like a breeze set against a hurricane. Release Caibre and Sianon and you will unleash a storm such as the land between the mountains has not seen in a thousand years." Rath's eyes fell heavily closed, and for a moment he didn't breathe. Nann put a hand to her mouth and looked up at Tuath. But then the old man drew a breath and then another: soft and small, like the breathing of a sleeping child.

FORTY-THREE

Lights appeared on the shadowed river—candles in storm glasses bobbing like fireflies. Where the Westbrook met the River Wynnd it forked around a small island, like the tongue of a drinking snake, and here the boats all converged, the candles inhaled into the mouth of the waiting serpent.

Tam elected to take the northern channel, and Fynnol, rowing the minstrels' boat, followed. They soon found this section of the small river shallow enough that they could pole themselves along against the lazy current. The stars appeared, blurred in the hazy sky, and the warm air was full of evening sounds: rousing insects, creaking door-frogs, and the calls of night birds taking to the sky. The moon, two days from full, silvered the eastern horizon. Its rim appeared in the faint lavender haze, and then it rose, near round, up into the deep azure.

Even Fynnol was hushed as they made their westing, and over the soft sounds of the evening, distant music drifted across the water.

"Have we reached the fair already?" Fynnol asked quietly.

"No, it is some way off yet," Elffen answered. The two boats were only a few feet apart, Fynnol and the story finder standing and poling them along.

Cynddl stopped, drawing himself up to listen. "It's a familiar tune," he said.

"Aye, 'Eventide', it's called," Elffen said. And then added softly, "Gartnn used to play it sometimes."

"That's how it's known to your people, but it's a Fáel tune as well. It would be 'River Night' in your tongue."

They rounded a bend and found the trees filled with brightly colored lanterns drawn aloft on lines. Against the shore, two men stood speaking softly, holding the leads of great Fáel horses, which raised their heads at the approach of the boats and then went back to their leisurely drinking. Cynddl called out to the men as they came near, and they answered in their own tongue.

The story finder turned suddenly to look at Tam, his face shadowed in the faint light. "Our journey's end," he said, his voice thick. He began to say more, but the boat slid up to the shore and eased to a stop on the soft mud. Tam and Fynnol looked at each other, and Fynnol closed his eyes and let out a long, slow breath. The Wynnd was behind them, and only the road north lay ahead.

"Come and spend the night with the Fáel," Cynddl said. "I'm sure they'll make you welcome. There might even be some you know from that cold winter."

The three Valemen glanced at one another. Cynddl was being kind. They all knew that it was unlikely they would find a welcome among the wanderers.

"We'll stay this one night," Tam said.

Cynddl gave him a bitter smile and nodded. "Yes . . ." he said softly. He looked up into the camp, where fires burned and the strange vowels of the Fáel language sounded. Tam had a feeling the story finder both wanted to go and stay. They'd become unlikely friends over the course of their journey.

"Let's go up into the camp, Cynddl. Perhaps you have friends or kin here."

They stepped out onto the bank, Elise and Elffen quickly and with a sense of relief, but Baore came out last and slowly, looking back once at the river, where his gaze lingered a moment before he stepped up the bank and into the shadows of the trees.

Word spread quickly through the Fáel camp that a story finder had arrived from the river. And if that were not strange enough, he was in company with three men from the far north and two lady minstrels.

Children gathered around the strangers, watching, dark-eyed and silent, and then a man approached. "Rath is asking for you," he said to Cynddl.

"Rath is here?" Cynddl stopped completely.

The man nodded and gestured for Cynddl to follow. But Cynddl hesitated, and his guide stopped, raising an eyebrow. "These men were my guides down the River Wynnd," Cynddl said, "and saved my life when we were set upon by brigands. Will you see to their comfort while I'm called elsewhere?"

The man bowed his head, and Tam remembered his

grandfather saying that story finders were held in high esteem among the Fáel.

Fynnol caught Tam's eye. "Who's Rath?" he mouthed, but Tam only shrugged in reply.

Cynddl was led to a large tent, well lit within, and admitted through the flaps by two men who stood watch outside. He hadn't met with Rath in perhaps five years and wasn't prepared for what he saw: a wisp of a man lying in deep coverlets on a wooden bed. He looked so small and frail—like a feather, Cynddl thought suddenly, and found himself fighting back tears.

The tent had a stale odor, like sweat and the faint smell of urine, though this was partially masked by the scent of freshly laundered bedding.

Rath was propped up on pillows, and two women sat by his side: the ever-practical Nann and another woman white as snow, pale eyed and slight. Cynddl thought her ghostlike or like a lady made of moonlight. The nagar came immediately to mind. He had a sudden strange feeling that she was there to bear Rath's spirit away into the world beyond.

"Cynddl," the old man whispered, and a tiny smile appeared on his face. He was as dark as the ghost woman was pale, but Cynddl thought his former teacher looked terribly ill all the same. "You've been seeking sorcerers?" the old man said.

Cynddl kissed Nann's hand, and bowed to the ghost

who sat beyond the bed. "I've found only parts of their stories. But the River Wynnd whispers many unexpected things."

"It is a strange old river," Rath said, "like an open vein bleeding the past out onto the land between the mountains. Staining it with forgotten history." He looked up at Cynddl suddenly, his dark eyes filled with cloud. "Tuath is a vision weaver," he said, reaching out a bony hand to the ghost woman, who took the dark, wrinkled flesh within her grasp of snow. Cynddl shuddered.

"She is a vision weaver," Rath said again, "and she has seen Caibre, carried back from Death's gate."

Cynddl nodded. "Caibre and his brother. That is what I've come to believe."

Rath's eyes closed. "Tell us your tale," he said.

"It is difficult to tell," Cynddl said. "So much isn't clear."

Rath's eyes opened. "Then we'll try to make sense of it together. You will need a chair, I think." He looked around. "Can no chair be found for our guest?"

A moment later a man came through the flaps, bearing a bent-willow chair for Cynddl. The story finder settled himself.

"Leave the flap open a little," Rath said testily. "Let our guest have some fresh air, at least." He nodded to Cynddl, a faint smile of affection appearing on his aged face.

"Nann has told you why she sent me north . . ." Cynddl began. Cynddl left out no detail that he thought might be the least significant, and several times believed his former teacher had fallen asleep. But whenever Cynddl paused, the old man would stir a little and whisper, "Go on."

Candles had burned to stubs by the time Cynddl was finished. The moon had drifted up into the heights of the western sky.

Rath lay still for a long while, his breathing terribly shallow. Cynddl glanced at Nann, wondering if this disturbed her as much as it did him.

"Much of what you say frightens me," Rath said suddenly. His eyes remained closed as though the faint light hurt them. "The nagar most of all. Do you know the story of the children of Wyrr?"

Cynddl shook his head.

"It isn't well known. I found it long ago and have told it to few. Wyrr was a great sorcerer . . ." Rath told a story of Wyrr and his children—Caibre, Sainth, and Sianon—and of the gifts Wyrr had given them.

"Our nagar was Sianon, do you think?" Cynddl asked.

A bony hand appeared from beneath the blanket and the fingers were pressed against the forehead, which was clearly the source of much pain. "It could perhaps be another—there were other sorcerers, many of them powerful, who lived in the Greensprings—but with what has already occurred I think it unlikely. It must be Sianon."

"But why did she follow us?" Cynddl said quickly. "And how did she manage to escape the Greensprings?"

Rath shook his head, and winced. His eyes were pressed tightly closed, his face contorted with the pain. Cynddl wondered that he did not cry out. "The nagar are a mystery to us, Cynddl. From Death's gate you say that Caibre came, but who has ever escaped the last gate? No one. And no one can. Yet Caibre is among us."

"He was not dead," Cynddl said quickly. "That is what I think. He was in some netherworld—not in the world of the living—but he'd not passed through into the world of the dead, for no one returns to tell what awaits us there." Cynddl saw the ghost woman shudder.

"Sustained by the love of his father," Rath muttered.

"Or his own hatred," Nann said bitterly.

Rath's eyes flicked open to rest on Nann, then shut again. "Tuath and her sister foresaw this," Rath said, "but we weren't wise enough to understand. This flute the old man gave you—do you have it still?"

"Yes, I carry it with me always now, for fear it might be stolen." From inside his vest, Cynddl removed the wooden box and opened it gently.

Rath's fingers trembled a little as he took the flute. He held it away from his face, turning it slowly in the poor light.

"Eber thought it might be very old," Cynddl said.

"Old?" Rath whispered. "No. It is ancient." He held it toward Nann, who leaned forward to look, but she did not touch it. Tuath also leaned forward. It occurred to Cynddl that she was the most wraithlike woman he'd ever seen: beautiful but haunting.

"It could be a smeagh," Nann said, and closed her eyes.

"We have been trying to remember every story we've ever heard about the nagar, Nann and I. In one or two you will find the word 'smeagh.' We don't know what it means precisely, but it seems to be an object to which a nagar is attached: like an anchor set in our world and to which they cling." Rath set the flute down on the coverlets and let his trembling hands fall by his sides. He laid his head back as though the effort of examining the flute had exhausted him.

"Then this is a magical object?" Cynddl said.

Rath shook his head. "No, not really. It is the nagar that have abilities we don't understand. The smeagh is merely something they've owned."

"What if we were to shatter this flute or burn it?" Cynddl asked.

"Oh, I think you would bring a curse upon yourself and your descendants for many generations. Perhaps you would find the nagar had attached itself to you. No, I would not trifle with a smeagh."

Cynddl looked at the flute. It didn't appear to be merely an ancient instrument now, but something terrible—like a sword that had been used in a murder. "You think the nagar has been following this, not us?"

Rath nodded.

"But we saw it further north, before we ever met Eber and learned of the flute's existence."

"And didn't you tell me that you ran up on this island—what did you call it—?"

"Speaking Stone."

"That you ran up on Speaking Stone at night? A place that is not only on a secret branch of the river but even, you said yourself, that the current should have drawn you past it."

Cynddl glanced at Nann and then at Tuath.

"The nagar might have led you there," Nann said slowly. "We don't know what they might be able to do."

Cynddl felt as though the world had shifted around him. He'd been carrying that flute ever since Speaking Stone; tucked near to his heart. He nodded at the instrument. "This once belonged to Sianon?" he said foolishly.

Rath nodded. "Tell me again about this man your companions met in the north . . . You say he had visited there once before?"

"Yes, he had been to the Vale and was curious about given names that were passed down through the families there. I think now that he was looking for descendants of Knights of the Vow. I had a vision of Knights crossing Telanon Bridge—Knights that had escaped the slaughter of Cooling Keep. Two nights past I saw the same Knights within the ruined tower by Telanon Bridge. They were honing their weapons. Six grimmer men you have never seen. I think now they carried something away from Cooling Keep."

"Perhaps this flute you've found," Rath said softly.

Cynddl suddenly wondered if Alaan had found the flute in the possession of someone in the Vale. "At the keep itself I found part of a story: the Knights burned all their books and scrolls before the Renné overwhelmed them." Cynddl stopped. "But since then, when I see that great blaze of knowledge, I perceive another fire in the same place. It has taken me these weeks to find some bits of this story. The Knights burned one of their own grand masters—long ago it seems—burned him for some heresy or the breaking of some vow. They did much to hide this act, and I've never heard tell of it before. Why they did it is still a mystery."

"For making a pact with a nagar," Rath whispered, his eyes still closed.

"What are you saying?" It was like Rath to make such an intuitive leap. It was one of his greatest gifts as a story finder.

"The Knights had some way of bending the nagar to their own ends. Some secrets of dealing with them. But that is all passed now. Nagar are among us, returned from the netherworld, like a tempest springing up from the darkness."

FORTY-FOUR

The Valemen and the minstrels were given a cold supper and left on their own. Fynnol spread one of their blankets on the riverbank, and they ate their cold shoulder in awkward silence. The parade of lights continued past: boats going to the fair, most laden down to within a handsbreadth of their gunwales.

Three women came and stood not far off, gazing at the strangers and whispering among themselves.

"I'm glad we are providing them with some amusement anyway," Fynnol said.

"They're deciding which of you gentlemen they will devour tonight," Elffen growled.

"It's you they're looking at," Tam said, glancing at the Fáel women. "You and Angeline."

"Perhaps their appetites aren't so common, after all," Fynnol said, earning him a gratifying look of shock from Angeline. She turned toward the river so that she couldn't be easily seen from within the camp. Tam saw a look of concern pass over her face, and she shook her hair free a little so that it hid her face.

A horse nickered and shifted in the dark, and was

answered by another. A breeze whispered down the river, waking the trees which hissed and murmured.

Cynddl appeared, his now-familiar silhouette striding across the encampment. A woman approached just then, intercepting Cynddl as he was greeting his companions. The woman was perhaps thirty, dark and lithe and lovely, as in Tam's mind all Fáel women were. She bowed to Cynddl. "The players who will enter the contest at the fair would like to invite the minstrels to hear them play and to judge their worth," she said.

Cynddl glanced at Angeline and Elffen. "It is a compliment to be asked to judge Fáel players," he said.

"Of course we will be delighted to hear them play," Angeline said graciously, "but we wouldn't presume to judge."

"If you have eaten, then . . ." the woman said.

The Valemen had all risen to their feet as the Fáel woman approached, and they continued to stand politely, even though they'd been excluded from this invitation—which would have been an act of terrible rudeness in the Vale. They watched Elffen and Angeline disappear into the encampment.

"They could have invited us as well," Fynnol said, "but I suppose we shall hear it from here anyway."

"Not likely," Cynddl said. "The music will be made on the far edge of the camp. No one wants to disturb Rath."

"Who is Rath?" Fynnol said, sitting down again.

Cynddl too sat down and stretched his shoulders as though he had been immobile for too long. "Rath is the most famed story finder of our time. For many years he was my teacher. But he is old now and sickly, and no one wishes to disturb his rest." Cynddl looked down as he said this, and Tam thought he heard a note of deep sadness in the story finder's voice.

A horn sounded, tearing through the sleeping silence of the encampment. Dogs began to bark madly, and the great Fáel horses reared and plunged in alarm. Over the chaos, Tam heard the deep drumming of running horses.

The companions leapt to their feet, in disbelief for a moment. Mounted men-at-arms thundered into the encampment, cutting down Fáel women and men as they stumbled from their tents.

"They've found us again!" Baore shouted, and sprang to the boat, tearing free his shod staff. Tam and Cynddl snatched up their bows and began firing arrows at the black-robed riders.

There was a moment of utter confusion, men riding in circles and people running in all directions. Twice riders came toward the Valemen standing by the river-bank. Twice they were toppled from their horses by deadly arrows. Baore charged out into the melee, trying to protect the unarmed Fáel emerging from their tents. Tam half registered the big Valeman driving a horse to the ground with a single blow to its forehead, the rider swept from his falling mount. Behind Baore a small figure waved a sword and screamed in defiance: Fynnol protecting his cousin's back. More bows began to sing.

A horn sounded retreat, and suddenly only riderless

horses wandered aimlessly about the encampment. The raiders were gone, disappearing into shadows cast by the moon. All that remained was the weeping of the Fáel and the cries of the wounded.

Tam found Baore standing, dazed, in the center of the encampment. The big man stared unblinking at a kneeling mother who held an unmoving child to her breast.

Fynnol took his cousin's arm. "There's naught to be done here," he said softly.

"Death's gate . . ." Baore muttered.

"What are you saying?"

"I've seen it grind open," Baore said, not moving. "No child should ever go there, not alone."

"Who is Cynddl?" someone asked. A young Fáel stopped before them, bow in hand. He too stared down at the weeping woman.

"I'm Cynddl," the story finder said.

"Then come with me. And bring these others."

They crossed the field of carnage, stepping over horses and dead men-at-arms, over Fáel who'd been ridden down or killed by a single stroke. On the edge of the camp their guide stopped before a figure lying limp and still in the shadow of the trees. Someone approached with a lamp, and the faint light crept slowly over the still form——morning light over mountains.

"Elffen," Tam said, the air jolted from his lungs.

Cynddl pulled off his long vest and laid it over the dead singer. Fynnol took a few steps away out of the light, and covered his eyes for a moment.

"But where is Angeline?" Tam asked.

"The other woman . . .?" the man who led them said. "But she was Lady Elise, the daughter of Lord Carral Wills. Some of the instrument makers recognized her from their visits to her father."

"She is a Wills!"

The Fáel bowman stared down at the still form of Elffen. "Yes, but these riders carried her away."

FORTY-FIVE

Prince Michael watched his father's counselor with his usual patience and persistence. Hafydd did not appear to care. Nothing galled the Prince more than the blatancy with which Hafydd went about his business—as though he believed the Prince of Innes too stupid to ever notice or question his counselor's motives. And apparently Hafydd was right—as he was about so many things.

"What is it you want?" Prince Michael whispered.

They were riding into the village of Westbrook, or rather what the village became once a year. The village proper was a tiny collection of houses and a few shops, not unlike a hundred other hamlets of similar size in what was once the One Kingdom. But for a few days at midsummer the village swelled out into all the surrounding fields. Pavilions were erected; market stalls sprang up. Carpenters built stands beneath awnings so the nobility could watch contests in comfort. A barrier was built on the tilt field, targets erected for archery, and a sand floor made for the swordsmanship contest. Paddocks appeared, as did wattle pens for ducks and sheep, swine and cattle. Butchers sharpened their knives, and ovens were built brick by brick.

Everywhere he looked Prince Michael saw people rushing about their business. The nobility were only just beginning to arrive, and a few knights and their retinues wandered about looking for their lodgings.

The Prince of Innes would set his pavilions out by the river on a piece of ground he'd purchased years before. Here he could have built a house, but there was something grand about coming to the fair and sleeping under canvas. It almost never rained during high summer at the Westbrook Fair, and the air was sweet with the smells of new-mown hay and clover.

Suddenly Hafydd looked around, saw Prince Michael, and slowed his horse to await him.

"My Prince," Hafydd said, barely bobbing his head.

Prince Michael acknowledged him with a bow which was even more fleeting.

"Do you remember our quest through the estates of the Wills family earlier this spring?" Hafydd asked.

"I do."

"The man I sought will be here, at Westbrook."

The Prince waited for Hafydd to finish his thought, but there was apparently nothing more.

"How do you know this?"

Eremon/Hafydd looked off toward the river. "I know him like a brother. Once, many years ago I chased him down, despite all his tricks, and captured him."

"But he escaped apparently," the Prince said.

Hafydd turned his unsettling gaze on Prince Michael. "No. He didn't escape," he said. "I executed him . . . with my own hands. And yet here he is again. And here am I. The world is stranger than you know, and more brutal than you realize."

The knight spurred his mount and rode on, leaving the Prince to stare at his retreating back. Hafydd was not only frightening, Prince Michael had begun to think, but he was macabre. Why in the world did his father tolerate him?

"Because he is a fool with no imagination," he said softly. Men with no imagination made the best warriors, the Prince was convinced. They could not even begin to imagine what horrors might lie ahead of them. Prince Michael, however, was blessed with a fine imagination— or perhaps he was cursed.

The Prince pulled up his horse and let his father's retinue continue. He could see Hafydd and his men-at-arms pushing through the throng, bobbing up and down in their black robes as they went. The people parted before them instinctively; most even averted their eyes.

They have more sense than my father, Prince Michael thought.

But at least he knew why Hafydd was here: he was seeking the man he called his whist, a person the Prince had given over a great deal of time to in contemplation. The man had once been in his father's house—Prince Michael had deduced that much. About the time that Hafydd's obsession had begun a group of minstrels had been visiting, and had suddenly fled. All but one had escaped—and he had been taken by Hafydd and was never seen again. No one, apparently, ever asked after the man.

Hafydd was a sorcerer, or had some knowledge of sorcerers—there was no doubt of that. And the whist must be a sorcerer as well. How else could one explain the chase he had led them on through lands no one had ever seen?

This man, who was named for the bird of omen, had helped Elise Wills escape, and he was the enemy of Hafydd. That made him a potential ally of Prince Michael, or so he hoped.

Prince Michael found an ostler to mind his horse and set out to scour the fair. The fair at Westbrook was a comparatively safe place, especially by daylight—though like most young noblemen the Prince wore a blade and had been thoroughly trained in its use. Only his purse was in danger and that he tucked away inside his shirt where even the most light-fingered would be hard-pressed to find it.

The day was fine, perhaps a little warm, but a breeze swept down from the north and carried with it a little of the coolness of the faraway mountains, or so the Prince imagined.

He walked across the already trampled grass, searching among the stalls being built and the hawkers' stands.

He made way for a knight and his retinue, the man barely nodding to him as he passed. The Prince knew they would not all be so haughty by week's end. Most would have left their pride upon the tilt field, and many would have lost mounts and armor and more. Some would suffer hurts from which they would never heal. Others would be killed, for there were a few deaths every year—all accidental, of course, and much regretted by the conquering knights.

A blind man crossed his path at the center of a knot of men and women—minstrels, the Prince realized.

"Lord Carral?"

Only the briefest hesitation. "Prince Michael, is it?"

"It is, sir, and very pleased I am to see you."

"And I to hear you," Lord Carral said and smiled. "Have you come to enter the lists?"

"No, my father's physician says I am not wholly recovered from broken ribs so I will be forced to watch."

"Well, I'm sorry to hear you've been injured."

"Oh, don't trouble yourself over it. I'm perfectly hale. I bribed the physician so that I might avoid this madness. A man can be hurt on the tilt field. Even bruised. And to what end, I ask you?"

Lord Carral laughed. "To what end, indeed."

"And you, sir? Will you honor the fair by playing?"

"Hardly an honor. No, I am to judge the minstrels. The best will play at the costume ball on midsummer's eve. The rest . . ." He shrugged.

"Now that sounds preferable to entering the lists. The

wrath of the minstrels passed over will be nothing compared to an angry man-at-arms."

"Then come and hear the players with me. I should enjoy the company and——" Carral's face changed as he remembered. "But of course your family will not permit it."

"Oh, I will convince my father that it is the best thing possible. We shall lay to rest these rumors that your lovely daughter spurned me. After all, would I consent to judge the minstrels with the father of a woman who——what is the rumor?——ran off the day after marriage was proposed? Lady Elise is well, I take it?"

Lord Carral nodded but looked uncomfortable, even ill, at the mention of his daughter. "Then I will begin in the morning," Carral said softly, "in the Guildhall. Join me, if you will."

Prince Michael stood and watched the blind musician go, surrounded by minstrels who were honored just to be in his presence. Luck had smiled on him this day, and he took it as a good omen. Where better to look for Hafydd's enemy than among the minstrels? What better way to be among them than to sit at Lord Carral's elbow and judge their merit? He would have occasion to speak with them all. And he would find the whist before his father's counselor.

But what then? he wondered.

FORTY-SIX

Elise was bruised, disheveled, and frightened nigh to death. The air in her lungs seemed somehow very thin and she gasped terribly. The men who held her, one to each wrist, had no regard for her station or dignity but treated her like a common criminal. When she had tried to wrench one wrist free, he had cuffed her, and not gently.

Her feet seemed barely to touch the ground as she was hurried along between her captors. But even in this situation, images kept springing to mind.

Elffen had been cut down by a rider. Cut down! Pray that she was wounded and no more.

Elise had been taken up by one of the raiders and carried away from the Fáel encampment, the sounds of people being ridden down filling her ears: ridden down because of her. And now they were in a compound near the fair at Westbrook. She did not think she needed to ask whose compound.

The door flap of a small pavilion was swept aside and she was thrust in, her captors releasing her wrists and stepping back to bar her escape. The man standing behind a wooden table looked up.

"Sir Hafydd," she said.

He regarded her gravely. "How many people have died that you might take this foolish flight to nowhere?"

"As though you care that people die," she said.

"Oh, I do not care. You are quite right. I would murder a thousand to have you back. But what of you? Do these lives mean nothing to you?"

"They could never mean nothing to me," she said, looking down at her hands. *Poor Elffen*.

"Then do not try to thwart me again, for I would slaughter a town to find you." He came out from behind the table and stood before her, forbidding in his black robe. "Who are these people who helped you escape?"

She looked up at him, angry suddenly. "They are dead. What matter their names now?"

"I shall warn you only once, Lady Elise. I care nothing for your family or station. I will beat you until your pretty face is unrecognizable if that is what is required to have you answer my questions. Is that what is required?"

Elise hesitated for only a second, then shook her head.

"Perhaps you are not as foolish as you seem. Who were these people who helped you escape?"

"Minstrels: Gartnn and a young woman named Elffen."

"Had they no other names?"

"I'm sure they did but they did not tell them to me, nor did I ask."

He leaned back against the desk, folding his arms before him. "There were no others?"

"A man I met at Braidon Castle. A minstrel as well. Alaan he called himself."

"Did he keep a small bird as a pet?"

She nodded, not looking up.

"And you went with him willingly." It was not a question.

"Anything to prevent the war that you are planning."

Hafydd contemplated her for a moment. "You do not care that your family has been humiliated, reduced to country gentry by the Renné? Does that mean nothing to you?"

She met his gaze, which she found profoundly disturbing. "I would not see one life lost to change our situation," she said evenly, but could look into those eyes no longer.

"You are the daughter of a minstrel," he said with undisguised disdain. "There were others who aided you. Young men from the north and a Fáel bowman."

"They did so unknowingly. They rescued us when our boat came near to sinking, and they carried us down-river. They thought us to be minstrels, no more."

"Did I warn you not to lie?"

Elise backed up a step. "They told me they had befriended a traveler in the north, and that this traveler had been set upon by men-at-arms who these young men believed murdered him. Their attackers then hunted them through the wildlands and down the river, though they claimed not to know why. I believed their story, for they seemed innocent young men."

"There are very few innocent men, in my experience; and these ones were accompanied by a black wanderer, and twice they interfered with my guards. Tell me their names."

"Two cousins named Loell—Tam and Fynnol. Another named Baore, though I don't know his family name. The Fáel's name was Cynddl."

"What was their purpose, do you think?"

"They were seeking this traveler, who they'd learned was still alive. Apparently he had robbed them."

"Of what?"

She shrugged. "I know not."

Hafydd shifted. Elise could feel him staring at her. "What are you not telling me?"

She hesitated, not sure why, but Hafydd noted her hesitation and she went on quickly. "We were followed by something other than men-at-arms," she said, afraid to lie outright, but not wanting to tell Hafydd the truth either. "There was some kind of river spirit—a woman whom several of us saw in the water and on the river-bank." She glanced up to see if this meant anything to Hafydd.

His face did not really change, but he swallowed noticeably and became very still. "Describe her," he said softly.

"When she was seen in the water she was slick as a fish, with hair like seaweed and unsettling eyes: pure white but for a gray pupil at their center. But when she was seen on the shore her form was more human, though not wholly substantial. 'Ghostlike,' the others said, for I never saw her thus. Tam said she was dark haired and beautiful, but silent and sorrowful; though men are given to talking about women in this manner."

"Do you know what this was?"

"Cynddl named it a nagar, but he said that no one really understood what they were."

"Who among you did she follow?" Hafydd asked. He was speaking very carefully now, and listening with an intensity Elise found disturbing. "There must have been someone she was drawn to?"

She nodded. "Gartnn, I think."

"Gartnn . . ." Hafydd said and Elise nodded, casting her gaze down again. "And what became of him?"

"He was struck with an arrow and fell into the river. We never saw him again."

"Into the river . . ." Hafydd said, too softly.

Elise glanced up and thought he looked suddenly pale. She looked back to the floor, afraid that he might realize she'd seen this.

Hafydd called out a name and a guard appeared. "I will speak with Grithh. Immediately."

Hafydd pushed himself away from his desk and paced across the rug, upon which, Elise realized, was embroidered a scene of battle. She watched his black boots as they went striding over the fallen warriors, and she wondered why she felt such fear. Twice the boots stopped and Elise felt Hafydd's gaze burning her. Once he seemed to mutter, "Not a minstrel," but she could not be sure.

The tent flap opened and another black-clad guard appeared. He glanced once at Elise as though in recognition.

"You told me you killed a minstrel when you failed to seize Elise Wills," Hafydd said.

"Men in my company did, Sir Eremon," the guard answered, making a small bow.

"What became of him?"

The guard hesitated. "I——I don't know, sir. He pitched into the river. Perhaps his body washed up on the bank the next day, as they often do."

"Take a small company north and find out if this is so. If this minstrel was found and buried, dig him up and burn him. If they set him on a pyre and gave his ashes to the river, talk to the men who did it and be sure it was this minstrel Gartnn. Collect any possessions that he might have carried on his person. I will have them all——to the smallest thing."

The man bobbed his head. "Sir," he said, and swept out of the tent.

Hafydd nodded, staring down at the floor a moment. "Where did these young men hail from?"

"Somewhere in the north. On the river, I think, for they were skilled watermen and one was a boatwright. They mentioned a bridge . . . Telanine Bridge."

"Telanon," Hafydd said. "A great battle was fought there once, long ago——and even before that it was an important waypoint, for it lay upon the road from the northern mines. These men from the wildlands: they

must have given something to the minstrel Gartnn—
some object?"

"Perhaps, but I know nothing of it."

"And these young men are with the Fáel now?"

"They were earlier this night. Perhaps they are dead
now, for your minions swept through the encampment,
riding down everyone in their path." Elise forced herself
to look up. "What will be done with me?" she said
suddenly.

Hafydd looked at her as though she had just appeared.
"You will marry Prince Michael and bear him a child,"
Hafydd said, his mind still elsewhere.

"And what if we choose not to bear a child?" she said.
"What if we refuse to give you a son to put on the
throne?"

Hafydd fixed her with his unsettling gaze. "You may
bear Prince Michael's child," he said, "or mine. That is
your choice." He looked up at the guards and nodded.

They stepped forward and took her by the arms, and
she was led out into the moonlit compound. Somewhere,
far off, she heard minstrels playing, and a tear came
unbidden to her, tracing a cool track down her cheek.

FORTY-SEVEN

Lord Carral Wills sat playing an old Fáellute, as always, in awe of its complexity of tone. The notes had a warmth and depth that no other lute he'd ever heard could match. It was partly the workmanship, partly the woods—alollynda and rosewood—and partly the instrument's age. Two hundred years had done much to soften the sound, to add subtle overtones.

"Is it the instrument or the player?" a voice said. It came from the balcony.

Carral stopped. "It is the Fáellute," he said. "You have left the castle you once wandered. Or is it me you haunt?"

"I have no loyalties to men or to the places of men. My purpose does not allow it."

"And what is your purpose?"

"This night it is to bear bad news." He paused, and Carral did not like this silence.

"Hafydd has found your daughter."

Carral felt his fingers go slack on the strings. "Has—has she been harmed?"

"I don't know, for certain. I think not. Though he

struck you I don't think he will treat Elise the same. She is to marry the son of his lord, after all."

"I don't think Hafydd cares much what his master thinks."

"He needs the Prince's armies, yet."

Carral took a long, uncertain breath. "You failed," he said flatly.

"Yes. Yes, I did. My plans went awry and Hafydd found her—found her in a place I might never have looked myself. She was with the Fáel, and he sent a raiding party to steal her away."

"A raiding party into a Fáel encampment!"

"Yes."

"Where?"

"Nearby."

"*Nearby!?* But what of the Peace of the Fair?"

"As you say, he cares little for what others think."

Carral heard the light tap of footsteps as the ghost entered the room. His foot fell upon a plank that squeaked; and it did, just as it would beneath any man.

"My poor Elise . . . with that monster."

"There is some hope yet," the voice said, closer now. The sound of wine being poured came to him.

"And what hope is that?"

"I have hope that we might steal her back."

"Where is she?"

"In the compound of the Prince of Innes."

"Surely she is well guarded."

"Better than you know. But I have found my way into

more difficult situations—and my way out again."

"What will you do?"

"I am not quite sure, but Hafydd killed my confederates to have Elise back—and to taunt me. I shall see that justice finds him."

"Spoken like a Wills," Carral muttered, his anger subsiding a little. "Were your confederates ghosts as well?"

For a second there was no answer. Carral could hear breathing.

"No. They were minstrels. Very skilled ones."

"Ah."

"But perhaps they are ghosts, now," the voice said sadly.

Neither of them spoke for a moment. Carral heard the man moving about the room. The strings of a harp rang as someone ran a finger over them, notes tumbling into the silence of the room like light.

"I was told that Hafydd sought you," Carral said, "all across the northern reaches of our demesne. It is said he sought you out by means that could only be described as arcane. Who is this man Hafydd that he has such knowledge? And who are you that you can disappear from a high tower when the only door is blocked?"

The ghost stopped in his pacing. He was near the doors to the balcony now. "It's said the blind hear more than the sighted," the man said, and Carral could tell that he faced the garden. "Hafydd has discovered things that he should not. He's broken his word and allied himself with . . ." He paused. "He has made unwise alliances.

Hafydd is something beyond your understanding now, a monster of sorts. You do not know the carnage that he would cause to satisfy his slightest whim."

"You frighten me, ghost."

"Men are meant to be frightened of my kind. And better that they are."

Carral heard him slip over the balcony and land on the ground, light as a bird.

FORTY-EIGHT

Tam poured Elffen's still-warm ashes into the river. The stream of fine powder formed a chain of gray islands, then each island darkened and sank, turning the water to misty milk. How could this be Elffen, vibrantly alive but a day ago? Tam closed his eyes. He hadn't known her well—or Gartnn for that matter—and his sorrow seemed somehow out of proportion to what they'd meant to him. Perhaps it was the grief of the Fáel, who committed the ashes of their loved ones to the river in this same ceremony, some of the dead mere children.

The Fáel began a soft lament, beautiful and sad beyond measure. Tam thought the song alone would bring anyone to tears. As the last ashes spun into the river and the lament came to an end, a small bird began to sing in the branches overhead.

There was a moment of silence and then the Fáel began to whisper among themselves.

Tam looked to Cynddl.

"It is a whist," Cynddl murmured.

"But that is not the song of the whist," Tam objected.

"Not the warning cry that you know but its love song. Listen."

And listen they did for a brief moment. The song was repeated only once, then the bird took wing and passed quickly over the river, disappearing into the world beyond.

FOR†Y-∏I∏E

Despite the fact that the jousting, archery, and equestrian competitions would begin that morning the Guildhall was filled with the sounds of people who had come to listen to the music. Carral knew from the sound and the soft breeze that the long line of double doors down each side of the hall had been opened to the crowd gathered outside.

"Lord Carral," came a familiar voice. "I thought I should never win through—there is such a mass outside."

"Prince Michael? Your father agreed, I take it?"

"Oh, he was not happy, but he was convinced by my argument. Oddly his counselor took my side."

"Hafydd?"

"Eremon, he is called in my father's house. Sir Eremon."

Carral heard the scrape of wood as the Prince shifted his chair. "What a crowd!" the young man said. "I think I have never seen it so thick. The galleries are full, as is the floor, and the lawn outside is dense with people for a hundred feet. Certainly they won't be able to hear a thing." He paused for a second, perhaps looking around,

Carral thought, and then he laughed gently. "The minstrels are all dressed in their finery and putting on bold faces," he said, amused. "They seem to have forgotten the judge this year will not be able to see them." The Prince paused, and Carral could hear the awkwardness take shape in the silence. "I am sorry. I didn't mean——"

"It's all right," Carral said, laughing, "I am aware that I'm blind. This will be one year that the prettiest singer will not take all the honors because of her smile."

The Prince laughed a little too loudly at this.

Carral could hear the buzz of people waiting for the playing to begin. Many of the eyes were fixed on the judges' stand, he was sure, but there was no one within earshot, he was almost certain.

"Prince Michael?" Carral said, lowering his voice.

"Sir?"

"Hafydd has my daughter."

He heard the Prince's breath catch.

"Are you certain? He cannot have her within our compound without me knowing . . ." A pause. "I don't think."

"Within your father's compound, yes. I am most certain this is true. Do you still wish to thwart Hafydd in his plans?"

"Let us not speak of this here," the Prince said so close to his ear Carral felt his breath.

And so the competition began. Men and Fáel coming before the judge and his advisors. Winning the competition at Westbrook could make a minstrel's reputation, but to receive the praise of Lord Carral Wills as well . . . This would push someone into the first rank of minstrels, assuring their fame and fortune. For that reason the men and women who came to play were all more nervous than they normally would have been, and yet many noted that the great Lord Carral seemed little interested in the contest. Some remarked that, occasionally, he did not seem to be listening at all.

FIFTY

Prince Michael made his way through the currents and running streams of humanity. He couldn't quite accept what Lord Carral had told him, yet he was certain the man wasn't lying. What spies the Wills must have that Lord Carral would know Elise was being held within the compound of the Prince of Innes before Prince Michael himself knew!

Had Hafydd not the slightest thought for honor? Prince Michael's father had signed his name to the charter guaranteeing the Peace of the Fair. And now his counselor had broken that peace and attacked the Fáel!

The Prince entered his family's compound and crossed immediately to his father's pavilions, confronting the guards. "Where is the Prince?" he demanded.

The guard bowed. "He dines with the Duke of Varrn this evening."

Prince Michael considered only a moment. Hafydd had actually taught him a lesson: the fainthearted would perish while the bold would prosper. "I can't wait for him," he said. "Muster twenty armed men. I want them here immediately."

The guard bobbed his head. "But for what purpose?"

"We go to secure my bride."

"Your grace, I must have the permission of my superior before I muster men. Where might I tell him we go?"

"To clean the stables! That is where you will spend the rest of your miserable days unless you have twenty men mustered here within the half hour. Can you do that, or does life in the dung heap seem preferable to you?"

The guard snapped upright, his face suddenly crimson. "I can find twenty men," he said.

"Be certain they are wearing mail," Prince Michael growled and went off to find his own arms and a shirt of mail.

Half of the hour later he was marching across his father's compound at the head of a column of men, their boots landing in rhythm on the soft grasses. Torches lit the way, wavering like his will. He was afraid, both of Hafydd and of what he had set in motion. There would be no way to back down once Hafydd had been confronted. Blood could be spilled. The Prince wondered if he would have the nerve to carry it through.

Why were men all so afraid of Hafydd? Why was *he* so afraid?

A memory of Hafydd knocking Lord Carral to his knees surfaced unbidden. Not just a blind man who could not hope to defend himself, but a minstrel of such genius that Prince Michael counted himself lucky to be born during his time. At the thought of this a slow flame, which had burned long and secretly inside him, kindled, and he nursed it into a blaze of anger, shutting out all doubts and whispered fears. There could be no other way. He must be in a rage or his nerve would falter and break.

He stormed across the compound toward the pavilions of Hafydd and his guard, offended that the knight had set himself up as a lord within his father's compound—a lord, when he was only a landless man-at-arms.

Two of Hafydd's guards stepped before him as he crossed the invisible line into the counselor's domain. Neither of them said a word.

"I will speak with Hafydd," Prince Michael said, surprised at how much resolve he heard in his voice.

"There is no one by that name here," one guard said.

"Then I will speak with Sir Eremon. This is my father's compound and you have no rights here. Step aside."

The two men glanced at each other and put hands to their sword hilts, as though there were not twenty men standing before them. Their arrogance was intolerable, and the Prince drew his sword before he thought.

"If they will not step aside, cut them down," he said, and raised his sword. He heard twenty blades leave their scabbards behind him. The resentment of Hafydd's guards was great among his father's men . . . and the odds here were greatly in their favor, the Prince noted.

Hafydd's men drew their swords, but the Prince

lunged forward and cut into one man's hand before his blade was free. The other aimed a blow at Prince Michael's head but the Prince danced aside. Half a dozen men fell on this guard, and would have hacked him to pieces if the Prince had not intervened.

"Take him prisoner. He disobeyed my orders within my father's compound and turned his sword against me. Any man who does the same will go before my father, where he can explain why he felt it his right to murder his son." A quick motion and the point of his sword was against the other man's throat. "Shout, but choose your last words well."

The man swallowed.

"Where is Elise Wills?"

The man did not move nor did he offer an answer.

Prince Michael looked up at his men in the poor light. "There can be only two tents within the compound that are guarded—Sir Eremon's and the one I seek. Go in pairs, eight of you, and find these tents."

The men hustled off, the dull jingling of mail rings sounding ominous in the quiet night. They were not gone but a few moments when they returned.

"There are two guarded tents, one bearing Sir Eremon's banner, the other the double swan of the Wills."

"Well, there is an odd mark of respect!" the Prince said. He motioned to Hafydd's guards. "Take these men away. My father will see them when he returns. Now lead me to the pavilion with the double swan banner."

It was a short distance. Two more black-surcoated

men-at-arms stood guard here, and when they saw the Prince approaching at the head of a column of men, one dashed off. The other stepped forward, but Prince Michael was not about to be stalled. "Encircle him," he ordered. "Cut him down if he resists."

But the man was no fool and read the situation quickly. His sword went back in its sheath and he held his hands palms out. The Prince hesitated by the flap of the tent, then cleared his throat.

"Lady Elise?"

A second later the flap was torn aside and Elise Wills stepped out into the flickering torchlight.

"Oh, Michael, you found me," she said, and tears glittered on her lashes.

"We haven't a second to lose. Leave everything and come as you are. Hafydd knows what I do."

Elise dropped the flap of the tent behind her and set out, trotting along beside him, the men falling in behind. The prince felt his hopes begin to rise. Another twenty yards and they would be out of Hafydd's realm and into his father's. Let Hafydd try to take Elise back then!

They rounded a tent and found Hafydd standing before a dozen of his ghostly guards, all with swords in hand.

"Prince Michael?" Hafydd said, as though he thought this must be some other. "What is this you do? One of my guards has been injured, I'm told."

"I will take my bride to lodge with my aunt, who will be her chaperone."

"That is a perfectly acceptable arrangement. I have been

waiting for your father to make his wishes in this matter known. Certainly Lady Elise cannot lodge here with me." Hafydd's brow wrinkled up quizzically. "But why would you not merely come and speak with me of this? Why come with armed men, and injure one of my guards?"

Prince Michael felt his grip tighten on his sword. Hafydd *would* try to make what he did seem foolish and juvenile.

"Because I know who you are, Sir Hafydd, and who you once served. I know what it is you do here, in my father's compound. Counselor, you call yourself! You would counsel my father to his ruin if it suited you. Stand aside. We will deliver my bride."

Prince Michael forced himself to go forward, skirting Hafydd and his man, avoiding a direct confrontation. As he passed, Hafydd glared at him, but the Prince tried to act as though he did not notice. The truth was that he could hardly breathe he was so frightened.

The Prince released a long sigh as they passed back into the area under his father's control. Elise put a hand on his arm.

"He would never have given me up if you had not come with men bearing arms," she said. "Do not be fooled by this sudden pretense that he is a reasonable man. He is not."

They sat on chairs just beyond the awning, looking up at the moon and stars. Elise pulled the borrowed shawl close around her shoulders. Not a dozen feet away Prince Michael's aunt sat, embroidering, just within the pavilion's half-opened flaps.

"Were you really abducted from the Fáel?" the Prince asked, keeping his voice low.

She nodded. "And one of my companions—one of those who helped me escape—was cut down . . ." She closed her eyes and felt hot tears well up. A hand took hers gently. For a long moment she cried, unable to control it.

"You must think the worst of me. Such a display . . ."

"I think the best of you. Such a display of loyalty and grief. It is like Hafydd to avenge himself on those who thwarted him. So he hunted down this man he calls the whist after all."

"Alaan," she said. "No, he wasn't with us. Only Elffen and me." Tears appeared again, but she fought them back. "What shall be done with me now?" she asked, mastering herself and sitting up to wipe her eyes. A square of linen was placed in her hands.

The Prince slumped down in his chair. "I assume my father will send word to your family that you've been found, but, to be honest, I see little chance that he will give you up now."

"I expect you're right," she said, thinking what a mess she must look and how perfectly dressed and composed this young man appeared. She had forgotten how beautiful he was. Beautiful, but at the moment he looked anything but happy.

"I can't tell you how sorry I am that you've been brought into this affair against your wishes," he said suddenly.

"I can't tell you how sorry I am that we are both so immersed," she said. "They will make a war, my foolish relations and your ambitious family. They shall make a war, and you and I will be part of it. You and I and this child your father wants to place on a nonexistent throne."

The Prince sank a little lower in the chair, as though the weight of what she said pressed down upon him. "Oh, it is not my father. No, that is not precisely true. He would remake the old kingdom and place his grandson on the throne—that is his dream. But it is Hafydd who drives him on. Without Hafydd my father's dreams of glory would never have seen the light of day."

Elise closed her eyes, remembering the words of Hafydd. "He threatened me," she said very quietly, as though Hafydd might hear. "He told me that if we refused to produce a child . . . that I could bear your child or his. That was my choice."

The Prince sat up suddenly.

"And something else," she said. "I'm very frightened for these young men who helped me. Hafydd is so vengeful, and they are innocent young men from some small village."

"I will send a warning to them," the Prince said quickly. "Where are they?"

"They were with the Fáel," Elise said. Then, in a very small voice, "Is there no hope that we might resist him?"

The Prince took a long breath and was about to speak but stopped. He had intended to offer platitudes, but felt that was beneath both of them. Elise Wills was smarter than that.

"I don't know, Elise. That is the truth. If Hafydd has a weakness, I've yet to learn it."

FIFTY-ONE

The four men-at-arms were laid out on tables in the old icehouse. A half-opened fan of sunlight streamed through the door illuminating the dead, who lay in their black surcoats, faces waxy pale, the blue-gray of death lurking beneath. By each man's head a helm was laid, and by his side a sword. At his feet was set a black shield with no coat of arms. From two of the shields, arrows protruded.

The plainness and uniformity of the men's armor and arms struck Dease. With their neatly trimmed beards and identical accoutrements there was little to distinguish them. He picked up one of the swords, unadorned but of fine workmanship. Even the metal appeared to have a dark cast, as though steel and smoke had been fused in the forge.

"Who are these dark knights?" Dease asked, afraid they were assassins. Had someone tried to murder Toren? Why else was he being so secretive?

"They are members of the guard of a counselor of the Prince of Innes."

"Why would a prince's counselor need his own guard?"

Toren stood staring down at the motionless men. "A question I have asked myself. It would appear that this man Eremon has assumed prerogatives few princes would allow. It also seems that Eremon is not who he claims. He was once known as Hafydd."

Dease gazed at his cousin, thinking that he suddenly had ceased to make sense. "That isn't possible. Hafydd died twenty years ago or more."

"If that is true, then he is reborn as Eremon, though I prefer to believe he did not die but escaped somehow. He has taken up with our enemy, or the ally of our enemy." He kicked a pile of straw, the golden blades spinning up into a shaft of sunlight, then settling back like slow-falling leaves. "Whatever the explanation, he is now a counselor to the Prince of Innes and plots against us."

"But how came these men to be here?"

Toren gazed at him and grimaced oddly. "Do not look so, Dease; they were not assassins." Toren gestured at one of the shields. "Have you seen arrows such as these before?"

Dease reached out to touch the feathers of an arrow. "But these are Fáel!"

Toren nodded. "You remember the rumor that Elise Wills had run away to avoid marriage——"

"To the Prince of Innes' son."

"Yes. It seems the rumors were true. She was lodging with the Fáel, who didn't realize immediately who she was. Hafydd's men attacked the camp and abducted her."

"Not here," Dease said quickly. "Not at Westbrook."

Toren nodded sadly. "At Westbrook, yes."

Neither man spoke for a moment. The light streaming into the icehouse seemed to be coming from far away—from another season or perhaps another age, an age of peace.

"If the Wills forge an alliance with the Prince of Innes," Dease said, returning his gaze to the dead knights, "the plan to return the Isle of Battle to the Wills must be abandoned."

Toren reached up and took hold of one of the low beams. He slouched down and let his arms take part of his weight. "That is the excuse they're looking for to begin a war," he said softly.

Dease looked at Toren in horror. "You don't intend to go through with it . . . They've broken the Peace of the Fair! We should look weak and foolish to cede them the Isle now!"

Toren continued to support his weight on the beam, staring at the row of dead men-at-arms. "If we do not go through with it we will have war."

"We will have war either way!" Dease almost hollered in frustration. "That is what the Prince of Innes plans."

"And he is far better prepared for it than we."

This stopped Dease for a moment. "You think to cede them the Isle to give ourselves time to muster an army?"

"Yes, or we might find some other way to avoid the war."

"There is no way to avoid the war but to surrender to the Prince of Innes and Menwyn Wills. I prefer war to that."

"Do you indeed," Toren said. His voice was soft and laden with sorrow. "Look at these men. They are dead because of the feud you all ask me to pursue. Imagine they're your cousins, Dease. That is what you are asking for."

Dease looked down the row of still men. "Death awaits us all," he said. "There is no place one can hide from it. You know I'm no more desirous of war than you, Toren, but we can't let down our guard with the Wills and their allies. Better to die on a field of battle than of shame in some prison. It is our survival or theirs. There is only one choice."

Toren did not answer but swayed back and forth, his heavily muscled arms still supporting part of his weight. He stared at the four dead men-at-arms so sorrowfully that Dease could have believed they were his cousins.

"What will you do?" Dease asked finally.

"I'll alert the marshals of the fair. It is their duty to deal with breaches of the peace."

"You know they have no power but for the resolve and strength of the Renné who stand behind them. This is no time to appear fainthearted."

"Nor is it a time to let the Prince provoke us into war. We are not prepared—the Wills have been weak for so long."

Dease looked at his cousin, who didn't meet his eye but only stared at the dead knights before him. "Toren, you know how the rest of the family will feel when they hear of this."

Dease realized that Toren must be keeping this from everyone in the family but him for this very reason.

"Yes, I know how they will feel. But only a fool is quick to go to war." Toren continued to stare at the dead knights. "Think of this number dead ten thousand times over."

Dease could hardly bear the pain in his cousin's gaze, and looked away. The dead lay before him, and it took little imagination to see a field so littered, the carrion crows calling from tree to tree.

"I will send the marshals of the fair to confront the Prince," Toren said. "They will bear these dead knights with them as proof of what occurred. They will demand the release of Elise Wills and the surrender of Hafydd so that he might face judgment. There can be no other course."

"But of course they will be refused, and what will you have accomplished but to make the Renné look weak and foolish?"

"I will have demonstrated to everyone who is guilty and who is in the right."

"What care we if people think we are in the right!?" Dease thundered, his voice echoing between the stone walls.

"What care we if people think we are foolish?" Toren said softly. "We will send the marshals to do their duty. We will abide by our own laws."

"Live by them and die by them, I fear. Sometimes war is carried to you and there is no choice but to take up arms. I fear such a disaster is only days away. Perhaps it's upon us now and we cannot see."

"Maybe, Cousin, but I will not choose war while I still can choose. If history proves me wrong . . . well, there is little one can do about the judgments of history."

"Yes," Dease said, "may history not judge us too harshly, for we do what appears right in the moment, though we can see but a little distance into the future."

His eye came to rest upon the still forms of the knights. How peaceful they looked in the streaming light, how removed from cares and worries, from the scheming and treachery of living men.

FIFTY-TWO

Prince Michael had managed to elude the guards his father had watching over him—and the men Hafydd had spying on him.

The town ostler let him have a horse for an exorbitant price, and he set out to cross the Westbrook Bridge and find the encampment of the Fáel where Elise had last seen the young men who'd aided her flight.

At the edge of the Fáel camp armed men appeared out of the bush before him. They regarded him with deep suspicion, their looks hostile.

"Have you business with the Fáel," the eldest man said, "or are you lost?"

"I have a message from Lady Elise Wills for Tamlyn Loell or for one of your people named Cynddl."

The Fáel whispered among themselves, and then the older man turned back to the Prince. "Tell me your name."

"Prince Michael of Innes."

The Fáel looked at one another in wonder, and then one ran off, leaving the others muttering among themselves in their own tongue.

It was a moment before anyone returned, and then Prince Michael was beckoned on, a Fáel taking the bridle of his horse. As he passed, the Prince realized a bowman peered down at him from a tree, an arrow nocked and aimed at his heart.

His horse was taken in hand as he dismounted and a woman appeared, introducing herself and curtseying gracefully. "Lady Elise has sent you, you say?"

He nodded. "Yes. She fears that three young men who aided her are in danger. I carry this warning to them in her name."

The woman nodded, gazing at him thoughtfully.

"Come and speak with Rath and Nann. They will decide what should be done."

The Prince fell in with this woman, pushing down his resentment of her suggestion that he would be judged. He was among the Fáel now, and they would care little for his station or name. He was led before a frail-looking ancient man and a woman seated beneath a spreading tree on the riverbank. No chair was offered him and he stood, like a truant, awaiting their pleasure.

"You are the son of the Prince of Innes?" the woman said at last. There were no introductions, but this must be Nann.

"I am."

"We were attacked by men-at-arms who serve your father's counselor." She looked at him very directly. "Is it possible that you didn't know this?"

"I knew nothing of it nor did my father, I assure you.

Our family respects the Peace of the Fair and the peace between our people and yours."

"Then how will your father deal with this renegade counselor?"

"I don't speak for my father," the Prince said. What was he to tell them? He didn't believe his father would have approved of Hafydd's attack on the Fáel, nor did he believe his father would censure his counselor in any way. How to explain that?

"I see," the woman said. "Then why are you here?"

"I carry a warning. Lady Elise was questioned by Hafydd—my father's counselor. He is known as Eremon—"

"We know who Sir Hafydd is," the old woman said.

"Lady Elise was questioned," the Prince continued, "and fears that she might have said things that will endanger these young men who aided her. If these men are with you still I must warn them."

Nann looked down at her hand and shook her head. "If your father seeks these young men it seems a clever ploy to send you to find their whereabouts."

"Then tell me nothing of them, but only carry my warning to them. I've given my word that I would do this."

"Then consider your duty discharged." The Fáel elders continued to stare at him with mild distaste.

"I regret what happened," the Prince said quickly. "I regret any harm my father's counselor did among your people."

"Do you?"

The Prince nodded. The elders glanced at each other. "Then perhaps you will make it your duty to redress the wrong done us?" Rath said.

"I'm not sure what I can do, and I will tell you truly, I feel little obligation to make amends for wrongs done by others, especially those who seek neither my counsel nor my approval."

"We don't ask for silver, Prince," the woman said. "We only wish to know more of this man who displays so little respect for the treaties signed by your people. Does honor mean so little to Hafydd?"

"It means nothing to him. I have come to believe he would murder innocent children to get what he wants, even were it something trivial. He is a man unlike any I have known in this way."

"Is there no one he cares for? A woman? A son or daughter?"

"No one. Nothing but his own schemes, his own substantial pride."

"And what are these schemes, your grace?"

"I wish I knew. Clearly, he has my father making an alliance with the Wills so that he might make war upon the Renné, whom he hates. He wants a child from my marriage with Elise Wills. This child is destined for a throne, I think—or so Hafydd hopes." He shrugged. "Hafydd keeps his own counsel and harbors desires I can't fathom, for they're foreign to me. I wish to revenge myself on no one, and I don't want to put my son upon a throne, where he'll be in danger every moment. No, let us live in peace. Let there be peace between men, and between Fáel and men. That's what I say."

"And that is what you would say if you wished to ingratiate yourself with the Fáel," the woman said. "What has been done with Lady Elise?"

"She is unharmed. I have spoken with her. Unharmed, though frightened."

"And now what will be done with her?"

"She'll be forced to marry me—and I her."

"Forced? How can you be forced?" the man named Rath said. "Have you not ridden here of your own choosing? Ride on, if that is so."

"He would find me. You know what Hafydd did to have Lady Elise back. He would do no less for me, and I don't wish to have that blood on my hands. Elise suffers it already."

This gave the Fáel elders pause.

The river flowed behind them, murmuring like a sleeping child. Rath turned his clouded eyes upon the Prince after a moment of thought. "And if war comes, what will you do?"

"I am the heir of the Prince of Innes," he said, his mouth going suddenly dry. "What choice have I?"

Prince Michael rode from the Fáel encampment, the question echoing in his mind.

What choice have I?

Certainly he could not side with his father's enemies,

his family's enemies. Yet this war his father and Hafydd contemplated was repugnant to him. A war of aggrandizement. The ambitions of men seemed petty and hollow.

Not far ahead he could see a man sitting against the bole of a butternut tree, his horse grazing at the roadside. The prince loosened his sword in its scabbard and looked up among the trees for other men. This is what came of riding off alone. The Peace of the Fair was a thing of the past. Who was not in danger now?

The man lounging by the roadside was well dressed, the Prince could see, though in clothes for travel. If he bore a blade it was not in sight. As the Prince drew near the man looked up: dark hair and beard, a passingly handsome face.

"I know you, sir," Prince Michael said, drawing up his horse. "But where is your whist?"

The man nodded, though he didn't rise but continued to lounge by the roadside. A few feet away the river flowed. "Oh, he is off somewhere, bearing his single message, which is always ignored."

The Prince could not help but smile. What audacity this man had! "For days we chased you. Had I known you'd be sitting here waiting for me I could have saved myself a great deal of discomfort. But then I wouldn't have seen Hafydd fail. How he cursed you! I can't tell you what pleasure this gave me."

The man held a small stick in his hand and scratched marks in the earth. "Hafydd murdered two of my friends because he knew I mocked him. I was foolish and vain."

He looked up. "You've been to visit the Fáel, though Hafydd's guards attacked them last night. Did you carry your father's regrets to the people his servant injured?"

Prince Michael shook his head.

"I didn't think so. Yet you went there anyway, though you knew you wouldn't be welcome. What could have led you to do this, I ask myself?"

"You ask the wrong man, it seems," the Prince said.

The man's look was dark. He had lost friends to Hafydd and was in no mood for jests.

"I went there to carry a warning."

"You do realize a warning is quite distinct from a threat."

"I'm told I have a way with words—and it's true that I respect them more than most men."

The man nodded, continuing to toy with his stick. "Do you know, I watched you when I was in your father's house. I was there for that purpose."

"You posed as a minstrel," the Prince said, "but to watch Hafydd, not me."

"Oh yes, to watch Hafydd, but I was also there to observe the Prince of Innes and his family. Hafydd serves a prince who has ambitions but no imagination, who could no more conceive a grand strategy than write a ballad. Hafydd is his strategist, though it is a strange marriage. Hafydd's title is counselor, yet he is more an ally and acts as one—as a near equal." The man smoothed the sand he had been scratching in. "But that is just how things appear on the surface. In truth, I think Hafydd holds sway over the Prince of Innes. Your father has ambitions I don't condone, but he has some regard for the concept of honor. Hafydd disdains honor and thinks any who believe in it are fools and weaklings." The man looked up. "You are your father's son. You believe in honor as he does. But there's a difference: you have both imagination and humanity, which makes you twice the man your father is, even if you don't know it."

"You forgot to mention that I've known flattery all my life. As a man of words, I've mastered its uses myself."

The minstrel smiled. "Then I'll come to my reason for waylaying you." He bent over his circle of sand again, making quick marks with his stick.

"Hafydd has no concern for your father, his family, or his honor. You know this. Hafydd has his own purposes, and for him people exist only to serve those ends. Anyone who will not serve is his enemy." The man looked up at Prince Michael, his manner suddenly very grave. "You must choose: either you are Hafydd's servant or his enemy. Which will it be?"

It was like a slap in the face. The man was speaking the truth that others dared not. "I will not be Hafydd's servant," the Prince said softly.

"Then you are his enemy, Prince Michael of Innes. And if you are his enemy you must help me steal Elise Wills away. Talk to Lord Carral Wills. He'll agree to announce your engagement to his daughter. Have him also say that people may carry their best wishes to you at the Renné costume ball, for both you and Lady Elise will attend."

The Prince shook his head. "It will never work. Hafydd will see what you plan, and he'll not allow Elise out of my father's compound."

"Of course he will see, but how else will he find me? He must use Elise to draw me out." The man stopped making marks with his stick. "See that Elise's costume is made by Mrs. Rowan. Her tent is in the market. That's your part. Oh, and you must alert Elise to our intentions. Can you manage to speak with her?"

"If I so choose, I can."

"How effective are your father's spies within Castle Renné?"

"Effective enough."

The stranger seemed to weigh this response a moment, then rose lithely to his feet. He fixed the Prince with a stare that was shrewdly measuring. "This is what I observed when I was a minstrel in your father's house: you are wiser than he. And whether you think I flatter or not, you know it's true. Help me steal Elise Wills away."

"I will help you, but it will not stop the alliance between my father and the Wills. What is it you hope to accomplish?"

"I will save Lady Elise from Hafydd: is that not enough?" He thrust his stick into the earth, and beckoned his horse, which came at the sound of his voice. As he went to put a foot into the stirrup he turned to the Prince.

"You can't stand on the field between two armies, undecided. I know what I'm saying in this. When the armies clash you will be their first victim. Treachery, I'm sure you know, is all a matter of which side passes judgment." The man swung into the saddle, nodded, and began to turn.

"What is it Hafydd knows?" the Prince said quickly. "How has he returned from the dead to haunt us?"

The minstrel stopped, turning in his saddle. For a moment he gazed at the Prince silently. "Hafydd has learned things he should not and now he is more dangerous than you realize. Or perhaps you have come to suspect?"

"I saw him strike his sword on a rock so that it quivered and moaned whenever it was pointed in the direction his enemy fled." The Prince paused. "But I also saw how you stayed before us, riding through lands no one had ever seen. Who should I fear more?"

The man looked out at the river for a moment. "Fear is despised in our society, your grace, but I think it a sign of wisdom. To falter and break when circumstances demand courage; that is shameful. But fear . . ." He tilted his head to one side and shrugged. "Fear is wisdom."

The man urged his horse into a canter and was quickly distant on the narrow road. When he was almost out of sight the Prince dismounted and led his horse forward. There on the ground, where the minstrel had thrust his stick, was a line drawing of a small bird, its bill open in song. Prince Michael did not have to ask what its call was.

FIFTY-THREE

The night whispered, fashioning words from the rippling of the tent, from the hissing of the grasses. Elise woke to the sounds, disturbed, certain she had been listening to a voice.

Dreams, she told herself.

She lay on a cot, moonlight setting her pavilion aglow. She rolled from one side to the other, warm in the coverlets, not quite awake. If only she needn't wake at all. Any nightmare would be better than the one she lived.

The night breeze rose again, the sweet scent of grasses finding its way inside. The fabric of her tent moved, and she heard words as she slipped into a dream. Moonlight cast a shadow on the wall of her tent; a woman, erect and graceful, moving as slowly as the moon in its course.

"Who are you?" Elise asked.

"Who was I, you might ask, for I was once like you," the breeze whispered—the shadow of a shadow's voice. "I once lived beneath the heel of Caibre."

"Who?"

"You call him Hafydd." The shadow raised a hand to

brush back its hair. "It is time to choose, Elise. If you don't take up the quill and write the story of your life, others will write it for you. Do you want Hafydd to write your tale?"

Elise did not answer.

"I have come to offer you a quill that will allow you to write a story of greatness. It will allow you to break free of everyone who oppresses you and to protect those whom you love. I have come to offer you this quill, though at times it will appear to be a sword. Write the story of your life, Elise Wills, or let Hafydd fashion it for you. In Hafydd's tale he will take your children at birth and use them for his own ends. He will cast them aside when they are no longer needed—and you as well. Is that the story that you would choose to write?"

Elise shook her head, tears appearing at the corners of her eyes. "No," she whispered very faintly.

The shadow nodded once.

"But what will be the price of this gift you offer?" Elise asked.

"Part of your life will be mine," the nagar said, a whisper like cold wind.

"That is too great a price."

"Then give all your life to Hafydd. And the lives of your children, as well."

This stunned Elise to silence.

"Give some part of your life to me," the nagar said softly, "and I will cherish and protect you—you and your children, and their children after them."

"What choice have I?" Elise said, speaking her thoughts aloud.

"None."

She hesitated, then said in the smallest voice, "Then I must give some part of my life to you."

The nagar touched a hand to her heart, then to her lips as though she blew Elise a kiss. "Baore Talon will bring you a gift. Carry it into the river, and I will await you there." The shadow on the tent wall turned away.

"But I will drown!"

The shadow glanced back. "I will not let you pass the final gate. Do not fear."

A breeze sighed through the compound, disturbing the sleep of the trees. The fabric of the pavilion rippled like a wave, and the shadow was gone.

Elise woke with a gasp, sitting up in the darkness. There was a sound—soft, repetitive. A summer rain fell upon her pavilion like finger drumming, though the moonlight endured.

Outside, a guard cleared his throat.

Elise put a hand to her belly, caressing the soft curve of it, wondering if one could feel a second heart beating within.

FIFTY-FOUR

Llyn sat in the window of her room, worrying at a ring of embroidery. No significant progress was being made, for her attention was repeatedly drawn to the window and her garden beyond. Somewhere over the wall the second day of the fair drew to a close. Men, thrown from their horses, lay within their pavilions, some with injured pride, others with worse. She could only imagine what it was like.

Despite having made a life within the walls of her own rooms and her garden, there was still, somewhere buried inside, a small, almost extinguished yearning to be part of the larger world. To dine with her foolish, passionate family, to walk beneath the sun, unafraid, perhaps even to be courted before she grew old.

She drew a long breath. Such desires might not have been entirely extinguished, but they had been mastered long ago. It was her great strength and solace: unlike her cousins who were ruled by their passions, she had conquered desire. Nothing ruled Llyn Renné but the most dispassionate reason.

Oh, there had been that one evening of madness: the

costume ball that Dease had enticed her to. Only Dease would have thought of such a thing. Perhaps only he knew how truly lonely she was. But then Dease had never seen her face.

The sun fell behind the western towers, setting the sky aflame in a way that it did only a few times each year. She sat for a moment transfixed, her convictions wavering. It seemed even the sky must have a moment of passion, now and then.

She rose from her chair as the maid came to draw the curtains. No looking glass was allowed in her rooms, and Llyn never sat by a window when it might find her reflection. Llyn knew what she looked like; she did not need to be reminded.

The evening air slipped down the nearby hills, wafting over the wall like a soft, cool wave. She opened the door to her garden and stepped out onto the landing from which the stone stair descended.

"I am below," a voice said, and she almost jumped back.

"Who is that?" And then she realized. "Where is your fearsome herald?" she asked.

"That is what my brother asks, 'If your herald is the forecryer of death, who are you?' But Jac is off on some errand of his own this night, and I have taken the great liberty of sitting in your garden, waiting to speak with you."

"It is more than a liberty. It is a terrible discourtesy."

"For which I apologize humbly. It is difficult for me

to arrange an audience. Have you found the trail of my Knights?"

She dared to peek over the balustrade, hoping to catch a glimpse of this man, but he was seated too near with his back to the stone. Emboldened, she wandered down two of the ten steps.

"I have found the trail but not the Knights. Not yet. I know the name of the lieutenant in the Renné army who sent men north seeking your escaped Knights. I have the names of at least three of the men-at-arms who were sent. Whether any of these men recorded the fate of your Knights, I have not yet learned."

"I thank you for your efforts, but please don't give up yet. The knowledge is more valuable than you know."

"I am like a hound on the scent when I begin such a quest. You don't know how dogged I can be."

Alaan laughed at this poor jest. "I think I can imagine," he said. She heard him hesitate.

"What else have you come to ask of me?" she said flatly.

"I have come to beg your assistance."

"Beg?"

"I will beg if it's required, for what I must do is more important than anything I have attempted before."

Llyn sat down on the step. "Both you and your bird are harbingers of woe, it seems. I cannot bear suspense. What is the nature of this assistance you require?"

"Lady Elise Wills shall attend the costume ball here in Castle Renné."

"How very kind of her."

"She will be accompanied by a man . . ." She heard him take a long breath. "You know the history of your family. Have you read of a man named Hafydd?"

"Yes, he was an ally the Renné betrayed. He died at the Battle of Harrowdown, I believe."

"Your reputation as a scholar is well earned, I see. But your knowledge isn't quite complete. Hafydd still lives. He calls himself Eremon now and is a counselor to the Prince of Innes."

"But isn't this the man they say attacked a Fáel encampment and broke the Peace of the Fair?"

"The very one. He holds sway over the Prince. He swore he would find Elise Wills after she ran away and he did, unfortunately. But if I can steal her away again, the Prince will be angered and his counselor will lose face. Perhaps he will even lose his place in the Prince's household. Without Hafydd to goad him on the Prince won't be quite so ready to go to war."

"And what part could I possibly play in this, shut up here in my rooms as I am?"

"You have the same hair as Elise Wills, and are like enough to her in size and manner. Masked and wearing the same costume you could, very briefly, appear to be her."

"You require someone other than me," Llyn said firmly, her mouth suddenly dry, anger dousing all amusement.

"I dare not ask anyone else. I require a woman of such standing, and . . . sympathy, that even Hafydd would not dare harm her."

"What are you saying? That Hafydd will take pity on me because I am disfigured?" She was on her feet in an instant.

"Do not be insulted. It is true that you have the sympathy of all who know of you. It is not pity."

"It is pity! Do you think I am unaware of it?"

She could hear him breathing below—thinking of some new argument to get his way. Why did she not leave? Why did she not call for guards to carry him away?

"Two minstrels helped me whisk Elise Wills away from Braidon Castle. Hafydd had them murdered. I shall not put others at risk again, if it can be avoided. But he dare not do the same to the Lady Llyn Renné. There is enough honor among the nobles he requires as allies that he would not dare alienate them by such an act. You are safe from him. I can think of no one else. No one else who might be brave enough to do it." He paused for a beat. "Tell me this, at least. Do you never wish that you might play some part in the events of the world? That you might break out of your rooms and act, as Toren does, or your fair Dease?"

"Leave my cousins out of this," she said.

"I have left them out. It is only your services I require. I will not say that war will be averted if we are successful. That would be a lie. But if the Prince of Innes was to cast out his counselor he would be much weaker for it. The Prince has neither intelligence nor imagination. Without Hafydd he is greatly weakened."

Llyn drew a long breath and released it as a sigh.

"Usually only rogues are this convincing," Llyn said.

"Rogues and men who speak the truth," the stranger answered.

She sat down on the step again. "What do you require of me, other than I dress in a costume identical to Lady Elise's?"

"You will wear your costume concealed beneath a robe. Attend the ball, dance if you wish. When the moment comes I will switch you with Elise Wills."

Very softly she said, "But how long am I expected to maintain this charade? They will unmask me."

"They will not. Trust me in this."

"Are you certain?"

The smallest hesitation. "Nothing is utterly certain in this life."

She closed her eyes.

"Many lives might be spared if I am successful," the stranger said quickly. "Perhaps those of your own cousins. What would you not do to save Dease or Arden?"

"You are an awful man!" she said. "You know I would do anything to save them. I would show my disfigured face to everyone in the land if it would save a single life, though I fear that is an ordeal I would not survive."

"I would not insult you with a lie."

"No, you would insult me with the truth. I am an object of pity to all who know of me."

"There is a way to escape that," he said.

"And that would be?"

"To live among your fellow men and women."

She almost choked. "Better unwanted pity than undisguised horror. But then you have asked me to wear a disguise, haven't you?"

"Will you help me?"

"I don't even know your name."

"Alaan."

"Alaan. What a cruel and hateful man you are." She stood. "One of my maids is just my size. She takes all of my fittings. Now may I have my garden back?"

"I am gone," he said.

For a moment she stood listening. She heard nothing but the soft sounds of the breeze.

"Alaan . . .?"

She descended a few steps and peeked quickly around the corner. He was not there. She went seeking through the garden, but he was gone. Utterly and mysteriously gone.

FIFTY-FIVE

The Valemen took seriously the warning Elise had sent to the Fáel. They'd left the wanderers immediately and planned to move their camp at least every day, much as they had for the long journey down the River Wynnd. Cynddl had chosen to stay with them, perhaps concerned for their safety, and Tam thought that, to the eye, things appeared much as they had for the past weeks. They made their camp beside the river, though the Westbrook was not so broad and flowed lazily by as though it knew the sea was near. There was no need to hurry.

The thought of the Westbrook Fair unfolding only a short distance away frustrated them a little. It seemed a cruel joke that they had traveled so far and would not see the famous fair.

Cynddl bent over the bed of coals, tending his cooking, while Tam fletched an arrow. Baore was nodding, near to sleep, against the bole of a birch; and Fynnol sat off by himself keeping watch on the quiet river. Small gulls and terns went winging by, aloft on the day's last light; and flights of ducks slid, then settled, on the darkening waters.

The camp was far enough down the Westbrook that they were away from the masses who attended the fair. They had also taken some pains to hide themselves, though the fire was hardly secret. It would be put out completely after Cynddl had produced their meal.

"I wish I'd been present when you spoke with Rath," Tam said. He and Cynddl had been discussing, yet again, the story finder's meeting with his former teacher.

"I wish you had been, too. I was telling parts of your story secondhand. I'd rather he'd heard about Alaan from you." Cynddl turned the fish on a thin slab of stone set on the coals. "Baore seems very tired these days, Tam. One would think he didn't sleep at night."

"I'm afraid he doesn't," Tam said quietly, "not well, anyway. It's been a disturbing trip, all in all. And it doesn't seem to be turning out any better."

Cynddl nodded. "What will you do now, Tam?"

The question Tam had been asking himself. Get off the river: that was all they'd thought about. There was no more talk of finding Alaan now. "I'm not sure. Buy horses and make a dash for home, though I'm not certain this is the wisest course. Perhaps it would be better to stay here in the south till spring." Tam sighted along the arrow and spun it slowly. "No doubt we'd find some work to tide us over. Baore has his skills, and Fynnol and I can do an honest day's labor. Many's the time we worked in the fields of the Vale. There will be a harvest soon hereabouts."

"Yes," a voice behind Tam said, "you could spend your

days scything grain with noble peasants or plucking rosy apples, but it doesn't seem like much of an adventure, does it?"

Tam was on his feet. The man who stood at the edge of their encampment was only a silhouette, but Tam would have known that voice anywhere. "Alaan!"

The man made a tossing motion, and a small leather purse landed at Tam's feet.

"That's part of what is owed you. The rest I'll pay you when the fair is over."

Tam made no effort to retrieve the purse. Baore had wakened and rose, rubbing his eyes. All but Cynddl looked as though a ghost had drifted into their camp.

"You were more welcoming when last we met," Alaan said.

"You hadn't robbed us then," Fynnol answered, stepping forward and scooping up the purse.

"Robbed you?" Alaan took two steps out of shadow and into the faint light of dusk. "I held Telanon Bridge so that you might escape, and then I went into the river. Having lost my horse, belongings, and blade, my only hope of escape was your boat. Once I'd set off in that there was no turning back. The river flows only one way—especially in the far north. But even so, I would have brought you your silver one day. I always discharge my debts."

"Or partially discharge them, as in this case," Fynnol said. He had opened the purse strings and counted the coins.

"Rest assured, good Fynnol, I got a better price for your goods than you would ever have managed yourself."

"But will we see it all?" Fynnol said, not caring much if he insulted their visitor.

"Every eagle, Fynnol Loell. You can be certain of it." Alaan sat down on a rock and bent forward, elbows on his knees. Tam thought he looked a little leaner since they'd last met, not quite so well groomed. "But I have yet another reason to seek you out."

"Someone else you need robbed?" Fynnol said quickly.

"Have a care, Fynnol," Tam said. "He has come with our silver, and his accounting is sound enough. Alaan held the bridge so that we might escape. I've not forgotten that."

Fynnol held his peace, though not happily.

Alaan looked up at the Fáel. "I'm Alaan."

The story finder nodded. "And I am Cynddl."

"It is a pleasure to meet you. Pwyll told me of you. He said you are all archers of the first rank, though poor Gartnn was lost even so."

"You knew Gartnn?" Fynnol said.

Alaan clasped his hands together and looked down at the ground. "He was my friend. Gartnn and Elffen helped me spirit Elise Wills away."

"Then she really was Elise Wills?" Fynnol said. "The Fáel were not mistaken?"

"They were not mistaken in the least," Alaan said sadly. "But I was mistaken. Many people died. At least Gartnn and Elffen knew what the dangers were and accepted them. The others . . ."

The fire popped and sent a spray of sparks arcing into the air.

"What is it you've come to ask of us?" Baore said softly.

Alaan took a long breath and looked up at the big Valeman. "The men-at-arms who attacked us at Telanon Bridge served a man named Hafydd—"

"And they chased us down through the wildlands, almost killing Baore!" Fynnol said, unable to contain himself.

Alaan looked directly at Fynnol, and there was compassion there, even regret. "Yes, Hafydd is vengeful," he said evenly. "He killed Elffen for no other reason than that she aided me, and he will do the same to you, if ever he finds you."

"But we did not aid you!" Fynnol protested. "We merely let you share our fire."

"That is the truth, Fynnol, but Hafydd thinks otherwise. You were seen to defend Elise from Hafydd's men, aiding her escape. He is sure you are allies of mine now, and I will tell you: this places you in grave danger." He drew another breath, as though what he had to say was difficult. "You might manage to return to the Vale and you might even live in peace there, but I think it unlikely. Hafydd's desire to eliminate all who oppose him is inhuman in its depth and passion. I think he will eventually find you, and perhaps you will not be the only victims."

The Valemen said nothing, and then looked from one to the other, their faces shadowed in the failing light. "Then what are we to do?" Baore said, almost in a whisper.

"I will steal Elise Wills back from Hafydd." Alaan hesitated. "And if I can I will put an end to Hafydd's desire for vengeance."

"You will kill him, then?" Tam said.

Alaan nodded.

"Why should we be party to murder?" Cynddl asked.

Alaan looked up at the story finder. "To save your own lives and because Hafydd has killed many, or had them killed. You saw what was done in the Fáel encampment. How many innocent people died that night? Many thousands more will die if Hafydd is not stopped." He looked from one man to the next. "What say you?"

"I say we are not murderers," Tam answered slowly.

"Then you will be the victims of a murderer," Alaan said, "you and whoever else might be nearby when Hafydd's minions find you." He sat up, scuffing his feet and lifting his hands as though agitated. "I know it's a terrible choice I've come to offer you, but you have a right to defend yourselves and your families. You can do that at a time and place of your choosing or a time and place of Hafydd's choosing. I don't think I need to tell you in which situation you will have the advantage."

"It will be a time and place of your choosing, I think," Fynnol said.

Alaan nodded. "That is true, but I know Hafydd better than you. Would you rather choose the time and place? Would you even know how to begin?"

Fynnol shook his head.

Tam glanced at the others, who all were grim and

stone-faced. "We need time to consider," he answered.

"There is no time to consider. You are either Hafydd's enemies or his victims. Which will it be?"

The silence stretched like a strand of web, and finally it was Baore who broke it.

"I will help you," the big man said. "Perhaps you don't need the others."

"Noble of you to hold such hopes, Baore, but I need bowmen." He looked from Tam to Cynddl. "Enemies or victims? Which do I see?"

"Enemies," Tam heard himself say, and Cynddl nodded his agreement.

Alaan bowed his head in acknowledgment.

"But don't show your face again without the rest of our silver," Fynnol said angrily. "When we told Eber son of Eiresit that you were dead he gave us your flute to deliver to a man named A'brgail. We have it yet and will trade it for the rest of our silver."

Alaan's gaze flicked to Fynnol like the point of a sword. "You found Eber's house?" he said incredulously.

They all nodded.

"He didn't give you my flute!"

"Oh, but he did!" Fynnol said, and not without a certain glee. "Show him, Cynddl."

Cynddl reached inside his vest and removed the wooden box polished by age. Alaan looked as though he would lunge forward and grab it, but Baore stepped nearer, catching Alaan's eye. The traveler stayed where he was.

"We know about your flute and the nagar," Fynnol

said. "If you want it back, deliver our silver."

Tam thought Alaan looked unsure for the first time since they'd met. "Keep it safe," he said, "and whatever you do don't let it fall into Hafydd's hands! I will bring your silver, do not fear."

Alaan stepped carefully out into the dark wood. For a long time no one spoke, then Fynnol said, "Is this where our journey from the Vale has led us? To committing murder?"

"The Vale is a long way away," Baore said. "A long way on a strange river. We are caught in the middle of some other men's war. We do what we must to survive." Saying this, he took his whetstone from his bag and began honing their weapons.

Tam woke to the sounds of whispering, and found the moon had lit in a nest of cloud.

"Tam?" Cynddl stood a few feet away.

"Yes?"

"Baore is gone."

Tam was up at once, pulling on his boots. His sword slid silently from its scabbard, and he and Cynddl went to the edge of the running water. The moon fledged from a nest of cloud and its pale light swept over the river.

"The boat is still here," Cynddl said. "I would guess he's either up the bank or down."

"Up," Tam said, and they set off along the narrow beach, Cynddl in the lead.

They'd not gone fifty paces when Cynddl suddenly crouched. Over the story finder's head Tam could see a shirtless Baore, kneeling on a rock. Before him in the water was the nagar, ashen and ghostly. She reached out her hands to him, and reluctantly Baore reached out to her.

"Baore!" Tam shouted without thinking. The nagar spun toward them, baring its teeth in a hiss. And then it was gone, the waters closing over it with barely a ripple.

For a moment Baore stayed as he was, and Cynddl and Tam scrambled along the bank to him, though they kept an eye on the river. Tam noticed that Cynddl seemed to shy back from the water a little. Baore still crouched by the river, gazing at the moonlight playing over its surface.

"Baore?" Tam said softly.

Baore nodded, but it seemed difficult for him. He shook his head a little and tried to rise, but lost his balance. Tam and Cynddl supported him.

"Did you see the nagar?" the big man rasped.

"It was here in the water before you," Tam said, trying not to let his fear sound in his voice.

Baore nodded. "It seems so much like a dream."

"Baore, tell me you didn't make a bargain with the nagar," Cynddl said.

Baore turned toward the story finder, his eyes focusing finally. He looked so different from the young man who'd left the Vale: wan and gaunt and haunted, Tam thought.

"I made no bargains, but it was she who carried me back to life. I owe her that, even though I refused her. One small task is all she asks."

"And what might that be?" Tam said, the entire idea leaving him cold.

Baore shook his head. "Don't meddle in the affairs of the nagar, Tam. I don't say this lightly."

Baore brushed past them and set off back toward the camp. Tam and Cynddl stood and watched him go, a massive, dark silhouette passing quietly along the river-bank. *A night animal,* Tam thought, *silent and secretive.*

FIFTY-SIX

There was, at the Westbrook Fair, entertainment every night after the day's competitions. Some of these entertainments were official, but most were not; for there would be dancing on the green and minstrels playing at the inns, in the square, on boats, and beneath the trees. Lords invited guests to their pavilions for suppers and music and dancing as well. Heroes were toasted and had the smiles of all the young women turned upon them, and the vanquished attempted to be gracious in defeat and to put on a brave face—which often took more pluck than meeting their opponents on the field.

At the end of the day's competitions there was a celebration in the Guildhall where the minstrels had taken their turns before Lord Carral Wills and his judges. Now it was the turn of the gathered minstrels to measure the skills of the judge.

"It is only fair that I should take a turn. That I should set myself up to be knocked down." So Lord Carral had said to Prince Michael.

The Prince found Lord Carral waiting in a small room

the guild used for business. He was bent over his Fáellute, performing exercises to limber his fingers.

"Lord Carral," the Prince said.

"Ah, Prince Michael!" Carral's face lit in a stiff smile. "Have you not had enough of minstrels for one day?"

"Not when the minstrel is you, sir. But I have come for another reason. I need to speak with you and have not had a moment to do so all day."

Carral's face changed, returning to its customary blankness. "If you don't mind," he said to his servants and several admirers who had managed to find their way into the room.

When they were alone, despite having rehearsed his speech a dozen times, Michael did not know what to say. That he had met a man upon the road and this man had asked that he approach Lord Carral to announce his daughter's betrothal? Anyone speaking thus would have to be daft.

"I have a plan to save your daughter," he said instead, plunging in.

Carral's face remained impassive, but his hands found each other. "I had hoped someone would. I have no way of doing it alone."

"I need your help, however."

"Whatever I can do, I will, but you must be careful not to ask me to play the part of a man with sight."

"No, nothing like. You need only make an announcement." It was impossible for the Prince to read the blind man's face, it was so devoid of normal expression. "This very night you must announce that Lady Elise and I are to wed."

The blind man seemed almost to twitch, he moved so quickly, reeling a little in his chair. "But is this not the very thing we've tried to avoid?"

"Yes, but there is no choice now. You must make this announcement and say also—and this is critical—that all may bring their best wishes to us at the Renné ball."

"What in the world are you thinking, Michael? It is enough that Menwyn and your father make this alliance, but do they need to slap the Renné in the face as well?"

"I'm afraid that can't be helped. If she is at the ball, in costume, we might find a way to slip her out."

"We?"

"There are others."

"Well, she is my daughter. I have a right to know what danger you might put her in. I'm blind, you know, not stupid!"

The Prince plopped down in a chair, staring at the man before him, touched by his concern and frustration. How terribly helpless he must feel at times.

"Lord Carral, I will confess to you that I don't know the plan myself. I—It has been arranged by others."

"Oh, you've not been visited by a ghost as well!"

"Sir?"

"Who has arranged this?"

"I don't know the man's name."

Lord Carral set his Fáellute aside. "Tell me about him." The Prince took a deep breath, certain this story would insure Lord Carral's refusal of cooperation. "I met him at the side of the road as I returned from visiting the Fáel. He seemed to be waiting for me." Prince Michael found he could not continue like this. "He was the man Hafydd pursued from Braidon Castle, Lord Carral."

"Ah," Lord Carral said, and put a hand to his face, a gesture a sighted man might make.

"Hafydd calls him his whist. I know no more than that."

"I know little more myself, other than that he failed once and people died as a result. I don't know if I will trust him again. Though it likely won't matter—your father will never let Elise come to the ball. Why would he? Your plan is too transparent. If she were at the Renné ball surely she would try to escape."

"Oh, the plan is meant to be transparent. Hafydd will bring Elise to the ball to draw this man, the whist, out of hiding. My father's counselor has a hatred for this man that is beyond description."

"And Elise will be in the middle of this feud?"

"She has been in the middle of a feud all her life, though you've tried to protect her from it. I don't know that we have any other course, unless you can devise a better plan. I have talked to Elise. Hafydd told her that she must marry me and bear a child. When she suggested that we might not comply, Hafydd told her plainly that she could bear my child or his. We must get her away."

Lord Carral sat very still. "It is a good thing I have no

sight, Prince Michael, for I would murder my own brother, who has offered up my precious daughter like a sacrifice to this demon. And then I would slay this monster Hafydd, no matter what it cost me."

Prince Michael stood before his father and Hafydd, having told them of Lord Carral's announcement. His father's rage was immediate, requiring not an instant of thought.

"What in the world is this blind man up to? And what did you say to him?"

"Why, nothing, Father."

His father's rather narrow eyes went wide. "We will not let her attend so that she can denounce us and accuse us of abducting her and attacking the Fáel." He glared at Hafydd as he said this. The counselor didn't seem to notice.

"This minstrel must think us idiots," the old prince went on. "Has he conspired with the Renné, do you think? He and Toren Renné would make a good marriage. They haven't a spine between them."

"I think she should attend," Hafydd said, his voice calm.

Prince Michael thought he saw a hint of a smile flicker across the man's face. His father stared at his counselor as though he thought the man had gone mad.

"She will run off," the old prince said. "In a room full of masked revelers, after all, it wouldn't be difficult."

"Oh, I think we can prevent that," Hafydd said evenly.

"We'll have sufficient numbers there to watch over her. Think of it, my Prince, all the nobles in the land will bring their good wishes to the happy couple. And the Renné can watch us cement our alliance in their own hall. That will be the greatest triumph at the Westbrook Fair—far greater than Toren Renné's. How shall we costume them?" He feigned to think. "Who were the children of Easal and Llynn?"

"Elyse and Mwynfawr, as you well know," Prince Michael said. These were the children of the swans, hatched from stones, from whom the line of kings was said to descend.

"That is it," Hafydd said. "You see, your learning is good for something. You will go as Elyse and Mwynfawr."

"And shall we take a brace of crow, broiled and basted, for the Renné to eat as well?" Prince Michael asked.

"I should not go to so much trouble for the Renné," Hafydd said. "Let them eat their crow raw and feathered."

They spoke in whispers so that Prince Michael's aunt would not hear.

"It seems all too obvious to me," Elise whispered.

"Certainly Hafydd saw right away that the announcement was contrived to bring you to the ball, but he is so fervid in his pursuit of this man he calls the whist that he doesn't care. Only bring this man within his grasp and Hafydd would sacrifice everyone and everything. That is how it seems to me."

"That is what Alaan said as well. I wonder why?" Elise seemed young and frail to him that night. A child in need of comforting.

"I don't really know. Hafydd doesn't brook interference in his plans and is vengeful like no man I've ever known, but somehow I sense it is more than that. I don't know why."

Elise nodded. She had sunk down in her chair and laid her head against the back, leaning near to the Prince so that they might whisper. Her mane of hair framed her pale face—pale and frightened. "It seems we have no choice but to go along with this plan," Elise said, "whatever it might be."

"I can't argue against that," he said. "We are to go as Elyse and Mwynfawr."

She shook her head. "Hafydd is more vengeful than any Wills."

He nodded.

"How fares my father?"

"Well enough, though worried about you. He is reluctant to trust this minstrel again. He has failed once."

"Were there another choice . . ." A brief silence. He listened to her soft breathing. "Michael? I am afraid of Hafydd."

"I have been told such fear is wisdom."

It was the shortest night of the year, yet full of dreams. Elise kept drifting in and out of sleep, sinking down into the river of her dream world, then bobbing gently to the surface. She would open her eyes, see the moonlight on her tent, hear the night sounds, then drift off again on the currents of sleep, spinning slowly beneath a dreamer's moon.

The sounds of the breeze mingled with the river sounds and the song of the moon, creating a voice. A voice which seemed to whisper across the leagues of history. It was the nagar's voice, cunning and pleasing, offering her escape. Escape into the depths of the river, into a sleep like oblivion.

FİFŤY-SEVEΠ

The news came like a sudden, hard frost, spreading across the valley of the Westbrook and killing the blossoming joy of the fair.

The Fáel had been attacked and men had died.

The marshals of the fair had gone to the Prince of Innes, accusing his counselor of the crime, demanding he be surrendered to justice. But the Prince had denied all accusations and refused the marshals, turning them away from the gate of his compound.

The Renné descended on Toren the moment the news reached them, four of them arriving at almost the same moment. They gathered in the courtyard beneath a spreading oak, hot after their day's exertions in the tournament.

"What were you thinking, Cousin?" Beldor asked. He stood, too agitated to sit.

Toren returned the anger of his cousin's stare with a mild look. "That the Peace of the Fair had been broken, and that this was wrong. Wrong for the Prince of Innes, hence wrong for the Renné to do the same. The marshals are the law for the duration of the Westbrook Fair. I sent the legitimate representatives of justice."

"The Peace of the Fair has already been breached," Samul said, "and not by the Renné. We did not begin this, Toren. Now, while we have enough force and the Prince of Innes is weak, we should put a stop to this alliance that threatens us." Samul sat stiffly on a bench, staring at the others, his face drawn and pale like a man who had suffered terrible insult.

Toren stood, not in the least intimidated by his cousins. Dease had to admire his conviction, his belief that he was right.

"The Renné are not only signatories to the Peace of the Fair," Toren said, still not raising his voice, "but our family wrote the document. A peace that has lasted more than a hundred years. If we break it now, that peace will be gone forever. Do you not see? We forged a peace here, in this tiny corner of old Ayr, by allowing the law to replace ill-considered reprisal. If we can do that here we can do it in the larger world. It only takes the will. But throw away the law and revert to vengeance and retaliation and we return to the feud that has lasted nine generations. Yes, Innes has done wrong. Yes, he should be punished, but we do not have the right to ride into his encampment in force and enact our will. The Renné are not the marshals of the fair. Innes will be banned from the fair in the future. I'm sure that is what the marshals will decide. That is all that can be done."

"He forges an alliance against us!" Beldor almost hollered. His customary manner of a man about to lose control of his rage was exaggerated this day. Dease stood ready to spring to Toren's defense, for it was all Beldor could do to not commit the murder at that moment. "Samul is right. We should mount what force we can and ride on the Prince's compound. This toady Eremon plots against us; everyone knows it. Let him pay the price of attacking the Fáel. Then the peace will be preserved, for others will know the cost of breaking it."

Toren looked to Dease, exasperated. "Eremon is our old friend Hafydd, Beld. At least know who you will go to war against."

"Hafydd died upon the field twenty years ago."

"He did not die. He was delivered from the Renné who betrayed him, and now he will have his revenge upon us. But there is more: Hafydd has uncovered some of the secrets of the Knights of the Vow. We dare not ride against him until we know more."

"Now there is a story to frighten children!" Beld said, a smirk spreading over his face.

"How do you know this, Toren?" Samul asked, looking wary suddenly.

"It has been reported to me by a man whose honor and loyalty are beyond question. I can tell you no more than that."

Samul glanced quickly at Dease, as though asking him to confirm this information. Dease shrugged.

Beldor looked around at the others, his look dark. "And so we are to accept this? Accept that we should do nothing, and let the Prince of Innes think us fainthearted? The strong prey on the weak, Toren. It is the way of the world. To appear weak is to invite attack from one's enemies. I say we muster our men-at-arms and ride on the Prince of Innes this night. Let the Prince see that we do not hesitate in the cause of justice. Let his counselor pay for his crime, and the Prince will go back to his keep and think again about this alliance he makes with Menwyn Wills."

"It is not your decision to make, Beld," Toren said calmly.

"Nor is it yours!" Beld shouted.

"It is mine. I stand in my father's place, and I will not breach the Peace of the Fair. Let it not be said that the Renné have as little honor as the Prince of Innes and his counselor."

"Yes, let them say instead that we are craven and that we are led by a man who preaches peace but is too timid to uphold it. That he let it slip away and brought war upon all the lands because he was not resolute when it was needed. Let them say that, for it will be true!"

"Beldor!" Dease cautioned, moving to place himself between his cousins.

Toren and Beldor stood glaring at each other, Beld with his mouth hanging open, his eyes wide, and his fists in knots. Toren cold and imperious.

"You have called me coward too often, Cousin," Toren said, his voice even and perfectly controlled. "Perhaps we will meet at the tilt tomorrow and you can show the others how fainthearted I am . . . That is if you can keep to your saddle that long."

Toren spun and walked back indoors leaving the others to push Beld out the gate.

"Clearly it was a mistake to wait until now to do what had to be done," Samul said.

Arden sat with his back against the tree, apart from the others. He had said almost nothing, and Dease did not like the way Arden's gaze kept slipping to the ground whenever any of the others spoke to him.

"We waited until now so that we could make it seem as if the deed had been done by the Wills," Arden said flatly.

They sat upon Summer's Hill, the very place where they had first made the decision to slay their cousin. The land rolled out beneath them, the roofs of Westbrook among the trees near the distant river.

"Though it will never be believed, now," Dease said. "Toren's inaction serves the Wills' purpose admirably. They would never murder a man whose beliefs so aided their cause. No, it will seem much more likely that Toren was murdered by one of us, who oppose him. That is what anyone with half a wit will believe."

Beld pointed a finger at him. "I knew you would not go through with it, Dease," Beld said, his voice filled with disdain. "I knew your nerve would break. But mine will not."

"It is not your nerve which carries you forward, Beldor," Dease said. "It is your hatred and jealousy. Do not try to convince us, who know you, that you do this to save the Renné."

"Enough of this!" Samul said. "Dease, it doesn't matter what others think. The arrow will belong to a Wills. Nothing else will be known. It is enough. We must go ahead. It is more important than ever. Menwyn Wills and the Prince of Innes prepare to go to war against us and we do nothing. Our allies are uneasy, afraid that Toren will delay too long, trying to make peace, and then it will be too late to make a defense. And what will happen to our allies then? Some will change allegiance rather than be overrun. We must go ahead with our plan or the Renné will be in danger of being eradicated at last." He looked at Dease. "Have you lost your taste for it, Cousin?"

"I've never had the taste for it, Samul, but you are right. We must go ahead, and if we are accused . . . well, accusations are not enough to condemn us. Tomorrow night as we planned. I have arrows stolen from one of the Wills who is entered in the archery contest. He feathers them in the manner of the Fáel though in the Wills's colors. They will be easily recognized."

Samul nodded. "Then we will continue as we agreed. Dease will do what must be done, and Beld will witness. Arden? Are you with us yet?"

Arden lifted his head, hesitating a moment. "Aye, though my heart is heavy with the weight of it." He turned to Dease, fixing him with a watery gaze. "I pity you, Dease . . ." He would have said more, but he shook his head and turned away, hiding his face from the others.

FIFTY-EIGHT

Midsummer's day was hot with only the smallest breeze to flutter the banners flying over the tilt field. Sand swirled up like whirling spirits who careened around the yard and then collapsed suddenly as though the spell that sustained them had broken.

The day's jousting was nearly done, Arden, Beld, and Toren defending the Renné honor at the tilt. Only one knight remained to stop their virtual sweep of the field; and he was an unknown, having appeared on the first day and won several mounts and suits of armor from those who opposed him. Dease had withdrawn after taking an errant lance strike to his knee, and he limped terribly about the field, watching. Without proper use of his leg he could not control his mount.

The truth was, Arden did not care who won or lost that day, for all the joy had gone out of the tourney for him. His cousins had chosen to go ahead with their treachery; and Arden had been awake all that night, walking along the riverbank until he was far from Westbrook. The drifting moon had lit his way, pacing him along the river, casting its light down upon the surface in a silvered path. Arden had wished that he could walk out onto that path and up into the silent heavens. Anything to escape the infamy to which he had assented.

Dease and Samul were right—Toren would lead the family to ruin with his intractable belief in honor and his naive pursuit of peace. All well and good in stories of chivalry, but leaders in the real world could not afford to be so idealistic.

Yet Toren was also right. Once you surrendered your honor where would it lead? To treachery and murder, it seemed.

Treachery and murder.

The marshals were signaling the heralds to blow their horns and call the next riders forth. Arden was to ride against the upstart, and Toren against Beld. Arden might no longer care if he won or lost, but he was sure this was not the same between Beld and Toren. Both would be determined to unseat the other. Pure strength would be matched against skill, for Toren was the consummate horseman and could aim a lance, at speed, with a precision Arden had never seen before.

The horns sounded and he spurred his horse forward. Three passes they would ride. The marshals would tally the lances broken, unless one was unhorsed, which would end the contest. The rider at the far end of the tilt—the long barrier which divided the riders from each other and eliminated the possibility of collision—dipped his lance to Arden, who returned the salute.

The marshal raised his flag, held it aloft. A bead of sweat ran down Arden's forehead and collected on the tip of his nose. Through the slits of his jousting helm he concentrated on the rider at the other end of the tilt, the marshal's flag just visible out of the corner of his eye.

When the flag fell he spurred his horse forward, trying to bring all of his attention onto the rider bearing down on him, but his focus would not hold; and in a moment a lance splintered against his shield, throwing him back, while his own had glanced ineffectively off the other rider's shield.

A cheer went up from the crowd. A mark would be recorded by the marshals for the upstart. Arden rode back, and found Toren waiting for him with a lance in his hand.

"Take this," he said, passing the lance up to Arden. "That last was of little use." Toren stood a moment in silence, his burnished face aglow in the sun, ringed by a hood of mail. His surcoat of Renné blue rippled in the wind, the swans on his chest seeming to be reflected in moving water.

How vital and alive he looks, Arden thought.

"I don't know what is on your mind, Cousin," Toren said, "but this stranger is formidable. You will not best him with your thoughts elsewhere, that is certain. Whatever it is that distracts you, put it aside until the joust is complete. You can wool-gather all you want then." Then his serious face split in a grin. "And if you do not, I shall miss my chance to topple you once more before the season draws to a close."

The heralds sounded their horns, and Arden returned to the tilt, trying not to smile. Toren usually knew what to say and do to pull Arden's attention back to the moment, but this day nothing mattered to Arden. He did not seem to care if he was injured or even if he was killed. In some ways it would be better if he was.

Yes, he thought, as he stared at the knight opposite, *spare me my infamy for what will be done.*

The flag fell and Arden spurred his horse forward. He tried hard to concentrate his mind, if only to not disappoint Toren. The rider bearing down on him was moving at ferocious speed. Arden set his lance and at the last second stood up in his stirrups, thrusting forward.

A lance struck his shield, knocking Arden askew in his saddle, but he pulled himself upright and realized his own lance had shattered. A better effort, though he'd nearly lost his saddle.

Toren waited for him again, lance in hand, but a runner from the marshals interrupted them.

"The marshals send a reminder to drop your lance immediately upon its breaking, Lord Arden."

Arden bowed his head. "Take them my apologies. I shall drop it the instant it shatters."

"Do that, Arden," Toren said. "Don't forget what befell our uncle." He shook his head. "You've not held on to a shattered lance in three years." Toren tapped his temple. "I will knock you from your saddle in one pass, if you're still asleep when we meet."

Arden returned to his place. His opponent's horse

danced in place, impatient to begin. Arden seemed to notice the man at the far end of the tilt for the first time: large and strongly knit. His arms and armor looked well used, as though he'd been off fighting in some unknown war. And his horse was astonishing—perhaps the best horse in the tourney. For a brief second greed kindled in Arden. How he'd like to win that beast!

The heralds sounded their horns and Arden tried to pull his focus back. At the other end of the tilt the knight leveled his lance to do Arden harm. *What madness this is,* he thought. *Why do I engage in this brutal sport when I could be courting women and listening to minstrels and storytellers?*

The flag dropped and Arden sent his mount forward. It was all he could do to aim his lance, the entire endeavor seemed so foolish suddenly. And then he seemed to hit a wall, and he was bent cruelly back, tumbling from his saddle. He hit the sand, gouging a furrow, and then rolled, the world spinning through the slits in his helm. When he came to rest he had sand in his eyes.

His first thought was not *I have failed at Westbrook*, but *thank all the spirits that it is over.*

Dease sat in the stands, cursing the knight who had disabled him, the pain in his knee causing him to grit his teeth so ferociously that his jaw throbbed almost as fiercely as his leg.

Samul took a seat beside him. Dease acknowledged his cousin with a grimace.

"I do not think you will be dancing this evening," Samul said. "Will you have to withdraw from your obligations?" He gazed fixedly at his cousin as he asked this.

"I can hobble as fast as Beld can run. Do not be concerned."

Samul nodded. "I have just spoken with Beld."

"How fortunate you are."

"He is concerned about Arden."

"He is concerned about no one, Cousin, and you know it."

"He thinks Arden has lost his nerve," Samul said, gesturing to the tilt field. "I have not seen him joust so poorly since he was a boy."

"Beldor is suspicious of everyone. What do you propose be done?"

"I don't know. There is no way of releasing Arden from his . . . responsibilities."

"That is true." Dease pitched his voice low. "He is racked by guilt and misgivings—as am I. Do you doubt me as well?" Dease turned to his cousin, not meaning this to be a challenge.

"I do not doubt you, Dease," Samul said softly.

"Then we should not doubt Arden. He is the most honorable of us. Treachery does not come as easily to him as it does to some."

"Speak quietly, Dease," Samul cautioned.

"It is my leg, Samul. It makes me short-tempered." He took a few breaths to calm himself. "Arden is unhurt?"

"Bruised ribs and pride, though I don't think he much cared."

Dease considered a moment. "Perhaps you should keep Arden under your watchful eye the rest of this day and this evening."

"I thought you trusted him?"

"Yes, but I trust him because he is honorable."

Samul was silent a moment. "Here is Beldor," he said finally.

And indeed, their cousin had taken the field. And at the opposite end of the tilt, Toren sat very erect on his horse.

"He is proud, isn't he?" Dease said.

"He is enraged," Samul answered. "And you know how Toren gets when he is so. Beldor is blinded by his hatred of Toren. But Toren's anger only concentrates his mind. He is more deadly now than ever. Beldor thinks his rage will give him strength, but it will not matter—not this day."

The heralds sounded their horns, and lances were lowered. Dease closed his eyes a second as pain gripped his knee in its jaws. When he opened his eyes Toren and Beldor were hurtling toward each other.

In his rage Beld had urged his horse to speed, and, never a proficient horseman, he bounced in the saddle like a sack of turnips. Toren, on the other hand, sat with grace, his gray making a speed equal to Beld's. Plumes fluttered in helms. Sand flew from hooves. And then there was the shock of their collision. Beld was thrown back, grasping for his pommel, his own lance bouncing harmlessly on the ground.

Toren had broken a lance, which the marshals duly recorded. "Toren toys with him," Samul said. "Did you see him knock Beld's lance aside with his own, and still he shattered a lance upon Beld's shield? Could you manage that at such speed?"

Dease shook his head. He would have said that no one could.

On the second pass Toren lifted his shield at the last second and batted Beld's lance tip aside, while cleanly breaking a second lance. This display brought a great cheer from the crowd, for Toren was their favorite and Beld was disliked, as was his lot everywhere.

Dease and Samul glanced at each other.

"Beld should never have called him coward," Dease whispered as the cheering died away and the knights rode back to their places again. Toren must have said something to Beld as they passed for Beld shook his fist at him and shouted a curse that could be heard at the top of the stands.

Again Dease and Samul shared a glance. Who would be thought most likely to hate Toren after today's encounter?

The third pass was signaled and the horses sprinted along their respective sides of the tilt fence. It seemed to Dease that, despite the speed of the horses, they took an unusually long time to meet. And when they did Beld was hurled violently from his saddle, turning completely in the air so that he landed upon his face, where he lay very still.

All the crowd stood and, after the initial cheer, were silent, watching the equerries run out onto the field. They bent over Beld, who still had not moved, only the breeze rippling his surcoat.

But then the big man moved his arm and raised himself shakily to hands and knees. His squires removed his helm and he sat back on his haunches, hands to his head. With assistance he stood and made his way off the field, as Toren rode before the Renné box to receive the favor of his own mother.

Samul turned to Dease and raised his eyebrows. "Perhaps Beld will be unfit for further activity this day," he said.

"I rather doubt Beld will miss what is to come. He has dreamed of it his entire life." Dease rose from his seat suddenly.

"Will you come to the ball?" Samul asked.

"Yes. Nothing must appear amiss. But I have two costumes: the messenger of death and an ass. Which shall I wear this night?"

"Come as a man who would sacrifice even his honor to preserve his family."

"Now that would be a masquerade, indeed," Dease said, and left Samul standing among the crowd that was cheering their cousin as a hero. Cheering him as though he were their own loved brother.

* * *

Tam and the others had ventured forth from hiding, lured by the last day of the Westbrook Fair—and the final contest of mounted knights. Seeing the size of the crowd, Tam wondered if they had not been too timid. How would this man Hafydd and his black-clad minions ever find them among such a sea of humanity? It would be like looking for one particular wave upon the open ocean.

At least they would have this story to tell: they would see the greatest tourneyer of their time, Toren Renné, ride against an upstart.

The four of them sat on a hill, overlooking the tilt field, the stands, and the river beyond. The day was midsummer warm, though relieved by a soft breeze laden with the sweet scent of fresh-cut hay. Clouds bubbled and tumbled into the distance, chasing their shadows across wood and meadow. It was a glorious day for a fair, Tam thought.

Fynnol suddenly pointed to the field. "Do we not know that horse?" he said.

The knights had taken the field for the final contest— Lord Toren Renné against a man whose name no one had known but two days before.

"Alaan's messenger!" Tam said. "What did he call himself?"

"Pwyll," Cynddl said. "Certainly that is his horse. There can't be two such animals in all of Ayr."

The stranger wore a round, flat-topped jousting helm that hid his face. There was nothing to mark him as Alaan's messenger but his magnificent horse. The muscles and shining copper coat showed where the trappings did not cover. But almost more than that it was his bearing and manner of going that marked him, for he was lively and alert as few horses were. Even Cloud, the great gray of Toren Renné, did not compare.

"If they were jousting wide," Cynddl said, "without the tilt fence, I should say that Alaan's messenger could simply ride his opponents down—though, of course, it is not allowed."

"Pwyll Stagshanks," a young man sitting near them said. "That's what they call him. He's come from some distant duchy and has triumphed over the best knights at Westbrook. Some are saying he will stand first at the end of the day."

The heralds sounded their horns then, and the riders dipped their lances in salute. The stranger wore a surcoat of white trimmed with crimson, a shining black horse-tail on his helm. His saddle was plain, and his shield bore only a high-stepping charger upon a field of gold and nothing more.

Toren Renné wore the sky blue of the Renné, the double swan upon this shield. His saddle was trimmed in silver, and sweet-voiced bells jingled on his harness. A caparison of the same colors covered his famous gray, and his jousting helm was damasked with the gold figures of an eagle and a swan.

"Let us wager," Fynnol said. "I will take the stranger over this coddled lord. What say you, Tam? The loser shall buy ale all around."

"Then I have no choice but to take the Renné," Tam said. "But it's not the horse that levels the lance, so I'm happy."

The flag dropped, and both riders spurred their horses forward, closing at a speed that took everyone by surprise. The sound of wood shattering could be heard all up the hillside, and when the marshals collected the lances from the ground it was found the stranger's had shattered well up its shaft, while the Renné's had broken only at the tip. A mark upon the cheque for Alaan's messenger.

"Now you see, Tam," Fynnol said, "when a man saves your life you must not abandon him and place your hopes with another. Alaan's messenger will carry the day. You will regret your choice."

"But what kind of wager would it have been had we both placed our hopes on the same rider?" Tam laughed.

"A thin excuse for disloyalty, Cousin. A very thin excuse."

"I think the Renné was betrayed by bad wood," Baore said. "His equerry should read the grain of his lances more carefully."

Tam and Fynnol glanced at each other. Baore had spoken so little these last weeks that showing an interest in anything at all encouraged them.

There was an odd hush among the onlookers, and Tam could feel their tension. Could their champion lose to an upstart? Toren Renné had carried victory with him everywhere this season. Many said he was the most skilled tourneyer in half a century.

The horns were sounded for the second pass, and the marshal raised his flag. It dropped, and the sound of hooves pounding over sand was all the noise to be heard.

The knights pressed their horses forward even more quickly this time, and it seemed certain that such speed would see one of them hurled from the saddle. But when they met there was only the sharp crack of breaking wood, and the horsemen passed each other by.

This time the mark went to the Renné, who splintered his lance on the other's shield. Pwyll Stagshanks had managed only a glancing blow. And the crowd roared its approval. Flowers rained from the stands, and the crowd on the hill took up Toren's name as a chant.

"I don't think either of these riders can unhorse the other," Cynddl said over the noise. "They're too strong and sit upon their mounts as though they had grown there."

"Can there be no winner?" Fynnol asked.

"No. If both were to shatter their lances on the next pass they would run three more, and then three more again until a winner was declared. It is uncommon for any contest to exceed three passes, and almost unheard-of for one to require more than six—though there was a famous contest, here at Westbrook fifty-some years ago, where the knights rode nine passes before a winner could be named. Nine passes!"

"Then I think these knights might ride twelve," Tam said, "for I believe we're watching a passage of arms that will be celebrated in song for years to come."

The knights took their places again, their horses prancing with excitement. The crowd fell silent, and Tam could feel them all leaning forward in anticipation. Again the flag was raised—and fell like a standard in battle. The knights appeared to have lost none of their eagerness, for they rode again as fast as they had.

The collision was like a hammer splitting stone, and in the rush of the horses passing someone was hurled from his saddle. Everyone jumped to his feet.

"It is both riders!" Cynddl cried, pointing.

And he was right, for the horses went on riderless, equerries running out to catch them and others racing toward their masters. Silence again descended, but everyone remained standing.

"Who will not rise?" Fynnol said.

But both knights rose, lifting up a gauntleted hand to indicate they would continue.

"Well, I have never seen that before," Cynddl said. "It is more uncommon than riding nine passes, I think. Especially among knights of such prowess."

The two men-at-arms stopped at the tilt fence and spoke for a moment and then saluted before returning to their places.

"Do you see, there?" a broad-faced old farmer who sat near them said. "These be nobles as nobles once were. Upon this morn, Lord Beldor Renné cursed his own cousin and foretold his doom upon the field. But it were the gracious Lord Toren who triumphed, and the foul-mouthed cousin who rode a saddle of sand. But these men speak fairly and salute when they part. They be not rabble but courteous, fair-spoken men each deserving of the prize."

Tam looked down at the scene spread before him and tried to fix it in his mind so that he might recall it when he was as old as their neighbor: the canopied stands where the nobility sat in all their finery, the tilt running along the center of the strip of sand like a strange fence. At either end of the field were pitched the pavilions of the knights who came from far and wide; and before each pavilion banners flew: golden lions and eagles and hunting hawks, flowers common and imaginary. And over all, the double swan of the Renné upon a sky of blue. And there, toward the end of the stands, the same double swan but on a dark field: the emblem of the Wills family, who would not relinquish their claim to the throne of a nonexistent kingdom.

Westbrook had once been far from the center of the old kingdom of Ayr, but now they lived in a world with no great center but many lesser cities, some hardly more than villages, and the culture was spread and thin.

Tam thought only the minstrels retained some of the culture of the old kingdom, for they knew all the stories: the names of the kings and their ladies, the celebrated knights and the great lords of ages past. It was as though each minstrel carried some part of the old world, and one day, perhaps, they would gather together and sing every song they knew, and by some strange magic, it would all be made real again.

The heralds announced that three more passes would be run after the knights refreshed themselves. The Valemen sat watching the scene below, talking among themselves. They bought cups of ale from a father and son carrying buckets on yokes across their shoulders, and none of them mentioned the deed that Alaan would try that night, though all thought of little else.

"Do you see?" Cynddl said suddenly, pointing. "There in the box near the western end. Is that not Elise Wills?"

They all strained to see at the distance, but the old farmer turned toward them again. "Aye. That be her. Sitting with the Prince of Innes and his son who is her intended."

"And the knight dressed all in black . . .?" Tam said, nodding toward the stands.

"The Prince's counselor, whose name I misremember."

"Sir Eremon," someone else offered.

The companions all shared guarded looks, and Tam felt them all draw their limbs closer as though they could make themselves small and go unnoticed.

"Are you from far?" the broad-faced man asked.

"Beyond the Wold of Kerns," Fynnol said, and Tam gave him a withering look. Better not to tell anyone about themselves—not even a kindly old farmer.

"Well, guard your purses," the old man said. "The Westbrook Fair draws pickpockets and thieves from every nick and crenny throughout the land between the mountains. It be said that during the Westbrook Fair, all the surrounding lands enjoy a few days when one might safely leave one's most valued property on the doorstep without fear of loss."

Tam turned his attention back to the Prince of Innes's box. Beneath the banners Tam could see the knight in his dark robe, two of his guard standing behind. Gray-headed, the man appeared, and haughty in his bearing. There were also several men-at-arms in the purple trimmed in black of the Prince of Innes: the other men who had waylaid Alaan and then pursued them down the River Wynnd. Tam ducked his head a little.

The horns sounded for the contest to begin again, and the rumbling of the crowd subsided as the two riders took the field.

"Will the fourth pass decide it?" Fynnol wondered, though he did not really seem to expect anyone to answer.

The flag sent the riders on, and they hurtled toward each other with renewed energy. Both knights shattered their lances and a point was recorded for each.

"They are too evenly matched," Cynddl said. "How can there be a winner between such men?"

The fifth pass saw the stranger make a point and the Renné lord miss his mark, which set the crowd to muttering. Did he tire? Would the next pass see their champion fall?

But the last point was Toren Renné's, and there was still no decision. The knights signaled their willingness to continue; and the marshals announced that three more passes would be run.

The caparisons of the horses were wet with sweat now, and the horses' great chests heaved from their efforts. Six times they had charged at speed, bearing their riders in full armor. And now a seventh would be asked of them, and then two times more.

Tam saw the equerries pass lances to their masters and tighten saddle girths. The day was wearing on, though the heat had not yet begun to abate. A crowning cloud cast a shadow upon the field, shading the fluttering banners and giving relief to the crowd and the two riders at the tilt.

The seventh pass was sounded by the heralds and the knights took their places. Lances were lowered, and the signal flashed. The horses raced along the fence, running true, both confident of their business. And then the splintering crash. For a moment it seemed the stranger would lose his seat, for he was flung back and bounced half out of his saddle, but he found the pommel and pulled himself upright.

But his horse limped terribly and the equerries ran out to take hold of its head.

"Ah," Cynddl said, slapping his thigh, "he's lost his great horse. Certainly he can't have another as good. Perhaps you'll win your bet, Tam."

The word passed up the hill like a breeze: the charger had a lance splinter driven into its foot. He would not run again that day. And then a second breeze, more urgent than the first: the stranger had no other horse. Toren Renné would be declared the winner!

But the Renné lord had rounded the tilt and stopped his horse before the marshals of the fair. Waves of cheering rose, then died away as the crowd expected their champion to be proclaimed the victor. Toren removed his helm, which produced a cheer from the onlookers, but then they saw that he shook his head repeatedly as he spoke with the judges and then suddenly he rode away— not staying to receive the adulation and prizes he was due.

Finally the heralds were sent out to their places around the field, where they blew their horns and proclaimed: "Lord Toren Renné refuses to be named victor in this contest." Nothing more was said, which caused waves of muttering and murmuring. The marshals huddled together, conferring, for knights did not often refuse their spoils.

"Well, here is a joust that won't soon be forgotten," Cynddl said. "Seven passes and then the victor refuses to be proclaimed. You'll have stories to tell back in the Vale, that is sure."

But then it could be seen that Lady Beatrice Renné beckoned the marshals and they made their way up to her. Everyone hushed as though they might hear what was said. For a moment the field was utterly silent, and then the marshals returned to their places.

Heralds were sent out again and horns sounded. The crowd fell silent, listening. A small breeze swept the heralds' words away, but the report passed up the hill, followed closely by cheering: both knights would be named champions and the prize split between them.

The crowd roared approval, coming to their feet. Then the onlookers began to shout wildly as Toren Renné appeared on his gray leading a second horse. This he took to the stranger so that they might both come before the marshals on horseback as was the custom.

Lady Beatrice descended to the rail and on each of their raised lances she dropped a ribbon of red to show her favor and a wreath of flowers, also. The proclamation of the heralds was lost in the wild hooray, and the two champions rode slowly about the field, side by side, the people from the hill rushing out to surround them. The shading cloud passed and the sun slanted into the field, casting long shadows and gilding everything with the warm light of late afternoon.

The tourney at Westbrook was over, and Tam's eye was drawn away from the scene of triumph to the box of the Prince of Innes. The man Alaan called Hafydd stood in his place still, unaffected by the celebration. His head turned slowly as though he surveyed the crowd. A strange wave of fear passed through Tam again and he had a strong desire to get away, a feeling that they were in terrible danger.

FIFTY-NINE

L lyn spread the costume on her bed and gazed at it, a strange storm of feelings whirling inside her. She felt she might burst into tears of sadness and joy and confusion. It was a very beautiful gown, pure white with a swan headdress of white and gold, and should not have reduced anyone fortunate enough to wear it to tears. But it did.

"What a cruel trick has been played on me!" Llyn said with feeling, though even she was not quite sure what this meant.

Lady Elise Wills, it appeared, would attend the ball as the mythical Elyse, mother of the kings of men. And no doubt she possessed the kind of beauty that such a part required.

Llyn turned her eyes away from the gown.

Carral Wills had given his daughter the name Elise, and now the Wills would make their claim before every-one: they would put Elise's child upon the throne. With the very considerable aid of the Prince of Innes, who would be the child's grandfather.

A child, she thought, and closed her eyes. A long, calming breath helped.

"And we shall stand idly by and let them make this proclamation at our own ball." She shook her head sadly. How could war be avoided now?

Her eye lit upon a note pinned to the collar of the gown.

> You must wear the cape over the gown and
> hide your hair beneath the headdress. I will
> find you at the ball. You are more courageous
> than any man-at-arms.

There was no signature.

She found the cape, carefully wrapped. It was dark blue and embroidered with silver moons and stars: the cape of a sorceress. Holding it up she could see that the hood would enclose the headdress so that only the mask could be seen. She could go into the ball thus and not be seen to wear the same costume as Lady Elise—or Elyse.

"Well," she said aloud, "first I shall be a sorceress and then I shall transform myself into another. It is not often a disfigured woman is asked to play the mother of the kings of men."

She felt a pang of anxiety and looked out the window. The sun had set rather hastily that evening. The ball would begin in about two hours. She looked back at the costume and felt again the strange desire to cry.

A soft knock intruded upon her thoughts, but it was from the door to her garden. Why would one of her servants be in the garden? And then she realized. She went near the door.

"And who could be so presumptuous as to come to my garden door?" she said.

"I fear you know the answer," a voice beyond the door said.

"Alaan?"

"Yes. I've come to disturb your contemplation once again."

"And what would you have me do this time? I fear to ask."

"I have merely brought you your gown for the ball."

"But I have a costume, and a rather beautiful one at that."

"Yes, but Hafydd knows of that one and of the cloak that goes over it. He will be watching for you."

"But how is that—" She stopped abruptly. "You have arranged it so he would know."

"Let us say I did little to hinder his finding out, but you should know that Hafydd has spies within your house."

"Not my servants surely!"

"No, though one of them is not so discreet as you formerly believed. You might caution them all, for they love you dearly and wouldn't do you harm knowingly." She heard his feet shifting on the stone outside. "Here is a second costume and different cloak to cover it. You say you have a maid who is just your size? Call her in and dress her in the swan costume and have her wear the cloak over it. She will accompany you to—"

"But this man you speak of will think she is me!"

"That is why she'll be in no danger. Hafydd must think you are there and that we plan to switch you with Elise somehow. That at least he doesn't know: how we will switch the two of you."

"But what shall I do?"

"Be on the floor for the last dance and get near Elise Wills. Tell your maid to keep a distance from you. Hafydd's minions will stay near to her. The room will suddenly go dark."

"That room will be lit by a thousand candles!"

"Nonetheless it will grow suddenly dark. At that moment you must throw your cloak over Elise Wills. Both she and Prince Michael will help you arrange it. Then you and your maid must disappear with all speed, back up to your rooms."

She was silent for a moment. "And that is all?"

"Yes, that is all."

"Then I shall not be a princess this night?" she said, her voice coming out small.

"No, you shall be something else." The door creaked open a crack, and a man's hand came through holding a package.

She hesitated a second and then reached out and took it. Alaan's hand found hers, and pressed it once before withdrawing—his skin warm and rough. The door creaked shut, but she reached out and grabbed the handle before it closed.

"The six Knights of the Vow," she said in a rush, "fought

to the death in an old keep near Telanon Bridge. Their bodies were buried beneath a mound, but everything they possessed was carried south to Aschen Renné."

"Not everything, I think," Alaan said softly, and she heard him turn to go. "Thank you, Lady Llyn."

"Will you ever visit me again?" she said, though her common sense told her to keep silent.

"If I can." He said this with such lack of conviction that Llyn had a sudden flash of fear. Alaan was going into danger this night. He didn't really believe he would survive.

At dusk Pwyll arrived bearing costumes. He was dressed as Tam had first seen him, leather vest over a well-worn shirt, a band of cloth binding back his hair. A woodsman he seemed, not a champion of the Westbrook Fair.

"I hope this meeting ends more pleasantly than our last," he said. He didn't look particularly elated or proud at having been declared a champion of the fair alongside Lord Toren Renné.

"Congratulations on your victory," Cynddl said.

Pwyll only shrugged his great shoulders. "It was a way to gain us all entrance to the ball. I hope these costumes fit. Alaan had to guess your heights and weights."

To each of them he passed a neatly wrapped package. Tam took his, but made no move to open it. The others hesitated also.

Pwyll looked up. "Alaan said you had decided to aid him . . .?"

"We seem to have little choice," Fynnol said, "but we don't really know our part. What is it we're expected to do exactly?"

Pwyll stood—taller than all but Baore. "You will attend the Renné ball, bearing arms. Near the end of the evening we'll gather by a door—I'll point it out after you arrive. When Alaan is ready he will alert me. It is up to him to lure Hafydd out into the garden . . . and beyond." He shrugged. "Alaan will deal with Hafydd. That will not be up to you, but Hafydd must be separated from his men-at-arms, who guard him with their lives."

"But they are trained men-at-arms and we are farmers and craftsmen from the Vale," Fynnol protested.

Pwyll almost smiled. "How many times have you met Hafydd's men now? Three times? Four? How many of them have been wounded or worse, yet you are all still hale? Your fathers trained you better than you know."

"And you?" Fynnol said. "What will you do?"

"I will stand with you or aid Alaan, whichever is needed."

"And what of Lady Elise?" Baore said. "Are we not to rescue her?"

Pwyll shifted from one foot to the other. "That will not be our part."

The three Valemen looked around at one another. All of them were as grave as mourners, their faces rigid, eyes dull and narrowed.

So this is what men feel before they go into battle, Tam realized. He thought of them first at Telanon Bridge, planning a trip to Inniseth to sell a few trinkets they had dug from an old battlefield. How had such an innocent journey come to this?

Without a word Baore began unwrapping his costume, and the others did the same. In a few moments masks hid their faces, though Tam thought the costumes did little to hide their fear.

Pwyll, who wore no mask, looked around at them. "Come!" he said. "We are going to the costume ball at the Westbrook Fair, not to your hangings! You are the envy of all of old Ayr! It is the event of the year."

"We are not going there to dance and court," Fynnol said. He rearranged a green hood over his face—a highwayman.

"Oh but you are. Until such time as Alaan needs us we are to act like all the other guests, and I will tell you, there is something about a mask that liberates people in strange ways. You will see."

Tam pulled the long, sleeveless cloak over his costume. It was embroidered in a thousand colors, apparently. "And what am I? A walking rainbow?"

"King Attmal, I should guess," Cynddl said.

"Attmal?"

"He was a king who wanted every color of nature in his royal cape. He was not merely flamboyant, though, but a great king as well. History has been kind to Attmal and all his endeavors." Cynddl shook his head. "I can never quite believe you know so little of your own history."

"Oh, Tam knows a great deal," Fynnol said. "You should talk to Baore and me if you wish to meet ignorance dressed and walking." This attempt at banter fell flat.

"More important," Pwyll said quietly, "Attmal was famed as an archer, so you can carry your bow and quiver as well as a blade."

Baore stood up then, taller than they had ever seen him. He was costumed as a mountain giant, but because the shoulders and head were merely stuffed and he looked out through cleverly disguised eye holes in the shirt, he appeared to be enormous.

Despite their mood, Tam and Fynnol laughed at the sight of their companion. "I think the mask upon the stuffed head a clever touch!" Tam said.

Cynddl was dressed as a minstrel, but not just any minstrel. He went as Ruadan, the man who had owned a magical pipe with which he'd won the love of a princess.

"I will leave you here," Pwyll said, mounting the horse Toren Renné had lent him. "As a champion of the fair I have other obligations. Alaan or I will find you at the ball." He wheeled his horse and went off along the trail that ran beside the river.

They had found a maidservant to help Elise with her costume, but she was just presentable when two of Hafydd's guards appeared and dragged her summarily away, the maid running along behind bearing her head-dress.

It was into Hafydd's tent she was thrust a moment later, and there she found the gray-haired knight awaiting her. He looked up and she could see the cold fire of anger burning there.

"I have begun to think you have lied to me, Lady Elise. And I do not care to be lied to." He stalked out from behind the table. "I sent men north and they found the body of your minstrel lying in an shallow grave. It was not Gartnn the nagar was drawn to, was it?"

Elise could feel her heart pounding. Her body leaned back of its own will, out of fear of this man. She went to speak, but Hafydd raised his hand and stopped her.

"You have lied to me enough," he said and turned to the table. Elise could not quite see what it was he did there, but when he turned back he held a goblet. Floating on top of the wine was an oily silver film, like melted metal.

"Drink this," Hafydd said.

Fear overwhelmed Elise and she spun toward the door, but the guards were quicker and caught her by the arms. Roughly, Hafydd took hold of her hair and forced her face up.

"You will drink it," he said, "though you may choose how much pain will precede the drinking."

Tears stung her eyes so that she could not see, but a glass was pressed to her lips and liquid tipped into her mouth. She gagged on it: a taste like wine and mercury.

It seemed to coat her mouth and tongue with a sickly film. And suddenly breathing was difficult.

Hafydd stepped away.

"Did you really see a nagar on the river, Lady Elise?"

She felt herself lowered into a chair, where she hung her head a moment, unable to catch her breath.

"I have never been known for my patience," came Hafydd's harsh voice. The threat in it made her lift her head, but when she tried to speak no words came.

"Yes, your mouth is dry, but you cannot have water yet. The nagar, my lady?"

She nodded. "We saw it," she said, the words tearing at her throat like shards.

"Tell me again who it was drawn to, for it was not Gartnn. He is dead, his body fished from the river and buried in the ground."

"I don't know," she croaked, frightened by the sound of her voice. Suddenly, the already shrunken opening through which air passed into her lungs seemed to constrict. She heard her breath coming in terrible little whistling gasps.

"Did I neglect to tell you the effect of this libation? With each lie your airway draws tighter. Three lies is usually all anyone can manage before suffocation, though I once saw a minstrel speak five." Hafydd held out a glass. "A sip of this and the spell will be broken. But the answers to my questions first."

Elise was being supported by the guards now, and she felt her head swimming. A sudden heat enveloped her, as though she stood too near a blaze. How terribly she labored to get even a little air into her lungs.

"One of the . . . northerners," she managed and thought she could breathe a little more easily.

"Ah, you see what a wonderful thing the truth is. Which of them?"

"Baore . . . I think."

"And which is he?"

"The tallest . . ."

"And has he been injured or ill of late?"

She shook her head.

"Lady Elise, suffocation is unpleasant to watch."

"I don't know."

Hafydd held the glass toward her, but just as she was about to grasp it he pulled it back.

"Who is it plans to rescue you this night?"

She stared at Hafydd, her breath still coming in gasps, little ink-black blobs running down the edge of her vision.

"Take your time," Hafydd said. "I am not fond of balls."

"Ala—" but she could not say more.

"The man who arranged your flight from Braidon Castle?"

She nodded.

"And Prince Michael is his collaborator?"

Elise hung her head again, fighting to pull air into her lungs, but she did not answer.

"Can it be that there is actually someone you won't betray? I would have thought you'd sacrifice your beloved father rather than suffer a little discomfort. It does not matter. I know the depths of Prince Michael's treachery."

She was lifted up roughly and felt water pouring down her throat. Elise choked and bent double, coughing, but then she could breathe.

"Have the maid come in," Hafydd said.

Elise sprawled in the chair on the edge of unconsciousness. She felt a hand gently patting her cheek, and air moved sweetly against her face. Someone employed a fan.

"Find me this northerner," she heard Hafydd say. "I will know how he can be Sainth's ally and yet draw Sianon."

The road leading to the main gate of Castle Renné was lined with several thousand people who were not fortunate enough to have been invited to the ball but who didn't want to miss the pageant. The way was lit by lanterns, though the light of the moon was very bright.

Lords and ladies rode by on magnificent horses, their trains following behind. The knights who had acquitted themselves well in the tourney rode their chargers, and the onlookers cheered them and threw flowers in their paths. A few, too old to ride, arrived in carts, or even borne in sedan chairs, but most walked. It was, after all, not far from Westbrook to the castle and the evening was so fair it seemed to call for a parade.

The spectacle was not to be missed, for there were several hundred people attending, and no expense had been spared on the costumes, for even here the spirit of competition burned.

Jesters, kings, spirits, lions, birds of the air. Sorcerers, warriors, wanderers, giants, and tellers of fortunes. There was no end to the inventiveness of the costumers, Tam thought. A knight rode upon a stuffed horse that had been cleverly sewn about him. A silveroak tree walked stiffly by, shying from torches.

"And what costume is that?" Fynnol said, nodding to a woman in a gown of gold with an elaborate crown upon her head.

"She is a princess of the Lost Ones," Cynddl said. "You of all people should know that, Fynnol."

A troll lumbered by, eyeing Baore and making rumblings in its throat, for the giants had warred with the trolls, driving them deep into the mountains.

A dragon with eight pairs of legs snaked its way through the parade, snapping its massive jaws and snarling hideously. A fool scurried past, bells ajingle, juggling balls of colored glass. And everywhere minstrels played and sang songs of the characters they encountered.

> The giant hid within a tree
> To snatch the travelers, all three.

"I had not in all my years imagined such a thing," Fynnol said suddenly. He looked around, eyes dancing.

"It seems that everyone has spent a year of thought and effort on their costumes."

"A highwayman!" several Knights of the Vow shouted upon seeing Fynnol, and Baore was forced to come to his cousin's aid, for the Knights would have trussed him up and gone looking for a marshal to judge him.

> The highwaymen, the highwaymen
> What would be awaiting them?
> A Knight upon a pure white steed,
> A rope upon a withered tree.

Despite the true nature of their endeavor, the Valemen were astonished to find themselves in such a procession and gawked like the people lining the lane. One would have thought they were not on their way to the ball themselves.

Tam thought that even Baore moved with a more relaxed gait that night. Several times he ran, roaring and waving his staff, toward people standing on the road's edge, and they scattered, laughing. Baore laughed as well, much to Tam's amazement: a sound he'd not heard in so long he hardly recognized it.

And then, all at once, they were at the castle gate and passing inside. Into the keep of the notorious Renné.

White horses were found for them, Elyse and Mwynfawr. And in their elaborate dress they looked, indeed, like a king and queen of ancient times, though young and fair.

But Prince Michael did not feel like a king, or even like a father of kings. He was apprehensive in spite of himself. Elise rode beside him, trying hard to keep her head up, though it seemed a struggle.

"Lady Elise?" he whispered. "Are you well?"

She didn't answer but only nodded, straightening her back.

They rode in procession: his father and several important lords in the fore, followed by a company of his father's men-at-arms. Around them minstrels dressed in white played and sang songs of Elyse and Mwynfawr. Behind came Hafydd and his own dark knights, and where they passed all the cheering and laughter stopped.

Everyone recognized the purple livery of the men-at-arms as that of the Prince of Innes. They also recognized the costumes that Prince Michael and Elise wore, and understood the meaning.

"Peace breaker!" someone shouted, and it took Prince Michael a second to realize this insult was hurled at Hafydd.

Hafydd, however, did not seem to care or even notice. He rode in the center of his men upon his usual horse, his dark robe arranged about him, head high. The Prince thought Hafydd looked rejuvenated this night—this night when he would begin his revenge upon the Renné. What did he care what the rabble thought?

Will he always be so haughty? Prince Michael wondered. *Is there no one who might bring him down?*

There was only this man Hafydd named the whist, and the Prince was not confident that even he would elude Hafydd forever. The knight was dogged when pursuing his fixations. Even the whist must land one day. But would it be tonight, or would he surprise Hafydd and switch Elise with some other?

The Prince's horse threw up its head suddenly as something was tossed from the roadside.

"It was not directed toward you," Elise whispered.

And again the cry "peace breaker" was heard. The Prince was not accustomed to such hostility from the common people.

This is what comes of allowing Hafydd sway in their lives, he thought. How different this reception from the people's reaction to Toren Renné. When the lord had insisted upon sharing the prize at the joust the crowd had surged down onto the field, crying his name. How easily he could have made an army right there and then, and how willingly they would fight for such a man. Hafydd didn't understand that. He considered Toren Renné weak and foolish.

And honorable, the Prince thought. *Hafydd has taken our honor away. My honor.*

And he did not know how honor, once lost, could ever be retrieved.

Dease was limping and thought a crippled sorcerer particularly difficult to believe in. But there he was, nursing his hurt from the joust and cursing under his breath. He descended a stair toward the main hall where the ball would be held, or at least where the dancing would take place. There were any number of rooms involved, and guests would wander freely through them and out onto the terrace, for the night was fine and all the doors would be open.

The most useful feature of his costume was the sorcerer's staff, upon which he could lean and take some of the weight off his injured knee. He had made some effort to be sure that no one knew what costume he would wear, for discussions with his cousins were the last thing he wanted this night. What he *did* want was a glass of wine or two, just enough to quiet his nerves but not enough make his hands unsteady.

He found that he had stopped on the stair without ever meaning to.

I will do this thing—his words came back to him—*for I love him best.*

"Sir?" A servant ascended toward him, bearing pillows. "Have you slipped?"

"No. No, I'm merely resting. Time catches even sorcerers, it seems."

The man nodded. "There is nothing I might do?"

"I have my staff and the rail. I need nothing more. But someone it seems has need of sleep. Bear your pillows on."

The man held up his burden. "The fat man hasn't girth enough, though this should fill his larder."

The servant went on. Three young women swept by, giggling and whispering—courtiers from ancient Ayr. A seemingly dejected frog sat upon the bottom step, and when Dease paused to rest his throbbing knee, the frog looked up.

"Awaiting a princess's kiss," it said rather forlornly.

"As are we all," Dease answered and hobbled on.

He didn't know what costumes his cousins had chosen, though Toren would be unmasked early in the evening when the champions of the fair were celebrated. Arden could be found, for he was easily the best dancer among the young men at Westbrook. Beld could not be mistaken, for his shape and lumbering gait could belong to no one else. Beldor was the only person he knew who could appear sullen and resentful even when hidden behind a mask, his body disguised beneath layers of fabric. It was as though a spirit of spitefulness had possessed him and would never let go.

Samul he would not find, of course, for Samul had perfected the art of concealing himself within the presence of others. Almost no one knew how much influence Samul had over Renné policy, for he planted his ideas in the minds of others and seldom spoke out in larger gatherings. The perfect costume for Samul would be a shadow—someone else's shadow.

The ballroom was lit by chandeliers bearing countless candles, and beneath the warm light the revelers glittered. It was customary for attendees to make their entrance into the main hall by the south doors and pass over the open floor to the foot of Lady Beatrice's dais, where they would be graciously welcomed. They would also be gently mocked by the gathered fools, for there were always a number of these, vying with each other to be the wit of the fete.

Dease, however, as a resident of the castle, slipped in a side door and avoided this altogether. Two fools had taken up stations by the main entrance and were grandly announcing guests as they arrived.

"An enchanted frog and a stagger—I mean—walking oak tree," one of the fools called out pompously.

The mood of the guests was gay, the room abuzz with excitement and expectation. It always impressed Dease that a mask could be so liberating. At the end of the evening, when the masks were removed, one often found that the most outspoken were those who were commonly silent, and the most flirtatious were known to be shy.

"A dancing bear and a Fáel princess of yore," one of the fools called out.

Dease intercepted a servant and rescued a glass of wine from a dangerously overcrowded tray. He had made certain to wear a mask that would allow him to both eat and drink.

"Elyse and Mwynfawr," the fool announced.

Dease turned to find a couple entering, surrounded by costumed minstrels.

"That is them," a woman nearby whispered to her companion. "The daughter of Lord Carral Wills with Prince Michael of Innes."

The news washed quickly the length of the room, a whispering wave that died at the feet of Lady Beatrice Renné. She raised her eyes to view this affront, though her face showed no indication of her feelings.

"Let us slip down the room and witness Lady Beatrice's greeting," Dease's neighbor said to her companion and they hurried off.

Dease continued to stare at the couple in the entrance. Behind them came two men, one in costume and the second wearing a knight's robe of black with a skull mask.

"The Prince of—" The fool coughed theatrically. "I mean, a humble woodsman and a knight."

The man in the black robe, obviously Eremon, the Prince's counselor, opened his robe and to everyone's horror, beneath wore a surcoat of Renné blue, though torn and stained. He leaned toward the fool and whispered.

"The ghost of Sir Hafydd," the fool announced, his voice trembling a little.

Dease felt his shoulders bunch into knots and he gripped his staff until his hand hurt.

They should be cut down here, before everyone, for their effrontery, he thought. *This is what Toren's policies had brought about. The Prince of Innes believed he could walk into the home of the Renné and announce his plan to put his grandson upon the throne and know that he would suffer nothing. That Toren Renné would protect him.*

Dease half expected to see the hunched figure of Beldor leap out of the crowd, sword in hand, to cut down this upstart prince. But all that greeted them was stunned silence.

An old man near Dease cleared his throat and said softly, "Never before have I seen war declared in such a manner."

And Dease nodded. Did everyone realize that is what this was? A declaration of war. The party passed the length of the hall, stopping before Lady Beatrice to bow and curtsey. Dease had never known such a silence at the Renné ball before.

"Welcome, Elyse and Mwynfawr," Beatrice said in her most gracious and regal voice. "And you, woodsman, and Sir Hafydd, come to haunt us, I see." She actually smiled. "Since you begat the kings of men," she went on, "much has happened, for the kings have been dethroned and many of their descendants are but coarse warriors without honor. I regret to inform you of this, for it is so difficult to see one's children amount to nothing. But no matter; you have descended here to be among us and we welcome you all. Be merry this night, for one cannot be sure of the days ahead, and too often events do not turn out as we expect." She smiled and bowed her head, turning her attention to those next to enter.

The silence lasted a beat and then the room erupted into a frenzy of whispering. Any comments by the fools gathered near Beatrice's feet were lost in the din.

Dease realized he had been holding his breath, and drew in a lungful of whispers. More guests arrived, though they were largely ignored, which must have seemed very odd to them, as they had not been witness to the recent events.

A slight man in an executioner's hood and robe stopped a few feet away, watching the spectacle. Dease felt a shiver pass through him, as though he saw himself suddenly. For a moment he could not take his eyes away, and then the man turned and noticed him, as though he had sensed Dease's stare. The executioner gazed at him a moment, blue eyes behind the narrow slits, and then he gave a small bow of acknowledgment to Dease and went off.

Dease closed his eyes a moment and the room seemed to shift beneath him. His eyes sprang open in panic.

Tam's attention was taken by the sight of the great hall and he didn't hear what the fools said who were announcing the guests. Something witty, though, for a few people standing nearby tittered.

But Fynnol, the highwayman, was never at a loss for a response. "If I were to rob you of your wit," he said to the fools, "I would carry away a wit of such little weight that a sack of feathers should seem a bag of lead when compared. But, even so, you could hardly be more witless than now." He bowed and waved his companions forward to applause from those gathered by the doors.

"Go easy on these poor southerners," Cynddl said. "They have not the advantages you enjoy, coming from the cultured and sophisticated north."

They went slowly the length of the hall to stand before Lady Beatrice, the Renné matriarch, who greeted them as though they were great lords, for this night no one's station was known.

"My good giant, welcome to our little hall. Do mind the chandeliers. I ask only that you keep all trolls from making mischief and from dining upon our guests."

Baore bowed.

"And you, sir, are a highwayman. Dare I trust you to refrain from your trade this night?"

"But I fear I have already committed such crimes as highwaymen do," Fynnol said. "I have robbed two fools of their wit and no one has remarked upon it—not even the fools. But I promise to refrain from such thievery the rest of this night. I shall steal no lady's beauty, no knight's courage. Each man shall retain his erudition, every gossip their prattle. Grace and good manners shall be left in place; and I promise to disturb no one's yearnings. Though I will confess, given the chance to steal a kiss, I might weaken."

Lady Beatrice laughed. "You have my permission to steal a kiss, but no more than two or perhaps three."

"But is the supply not boundless?"

She wagged a finger at Fynnol. "You are a wicked highwayman. Four kisses and that is my final word. Any more and I shall make you return them one by one."

She turned to Tam.

"You, sir, I should know. King—Oh, Llyn would know," she said.

"Attmal," Tam said.

"Yes. The cloak bearing every color of his garden, or some such thing. I am your descendant, you realize."

"And I am proud of you, granddaughter."

She laughed. "And I am so pleased to meet your approval." She turned to Cynddl. "And here we see another minstrel? But are you not some particular minstrel?"

"I am called Ruadan, Lady Beatrice."

"Then we will hear your magic pipe. Princesses"—she looked around—"be advised to block your ears."

Reluctantly Cynddl took out his flute—Alaan's flute. Tam could see that he hadn't expected this. The tone of the instrument was so haunting that everyone nearby fell silent to listen.

When Cynddl had done Lady Beatrice applauded. "Seldom does a minstrel come disguised as a minstrel." She gazed at him a moment. "But perhaps that is not your calling. Perhaps you are one of our wandering friends? But either way, you are welcome. You are welcome all."

The companions passed into the crowd, though not without a few remarks from the gathered fools, though none dared test Fynnol whose reputation was already made. They found a place at the side to watch the procession and for more than an hour almost forgot why they were there.

Horns were sounded then and cymbals clashed. The marshals of the fair stood up on the landing to Lady

Beatrice's right, and the crowd fell silent. A marshal, a famous knight of years gone by, stepped forward. "The fair at Westbrook is ended for another year," he called, "but there is one small matter left undone. We have not had our parade of champions. Come up now, all who triumphed at the fair. Take off your masks so that we might see you."

"What is this?" Tam asked Cynddl.

"The parade of champions," the story finder said. "Were you not listening?"

The victors began emerging from the crowd, removing their masks as they came. They mounted the two steps to the rostrum and took their place in a line of archers and knights and men-at-arms.

The marshals then had each man step forward and announced his name and his feats. Pwyll Stagshanks— not one of the noble names that most knights bore—could not boast a long list of tournaments won, but this didn't seem to matter much to the guests who cheered him almost as they had Toren Renné.

The champions were all directed to chairs, and no sooner were they seated than young men rushed forward to bear the chairs up. They were carried thus, three times around the hall, while everyone cheered them and sang a song Tam did not know. Young women threw roses to the victors as they passed, and by the third circuit Toren Renné was nearly smothered in them so that they fell upon the floor, leaving a trail of crimson where he passed.

Pwyll looked distinctly uncomfortable as he was jolted

about on his chair, high above the heads of the costumed men who bore him. Finally, and to Pwyll's great relief, the champions were lowered to the floor. He had come to rest not far from Tam and beside Toren Renné.

"What shall I do with all these roses?" Pwyll said to the Renné lord.

Toren gestured. "This servant will take them," he said. "Now don your mask again."

"But everyone knows who I am."

"It doesn't matter. You must be masked all the same. Only Lady Beatrice requires no costume. Now you must try to dance with every woman who tossed you a rose. You did note who they were, I hope?"

"I did not."

Toren shook his head and smiled. "Well, you will be considered terribly unchivalrous if you do not make a valiant attempt to do your duty."

"But, Lord Toren, I should still be dancing tomorrow night if I danced with them all."

Toren laughed. "It is unseemly to boast. But there will be two dozen short dances to begin, so that you may discharge most of your duty. You will be expected to dance every one and each with a different partner."

"But I do not know the steps."

"Too late to think of that now. They're not so difficult. Ah, here—the first dance. Find a partner, and good luck to you."

The dances were remarkably short and punctuated by much laughter and a rush to find new partners. All the uninjured men-at-arms participated, and the young women—some of them very young—were willing partners. Tam saw Pwyll dancing with a girl no more than six. She was dressed as a sprite and danced as one, too, to the delight of onlookers.

Tam found himself being gently pulled out onto the floor and danced with a princess, a sorceress, a cloud rider, a ghost. A huntress, a seamstress, milkmaid, a dwarf. He also danced with a bear, who he suspected was no lady at all.

And then as he stood, red faced and gasping, the serious dancing began, and he found himself suddenly standing on the side. A man dressed all in gray gazed oddly at Tam. "Meet me on the terrace, Tamlyn Loell," he said, and then turned and slipped back into the crowd.

Cynddl appeared just then. "Out of breath, are you?"

Tam nodded, his face hot beneath his mask. "I've just met our friend. We're to go out to the terrace."

"Ah," Cynddl said. "And so it begins."

Prince Michael watched Elise dancing with her father, who she guided with a practiced hand. Every movement, every gesture, spoke of her love for this man. One did not need to see her face to know that.

Lord Carral Wills had appeared, wearing a mask with no eye slits at all. He was a seer, predicting futures for all who asked. Prince Michael did not ask.

Hafydd and his guards were poised about the dance

floor, watching. Many men present, and even a few women, wore blades that night, but most of the others were merely painted wood. Hafydd and his guards bore steel.

A giant and a dancing bear lumbered about the dance floor together and actually jostled Elise and Lord Carral so that they stopped dancing. Prince Michael was about to go forward when he saw them all nod and bow, and then the giant and bear lumbered off.

A minstrel happened by just then, playing upon a small instrument called a traveler's lute. "Lord Mwynfawr," he said, bowing absurdly low. "You should not look so forlorn, my lord. Perhaps all will turn out well in the end."

He began to sing a familiar song, but as he passed close by the lyric changed. "Dance the last dance with your bride, and then apart shall you abide," the minstrel sang, and strolled leisurely on his way.

The Prince felt his mouth go suddenly dry. This stranger really would try to snatch Elise from beneath Hafydd's nose. He shook his head. Certainly it couldn't be done, not to Hafydd.

Elise was dancing with her father and holding back tears. How good it felt to have him near, someone who loved and cared for her. She had been so long among rogues and strangers and brutes. This thought made her feel suddenly that she must protect her father, for he knew so little of what went on around him. But this night it was she who was in danger.

"Hafydd knows what is planned," she said urgently. "It cannot work now. Alaan has failed again."

"Alaan . . ." her father said oddly. "Then what shall we do? I will take up with the Renné rather than let you go again."

Elise hesitated. She did feel a tear come to her eye now. It quivered on her lid and then spilled over and ran down outside her golden mask so that she did not feel it.

A giant jostled her just then, and her father almost fell. "I must find Angeline," the giant said to his partner. "Angeline A'drent. I have what she seeks." And then with a nod and an apology, he danced off.

Elise stood utterly still for a moment, and then took her father's hand again. She leaned close to him. "I think I've found a way to escape," she whispered.

"Elise, you won't do something desperate and fool-hardy?"

"Foolhardy? No," she said. "Father . . . would you love me if I changed?"

"What do you mean, changed?"

"If I went away and came back and you hardly recognized or knew me." The dance ended and the dancers all began to applaud. "Would you still love me?" Elise said over the din.

"I would love you no matter what," her father said.

She leaned forward to kiss his cheek, but instead felt her mask press against his, her lips touch the inside of her own outer face.

*　*　*

Beneath her robe Llyn wore the gown of a fairy princess, but the outer robe was that of an executioner, with its black hood and narrow eye slits. She attended the ball as a servant of Death.

What a wicked man this Alaan was, playing such a prank on her! As everyone would assume such a costume was worn by a man she danced with women, forgetting regularly that she should lead. As executioners were never supposed to speak, she was saved from having to try to disguise her voice.

She saw Toren doing his noble best to dance with all the maidens who'd thrown him roses. She longed to dance with him herself, but her costume would not allow it. Instead, she admired his grace and charm from afar, watching the young ladies blush and gaze at him raptly. It was almost more than she could bear. Toren, who was destined for a marriage that would strengthen the Renné. She took a long breath and it escaped raggedly.

"Everything proceeds as it should," a muffled voice said.

She turned to find a man dressed drably in gray.

"Do I know you, sir?" she asked.

"I am a traveler," the man said, his voice disguised by a layer of cloth, "a pilgrim, perhaps. Before me flies a small bird crying a warning to the sons of men—though they pay it no heed."

"It is always thus. I study history so that I might learn life's pitfalls, but no one cares to hear of this."

"Are you confident of your part?"

"No, but I will manage."

He bowed to her and swept away.

Arden thought the dancers that night looked like puppets, false and petty. Although he loved to dance he didn't step out among them and was thankful for the mask that hid his face. He had recourse to his wine goblet often, and felt a blessed blurring of his senses, the tiniest alleviation of his guilt.

An executioner stood nearby, he realized, and Arden thought there was something familiar in the man's stance. "Dease?" he said aloud without meaning to.

The executioner turned toward him quickly, and Arden felt a flash of panic. "What say you, good executioner?" he said jovially, waving his wineglass. "Have you come to ply your craft among the dancers?"

The executioner looked pointedly at Arden's goblet. "You shall regret what you do this night, Arden Renné. You shall regret it most deeply."

Tam found the others and shepherded them outside. Laughter came from the small gatherings of men and women scattered about the terrace. A few men had even pushed up their masks for a moment, revealing the flushed faces beneath. In their colorful costumes and in the faint light, Tam thought these people looked a bit like sea life stranded by an ebbing tide.

Alaan appeared at the head of a stair from the garden and gazed at them a moment before shaking his head. "A giant, a minstrel, a vain king, a thief. What a ragtag band I've formed." He caught Fynnol's eye. "For the highwayman," he said, and he tossed a purse to the Valeman, who caught it deftly. "That's all the gold I received for your goods, Fynnol," he said, "but satisfy yourself."

Fynnol shook his head and tucked the purse inside his costume. "It is enough," he said.

Cynddl produced the flute and gave it to Alaan, though he hesitated as though he didn't want to part with it.

Alaan took the box almost reverently and put it away without opening it. "Hafydd knows what costume I wear, though he doesn't know I've hidden that costume beneath this robe. When the last dance is announced I will appear dressed as Hafydd expects and he will come after me." Alaan turned and pointed out into the lantern-lit garden. "Do you see the rowan tree, there?"

A second of hesitation. "I see it," Cynddl said.

"There is a path that begins beside it and leads out of the garden. When the last dance is announced, meet me there. Don't be a second late, for Hafydd will not hesitate once he sees me."

"And what of Elise?" Fynnol asked.

"Freeing Elise is the task of others. Concern yourself only with our own duties." He looked at each of them. "Be warned," he said. "Hafydd's guards wear mail shirts."

Tam thought Alaan was about to say more, but then he nodded to them and disappeared through the doors and into the crowd like a man falling into water.

"Was there any sound of dancing in your dream of Death's gate?" Fynnol asked Baore.

The big man shook his head.

"Then let's find partners," Fynnol said, turning to go inside. "The dance doesn't last forever."

Tam lingered by a wall, watching the swirling waves of color. Somehow he didn't really believe he was at such an affair. It was like a macabre dream, legged snakes dancing with maidens, Knights of the Vow waltzing with stiff-walking trees. He could see Fynnol, the highwayman, dancing—desperately dancing—trying to steal a last few moments of this grand life for fear it would disappear forever.

Here is Fynnol's dream of the larger world, Tam thought. *The world of wit and wealth and beautiful women. But it will soon take a turn Fynnol hasn't seen in his dreams.*

He found Baore still standing by a pillar. The big man had been there for an hour, awaiting the call of the last dance. He seemed strangely calm to Tam, towering over everyone present, his shod staff in hand.

Cynddl he could not find, look as he might.

The party of the Prince of Innes gathered near a door, for the cooling breeze no doubt. Tam had heard that Menwyn Wills and his wife stood with them, taunting the Renné. How petty this seemed to him. Alaan appeared rather unconcerned about the Renné and the

Wills for a man who had gone to such lengths to steal Elise Wills away. Hafydd was his concern now. Hafydd, whose men had tried to kill them for the crime of associating with Alaan. Alaan, who Elise claimed was a sorcerer.

After what had happened at Telanon Bridge, they should have taken the advice of friends and family and stayed in the Vale. But they had been lured by Cynddl's promise of horses and a little adventure.

A little adventure.

As the dance came to an end, horns sounded and the grand marshal of the fair appeared on the rostrum. "The final dance, ladies and gentlemen all. The final dance of the Renné ball."

Tam felt suddenly warm from head to foot. He worked his shoulders to loosen them, checked that his sword slid easily in its scabbard, and set out across the room for the doors.

He spotted Alaan just at that moment, only a few paces off. The traveler shed his gray robe, and after a second of hesitation stepped out onto the dance floor within sight of the Prince of Innes's gathering.

Tam pushed his way rudely through the throng and ran for the door.

Anticipating the final dance, Llyn found her maid just before it was announced. "Go show yourself to the Wills, then retreat to the far corner."

Llyn turned to the nearest woman. "Have you a partner?"

The lady shook her head.

"Then please dance with me."

The woman nodded and the two spun out onto the
dance floor. Llyn's maid was wearing the costume Hafydd
was looking for, which unsettled Llyn more than a little.
It was one thing to risk herself . . . But Alaan had assured
her the maid would be safe. She prayed he was right.

There was disturbance near the door, some pushing
and grumbling, but it passed. Prince Michael and Elise
Wills were dancing, moving slowly out into the center
of the floor. Llyn moved to meet them. If only she knew
when this promised darkness would descend—and how
Alaan thought he would manage that!

A drunken giant, dancing without a partner, lumbered
by, narrowly missing knocking them down.

Bile suddenly spewed up her throat, and she
misstepped, almost tripping on her long robe. Perhaps
she was not such a heroine after all.

Tam and Cynddl arrived together at the head of the
garden stairs.

"There is Fynnol!" Cynddl said, pointing back to the
doors.

"He'll catch up," Tam said. But then, "Where is Baore?"

"Let Baore worry about himself," Cynddl said, grabbing Tam's shoulder and pulling him down the stairs. The

story finder tugged off his mask as they went, to the surprise of people ascending the stair. Their eyes went very wide when the Fáel drew his sword.

They took the main gravel path that split the garden, skirting the fountain and the flirting couples. They ran as though they were being chased, feet striking the ground hard, sending sprays of gravel to batter the bordering flowers.

Near the end of the path Cynddl leapt the flower bed and sprinted across the lawn. As they came to the rowan tree he pulled up, turning to look back. Tam caught him and did the same. Coming down the steps was a lone figure, drawing behind him a wave of men that appeared to topple and break down the stairs. Just past the fountain a small figure was running furiously.

"That is Fynnol in the lead and next Alaan, I think," Tam said. "But where is Baore? This is not like him."

Cynddl stared for a moment, his features set and hard. "Baore said he had some errand to perform for the nagar, Tam. I fear he serves no one else now. Even concern for his friends in need will not be greater than his duty to that thing."

Tam closed his eyes for a second, but then Fynnol shouted as he leapt the flower bed. "Where is Baore?"

"We don't know," Cynddl called.

Fynnol arrived panting, and turned toward the castle. Tam didn't think he'd seen a man run as fast as Alaan. The traveler blew down the gravel path like a breeze of wind, outpacing the men who chased him. In a moment he leapt over the flowers and came toward the companions across the grass.

"We've lost Baore!" Tam called as Alaan came up.

"No matter. String your bows." Alaan skidded to a stop on the dew-slick grass. He looked back, gauging the speed of their pursuers, perhaps counting their numbers, which Tam did as well. *Ten,* he thought. *And only four of us.*

"Follow close behind me. We'll play blind men for a moment. Put a hand on the shoulder of the man before you." He grabbed Fynnol's hand and set off into the shadows of the trees. Cynddl took hold of Fynnol, and Tam tagged on the end, glancing back once as they went. Black-clad men-at-arms trampled through the flower bed.

As Tam stumbled into the darkness a wind suddenly arose, funneling down the path they followed. It bent the trees back and tore leaves and branches free, sending them whirling down the path to batter against the companions. Tam's long robe shook and snapped like a sheetless sail.

They leaned into the wind, protecting their eyes with upraised arms. For a moment Tam thought the wind would blow them back, so fiercely did it howl, but then they seemed to pass through a narrow place and the wind dropped a little. They were stumbling down a moonlit slope among sparse trees. Tam could see suddenly. Before them appeared a great vista of jagged hills and high mountains.

Fynnol cursed and stopped so that Cynddl and Tam ran into him. "Where in the world . . ."

"Don't stop!" Alaan shouted. "They are behind us."

Tam pushed Fynnol on, and in a moment they came to a nearly flat cliff top that jutted out into the night like the prow of a great ship. Alaan was running again and they followed. All around them in the moonlight, the wind howled and screamed, rushing suddenly up the slope so that the trees waved their branches like crazed dancers.

Alaan dropped over a small edge and turned to look back. The rock had stepped down so that their chests were at the level of the prow of stone. A dozen feet behind them a chasm fell away to nothing.

Alaan bent down. "There are arrows here," he said, "many more than you've carried." He stood, stringing a bow of obvious Fáel workmanship. "There is a steep, narrow gully there," he said, pointing off to their right. "If things go wrong for us, go that way and make your way down. Don't follow me! Do you understand?"

Tam looked back toward the line of thin trees, thinking he saw movement. "But where is Pwyll?" he asked suddenly.

"Pwyll?" Alaan said. "Don't worry about Pwyll. He knows this place."

"Alaan!" Cynddl called over the wind. "Where have you brought us? Our bows will be nearly useless in this wind."

"That's why I brought the two of you. Finer archers

one cannot find. Watch, now! They're upon us." He nocked an arrow and let it fly.

The dark-clad knights came sliding down the slope like shadows, and Tam felt the coldness of the place seep into him. The wind veered and shrilled, plucking their arrows from the air and sending them off in different directions. Tam shot one arrow after another, all of them going astray.

But then the wind fell calm, just as the black-clad knights reached the base of the stone prow. Four archers let their arrows fly and these found their mark. The knights fell back, trying to scramble up into the trees, but in that instant of calm that betrayed them, arrows found them out of the darkness.

Tam heard only groaning and men crying out. One man crawled pitifully across the stone, a crimson river flowing behind. Alaan dropped his bow and yanked his blade free. He leapt over the edge that protected them and strode quickly across the stone, the others in his wake. It was eerily calm, though Tam could hear the wind howling far off.

Hafydd lay face up, still as stone in the moonlight. Alaan hesitated over him for a moment, then suddenly reached down and tore off his mask. There lay a young knight, not more than thirty, a stain of blood around his mouth.

"I did not think it would be so easily done," Fynnol said.

"This is not Hafydd," Alaan said. He stood, still staring down at the dead man.

"Then he has played some trick on you," Cynddl said quickly.

Alaan's head shook. "No. I expected this, or something like it."

There was a noise just then up the slope, and a figure could be seen moving. Tam and Cynddl raised their bows, but Alaan stopped them.

"That is Pwyll," he said.

Pwyll came sliding down the slope, sword in hand. He was red-faced and gasping.

"They are behind us!" Pwyll shouted.

And Tam looked up the slope. In the faint moonlight he could see a red-clad jester bearing a blade, and then a lion with a bow, and behind them any number of others, all costumed and armed.

Alaan dropped the skull mask he'd torn off the dead man. He looked at Tam, his face drawn and grim. "*Run*," he said.

A high, inhuman moan was heard beyond the hall, and then a cold gale of wind whipped in the doors, setting skirts and capes flapping wildly. The wind moaned and screamed, swelling within the massive room and swirling around the walls. All at once, the candles in the chandeliers flickered and died, and in the great hall there was complete darkness.

People lumbered into Elise, losing their balance in the darkness and the staggering wind. Unseen hands snatched at her, and she was pulled this way and that.

"Elise?" she heard someone call, but her shouted answer was lost in the din.

Someone very large suddenly took hold of her, sweeping others away. He found her hand in the darkness and a small box was pressed into her palm. She wrapped her fingers around it and pushed it inside her costume.

The wind was suddenly gone and Elise's eyes began to adjust to moonlight. Spirits and warriors and ghosts drifted by.

It is like a dream, she thought.

Then she saw shadow-black knights ranging about, searching. A woman tried to throw a dark cape over her, but Elise brushed it aside. "Flee," she said, grabbing the woman's hand. "Hafydd knows your plan." She pushed her away, but the woman stepped back into one of Hafydd's guards who took hold of her roughly.

Others came forward, blades drawn.

"Baore!" she warned.

She saw the big Valeman tear off the false head of his costume, the vast shirt settling around his shoulders. He took up the staff he held, and she thought he would run at the guards but instead he bolted for the doors. A woman screamed. And then a candle was lit, and then another.

Moonlight fell through the high windows and filtered past the doors. Shapes took on muted colors, and then they were humans, though in strange forms.

Llyn pushed her way through the milling crowd, though she was jostled and shoved. Suddenly Elyse and Mwynfawr were before her, hand in hand, looking about as if lost. Quickly she went to them, pulling off her robe.

"Lady Elise," she said. "Take my ro—"

But she was almost knocked to the floor by some enormous being, who pushed through to Lady Elise. At first Llyn thought he would harm her, but he only bent near for a moment.

Llyn gained her balance and forced her way forward again. Without a word she threw her executioner's robe over Elise, but the young woman brushed it aside, then reached out and grabbed Llyn's hand.

"Flee," she said grimly, and then something more that was lost in the general clamor. Elise pushed her ungently and she stumbled into someone who grabbed her arms. She thought this man had only meant to save her from falling, but he would not let her go.

A candle was lit, its light wavering, then growing. Then a second was lit from that. Then two from each of those. Everyone began talking at once.

She saw Lady Elise, the executioner's robe draped, unknowingly, over one shoulder. Everything had gone horribly, horribly wrong. She had only the briefest glimpse of a hall in ruin. People doffing their masks, revealing faces drawn and pale.

Llyn struggled to have her arms free. "Will you let me go!" she protested.

A tall man dressed as a Knight of the Vow stopped

before her. His mask had been removed and he was gray-haired and grim.

"This woman tried to give Lady Elise a robe, Sir Eremon."

The man gazed at her a moment, and before she could even try to turn away, reached forward and tore off her mask. Llyn saw Elise put her hands to her face in horror, then turn away and bury her face in Prince Michael's shoulder. All around there were gasps and cries of dismay. Llyn hung her head so that her hair might hide her.

"Let that woman go!" a voice said. And then, "I am Toren Renné. If you do not sheath that sword I shall cut you down where you stand." And her arms were suddenly free, and someone took hold of her gently and she was moving. The sea of gawking, appalled faces parted. Llyn shut her eyes and covered her face with her hands. In a moment they left the sounds of the hall behind, but she could still hear the gasp of horror from those who had seen. She was a monster. That was the truth. A monster who must be shut away.

They flew toward the gully Alaan had pointed to, not even looking back to see what Alaan himself would do. Arrows began sparking off the rock by their feet before they made the gully, and then they were going down, their way faintly lit by moonlight.

It was a steep gully, with loose rock here and there and tufts of grasses, gray in the dull light. Tam pulled his bow over his head and one shoulder, needing both hands to keep himself from falling. The gully twisted and turned so that they couldn't see who might be behind or how close they might be, but Tam was comforted by the knowledge that their pursuers wouldn't have free hands to take up a bow. A boulder struck stone just above his head and shattered, a shard of it striking his shoulder.

He cursed and pushed on. Pwyll was behind him. Just ahead was Cynddl, and Fynnol was in the lead, risking life and limb to make speed. Each of them had slipped more than once, skidding down a dozen feet, battering elbows and knees. But then they were up again, not slowing a bit, running for their lives.

The gully began to open up, the sides curving away, and then trees appeared. Suddenly there was soft ground among the rocks and trees all around them.

Cynddl brought them up behind a rock, bent double gasping for breath.

"Have you . . . arrows still?" he panted.

"Some," Tam said.

"Then let's stop them here for a while. They can't easily circle us, and we can drive them back and make them stop and think, while we catch our breath."

"There!" Fynnol called. He sent an arrow up the slope, and Tam and Cynddl quickly joined him. The few dark shapes they saw scrambled back up into the rocks above.

"Go on," Pwyll hissed. "There are too many of them. They will mount a charge and we cannot resist it here."

On they went, Tam bent over with a pain in his side

from running. In the shadows of the trees they tripped
and fell hard, pulled themselves up, and ran on. An hour
passed, and the wood became so thick and shadowed that
they were forced to go slowly.

And then they came out of the wood into pale light,
a soft summer night around them, a hayfield spreading
out before. A moon-silvered river flowed among poplars,
and a nightingale pealed its perfect song.

"That is the Westbrook," Cynddl said.

Pwyll nodded.

Tam turned and looked back. A low, wooded hill lay
above them, its gentle curve visible against the stars.
There were no mountains or high stone cliffs.

Pwyll had them take up a position behind a drystone
wall, but no one emerged from the trees.

"They've found some other track," Pwyll said at last,
and Tam saw the traveler's shoulders relax.

Tam replaced his arrow in his quiver and gazed up at
the low hill again. "I've been on the secret river," he said,
"but I don't know where I've been this night. Certainly
not in the land between the mountains."

"No," Pwyll said, "you've been in the land beneath the
stars and moon. The place only Alaan can find the paths
to, knowingly." He pointed off down the Westbrook.

"And where is Alaan?"

"Trying to separate Hafydd from his guard—all those
who did not follow us. That is his only hope. If he survives
we are to meet him near the town."

Fynnol shook his head. "We've fulfilled our bargain

with Alaan. We're looking for my cousin Baore. Pray nothing has befallen him." And Fynnol set off down the slope among the dark heaps of new-mown hay. In the faint moonlight Tam thought the stacks stood out like gravestones.

SIXTY

The strange wind, which had darkened the ball, carried cold air down from the hills and formed pockets of mist all along the Westbrook valley. Arden passed into one of these, slowing his horse, for there were still revelers coming from the ball and wandering drunkenly on the roads. A tree loomed before him, then sprang aside to be replaced by a lion walking upright and singing obnoxiously. His horse shied, but a steady hand and soothing words sent it on.

"Damn this fog and these foolish people!" he muttered. He had to get to Westbrook immediately. Arden could still see the executioner standing before him. *You shall regret what you do this night, Arden Renné. You shall regret it most deeply.*

He knew finally that he could not live with the guilt or the regret. Better to follow Toren and bring the Renné to ruin than take on this infamy.

All he had to do was reach Toren before Dease and Beld.

"Arden?" A voice sounded behind him, and then Samul loomed out of the mist, costumed revelers jumping out of his path. Samul rode up, the hood of his costume thrown back, his face flushed. "Ah, there you are. Where is it you go this night with such haste?"

There were other boats on the river. Baore could see their lights looming in the blear. The sounds of hushed voices seemed to travel from great distances, and the dip and sweep of oars ranged along the riverbanks like running echoes.

"The bridge did not seem so far, before," Baore muttered.

He was at the oars, driving the boat with greater speed than prudence suggested. He had left his pursuers behind in the chaos of the ball. The Renné had aided him in this, for they had drawn weapons when they saw Hafydd's guards doing the same. Baore wondered if the ball had ended with bloodshed.

He twisted around to look ahead, but could barely see the bow in the fog and darkness, though when he raised his eyes he could still see, faintly, stars and the westering moon.

Something broke the surface a few feet away.

"Row on," a voice hissed.

Dease shouldered his bundle and looked over at his cousin. What a lump Beld was—twisted by his jealousies and hatreds. How had he become such a creature of malice? Dease wondered. Had he not been loved and cherished just as his own sisters and brothers were? And yet look at him.

Dease shook his head. "Let's get this over with," he said.

Beld could not help himself: he broke into a smile of great satisfaction. "Yes, cousin," Beld said. "Let's put an end to Toren's foolishness before it is too late. You saw what the Prince of Innes did in our hall this night. Poor Llyn!"

Dease knew Beld didn't care what happened to Llyn but thought only that this reminder would galvanize Dease and raise his ire. Bastard! Instead Dease took a calming breath and tried to master his rage. He would not commit this act in passion.

They set out through Castle Renné, which remained in turmoil after the events at the ball. If Dease had had doubts before, they had all been erased that evening. If not when the Prince of Innes arrived with his son and future daughter-in-law dressed as the parents of the kings of men or when Hafydd revealed himself, then when Hafydd's guards had drawn their weapons and gone after guests at the Renné ball. No, Toren had failed utterly, and now they must quickly try to repair the damage he'd done.

Samul was preparing to gather the troops needed to storm the Prince's compound. Hafydd would be hung by morning, and the Prince's plans for marrying his son to a Wills would also be thwarted. Before the day was out Prince Michael of Innes would be wed to a Renné, at sword point if needed. Menwyn Wills and his ferocious wife would be ensconced in a Renné villa—"guests" of the family for some time to come. And that would be the end of the Prince's war. If only Toren could have acted so boldly.

They made their way into a small stair, almost never used now. Samul had already been down it to chase out any lovers or servants hiding away with a bottle of wine. It would not do to be seen this night, Dease thought.

Beldor held aloft a small candlebranch that cast its anemic light down the stack of worn treads. In a moment they were outside and off down a narrow lane, lit only by moonlight.

"Pull up your mask," Dease said.

"No one will recognize us in the dark," Beld protested.

"Nonetheless, do as we all agreed or stay behind."

Beld cursed softly and pulled up his mask. Dease did the same.

The world seemed suddenly far away, seen through the narrow eye slits—as though Dease were not part of it somehow, but watched from outside, like a spirit. It was an odd feeling, as if he were only vaguely attached to his body, which was animated by someone else.

Dease suddenly remembered receiving his first sword from his father, and swearing "By all of the Renné who have gone before and carried our feud to the enemy." *Tonight they walk with me,* Dease thought, *and within me.*

As they neared the river, a ghostly mist appeared,

clinging to the trees, forcing them to feel their way forward.

"We shall look fools if we get lost this night," Beldor growled.

But Dease was almost relieved. Perhaps the mist would foil their plan. He regretted deeply putting himself forward to do this terrible thing. But he could not give Beldor the satisfaction—he respected Toren too much. He also didn't trust Beld to perform the act cleanly.

I will do this thing, for I love him best.

But there was no going back, nor was there any way to erase the memory of what had happened that night in Castle Renné.

They came to the river, finally, and there found a small boat drawn up on the bank. They could not take the bridge for fear of being recognized on the road.

Dease set his bundle on the thwart, and ordered Beld into the stern. The boat clung to the bank a moment and then slid into the river, sinking down, then bobbing upon the surface. Dease shipped the oars and in a moment took them out into the stream.

"I'm lost already," Beld whispered.

"Look," Dease said. "There is the moon. Overhead the mist is thinner. We can navigate by the moon."

"I don't like this fog," Beld said. "It came with that foul wind which darkened our hall. That was no accident, nor was it natural."

Dease dug his oars into the black water, pressing them

forward, just as a dark apparition slipped past in the moonlit haze—a boat, its oarsman as silent as a ghost.

When they met the mist, Hafydd gave curt orders to one of his guards, who took hold of her horse's bridle. Elise went on thus, wedged between Prince Michael and Hafydd's black-clad guard.

What a terrible disaster the night had been, every plan seeming to go awry. And that poor woman! She was a Renné, someone had said. So all along Alaan had been allied with the Renné. Elise shook her head. The man hadn't really been interested in the cause of peace at all.

But she was lost, now. There was only one course left and Elise was not sure she could take it. It was too desperate and she hadn't the nerve. Ahead, in the fog, she could just make out the black form of Hafydd. He had fooled them all, sending one of his guards as "the ghost of Hafydd" and then wearing another costume himself.

The night had ended in chaos. From where she'd stood on the dance floor she'd missed almost everything. Swords had been drawn, someone said, and blood spilled. Hafydd and the Prince's men-at-arms had gone after Baore. And that was all her fault! She had not been brave and resolute but weak and traitorous. What kind of heroine was she? None at all, it seemed. But she had so little power in this world.

The hideous woman's face appeared before her, and she shut her eyes. Poor, poor woman.

But there was little room in Elise's heart that night for pity for others. Her own situation was black enough. And there was only one way to escape it. She looked up at Hafydd riding before her, and felt her hatred and fear kindle.

Perhaps she had nerve enough, after all.

It was with difficulty that Dease found their landing place, running the boat up onto a small beach. No one had camped in this place, they knew, and from here they could find their way into the village, keeping to the shadows of hedgerows that bordered fields.

Beld took the lead, hurrying along in the filtered light of an obscured moon. Dease thought his cousin looked like an evil dwarf, abroad on some errand of malice. But he followed along, trying not to think of what he must do, hoping that his hand would be steady when the time came.

The mist hung in patches here and there across the valley, and they went in and out of these like bandits slipping from bush to bush. Houses loomed up, sooner than Dease expected, and he felt his heart race and his mouth go suddenly dry. The village was still alive, but the back lanes were hardly the places for celebration and they went unnoticed but for the barking of dogs.

It was no time before they had come to the garden wall behind Toren's house, and here again Samul and Arden had been at work, leaving two barrels for Dease and Beld to stand upon.

They scrambled up and peered toward the house. As Dease had expected, they found candles burning and both sets of double doors opened to the terrace. It was Toren's custom to sit out on his terrace for a time each night before retiring. Toren called this his contemplation hour, and Dease thought this night there would be more than usual to contemplate. It even occurred to him as he stood there that Toren might finally be coming to his senses, and it would be both ironic and tragic that Dease would take his life this night.

He has had two years to come to his senses, Dease thought. *There is no reason to believe it will ever happen, let alone this night.*

Against the light within a silhouette appeared, walking slowly across the space between the doors. They heard hushed voices—Toren was not alone—but words echoed off the stone walls and were reduced to a jumble.

"There is your target, Cousin," Beld whispered as the silhouette appeared again.

"I am not so sure. That does not seem to be Toren."

"Of course it is Toren!" Beldor growled. "Take aim and do as you have pledged."

Dease drew his arrow back, but hesitated still.

"Look, Beldor . . . can you not see? That is some other."

"It is Toren and he'll be gone to bed if you don't perform your agreed duty—now!"

Dease took aim once again, but the silhouette moved a little and Dease was almost sure it was not Toren. He lowered the arrow.

"We must wait. That's not him." He glanced at Beld, who was staring at him, mouth raggedly open.

"*Dease*," he hissed, but Dease ignored him, returning his attention to the lit doors.

All at once there was an explosion of light and pain, and Dease felt himself slipping from his perch, though he never seemed to strike the ground.

Not a breath of air disturbed the mist, which clung to the branches and drifted over the road, concealing everything beyond a small circle. Elise looked over at Prince Michael, whose gaze had barely met hers at all this entire ride.

He feels that he has failed me, though the failure was not his.

The sharp rap of iron-shod hooves on stone rattled back between the trees. Elise took a long breath and quickly slipped her shoes off. She took hold of her pommel.

She wanted to reach over and touch Michael's arm but knew she should do nothing to catch the guard's attention.

The guard's horse reached the bridge, and a step later her own horse found the stone deck. The bridge arched up, the balustrade appearing in the mist, then she was looking out over the river, fogbound and moonlit.

The instant drew near and yet she did nothing. In a second it would be past.

"Think of your child in Hafydd's care," she whispered, and took a quick breath.

She pushed herself up and placed one stockinged foot just behind the guard's saddle. She grasped the man's shoulder to pull and steady herself, and though he spun around he turned only toward where she'd been. Elise was already behind.

A quick step and she was on the parapet; only a second's pause and she flung herself off into the moon mist. Elise felt a tug as a hand grabbed the skirt of her gown. A tearing sound and she fell into the slow-swirling white, and then into the cold, welcoming river.

Baore heard the splash but saw nothing. He pushed even harder on the oars, twisting about. There! There was the stone of the bridge. He wanted to call out Elise's name but was afraid arrows would find him. Instead he spun the boat slowly around.

Men were shouting on the bridge now. And some others came splashing along the shore. Men-at-arms, Baore thought, wearing heavy coats of mail—not that any of them could likely swim.

He remained still, letting the mist hide him. He felt light, sitting there without the whetstone he had carried so far. And he felt a terrible guilt as well that he had passed it to some other. He feared Elise didn't really understand the bargain she would enter into.

* * *

Elise felt the cold waters envelop her. She opened her eyes and found herself floating through liquid moonlight. And then the panic took hold. She began to flail, searching about. Where was the surface? Where? A pressure seemed to build in her chest. Breathe. She had to breathe. She felt a darkness pressing in at the edge of her vision and a strange ringing sounded.

And then she saw, floating a few yards off, the nagar, hair wafting like kelp, a terrible sadness on the pale features.

Baore held his position near the bridge, the mist licking around him. It seemed to him that half an hour had passed, though it could not have been so long. And then there was a terrible gasping for breath. He was up in a flash, reaching over the side to pull Elise from the grasp of the river. She came up, pale as the moon.

Water seemed to run out of her pores when he laid her in the boat. It streamed out of her hair and eyes and mouth. She gasped for breath and sobbed, adding salt tears to the streaming water.

She looked up at Baore as if noticing him for the first time. "I'm alive," she sobbed. "Alive again."

"Dease?"

He heard the word, but for a moment it seemed to have no meaning. There was such excruciating pain in his temple and his ears rang as though he'd put his head inside a bell.

"Dease? Can you hear me?"

His eyes opened and the light pained them so he shut them again.

"Toren?"

"Yes."

"I'm going to be ill."

"Here . . . turn on your side. There. You'll be all right."

Dease retched terribly, and then lay back. Someone pressed a glass of brandy to his lips and it burned in his already scorched throat. But it did not matter. The pain in his head made everything else insignificant.

"Dease? What happened?"

What had happened? Dease felt as though the world would not be still. It tilted this way, then that. His nausea persisted, and the pain in his head seemed to scatter his thoughts and memories like windblown leaves.

"Was it Beld?" Toren said.

"What?"

"Was it Beldor who shot Arden?"

Dease shook his head. "I can't quite remember. Toren? What of Arden?"

There was no answer to this. Dease dared open his eyes just a crack, and he saw the sorrow on Toren's face.

"*No,*" he heard himself whisper.

Dease felt a hand laid gently on his breast. "He had come to warn me, Dease. He'd had to fight Samul on the road here, killing Samul's horse and riding off." Toren took a long breath. "My own cousins . . . my own blood plotted my murder. Beldor, Samul"—a second of hesitation—"and Arden." The hand on his chest tightened a little, then relaxed. "Perhaps others. Arden was shot while he confessed. Can you not remember? Did you find Beld or Samul beyond my wall? Was there anyone else?"

Fragments of memory came back to him, stabbing into his mind like shards of glass. He gritted his teeth against the pain.

"Someone . . ." Dease grunted. "Yes, someone upon a barrel at your garden wall."

"You were coming to speak to me?"

"Yes." Dease racked his brain. "About what had happened at the ball . . ." Dease remembered now. *He* had stood at the wall and aimed the arrow. Not Beld. *He* was to have been the assassin. Had he killed Arden? But if so, what then had happened? Had he fallen? An image of Beldor came to him—staring at him in rage.

"It was Beldor," he blurted. "He must have struck me."

"Was he alone?"

"I—I don't know. Bloody hell, Toren, but it's all a jumble."

"It will come back. You'll be whole again. The same happens to men in the joust, sometimes. But it was Beldor. You're sure?"

Dease nodded his head. What was he saying? It was *him*. Though Beld had knocked him down and apparently taken up the bow. Dease had known it was not Toren in the door. He should have realized it was Arden, though. Who else looked so much like Toren? But Arden shouldn't have been there—not this night.

"Beldor must have shot Arden believing it was you."

"Yes. Or murdered Arden when he realized what he was doing—giving the traitors away." The pain in Toren's voice was almost more than Dease could bear. "I can't believe that Arden would be involved in such a thing. Beldor—yes, easily. He has hated me for years. Samul . . . Well, he has the courage of his convictions and never doubts that he is right." The hand resting on Dease's breast took hold of his forearm. "I have only you I can trust, Dease. Only you. The others shall pay for their treachery. I can't tell you what sorrow it brings me, but it must be so. There will be a war, I fear, and there can be no place among the Renné for traitors. We will hunt them down, Dease. They can't get far." Toren gave his arm a squeeze. "Only you," he said, his voice breaking. And then he began to weep, sobbing again and again, *"Arden. Arden."*

SIXTY-ONE

On the final night of the fair a sudden wind funneled down the Westbrook, blowing down tents and tearing away branches. The Fáel scurried around their encampment, driving home pegs and rigging ropes and poles to secure the tents to the ground. Tuath thought it felt like a cold breath from some ancient, sentient mountain. It made her shudder, and not just from the cold.

She had been working by candlelight, trying to capture a vision in threads. All Tuath had thus far was a fair woman with two faces, one perhaps a mask set on the back of her head, but it was hard to be sure.

When the wind broke upon the camp, she made certain her embroidery hoop was safe within a trunk and then ventured out into the wind-battered night. All around her tents were luffing like sails. A gust took hold of her and she bent forward, pushing against it, unable to look directly into the wind that threw broken leaves and grit into her face.

There were no lanterns that could hold a flame in such a wind, but the sky remained empty of cloud, so the camp was lit by frantic moonlight that fell between madly swinging branches. The horses were restive; and one or two had broken their leads and thundered through the camp, men chasing after them or leaping out of their way.

Tuath turned her back to the wind and the whole scene was revealed to her: hunched figures scurrying this way and that in the flailing moonlight, tents convulsing like strange animals in agony. The trees bent and creaked as their branches were forced back until many cracked and shattered, falling heavily to the ground.

And then it was over—as though a door had been closed against the storm, except that it was silent. For a moment nobody moved, so startled were they. And then a single oak leaf floated down before Tuath, and she set off at a run across the encampment.

She found Rath's tent half blown down, like a horse up on its hind legs only. Nann was there, trying to peel away the layers of fabric, pulling at them frantically with strong, pudgy hands. In a moment she found the door and pulled open the flap, throwing the fabric over her and swimming through it. Tuath was only a step behind.

"Rath? Rath!" Nann called.

They rolled the fabric back, to let the moonlight in, and there found the story finder, lying peacefully in his bed, his mouth open as though he would begin a story. But no breath escaped those lips.

Nann bent down and gently put her ear to the old man's narrow chest. Tuath saw Nann's eyes close suddenly and tears flow. Rath's spirit had fled, borne on the breeze. Around them the fabric of the tent moved to a small wind, and then it was still again. A final whisper, and then silence.

And now turn the page for a preview of

SEAN RUSSELL'S

THE ISLE OF BATTLE
Book Two of the Swans' War Trilogy

Alaan went down, too quickly, slipped and slammed his knee on the worn stone, tearing his fine costume. For a moment he slowed, the pain forcing him to take more weight on his hands as he slid and scrambled over the rock.

The wind funneled up the gorge with an agonizing moan. Alaan clung to his place while it shoved and tore at him, flailing his costume about his face. His arms trembled and his injured knee throbbed. Above, he could hear voices, the words shattered and swept up into the sky.

Is he among them? Alaan wondered. Had Hafydd come?

The wind dropped away, growling down the slope, and Alaan followed it, his knee stiff but bearing his weight now. An arrow sparked off the stone by his hand and he jumped, letting himself fall and slide a dozen feet to a ledge. Pulling his own bow over his head he nocked an arrow and shot the first man to appear above. The next he thought he might have missed, though narrowly.

He pulled his bow back over his head and shoulder and went on, the way widening and becoming easier. The advantage here was his, for he had been this way before and, as much as he could, had committed the path to memory, though by moonlight everything seemed different – steeper and more dangerous.

A ledge should slope off to the right not far below – though when it didn't he was possessed by a sudden fear that he'd passed it when he'd let himself drop down to avoid the arrows.

But no, there it was, much as he'd remembered, though appearing narrower now. He swung himself onto the ledge around a buttress of stone, and paused there a moment, gazing up. He didn't have to wait long. They followed behind, climbing down quickly, searching for holds and trying to watch for him at the same time. How the lead men must be expecting an arrow at any second.

Hafydd, if he were here, would not be among these. He would be safely behind, letting his guards suffer the risks. Alaan barely had the heart to use his bow, but he didn't want to make their pursuit seem too easy. Hafydd was suspicious by nature. So Alaan stayed there a while, and drove the men back up the draw, repelling two of their attempts to rush him. And then he went on, trotting quickly along the ledge, his battered knee having stiffened up again as he stood.

To his left the night world stretched away – shadows like shale, mountains of jagged moonlight. A cloud passed over the face of the moon, and Alaan was forced to grope forward, barely able to discern the ledge. It would be easy to misstep in such light, to be fooled, and find oneself suddenly a creature of the air – for a brief moment.

The cloud passed and he hurried on. Where the rock bent around a corner he stopped to look back. There they were, following quickly along, their costumes, in the stark light, lending a macabre air to the scene; like a madman's painting. Alaan pressed himself on. There was some distance yet to go, even to one who could find hidden short cuts.

The ledge led to another gully, though not so steep, with a sloping floor of loose rock, some of it large, most not. Alaan could almost run now, his knee loosening up a little. The trick was to keep his speed under control. The rock slid beneath his feet, and he stood upon its moving back like a trick rider at a fair. When it slowed he went on, leaping knee-high boulders, falling once to bloody his knuckles. Twice he paused to fire arrows back up at the men behind – keeping them at a distance.

The way he went offered them few branchings or even other passable tracks to take. Alaan did not want to lose Hafydd's guards – or Hafydd. Not yet.

Is he there? he wondered. *Does that aspect of Caibre survive in this stern knight?*

He pressed on, until he was down from the high cliffs and under the trees of a wooded gully. This place did not match with any view that could be seen from above, but Hafydd would not be much bothered by that. He had chased his "whist" before.

Beneath the trees the air was moist and cool, and the ground gave beneath his feet. Out of the dark, a little stream curled to bounce and burble along the gully bottom, as though it had come to keep him company.

This should allay Hafydd's worst fears, Alaan thought: *water*.

Streaks of moonlight swarmed over the ground as the wind whipped the trees to and fro, and Alaan went forward haltingly, trying to make sense of this mad moving land-scape.

The air rasped cruelly in and out of his lungs, now, and his mind seemed numbed, the sound of his breathing loud in his ears, punctuated by the dull thuds of his foot falls.

A shout from behind and an arrow buried itself in the ground near his boot. Alaan pushed himself on, dodging into shadow, the trees throwing stains of moonlight at his feet then stealing them away.

The slope began to level, and Alaan leapt the moon-silvered stream that only whispered, now. He stopped in the shadow of a tree, bent double, listening. The moonlight chased madly across the clearing. When the silhouettes of men appeared he showed himself, waited until he was seen, and then slipped into shadow.

The slope went steeply down again, and the smell of rotting vegetation wafted up the slope on a falling breeze. By the time he found the shore of the swamp he was out of breath, and stopped again, standing with one foot in the tepid water.

A man shot out of the shadow, sword raised. Alaan had barely time to pull his own blade and dodge a vertical stroke. He slipped on the wet bottom, having stepped back without thinking and fought to regain his balance, barely parrying a thrust at his heart. Alaan's own blade sank into the man's throat as he felt steel drive deep into his thigh above the injured knee.

The man, dressed as a toy soldier, reached up and grabbed Alaan's blade, choking as he did. In the pale light black fluid ran down his hand, and he fell to his knees. Alaan yanked his blade free and wallowed into the swamp, limping terribly. Across a few yards of open water he forced his way into the reeds, looking back to see his track plainly marked where he'd stirred up the bottom. The man lay at the swamp's edge, still gurgling and choking.

Alaan pulled his bow free, ducked down and nocked an arrow. Others appeared, catching up to the magnificent runner who lay choking on the bank. Alaan shot the first man and just missed another as they retreated into the protection of the trees and their shadows.

Alaan didn't wait to see what the men would do, but plunged into the reeds. His pursuers were too close now, and he was wounded. He bulled through the rushes, trying to balance on one leg, the sharp-edged reeds lacerating his hands. As his shoulders began to ache he pulled free of the cattails into open water.

"A staff," he muttered, barely able to go on. "I need a staff."

If anyone was close behind him now he would be caught out in the open, vulnerable. He slipped down into the water, and half-swimming, half-pulling himself along the bottom, crossed the pool. His bow string would be wet and useless now, but there was nothing for it. He had to put some distance between himself and his hunters.

In the sky goatsuckers dove and wheeled, crying forlornly, and frogs sang of their night of love. A snake slid silently by. His hunters would be difficult to hear in this place, but then he need not be so quiet himself, which had advantages when one was in a hurry.

Alaan reached a shallows and tried to stand on the soft bottom, lost his balance and toppled into the water with a splash. He crawled on, dragging his injured leg, cursing under his breath. A channel opened up to his left and he followed it, able to pull himself forward now, letting his body half-float, the weight of his sword and quiver dragging him down.

Alaan glanced up at the moon, hoping for cloud, but the moon, perfectly full, floated in a clear, star-filled sky. He dragged himself into the rushes again, forcing his way through, taking many turns and doing as little damage as he could. His bow was impeding his progress and should have been cast aside but he wanted to leave no markers of where he'd been. Again he found open water and went back down to his half-swimming pose, digging his fingers into the soft muck of the bottom, and propelling himself forward. He glanced over his shoulder often, afraid that he'd been found. Without the use of his bow he wouldn't have a chance. He wouldn't last long in a sword fight, not hobbled as he was.

Alaan felt like a hunted beast paddling through the swamp with tall, armed men in hot pursuit. Again he pulled himself into the reeds and forced himself through. The bulrush stands were dense and stood high above his head offering perfect cover. A snake slithered lithely into the reeds almost beneath his feet.

"Yes," he whispered, "I am a son of Wyrr. And thanks be for it."

He came to another channel but crouched down, having thought he heard some sound above the frogs. For a moment he stayed very still.

"If Welloh stuck him he didn't get him anywhere that mattered," a voice said. "He's kept on like a frightened hare."

Three men came into view then, wading down the center of the channel, swords drawn. Two archers followed behind.

"Oh, Welloh stuck him alright. The point of his blade was bloody. He'll slow down, by and by, our whist; that's what I say—"

"Keep your voices down!" another hissed. Two more men brought up the rear, swords in hand.

Alaan let them pass by. Seven men he'd counted. There seemed to have been many more than that. How did Hafydd slip so many into the ball?

When the troupe of men was out of sight, Alaan paddled across the channel, slipping through a narrow opening in the rushes. Something snagged his good ankle and Alaan was forced to stop and cut himself free. *Tanglevine.* He'd have to be more wary. The telltale blossoms, blood-red by day, closed at night and were hard to see.

He slunk on, stopping now and then to listen for men above the sounds of the swamp. He found a low island of soggy ground and lay down in the reeds. He'd rest here a bit, but not long. If Hafydd was among these men he'd be able to track Alaan no matter how cunning he was. Sorcerers had their means.

Taking out his dagger, Alaan slit his pant leg to above the knee. There was not much blood from the wound, which was already swollen and terribly painful. He pulled some rushes aside so that the moonlight illuminated his leg. He'd had worse — much worse — but he'd been near the healing waters of the Wyrr then. He cut some fabric from his now filthy costume and bound it over the wound. These stagnant waters were foul and not healthful, but there was nothing he could do. He'd be lucky now to escape.

A man shouted off in the distance, too far away for the words to carry, but the tone was clear – desperation. Someone had met one of the swamp's serpents, or perhaps a swamp cat. There were any number of dangerous beasts in this place.

Another call, in answer this time.

Hafydd, however, would survive. Beasts were wary of the children of Wyrr – they were smarter than humans in this regard.

He lay his head on his arm for a moment and when he opened his eyes again the moon had washed into the west. He was wet through to his skin, where he lay on the soggy ground, which seemed to have subsided under him. He sat up quietly. Listening.

"He is not here," he whispered to the singing frogs. "He would have found me by now."

With difficulty he staggered to his feet, but his right leg would only bear weight with considerable pain. A staff – he needed a staff. His sword just sank into the soft swamp, making a useless cane. What had happened to the men-at-arms who followed? Wandering in circles through the swamp no doubt. He'd need to find a couple of them and lead them out. Not so easy now with his wounded leg.

He waded back into the swamp, but was soon down on his hands and good knee in the water again. He hadn't gone far when he heard calling, not so desperate now. More muffled and despairing.

He followed the cries, which were separated by long periods of silence. It took him some time in the pale moon-light to locate the source. He parted the reeds and found a man, dressed as a Knight of the Vow, lying a few yards away, his head barely out of the water, hopelessly entangled in a web of fine chord.

The two regarded each other a moment.

"You've not heard of tanglevine, I take it?" Alaan said after a moment.

The man was tiring fast. He wouldn't be able to keep his head above water much longer.

"Gloat if you must," the man said, "but my fellows will do for you yet."

"They can't even find you when you're calling. How will they ever find me? No, your friends have fallen to the same fate as you. Or have met with some of the swamp's other perils. Or have wandered off into further reaches and will not find their way here again." Alaan reached out with his sword and tugged at a loop of vine. "I once tried to count all the little spines in a short length of tanglevine but soon gave it up. They're sharp as glass, as you've no doubt learned, and once they tighten cannot be made loose again." With the tip of his sword Alaan pointed toward a closed blossom. "Do you see these flowers? They are like those plants that eat flies. At dawn they will open and slowly search about until they have found you, alerted already by the tugging of the vines. Their kiss burns like no passion you've ever known. They digest their prey a bit at a time, alive at first, and then the carcass. They don't seem to care much if their food is alive and wiggling or dead and rotting. They haven't much refinement in this regard."

"They say you are brother to that bloody Eremon, and now I believe it."

Alaan tried to smile. "You shouldn't talk so to the man who will set you free."

Hope flashed in the man's eyes. "Why would you do that?"

"You don't look like one of Hafydd's guards. I assume you serve the Prince of Innes?"

The man nodded.

"I have no argument with the Prince, though I think he's an ass. You've been hunting me, but I'll forgive you that. You are a man-at-arms and have no say in who will be your foe, who your friend."

The man gazed at him now, wondering, hardly daring to hope. Did this stranger torment him?

"I will have your oath, though. If I set you free you will do me no harm and do as I say. You cannot survive this swamp without me, I will tell you that. It is more fierce than you."

The man continued to watch him closely, but said nothing.

"You will not keep your head up much longer. Choose, man."

"What will you have of me?"

"Have of you? What have you to offer? I will have your word that you will harm me not. Yeah or nay?"

"You have it," the man said, his tone saying that he still believed Alaan toyed with him.

Alaan raised his sword and when he brought it down the man turned his head and closed his eyes. But when he felt some of his bonds loosen he looked back again.

"Who are you, then?" he almost whispered. "Who are you who sets his enemies free?"

"You? You aren't my enemy, man-at-arms. Hafydd, whom

you call Sir Eremon, is my enemy. But you . . . you are but a sword with a man attached. There are ten thousand others like you. But I will spare your life — out of pity for you, who have no thoughts of your own."

Alaan continued to slash away at the vines that held the man until he could move again, though his arms were still pinned to his sides. With some difficulty Alaan hauled the man up and cut free his legs and feet.

"What about my sword?"

Alaan poked around in the water and rushes until he felt something solid, then fished out a sword. He assured himself that the man's arms and hands were immobilized by the tanglevine and then slid the man's sword back into his scabbard.

"Why did you ask for my word if you were to keep me bound?"

"Because I take no more risks than I must, man-at-arms. This way . . ." he pointed with his sword. "Let me put a hand on your shoulder."

"Welloh did wound you, then . . . before you cut his throat out."

"He would have murdered me on the spot — me, who had never done him harm or even known his name. Any man would have done what I did. Even you." Alaan waved his sword. "This channel."

They turned down a narrow, open channel, the man's gait awkward from his bound arms, and Alaan leaning on him and hobbling like a cripple.

They did not talk as they went, Alaan silent from the pain, the other still suspicious and harboring his words,

Alaan guessed. They staggered down an open channel in thigh-deep water, bubbles rising where they disturbed the soft bottom. A breeze set the reeds to hissing.

It was a long hour of going and stopping to rest Alaan's wounded leg. Twice he sat down in the water, overcome by pain. The man at arms standing docilely by.

"Your wound must be deep," the man-at-arms said, gazing at him.

"To the bone," Alaan answered between clenched teeth.

"I am a man of my word," the other said, "free my hands and I will do what I can to help you."

"Perhaps you are, but I will not take that chance." Alaan reached down and touched his leg. "Hafydd did not venture forth with you, I take it," Alaan said, the pain in his leg subsiding a little with immobility. He forced himself up, stiff-legged and dripping.

"Hafydd; that's what you call Sir Eremon?" the man said. "There were some among the Prince's men who said that: that he was Hafydd, and had once served the Renné."

"To say that he served the Renné is less than true, I would think, but he was their ally – as much as he was any man's." Alaan put his hand on the man's shoulder and they set off again.

"But it is said that Hafydd died upon a battlefield, murdered by his own allies."

"He did not die. Not there. Though there was barely life left in him; only a tiny spark that was fanned back to a flame. A flame of hatred. And how do you and your fellows like to serve this man?"

The man was silent for a moment. "We like it not," he

said softly, his voice bitter. "I have seen him strike his blade upon a rock so that it rang and screamed like a tortured spirit, and then he followed where it pointed. The lands we rode through were strange — as they were this night — and no one had seen them before, not even men who had spent their lives in those places. He is a sorcerer come back from the dead, that's what many say — though they say it low for none would face him with such accusations. None of the men who say he should be burned would dare stand before him and draw a sword. He is feared. I have never known a man to be so feared."

"Yes, he is feared: a strange gift to ask of one's father. What will you do when I let you go? Will you strike out on your own — they will certainly believe you dead after tonight, for I would guess most of your fellows are."

The man looked at him in the moonlight, then shook his head. "I have taken an oath to the Prince of Innes. My father served his father, my grandfather his."

"But now you fraternize with his enemy. Does your oath allow that?"

The man shook his head. "I'm your prisoner. My duties to my lord change when that is so."

Alaan snorted. "We are almost at the swamp's edge. You will be on your own from there. If you are foolish enough to go back to serving the Prince of Innes, that is your business."

The shore rose up out of a thin mist, dark and over-shadowing. Alaan cast the man's blade up on the hard ground and then cut him free with the tip of his own sword.

"Carry on along the bank for about an hour in that

direction. You'll find a dry stream going up the hillside. Follow it over the crest and then make your way down the other side. You will come out somewhere near Westbrook. I can't say exactly where."

The man turned to look at him, incongruous in the grey robes of the Knights of the Vow. "And what of you?" he asked. "What will become of you? Your wound is septic. You should come with me."

"No, it is safer for me here, until I've healed. Before you go cut me a staff from that tree."

The knight looked at him a moment then found his sword and cut a heavy staff with it, hesitating only an instant before applying his perfectly honed blade to wood.

Alaan took the staff, leaned his weight on it and grunted his approval. "Beware, man-at-arms. There is a war coming and your oath binds you to the wrong side. Hafydd is more than just a sorcerer, he is ruthless and without principles. War is like air to him: he must have it to live. And war he will have unless I stop him. Do you want to do your duty to the House of Innes? Kill Hafydd. That would be an act of heroism — none greater."

The man cocked his head and looked at Alaan. "I am almost convinced that what you say is true. That is what Sir Eremon says about you, that you are a sorcerer of words."

"It is better than being a servant of Death, which Hafydd certainly has become."

The man saluted Alaan once with his blade, then set off along the embankment, working his stiff shoulders as he went, a Knight of the Vow whose vow would bring him sorrow.